A BET WITH BENEFITS

KAREN BOOTH

POWER PLAY

ANNA DePALO

MILLS & BOON

First Published in Great Britain 2019
by Mills & Boon, an imprint of HarperCollinsPublishers,
1 London Bridge Street, London, SE1 9GF

A Bet With Benefits © 2019 Karen Booth
Power Play © 2019 Anna DePalo

ISBN: 978-0-263-27193-5

0919

A BET WITH BENEFITS

KAREN BOOTH

For my sweet husband.
Every absurdly tall hero I write
is at least a little bit you.

One

Mindy Eden was doing far more than burning the candle at both ends—she was melting it from every angle. Her days were divided between her position as chief operating officer of her family's department store, Eden's, and her role as founder of her custom greeting card business, By Min-vitation Only, or BMO. Under Mindy's leadership, Eden's was rebounding after years of teetering on the edge, while BMO was growing by leaps and bounds. Money was rolling in, her to-do list was a mile long and she was sleeping about four hours a night. She loved every minute of it. This was no time to slow down for anything.

As she settled in the back seat of her car on her way to Eden's, her cell phone rang. She'd been waiting for this call from Matthew Hawkins, the interim chief executive officer Mindy had hired to run BMO while she helped her sisters get Eden's back on stable ground. "Matthew. Do you have news for me?"

"I do, and it's not what we were hoping for."

"Let me guess. They want more money." BMO had just made an offer on an amazing old warehouse in New Jersey. The Mercer Building. It was a massive space, and it would be a huge undertaking to move the entire company, but it had to be done. Right now, they had production running out of four different facilities, with the administrative offices at a fifth site and bulging at the seams. The Mercer would make it possible to streamline their entire operation and give them room to grow, and it would be an incredible space to work from.

"I wish it was as simple as that. The building has been sold," Matthew said flatly.

"What do you mean? I thought you were on top of this. You told me it was a done deal."

"Unfortunately, I think your personal life interfered on this one. Your *romantic* personal life."

Mindy was close to asking Matthew if he had his head screwed on right. There was no romance in her life. There wasn't much personal in there, either. Aside from the time she spent with her sisters, Sophie and Emma, at Eden's, she didn't have a spare minute to socialize. "Is this some sort of cruel joke?"

"Your ex. Sam Blackwell. He bought the building. Right out from under us."

Mindy was rarely caught off guard. She had a knack for anticipating problems and being a step ahead. But she had not seen this coming. Sam had been out of her life for five full months, since the last time she broke up with him and kicked him out of her apartment.

She'd never forget their last conversation.

You tell me to go and I'm not coming back. Ever.

My sisters need me more than I need you.

Have it your way, Min. Good luck with your dysfunctional family.

Mindy had broken up with Sam several times before that and he always found a way back. This time, he'd not only stayed away, he'd moved on to greener pastures. He'd been photographed with several gorgeous women in the tabloids, most recently with Valerie Cash, a former model turned executive fashion editor. That hadn't been easy for Mindy to take. She couldn't figure out what made him stay away this time. Unless, of course, it was because he'd finally believed her when she'd said that he was no good for her.

"Mindy? Are you there?" Matthew asked. "Sam Blackwell. Your ex-boyfriend."

"He was never my boyfriend." Sam never would've allowed himself such a label. He wasn't the type—his words, not hers.

"Look, I couldn't care less what role he played in your life. The bottom line is we have to start looking for something different. Maybe new construction. I can start meeting with architects and looking at commercial sites."

There was no way Mindy was going to give up on the Mercer this easily. "Are you insane? We're talking eighteen months on new construction, if we're lucky. We don't have that kind of time. And frankly, I'm a little shocked that you're suggesting it. That kind of delay could destroy everything I've built."

"With all due respect, I've built quite a lot since I've been here. I have a lot invested in BMO, as well."

Mindy had to stop herself from biting down on her own tongue. BMO was her company, not Matthew's. And he needed to stop acting this way. "I'm going to fix this. I don't want you to do another thing until you hear from me."

"How? The building is sold. If we try to buy it from Blackwell, he'll make us pay through the nose."

Mindy drew in a deep breath. Matthew was excellent at organization, but he wasn't much of a shark. She, however, was well versed in the art of getting what she wanted out of Sam Blackwell. Not that she was an expert. She'd failed at that before, but she at least knew his tricks. "Let me handle it. I'll let you know how it goes."

"This is technically my job."

And technically, I can fire you. "BMO is still my company and this affects our entire future. I want to get this done quickly, and I know how to deal with Sam."

"Good luck. I'd say you're going to need it."

Thanks for the big vote of confidence. "Goodbye, Matthew." Mindy leaned forward to speak to her driver, Clay. "Change of plans this morning. We need to make a stop before I head into Eden's. Eighteenth Street and Tenth Avenue. North side of the street."

"All the way down by Pier 60, Ms. Eden?"

"Yes, please. All the way down." *All the way down to see Sam.* Mindy sat back, glancing out the window and making a conscious effort to unclench her jaw and relax her shoulders. She'd spent the last five months wondering if Sam Blackwell would find a way to wander back into her life. Now she had no choice but to storm into his. She would not allow him to create problems for her from afar, pulling strings and making messes. He was going to have to do it up close and personal.

"I won't be more than fifteen minutes," she said when Clay pulled up in front of Sam's office building.

"Got it. I'll hang back and wait."

Mindy climbed out of the car, breathing in the crisp October day deeply, if only for a boost of confidence. She strode inside, sunglasses on and head held high. With no turnstile or guard in front of the elevator bank, she bypassed the security desk and nobody said a thing. Mindy had learned long ago that if you act as though you know where you're going, no one will question you. She did not want to give Sam even a minute to prepare for her arrival. She quickly scanned the directory and pressed the button for the seventh floor. Alone inside the elevator, she blew out a breath and decided to give herself a pep talk. "You got this. Sam Blackwell will not hurt you. Personally or professionally."

When the ding came and the door slid open, the reception desk was straight ahead, manned by a suitably gorgeous woman Mindy did not recognize. Behind her, a solid black wall was emblazoned with the words *S. Blackwell Enterprises* in gleaming chrome. The furnishings were sleek and modern, not so much as a stray paper clip in sight.

"May I help you?" the receptionist asked coldly.

"Mindy Eden for Sam."

"Is he expecting you?"

For an instant, Mindy considered answering honestly and saying no, but Sam had to be expecting her. He didn't do things like buy a building out from under someone unless he was expecting a response. "Yes. He is."

The receptionist picked up the phone and eyed Mindy as she spoke to Sam. "Yes, sir, Mr. Blackwell. Of course," she said before hanging up. "He'll be with you soon."

An eternity went by as Mindy paced in the reception area. Back and forth she went, but she wasn't about to sit down. She had too much anxiety coursing through her veins. The thought of seeing Sam made her nervous, a reaction she needed to stomp into submission. She would get what she wanted today. She would not let him control her.

She'd nearly convinced herself of it until all six feet and six inches of deliciously imposing Sam Blackwell appeared before her.

"Mindy." His voice was smooth and low, the sound filtering into her ears and quickly spreading through her entire body. It was like being gently shaken awake, something Sam had done to her countless times, rolling over in bed and pressing his long, lean form against hers. Sam was insatiable. He always wanted more of everything. Seeing him now made Mindy want to give him at least a little something. He was too appealing for words in black trousers and a charcoal-gray shirt, no tie, the sleeves rolled up to the elbows, showing off his firm forearms and his silver Rolex. His jet-black hair perfectly walked the line between tidy and messy. "I'd wondered when you'd turn up."

Damn him. So he *had* planned this. He'd lured her

here by buying the Mercer and she'd taken the bait. Maybe she should have let Matthew deal with this, but it was too late for that. She had to stay strong. Confident. She couldn't let Sam rattle her. "I need fifteen minutes. In your office."

"That sounds like a lot more fun than what I was just working on." His eyebrows bounced, and the corners of his mouth threatened to curve into a smile.

Mindy cursed herself for thinking exactly what he was thinking. Fifteen minutes was plenty of time to do a lot of sexy things to each other. "If I do it right, it will only be fun for me."

"I've had worse offers." Sam waved Mindy closer, waiting until she started down the hall first. "Last door on the right."

"I remember." Mindy led the way, ignoring the intoxicating effect of having her lungs filled with Sam Blackwell–scented air, hoping she could find the strength to outmaneuver him and get the Mercer Building, all with her pride and heart intact.

Sam had a definite opinion about most things, but he was uncertain how to feel about Mindy Eden showing up at his office. Judging by the tug in the center of his chest the instant he saw her, he'd missed her. As he trailed behind her down the hall, the tension building in his hips confirmed that at the very least he'd missed her body—every killer curve. But he didn't trust Mindy. Not anymore. By the third time you get kicked out of a woman's life, she's officially taken the gloves off.

"What can I do for you?" Sam asked, closing the door behind him.

Mindy dropped her handbag in one of the chairs opposite his desk. "I had hoped you and I were beyond guessing games."

"If we are, it's because I don't play them. I honestly have no idea why you're here." He rounded his desk but waited to sit. "Please. Have a seat."

Mindy shook her head, her russet-red hair a wavy tumble across the shoulders of her trim-fitting black jacket. Peeking out from beneath her lapel was something black and lacy. He loved that she worked in a fashion-forward business and could apply a sexy edge to her wardrobe. "I'm not staying. I'm here about the Mercer Building. You know, the historic warehouse out in New Jersey that I was about to buy? You snatched it out from under me. You're trying to meddle in my business."

"I might have bought it, but it had nothing to do with your business."

Mindy's pouty berry-pink mouth went slack with disbelief. "So what, then? Was this some attempt to get back together with me?"

Wow. He had *not* seen that coming. "Is that really what you think?" He rounded his desk and closed in on her, enough to smell her perfume and see firsthand the touchable texture of her skin. His mind and body began to wage a battle. There was no telling which would win out—the urge to keep her at arm's length or the one to wrap her up in them. "I don't hear from you for five months and you think that I'm suddenly so struck with affection for you that I devise some silly plan to lure you to my office? Believe me, Mindy. If I wanted to get back together with you, I would call you. On the telephone. And I would ask you out."

Mindy crossed her arms as if she was determined to keep him away. "I have a hard time believing you aren't up to something, and it's not my fault that I suspect it. That's what you do. You meddle. You've interfered with Eden's plenty."

If only Mindy knew that what she saw as meddling, he considered to be nothing more than a favor. "I'm not a gatecrasher, Mindy, no matter what you think. I had nothing to do with buying that building out from under you. I don't know why Eden's would want it anyway. You have enough space in Manhattan to build a cruise ship."

"It's not for Eden's. It's for BMO. My company. We need to find a single space for our entire operation. Having things scattered all over the place is killing our margins."

That was a different case. BMO was Mindy's baby, but she'd left it in the hands of someone else. Had she managed to worm her way out of her duties at Eden's? Was that why she was taking time to personally address this issue? "I thought you were letting the interim CEO take the reins."

"I'm still involved in the day-to-day. I'm not really capable of being hands-off."

The phrase made Sam want to thread his fingers through Mindy's hair, but he pushed the thought aside. "I get that. I'm the same way."

"It's only a little more than a year until I will have fulfilled my two-year obligation to Eden's and can hightail it out of there. I'm not going to stop putting my mark on the world with BMO."

He'd always admired Mindy's determination. When

she wanted something, she did *not* take her eyes off the prize. That had actually been part of the fun of being with her—trying to distract her. It almost always involved the two of them taking off each other's clothes. "Then how can I help? Do you want me to see if I can help you find a different space?"

"No. I want you to sell the Mercer Building to me."

He stepped back, perching on the very edge of his desk and stretching out his legs, crossing them at the ankles. He pinched his lower lip between his thumb and index finger. It wouldn't be a travesty if he decided to sell her the building, but Mindy was his key to an event he'd been certain before now he'd never get into. An event he needed to be at. "I need something in return." He didn't want to be greedy, but he also didn't want to be foolish. Why do a favor for Mindy? Out of the goodness of his heart? She'd ground his ego into the dirt with her stiletto heels. He didn't owe her a thing.

"A pile of money?"

"No. An invitation to your sister's wedding."

Mindy reared back her head, eyes wide with astonishment. "That's in a week. There are no invites to be had. Plus, why would you even want to go to Sophie's wedding? Half of the guest list doesn't like you."

Sam didn't hurt easily, but that wasn't an easy remark to hear. "It makes me look second-rate to not be attending the social event of the year."

"Since when do you care what people think about you?"

"A good businessperson always cares about their reputation. I've been concentrating my work in New York and I need to be firmly entrenched in those social circles if I'm going to get anything real done in this town." His sister, Isabel, had been the one to encourage him to stick closer to Manhattan over the last five months. She'd told him he couldn't outrun his feelings by buzzing to Prague or Buenos Aires or wherever the smell of money and big deals lured him. Logic said that the minute Mindy dumped him last time, he would want to be as far away as possible. The Eden family was impossible to ignore in this city. But he suspected Isabel was right. He couldn't avoid everything that caused him pain. Even when he'd had more than enough to last him a lifetime.

"I couldn't get an invitation for the queen of England right now. Sophie has been moaning for months about how tight the guest list is, and now that we're this close, she's perpetually freaking out."

Sam's mind immediately leaped to a solution. He cleared his throat and prepared himself for another potentially insulting answer. "Who's your date?"

A rush of pink colored Mindy's cheeks. She batted her lashes and looked away. "I don't have one. So what?"

"There's no need to be defensive about it." Sam had to fight the smile that wanted to cross his lips. He didn't want to be so happy that Mindy Eden, one of the most extraordinary women in the city, didn't have a date for her own sister's wedding. But he was. "I could fix that for you. You'd be killing two birds with one stone. Getting your building and a date."

"You'll really sell me the building if I take you to Sophie's wedding? That's all you want?"

Sam was surprised Mindy had asked the question,

a classic misstep in negotiations. Never let on that you think you're getting a great deal. "Take me to the rehearsal dinner, too. You know, make it seem like I'm really in the inner circle."

"I'm not sure this is such a good idea. You and I both know we don't work as a couple."

Sam shrugged and pushed off from the desk, taking his seat behind it. He was wary of the idea, only because he knew how frustrating it would be to spend time with Mindy and not be able to touch her. But he could get some real business done at Sophie and Jake's wedding. He might even mend a few Eden fences. "Like I said, not struck with affection for you. But I think I could be convinced to keep you as a friend."

Mindy's blue-green eyes were full of questions, and maybe disappointment, too. He was okay with that. She'd taken him down many notches more than once. Let her know how much it hurt. "Okay. If you'll sell me the Mercer Building for what you paid, I will bring you to her wedding."

"And the rehearsal."

"I'll have to figure out how to play it with Sophie, but okay. The rehearsal, too."

"For what I paid?"

"Yes. Not a penny more."

"And as friends."

She grumbled and plucked her handbag from the chair, hooking it on her arm. "If that's what we're shooting for, then yes. Friends."

Sam got up to walk her out.

"I can find my way," she shot at him.

"I know that. I just want to be sure you don't steal anything on your way out."

"Very funny."

"Okay, then. You go ahead. I'll just watch." He leaned against the door frame, grinning to himself. Their impromptu meeting had been a win for him, especially the last part. He'd come off like a gentleman, when really he'd been after only a spectacular eyeful as Mindy walked away.

Two

As Mindy left Sam's office, only one thought was running through her head: *What in the hell did I just agree to?* Letting Sam be her date to Sophie's wedding? On a long list of bad ideas, this not only belonged at the very top, it was the entire reason for making a list in the first place. Sam was trouble. Her family, for all intents and purposes, hated him. He was the king of underhanded behavior, which he always managed to explain away as somehow noble or good. Then there was the unavoidable fact that Mindy seemed to lose about fifty points off her IQ when she was around him. He had a real talent for making her do stupid things. Case in point, agreeing to let him take her to Sophie's wedding.

Judging by the way she'd felt during their short meeting, it wouldn't be hard for him to do it to her again. Her physical attraction to him was still off the charts. That was why she hadn't taken a seat, even when her brand-new Louboutins were killing her feet. She couldn't allow herself to linger or get comfortable, even when she'd wanted nothing more than to unbutton her jacket and ask him if he wanted to rekindle the flame between them. One more time. For old times' sake. But Sam was too sly and clever. Whip-smart and devious. There were plenty of reasons to stay away.

Of course, he'd been clear that attending the wedding together would be only as friends. That one detail of their agreement had helped her decide she could escape this scenario unscathed. So she'd be on the arm of a ridiculously hot guy for a few nights, she wouldn't have to go stag to Sophie's wedding and she'd get the building her business so desperately needed. This was a win-win-win. As long as she kept her clothes on and her head out of the clouds.

Clay whisked Mindy off to Eden's, dropping her off at the south entrance on Thirty-Sixth Street. She breezed through the store, past cosmetics and the perfume girls, through ladies' accessories to the back elevators that would take her up to the executive offices. She still hadn't figured out how to handle this news with Sophie, although she had an idea about an approach involving one of Jake's groomsmen, Gerald, and his wandering hands.

"Hey, Soph," Mindy said, knocking on Sophie's doorway, which was almost always open. "Do you have a minute?"

"Sure. I can't keep my mind on work right now anyway." Her sister pushed back from her desk, gathering her sleek red locks in her hand and pulling them in a bundle over one shoulder. Always fashionable and put-together, Sophie was wearing a jade green floral dress with dramatic bell sleeves.

Mindy was making herself at home on Sophie's gray velvet sofa when Emma appeared at the door.

"Discussing wedding stuff, by any chance?" she asked.

"Yes. Actually. That's exactly why I wanted to talk to Sophie." Mindy patted the seat next to her. "Join us."

"You guys want to talk about the wedding?" Sophie asked, incredulous. "I always feel like I'm jamming it down your throat."

Emma glanced over at Mindy and without words, conveyed their shared desire for the relief they would feel when Sophie's wedding was over. "Oh, no. We love to talk about the wedding," Emma said, putting on an excellent front.

"It's the best part of the day," Mindy lied.

Emma tucked her long chocolate-brown hair behind her ear and crossed her legs, showing off an incredible pair of cherry-red Manolo Blahnik pumps. The three sisters did enjoy outdoing each other when it came to shoes, although this was a daring choice for the other-wise more subdued Emma. Her charcoal tweed pencil skirt and jacket made a nice counterpoint. "Absolutely. Mindy, what's your news?"

Mindy wasn't about to stall. She wanted to get this over with. "I found a date for the wedding. If you can just let Jake know and have him somehow filter that news down to Gerald, that would be great."

"Why don't you tell Gerald yourself? Doesn't he text you four or five times a day?"

This was true. Gerald had been putting the full-court press on Mindy from the moment he met her at the first engagement party. He was one of Jake's business school pals, and Sophie had known him then, as well. He had it in his head that Jake and Sophie along with Mindy and Gerald would make the perfect pair of power couples. Mindy had been clear that she wasn't interested, but she'd delivered that news gently, only because she knew she was going to see Gerald a lot at the various events leading up to the wedding. Apparently she'd been too soft with her approach. Gerald didn't seem to be taking the hint.

"Yes. He does. I just don't know how to work that particular detail into a text conversation."

"Then call him," Sophie said.

"I don't want to encourage him. And this was all your idea in the first place. Telling me to get a date to send him a signal."

"So?" Emma knocked Mindy's knee with her own. "Who's the guy?"

Mindy couldn't afford to hesitate with her answer. "Sam."

The room went dead silent. Mindy braced for the fallout.

"No. No way," Sophie said. "Absolutely not."

"What? You can't tell me who I can bring as a date. I'm a grown woman."

"Not around Sam you aren't. And it's my wedding. I don't like Sam. My future husband despises him. And frankly, you shouldn't like him, either. Just think about the things he's done to interfere with our business." Sophie gestured to Emma. "Or our own sister, for that matter. He was the one who leaked the story of Emma's childhood to the tabloids."

"Which was ultimately a good thing, wasn't it?" Mindy turned to Emma, pleading with her eyes.

"It was." Emma looked back and forth between Mindy and Sophie, seeming stuck. "I just wish I would've had the chance to do it myself."

"See? There you go." Sophie sat back in her chair. "You are not bringing Sam Blackwell to my wedding. If nothing else, he is going to stomp all over your heart, and I am not going to watch that happen again."

"Ah, but see, that won't be a problem. We agreed that we're only attending as friends."

"Why in the world would you even want to be friends with him? Does he have any friends? Is he capable of it?" Sophie asked.

Mindy had been afraid of that question, but she'd anticipated it. She considered telling Emma and Sophie about the deal for the Mercer Building, but that seemed like news for after the wedding. She didn't want to give them any more reasons to question his motives. "Whatever you think of him, we were good friends. We understand each other, at least from a business standpoint. And I couldn't find a date. That's the very sad reality of my life right now. I know you think Gerald is harmless, but I'd like to keep him at bay."

Sophie nodded, seeming to think hard about all of this. Emma sat back and wrapped her arms around her middle.

"What, you guys? Just tell me what you're thinking. I can take it."

"Even if it all goes fine, even if there are no problems, I worry about you and Sam together, especially in a romantic environment like a wedding," Sophie said softly.

"It's true. It's hard not to get caught up in the romanticism. And you were so sad after the last time you and Sam broke up," Emma added.

"I broke up with him because I couldn't be in any way disloyal to you guys. I told him as much. And of course I was sad, but we've had five months apart and I think we're ready to be friends." Mindy doubted whether that was at all possible, but she had to try, at least to get the Mercer Building.

"I'm worried you'll fall for him again. Then you'll be miserable. Again," Sophie said.

"I won't."

"You will."

"I will not," Mindy insisted.

"Wanna bet?" Sophie asked.

"I told you I won't fall for him," Mindy restated.

"Then bet me. I know you and you hate to lose. So we'll make a bet and as long as you don't lose it, you won't get hurt." Sophie grabbed the pencil on her desk and began tapping it against a legal pad. "The question is what to bet."

"I know," Emma said. "The one thing Mindy doesn't want, to stay at Eden's longer than she has to."

Mindy was struck with horror while Sophie's expression became one of sheer delight. "Yes. That's perfect." Sophie clapped her hands together gleefully. "You promise me there will be no romance between you and Sam, and I will stop pestering you about staying on at Eden's beyond the deadline next year."

"And if I lose?" Mindy asked, wary of the whole thing.

"Then you have to stay for one more year. That should give Emma and me enough time to convince you to stay full-time."

Mindy was starting to feel trapped, a feeling she didn't handle well. Sophie and Emma had both been making their case for Mindy to sell BMO and stay at Eden's. But maybe this bet could be a good one. It would keep her from falling under Sam's spell. The very last thing she wanted was to spend an extra year at Eden's. The second-to-last thing she wanted was to deal with Sophie's and Emma's regular hints about her staying.

"We're talking a real bet, you two." Mindy pointed back and forth between Sophie and Emma. "You guys don't get to say one more thing to me about walking away from BMO if I'm able to keep Sam in the friend zone. Not a peep. No guilt trips. Nothing."

Emma nodded. "I'm good with it."

"Me, too," Sophie said.

"Fine. It's settled." Mindy got up from her seat, feeling pretty good about having gotten everything she needed out of a second meeting today. "Oh, and just so you know, I'm planning on bringing Sam to the rehearsal dinner."

"Seriously?" Sophie asked.

"Yes. Just think of it as one more chance for you to win your bet." Mindy stopped at the door and turned to Emma. "I almost forgot. Emma, did you have something you wanted to talk about?"

Emma noticeably winced. "I guess my mom and your mom had a phone conversation. It didn't go well. Your mom hung up on mine." Jenny Stewart, Emma's mom, and Jill Eden, Sophie and Mindy's mom, had a complicated relationship. They were sisters. Who didn't speak to each other. They'd also each had children by the same man, making Emma not only Sophie and Mindy's cousin, but their half sister, as well. It was a bizarre situation, to say the least. All three sisters had hoped that the occasion of Sophie's wedding and the fact that they were all working together now might be a reason for the moms to make amends. Apparently not.

"Is this going to be a problem at the wedding?" Sophie asked. "I don't think I can handle any more stress."

Emma shook her head. "I figure I'll handle my mom and Mindy can handle yours. As long as we keep them apart, it should be fine. There might be some steely silence, but that should be the extent of the drama. I promise we'll keep everything going smoothly."

Sophie took a deep breath, her shoulders rising and falling. "Okay, then. Let's hope this all goes off without a hitch."

Sam couldn't keep Mindy off his mind, even though he had a mountain of work to do. *This will be a good thing,* he kept saying to himself, although he wasn't 100 percent sure. Attending Sophie and Jake's wedding certainly had the potential to put Sam back into a few business and social circles he'd managed to spin himself out of. But he also worried there was something else to it.

Every time he read about the upcoming nuptials, it sent him into a downward spiral, thinking about Mindy's life and wondering what she was doing and—most important—whom she was dating. He'd jumped at the chance to stake his claim on Mindy the instant he realized she didn't have a date. But there was no claiming Mindy. She was her own person, through and through. Would this wedding just end up being an exercise in public humiliation? Quite possibly. But without risk came no reward. And he knew that his bad relationship with the Eden family had to end. It was keeping him from making all of the money he wanted to make.

Sam jumped when his phone line buzzed.

"Mr. Blackwell. Mindy Eden is on the line for you." It was almost as if she knew he'd been thinking about her.

"Mindy, hi. Two conversations in one day. I hardly know what to make of this."

"I won't keep you long if that's what you're worried about."

"Believe me, I'm not worried."

"I was calling to give you the details of the rehearsal dinner and the wedding. I tried to reach you on your cell, but some woman answered and told me to call you at the office. Please tell me that wasn't Valerie Cash I just spoke to. I refuse to go with a taken man to my sister's wedding."

Sam pursed his lips to stifle a laugh. Mindy did have a bit of a jealous streak. "Valerie and I are no longer dating. It was a very short-lived thing."

"Long enough to be in the tabloids more than once."

So she *was* jealous. If that was the case, why hadn't

she tried to beat Valerie Cash at her own game? He would've given in without too much of a fight. Okay... a little fight. But now? Months later? He wasn't feeling generous. "It's over. That's all you need to know." He swallowed hard and prepared himself for the question he had to ask. "How'd you manage to keep your love life under wraps that whole time?"

Mindy laughed quietly. "Cute, Sam. Real cute."

"What?"

"Nice attempt at digging for information. I'm not about to tell you what I've been up to. I'd rather keep the mystery alive. Also, I'd rather ask about the mysterious woman answering your phone."

"It's one of my assistants. My phone has been acting up, so she's out getting me a new one."

Several seconds of silence wound its way through the line. "Oh. Okay."

Sam couldn't help but notice how uncertain Mindy sounded. Had she really been bothered that much by his relationship with Valerie? Had that been what kept her away? "So the wedding. Do you want to just text me the details?"

"Sure. I can do that. You should know that since the wedding is taking place at the Grand Legacy Hotel, I'm staying there both nights. If you wanted to do that, you could book a room. It would just need to be a separate room. And I don't know what their availability is."

"Right. Friends and all."

"Exactly."

"I think I'll sleep in my own bed those nights." *It will save me the temptation.* "So how did Sophie take the news that I was coming?"

"She wasn't superexcited, but she was fine. Don't worry about my sister. She'll be too drunk on love and attention to know what's going on. You just play the part of model wedding guest and we'll be fine."

"I do know how to behave in social situations, you know."

"I know. I guess I'm just restating the obvious." Mindy blew out a breath of frustration. "I should go. My to-do list is ridiculous."

"Oh, sure. Me, too." For some reason, Sam couldn't bring himself to say goodbye and he sensed that Mindy was feeling the same way. "Big plans this weekend?"

"Sleeping, perhaps. Maybe brunch on Sunday. How about you?"

"Definitely the sleeping part. You know how I feel about brunch."

"You're the only person I know who doesn't like it." Despite her words, Mindy's voice was light and playful.

"Well, which is it? Breakfast? Or lunch? Make up your mind, brunch. You don't get to be both. Plus, it's basically cutting out an entire meal, which is a big downside for me. I will always eat."

"I actually noticed today that you were looking a bit skinny. Are you sure you've been eating?"

Sam ran his hand over his stomach. He hadn't weighed himself in forever, but he had noticed that his pants were getting a bit loose. "Clearly not enough if you think I'm looking scrawny."

"I didn't say *scrawny*. I said *skinny*. You're still all muscle."

Sam had to swallow back a groan. The thought of Mindy looking at him that closely was a definite turn-on. One he knew he shouldn't be relishing too much. "I'm not sure friends should be making comments about each other's bodies."

"It was just an observation," Mindy retorted.

"Fair enough. For the record, you looked perfect today." *Every last inch.*

"You're just sucking up to me because I'm taking you to the wedding of the year."

Not really. "You've always seen right through me, Mindy Eden. I can't get a single thing past you, can I?"

Mindy laughed again, a musical sound that made Sam feel a little lighter. "Nope. So you'd better stay on your toes. I'll call you next week so we can make a plan for the rehearsal on Friday."

"Sounds perfect."

Sam and Mindy said their goodbyes, but as soon as he hung up, his office line buzzed again. "Mr. Blackwell? There's a Ms. Parson on the phone. She won't tell me who she's with or what she's calling about, but she's very insistent that she needs to speak with you."

Sam was more than a little annoyed by this. Just when he'd been having fun talking to Mindy, he had to be smacked in the face with a less-than-pleasant call. "Put her through."

"Mr. Blackwell?" Ms. Parson asked.

"I thought I asked you to never call me at the office."

"You did, and I'm sorry, but I was unable to reach you on your cell phone."

"Yeah. Sorry about that. Long story."

"Well, I'm very sorry to bother you during the day. I was as discreet as I could be when I called." Ms. Par-

son had always kept Sam's business with her a secret,
at his request.

"It's fine. What can I do for you?"

"I know your involvement with our organization has
always been anonymous, but there's a potential problem with the couple who is underwriting and hosting
this year's big event. Do you know who and what I'm
talking about?"

Sam had heard inklings of this. "The senator and her
husband. Something about a sex scandal?"

"Yes. I'm afraid so. Obviously, if that continues to
play out the way it is in the tabloids, we're going to have
to ask them to step aside. Which means we will need a
new host for the event. You'd be the perfect person to
do it. You've been such a big contributor for so long."

Sam drew in a deep breath. He'd attended this event
many times and was well aware of what hosting it involved—getting up in front of a crowd of five hundred
people and asking them to open their wallets, usually
by telling a story that caused people to reach for a tissue. "That would require me to step into the spotlight.
I prefer to keep my personal life, especially my past,
out of the public eye."

"I know that, Mr. Blackwell. And we've always re-
spected your wishes. Always. But perhaps it's time to be
a bit more public about your involvement. People might
benefit from hearing your story, especially since your
mother was so young when she passed away."

"I'll think about it. No promises." Sam hung up,
swallowed hard and looked out the window. He didn't
like to think about this. It was too painful. He preferred to write a sizable check every year, try very hard

to forget the difficult parts of his past and to remember happier times. Those days were so far gone, it was sometimes hard to believe they'd ever existed. His sister, Isabel, was the only person on the planet still around to remind him that any of it had ever been real.

Three

Sam's driver dropped him off in front of the Grand
Legacy Hotel on Forty-Fifth Street, a few blocks west of
the bright lights and perpetual hustle of Times Square.
The night air held just a hint of cooler fall weather, but
Sam would take what he could get. Summer in New
York was insufferable. He was glad to see it gone.

Sam had always admired the Grand Legacy, an art
deco jewel brought back to life by fellow real estate de-
veloper Sawyer Locke and his brother, Noah. Sam was
hoping to get some face time with them both tomorrow during the wedding reception, along with many
other notable members of that business circle. Spending more time in New York over the last several months
had meant confronting a lot of his earliest misdeeds
in business. He could admit that he'd been a little too

ruthless more than once. He wished that hadn't been the case, but when you'd been on your own since the age of seventeen, you became a survivalist. You took as much as you could, even if it meant amassing more money than you could ever spend. Every dollar in the bank was another layer of security. Now that he was thirty-six, he was starting to see the errors of his ways. He wanted to mend a few fences, especially with Jake Wheeler, Sophie's fiancé.

Sam stepped into the lobby and straightened his jacket as he scanned the crowd ahead, a throng of people talking and mingling near the hotel's grand staircase, which led up to the main bar, the hotel's speakeasy during prohibition. He'd dressed in a charcoal-gray suit, white shirt and midnight-blue tie—quite a conservative getup for a guy who preferred to wear only the darkest colors, black if he could get away with it. For the first time in his life, he was making an effort to blend in rather than lurk in the shadows.

It took him only a few seconds to spot Mindy. Being a head taller than most people afforded him the luxury, and he took full advantage of the view. She was simply stunning in a black cocktail dress, her scarlet-red hair framing her flawless face in shiny waves. As he moved through the crowd to reach her, he saw that she was having a conversation with a man he didn't recognize. He knew that look on her face—her lips pulled tight in a thin smile. She wasn't happy. The man put his arm around her and kissed her cheek. Mindy recoiled and Sam was ready to push past several people to save her, but she turned her head and spotted him, her eyes flashing bright. She muttered something to the man, then quickly wound her way to Sam.

"You're here!" she exclaimed, throwing her arms around his neck and pulling him forward until he had no choice but to kiss her square on the lips. "We're going to have to abandon that whole just-friends thing," she muttered against his mouth.

Sam reflexively wrapped his arms around her waist, his lips buzzing from the kiss. Mindy flattened herself against his chest, making everything in his body go tight. "What happened?" he asked, mumbling into her ear. Her silky hair brushed his cheek. Her skin was so soft and warm. He knew then that no matter what she said to him next, this wedding was going to be a test.

Mindy released him from her embrace but quickly tucked herself under his arm, placing her hand on his stomach. "See that guy I was talking to?" she asked out of the side of her mouth.

Sam cast his sights down at her, loving the view the deep V of her neckline gave him. "I couldn't help but notice. He seems to like you." Sure enough, Sam casually glanced at the man, who was narrowly watching them while he stabbed ice cubes in a glass with a cocktail stirrer.

"That's Gerald Van Dyke. One of the groomsmen. For some unknown reason, he has a big thing for me. I keep telling him I'm not interested, but he thinks I'm kidding. Like he can't seem to fathom it."

"He's a good-looking guy. He's probably not used to women turning him down."

Mindy gazed up at him. "And he's loaded, too. So

I'm sure he thinks I'm nuts for not being interested, but he's just not my type."

"I wasn't aware that you had a type."

Mindy shook her head at him. "Take a look in the mirror and you'll know exactly what I have a big weakness for."

Sam appreciated knowing that he was at least physically what Mindy wanted, but that almost cast their past in a worse light. Had it been nothing more than sex to her? Her propensity for ordering him out of her apartment made him think yes. "Do you typically kick guys who are your type out of your life?"

"I had no choice when you were messing with my family. Especially since none of them are particularly fond of you because of it. And I still don't buy your excuse that you were trying to make me happy."

Sam knew then how little Mindy understood him. "Why? Do you truly believe that I don't care about the happiness of others?"

"It's not that so much as you don't seem like the kind of guy who would try to save someone. Especially more than once."

"There are lots of things you don't know about me, Mindy." He'd have to leave it at that.

"Yeah? Because I feel like you're an open book." She again made eye contact, her expression nothing but clear conviction. "It's one of the things I like most about you. You always tell me exactly what you're thinking."

Not even close. Out of the corner of his eye, Sam could see that Sophie and Jake were making their way closer to them. "This might be a conversation for another time."

"Right. Well, regardless, you and I need to pretend like we like each other a lot. Just until Gerald gets on a plane back to Miami."

Sam leaned down and kissed Mindy's temple, hoping Gerald would take the hint. "I think I remember how to do that." *I have a lot of practice.*

"Good." Mindy faced him again and smoothed her hand across his chest, sending a tidal wave of warmth through his body. This no-longer-friends plan of hers might kill him. "I hope you can keep it up for a few days."

Sam settled his hand in the small of her back and pulled her against him. Their physical proximity was doing more than make him miss what they'd had before. He felt almost desperate to reclaim it. If only for one night. "You know I can keep it up long enough to make you very happy."

One corner of her luscious mouth pulled into a smile. "Clever. I also forgot to mention that you might have to stay here with me tonight and tomorrow."

Now Sam knew he was truly in trouble. He and Mindy wouldn't last two seconds behind closed doors. It was a miracle they hadn't torn off each other's clothes a week ago in his office. "I feel like you're breaking every parameter of our agreement."

"I'm sorry, but Gerald's room is across the hall from mine. I'm not sure a do-not-disturb sign will be enough to keep him from knocking on my door or slipping creepy notes under it."

"So you need me to be your muscle."

"I prefer to think of you as a stunt boyfriend."

Sam laughed at the joke, but these were dangerous

waters to be wading into with Mindy. Why did he have to be so drawn to the one woman who was most likely to take everything she wanted from him with absolutely no guarantees of anything else?

Mindy was digging herself a deeper hole with every passing minute in Sam's very capable arms, but she had no choice. She'd never be able to enjoy her sister's wedding if Gerald was pestering her. However much she and Emma had complained about Sophie while she'd been planning the wedding, they both very much wanted it to be a perfect affair. This was a time for celebration.

"Sophie and Jake are coming this way," Sam mumbled into her ear.

Unfortunately, staying away from Gerald by staying close to Sam was only going to convince Sophie that Mindy had fallen under his spell again. For the moment, Mindy was stuck between the rock that was Sam and the hard place that was her sister.

"Jake. Sophie. Congratulations." Sam gave Sophie a quick hug, then shook Jake's hand. The two men were quickly locked in a steely-eyed staring contest.

"Thank you, Sam," Sophie said, bugging her eyes at Mindy. "Don't you two look cozy over in this quiet corner." It wasn't a question. It was a statement.

"The lobby is packed. Everybody's cozy," Mindy countered, knowing she'd have to explain to Sophie that she and Sam were canoodling in public only out of necessity.

Jake stood back and put his arm around Sophie. Sam stuffed his hands into his pockets. Mindy felt an urgent need to remedy the distinct lack of conversation.

"The rehearsal went well. I'm sure tomorrow will be amazing."

Sophie smiled, but Mindy could see the unease on her face. Was it prewedding jitters or did she truly despise Sam that much? "I hope everything goes off as planned. I don't want to have to stress at all."

"Everything will be perfect," Mindy replied. "If there are any problems, Emma and I will deal with them."

"So, Jake, how's business these days?" Sam asked. For a moment it felt as if they were all holding their breath, waiting for the answer.

Jake allowed the corners of his mouth to turn up, but it wasn't even close to being a real smile. "Better than ever, although I'm surprised you'd ask. It's one thing for you to show up at my wedding as Mindy's date, and quite another for you to ask about business. As if you actually care about that part of my life."

Mindy was shocked by Jake's tone. She knew he didn't like Sam, but this was more biting than she'd ever heard from him. She looked to Sophie for answers, but her sister was pursing her lips and avoiding eye contact.

"Come on, Jake," Sam replied. "That was a long time ago. You shouldn't hold on to animosities for so long. You're getting married to an amazing woman. This should be a happy time."

Before Mindy had a chance to figure out what was transpiring between Sam and her future brother-in-law, Jake had dropped his hold on Sophie and was nearly toe-to-toe with Sam. "You don't get to tell me what to do. Especially not about my work or my personal life."

"Jake. Stop. What is going on with you?" Sophie tugged on Jake's arm.

He cast an uncharacteristically mean-spirited look at Mindy. "Your sister brought a jerk to our wedding. That's what's wrong."

"Hey. Jake. That's not cool," Mindy said. "And don't talk like that. You'll just upset Sophie."

Sam reached for Mindy's hand. "No. No. It's okay." He then turned to Sophie while Mindy thought her heart was going to punch a hole in her chest. Her pulse was racing. "Sophie, apparently Jake never told you that he and I were almost business partners at one point. A long time ago."

"We were more than possible business partners, Sam. We were friends. And we never became partners because Sam talked me out of going in with him on what ended up being his first big deal. He made a mint and completely cut me out of the profits."

Was this the root of the dissension between Jake and Sam? It certainly sounded like something Sam would do. A person didn't get a ruthless reputation by being anything less than cutthroat.

From across the room came the sound of clinking glass. "Ladies and gentlemen, if you can all begin moving into the restaurant's private dining room, we'll be serving dinner soon."

"Look. We have to go." Sophie seemed nothing less than flustered, which Mindy hated seeing. "I guess we'll see you two later. Just, please, no drama."

Jake and Sophie blazed a trail through the crowd while Sam pulled Mindy aside.

"Maybe this wasn't such a good idea. I think I underestimated how much Jake is still holding a grudge."

"Did you really screw him over?"

Sam took in a deep breath through his nose. "I wouldn't characterize it quite like that. We were both getting our businesses off the ground. Neither of us really knew what we were doing."

Was this Sam covering his tracks? He had a way of seeing his own misdeeds in quite a different light than others. "Cutting a friend out of a deal is no small thing. And you're a smart guy. I don't buy for a minute that you didn't know that because you were only starting out."

He nodded in agreement, but the tension on his face was clear. "You're right. You're absolutely right. I had my reasons for doing it, though."

"Can you tell me what they were?"

"This was years ago, Mindy. I don't really want to dredge up the past."

"And I get that, but Jake is clearly still angry about it, and he's marrying my sister, so I feel like I deserve to know your side. So I can at least defend you. That is, if you deserve defending." She still didn't trust Sam completely, but she did feel like she'd learned more about him during their last two conversations than she'd ever known about him. She couldn't help but want to push for more. It was just her way.

"Tell you what. I'll explain it later."

"Later tonight? When you come to my room?"

"Yeah. About that. I'm not so sure that's a good idea. How about I walk you up to your room and sneak out when it looks like the coast is clear?"

Mindy hated the disappointment that came with Sam's answer, but it was the sensible choice and she was determined to be nothing but smart about Sam. "I'll take what I can get from you, Sam Blackwell."

"I expect nothing less."

Sam and Mindy made their way into the dining room and took their seats, across the table from Jake and Sophie. All Mindy could do was hope that Sophie wasn't feeling as on edge as she was, but judging by the number of glasses of champagne Sophie had downed, she was working hard to smooth her ragged edges. As difficult as it was for Mindy to imagine herself as the bride-to-be, she tried to put herself in her sister's shoes. If she was getting married, she definitely wouldn't want to endure any hostility between her groom and her sister's date. This was Sophie's time, and Mindy needed to stay focused on doing everything she could to help make it perfect.

As dessert was served, the toasts were announced by Jake's best man, who gently clinked a spoon against his wineglass. Mindy listened to his sweet and sentimental words for the happy couple, hoping she could measure up. She didn't want to let her sister down. When it came time for Mindy's turn, Sophie reached across the table and squeezed her hand.

"I hope you know how much I love you," Sophie said quietly.

Tears immediately welled in Mindy's eyes. She nodded eagerly. "Me, too. I love you so much." She stood and raised her glass, trying to run through her carefully crafted toast, while the realization of her predicament settled over her. Even if she took Sam and the bet with her sisters out of it, the reality was that she and Sophie and Emma were bound tight, and that bond was getting stronger every day. It was going to be ridiculously hard to walk away from Eden's in a year. Even when that had always been Mindy's plan. Even when that was what she'd wanted all along, there would be no easy way out.

"I want to say that I'm incredibly lucky to have the best sisters in the world. We don't always agree or get along, but at the end of the day, I know that they both have my back." She turned to Sophie, trying to ward off the lump that was forming in her throat. They had been through so much together, and it was time to recognize that. "Sophie, you and I have been thick as thieves since the minute Mom and Dad brought you home from the hospital. You have always been fiercely loyal and full of the best intentions. Nobody deserves to have found true love more than you. I know that you and Jake will have a long and loving life together, and I couldn't be happier for you."

Everyone in the dining room offered a hearty "Hear, hear!" Mindy knocked back the last of her champagne, then became fixed on the sight of Jake and Sophie. They exchanged a sweet kiss, then looked deeply into each other's eyes. It was so easy to see that there was nothing but love and admiration between them. Mindy didn't want to be envious, but there was an invisible force pulling at her and leaving her feeling empty inside. She turned to Sam, only to see that he was watching them, too. He glanced over at Mindy, shrugged, then slugged back the last of his drink. Did he think this was all unbelievably sappy? Too sweet? If so, what had made Sam so hardened to the world? Was it simply years of pursuing big deals with no regard for the toll? Had his immense success made him not care about the more important things in life?

As the guests began to dwindle, Sam got up from his seat. "I'm pretty tired, so if you're still wanting me to walk you up to your room, it would be great if we could go now."

Mindy saw that Sophie and Jake were deep in conversation. Emma and her fiancé, Daniel, had already left. "Okay. Sure."

They strolled back through the lobby to the bank of elevators. With no one around, there was no show to put on, which meant no hand-holding. Mindy reminded herself this was for the best. She'd navigate whatever rockiness there was tomorrow, buy the building from Sam and then decide if she and he could make a run at friendship. That seemed like something Sam really needed, especially after witnessing his run-in with Jake, even if he might not ever admit it. Still, friendship meant closeness, and that would require a delicate balance. It was a narrow path to walk with Sam. It was so easy to get lured back in.

Mindy keyed into her ninth-floor suite, Sam following behind her. Before he let the door shut, he took the do-not-disturb sign and hung it on the outside knob.

"Can I make you a drink?" she asked, again filled with this uncomfortable mix of hope and regret. She hoped he'd stay, but she regretted her inclination to think that way. Why did her brain have to go there?

He leaned against the wall and again stuffed his hands into his pockets. "I'm okay. I won't stay long."

"What if you run into Gerald in the hall?"

Sam flashed her a devilish smile. "I'll tell him I'm running out for condoms."

Mindy laughed, but she had to force it out of herself. Her ill-advised hopes had officially been dashed. "Well, thank you for tonight. I know it wasn't easy. Are you sure you don't want to tell me about the Jake situation?"

He shook his head slightly and stared down at the floor. "Not right now. It's not a big deal. He'll get over it or he won't. I have no control over what other people think of me."

Mindy wasn't used to this more somber side of Sam. "Okay. Well, if you ever want to talk about it, I'm all ears. Superunderstanding and completely nonjudgmental ears."

He smiled, a breathy laugh crossing his lips. "I appreciate that."

"Any time."

"Gotta be nice to the guy whose building you so desperately want to buy. Right?"

Mindy dropped her head to one side and stepped closer to him. "It's more than that. I hope you know that."

He nodded, but judging by the look in his eyes, he wasn't necessarily buying it. "I should head out."

"Okay. Sure. Thanks for coming tonight."

"Absolutely. I'll see you tomorrow." He leaned down and pressed a soft kiss to her temple, gently gripping her shoulders. That brush of his skin sent tiny shock waves through her—pulses of electricity meant to remind her that he knew how to make her unravel. He could be her undoing.

And just like that, Sam slipped through the door to her hotel room, the door thudding shut. Mindy wandered over to the bed, kicked off her shoes and flopped back on the mattress, staring up at the ceiling. Tonight had not gone the way she'd thought it would. Some parts were better. Some parts were decidedly worse. More than anything, she was starting to see Sam in a different light. She'd always thought of him as an open book. Now she was starting to think that she might have read only the first chapter.

Four

Sam had thought once or twice about skipping Jake and Sophie's wedding. It had taken far too much self-control to walk out of Mindy's room last night. If things had been different, he would have stayed. But he wasn't ready to be pulled back into Mindy's world, however much it made him look good to be at this wedding. He wanted her, but he didn't. Part of him wanted a fuller life, and part of him wasn't convinced it was worth the hassle. In his experience, people you dare to care about eventually leave, in one way or another. In Mindy's case, they banish you from their life and pull you back in only when it suits them.

He arrived at the Grand Legacy early. Which was a good thing, judging by the panic-stricken look on Mindy's face as she rushed across the lobby to him.

"I'm so glad you're here a little early. Gerald is being ridiculous. He won't leave me alone." She glanced back over her shoulder, seemingly making sure the coast was clear.

The situation *was* ridiculous. Sam had to put it to an end. "Where is he? Let me talk to him and tell him to back off."

"You can't make a scene, Sam. Sophie is already freaking out enough as it is. Plus, I don't think Jake will like it if you're mean to one of his best friends."

Sam grumbled under his breath and pushed aside his annoyance, instead taking his chance to admire her—she was breathtaking in a flowing dove-gray bridesmaid's dress that showed off her glowing sculpted shoulders and graceful collarbone. "I can't entirely blame Gerald. You look especially beautiful today, Min."

Mindy dropped her stressed facade for an instant, while her rosy pink lips pulled into a pleased smile. "Thank you. You clean up very well. I love you in a tux. I don't think I've ever seen you wear one before." She smoothed her hand over his lapel and dragged her fingers down the length of his arm.

"I'm not a huge fan, but I figured your stunt boyfriend would wear one."

"You're absolutely right. He would. Now come on. Stay close to me." Mindy grabbed his hand and began pulling him back across the lobby toward the bank of elevators. "Gerald's not our only problem today, unfortunately. I think we have a potential catfight on our hands."

"Our problem? Don't you mean your problem? I'd

been hoping to do some networking today. Reconnect with a few big fish."

"But I need your help."

Sam didn't completely understand why he allowed himself to be pulled into Eden family drama. He only knew that it happened with regularity. "Alright. I suppose you'd better tell me why there's going to be a catfight." If today was going to be torture, and wholly unproductive from a business standpoint, at least it would be interesting.

"There's trouble brewing between my mom and Emma's mom," Mindy muttered, stopping and pulling him closer. "They're already throwing around unkind words and I'm worried about what's going to happen when champagne starts flowing at the reception. This is only the second time they've been in the same room since our grandmother died and her will was read."

"You mean the day everyone found out they'd both had children by your dad?"

"Exactly."

Other than his sister, Sam had no extended family to speak of. His father had passed away when he was sixteen and his mom less than a year later. It was just Sam and Isabel from that point on and they'd had no need for family drama. It had been enough to figure out how to survive. "Okay. Sure. What can I do to help?"

"Can I have you sit next to my mom during the ceremony? My aunt is several rows back and I convinced Lizzie, the receptionist from Eden's, to sit with her. Emma and I can worry about them during the reception."

Several guests filtered past, carrying elaborately wrapped gifts and chattering away.

"This isn't going to be a particularly fun affair for you, is it?"

"By the looks of it, no."

Sam couldn't help it. It was his inclination to help Mindy whenever she was in a tough spot.

"Okay, then. Introduce me to your mom."

Mindy took Sam's hand and they wound their way through the crowd gathered to enter the hotel's grand ballroom. They ducked past the ushers and marched straight down the aisle until they reached the first row.

"Sit right here." Mindy pointed to the second seat in. "My mom will be the first one down the aisle after the flower girls."

"Who's walking Sophie up the aisle?"

"Reginald. Eden's creative director."

"The guy who designs the window displays?"

Mindy nodded. "He was one of our gram's closest friends. He's like an uncle to us."

"The store really is an extended family, isn't it?"

"Of course it is. That's why I feel so guilty about it most of the time."

Sam studied the look of worry on Mindy's face. He knew very well her inner conflict over Eden's. She loved it, but she didn't like being tied down or told what to do. It would have been a very different situation if she'd chosen to work at Eden's. But she hadn't. Her inheritance had been tied to it. "Well, don't worry about me. I will have no problem taking care of your mom."

Mindy leaned down and kissed his cheek, leaving

behind a tingle and probably lipstick, too. "You're the best. Thank you."

Sam took his seat. "You're more than welcome." He watched as Mindy walked away, her dress swooshing back and forth. She was easily the most complicated woman he'd ever had the pleasure to be with. He usually avoided complications. But there was something about Mindy that made them, at the very least, enticing.

Guests continued to file in and he took his chance to wave or nod at a few people he hadn't seen in some time. There was the Langford family, famous for their international telecom business—Adam and his wife, Melanie, and their twin boys. Adam's sister, Anna, and her financier husband, Jacob Lin, their little girl toddling between them. By the looks of Anna, there was another baby on the way. Joining them was Aiden, the oldest brother in the family, and his wife, Sarah, along with Aiden's young son.

The Locke family, owners of the hotel, were on hand, as well. Sawyer, the oldest, and his wife, PR whiz Kendall, along with their daughter. Noah, the youngest, and his wife, Lily. And real estate power couple Charlotte and her husband, Michael. Sam even got a glimpse of a few famous New Yorkers he'd never met, like British gin magnate Marcus Chambers and his wife, television personality Ashley George, better known as the Manhattan Matchmaker.

Soon enough, the guests had filled the ballroom. The processional music began. Along with everyone else, Sam stood and watched as two flower girls flung flower petals on the aisle runner and scurried to their parents as soon as they could. After that came Jill Eden,

Mindy and Sophie's mom. She had the same flame-red hair as her daughters, but with a stylish streak of silver in the front, and carried herself as a woman who had known nothing less in her life than money and luxury. Sam pushed aside the thoughts of his own mom—they always seemed to creep in at moments like this, when major life events were occurring.

Jill smiled at Sam when she arrived at the first row. "You must be my wrangler. I've heard a lot about you." She held out her hand and raised an eyebrow, regarding Sam with suspicion. He was more than used to that treatment from members of the Eden family.

"I'm your honored guest. Nothing more than that."

"I have to hand it to my daughter. You're smooth. And handsome."

Sam stifled a grin as they returned their attention to the bridesmaids marching up the aisle. Even now he could see Mindy at the very end and he found his heart thumping harder. It all seemed a little silly. He wasn't the type to fall for the romanticism of an event like this, but there was something in the air—a warm feeling he couldn't put a name on. She smiled as she gracefully stepped her way past the guests, nodding and silently greeting people she knew. But then her sights landed on Sam, their eyes locked and he felt a verifiable jolt in the center of his chest. At any other time in his relationship with Mindy, this would have been par for the course. She had no trouble getting his engine revving. But he'd promised himself he wouldn't get caught up in her again, and this was the surest sign that he was doing exactly that. He forced himself to look down at his shoes. He'd gotten himself into this and he was going to have to find a way to get himself out.

"You must be very proud," Sam said, leaning closer to Jill as Sophie made her slow march up the aisle on the arm of Reginald from Eden's.

She nodded. "I am. I just hope it lasts. My marriage was not a good one."

Sam found that an odd sentiment for the mother of the bride, but then again, Jill Eden had been burned by her husband, big-time.

"I should enjoy this while I can," she muttered out of the side of her mouth. "Sophie might be the only daughter I get to see married. Mindy's too independent. To her, it's a trap."

Sophie stopped at their row and gave her mom a kiss on the cheek. She ignored Sam, which was fine with him at this point. Then Reginald escorted her the final steps to the altar, where she took her place next to Jake. The officiant invited the guests to take their seats. Meanwhile, Jill's words about Mindy and her independence echoed in Sam's head. Mindy and Sam had never discussed marriage. In fact, the subject of commitment had never come up. Not that Sam had been particularly eager to go there, but he hadn't even had the chance to entertain it with her. It had always been Mindy who put up boundaries and set rules. She seemed to think that Sam had been entirely to blame in their many breakups, but the truth of their situation was that Mindy had always made the call. So perhaps her mother was right. Maybe Mindy saw all of this—commitment and love— as nothing more than an ambush.

The ceremony went off without a hitch, and it was

short and sweet, thank goodness. Sam spent most of the time studying Mindy, trying to resign himself to the fact that she would likely always be unfinished business in his life. He was the sort of the guy who either tied up loose ends or left them entirely behind. He suspected there would never be any winning with Mindy and not simply because he was still wary of being hurt. He couldn't imagine her ever letting him get close enough to try.

After Sophie and Jake exchanged their vows and said, "I do," the guests began to filter through a receiving line at the back of the room while hotel employees quickly moved the chairs and set things up for dinner. Not wanting to create tension with the bride and groom, Sam skipped the line and instead took his chance to exchange pleasantries with the various guests he'd most needed to reconnect with on a business basis. Thankfully, not a single person made a comment about Sam being a bit of an outcast with regard to the Eden family. Perhaps they had been discreet in their dislike for him.

Mindy and Sam were reunited when it came time for dinner and they were able to sit together, but there wasn't much opportunity for relaxed conversation. There were too many unpleasant undercurrents running through that room—Gerald shooting Sam the evil eye, Jake and Sophie ignoring him, Jill downing drinks a little too fast and Mindy preoccupied with everything being perfect.

"The ceremony was nice," Sam said.

Mindy wiped her mouth with a napkin. "It was. We're almost at the finish line."

Sam hated the fact that she wasn't enjoying herself.

He put his arm around her and leaned closer, speaking into her ear. "Relax. Everything is fine. Can I get you another drink?" Of course, Sam could do anything but relax right now, but he was fairly certain he was doing a good job of faking it. Being able to put his mouth so close to Mindy's neck wasn't helping him unwind. It only made his blood run a whole lot hotter. She not only looked stunning today, but he also had a real weakness for stressed-out Mindy. He knew how to unwind her. Again and again.

She turned her head toward his and kissed him on the cheek. "Gerald is watching us," she muttered.

"So I gathered." Sam didn't bother to look. He'd take Mindy's word for it. Instead, he took his chance to gaze deeply into her eyes, relishing the way they reflected uncertainty. She clearly had no idea what he would do next and how he loved the element of surprise. He leaned closer, and under the table, planted his hand on the top of her thigh, his fingertips just close enough to her center to send a message—he was hers for the taking. He placed a soft kiss on the corner of her mouth. Given the time and place, it was only a fraction of what he wanted to do, but he did make a point of being slow about it and allowing his lips to linger. It was chaste and sweet, when the thoughts running through his mind were of a more carnal variety. He wanted to pull her hair out of that neat twist, gather the gauzy fabric of her skirt in his hands and convince her to give in to him.

"You're so beautiful," he said.

"You're so bad." Mindy's eyelids fluttered and she showed him the most relaxed smile he'd seen from her all night.

Despite the need to keep Gerald at bay, Sam knew it wasn't good for him to be flirting with Mindy this way. The problem was, he no longer cared what was good for him. He only wanted whatever she did. "I'm only living up to expectations."

Sam was going to be the death of Mindy. Yes, they were putting on a show right now, but damn… It felt so real. It felt the way it had felt months ago, when things were fantastic between them, before they veered off course. His hand on her leg was one thing, but it was the kiss that really sent her into overdrive. It was enough to convince her that although they might eventually work as friends, for tonight, she needed more than that. She needed everything she'd wanted from him last night.

Unfortunately, that couldn't happen right now. Jake and Sophie were about to have their first dance. As the lights dimmed in the ballroom, Mindy took Sam's hand. "Come on. Let's go watch." She tapped her mom on the shoulder. "Mom. Join us. We'll be able to see better if we're up by the dance floor."

The three made their way closer to Jake and Sophie as the DJ told a few corny jokes and many more of the wedding guests followed their lead, joining them at the edge of the dance floor. There in the near dark, Mindy didn't hesitate to hold on to Sam's hand tightly. All she could think about was how glad she was to have him here. She couldn't imagine how little she would have enjoyed today if she'd had to do it all on her own.

Sophie and Jake looked so happy it was hard for Mindy to wrap her head around. She and Sophie had grown up with their parents' marriage as the only example of the way a couple should behave, and it had not been pretty. They had never been kind or sweet to each other. They only exchanged barbs and icy stares. Once Mindy and Sophie were old enough to have a better sense of what was going on in their parents' private lives, they quickly figured out that it wasn't just their father who was having many affairs. Their mother was plenty unfaithful. It was only last December, after Gram's will had been read and they learned that their cousin Emma was actually their half sister, that they also learned the most salient detail of the murky history of their parents' marriage. Their father's first affair had been Emma's mom, Aunt Jenny. The betrayal their mother felt over that would never go away, not even now, years after their father's death.

How Mindy hoped that Sophie and Jake would never reach that state with their marriage. She wanted to believe it wasn't preordained for their family. Sophie and Jake did genuinely love each other. That already gave them a leg up. Mindy wasn't certain that her parents had ever felt that way about each other. It was difficult to imagine how anyone would ever hurt someone they love so badly.

Sophie's and Jake's song wound down and the DJ invited the guests to join them. Mindy didn't even need to ask Sam if he wanted to dance… He was already leading her out onto the dance floor, his hand fully wrapped around her own.

She sucked in a sharp breath when he wound his arm around her waist and tugged her body against his. How she loved it when he took charge, but these were dangerous waters they were wading into. Every minute that ticked by seemed to be another tiny barrier breached— a touch, a warm breath, a kiss. She knew where that led with Sam... And he knew it, too. And she wasn't sure how they were going to handle their goodbye in a few hours, when the dances were done and it was time for her to go upstairs and for him to go home. Her sisters were sincere about the bet, and not just because they wanted to keep her at Eden's. They wanted to keep her from being hurt.

Reginald, in his pastel peach suit and one of his trademark plaid bow ties, and Mindy's mom joined the crowd on the dance floor, which made Mindy happy. She hadn't seen a smile on her mother's face in a long time. Sure, she was fairly certain she was drunk, but it didn't matter. Happiness was happiness. "It's nice to see my mom enjoying herself."

Sam glanced over at them. "I like your mom. She's different than I thought she would be."

"What do you mean by that?"

Sam shrugged. "She's not very sentimental. Most moms are, especially if their daughter is getting married."

"Do you really think most moms are that way? I think of moms as being tough and pragmatic."

Sam cast Mindy a look that seemed to suggest she was off her rocker. "Yes, moms can be like that, but in general, I've found most moms to be tenderhearted. Especially when it comes to their children."

Mindy shook her head. "Yeah. That's not our mom. Is your mom like that?" Sam never, ever talked about his family.

Sam's lips formed a hard, thin line. "My mom passed away when I was in high school. But she was like that. Before she died."

"I'm so sorry. I had no idea. Why didn't you ever tell me this before?"

"It never came up."

"More like you failed to mention it. I've talked about my mom dozens of times around you. The subject definitely came up."

"I don't want to argue about it, Mindy. It's personal. And private. And something I don't enjoy discussing."

Mindy had to choke back several follow-up questions about Sam's mother. It was clear from his tone that he was very serious about this. Plus, her aunt Jenny was currently trying to cut in on her mom's dance with Reginald.

"Oh, crap," Mindy said. "This is exactly what I worried about."

Sam seemed to know exactly what Mindy was thinking as he twirled them closer.

"Have a seat," Jenny said. "I want to dance with Reginald."

"You're drunk," Mindy's mom snapped. "Go away."

"Ladies, ladies. There's more than enough of me to go around," Reginald said. He wasn't wrong. Tall, spindly and unavoidable in his colorful suit, it did feel as though he could easily make time for everyone.

Mindy glanced over at Sophie, who hadn't yet noticed the drama unfolding before them. "Aunt Jenny, it's probably not the best time for dancing anyway. Sophie and Jake are about to cut the cake soon. We wouldn't want to miss that."

Aunt Jenny shot Mindy a look. "You're just like your mother. Bossy as hell. You can't tell me what to do." She closed her eyes and her head bobbed back and forth. Mindy knew for sure that her aunt had enjoyed a few too many glasses of champagne.

Mindy wanted to fight back, but this was all about de-escalation. "Um, I'm sorry. I'm just thinking about what Sophie would want. It's sort of my job as maid of honor."

Sam let go of Mindy and set his hand on Jenny's arm. "Ms. Stewart. I'm Sam Blackwell. I don't believe we've had the chance to meet. I'd be happy to walk you back to your table."

"I don't need your help!" Jenny shouted, yanking her hand back. The sound of her voice pierced all noise in the room, even the music. Everyone seemed to be staring at them.

Sophie and Jake let go of each other and started making their way through the crowd on the dance floor. Mindy's heart was about to pound its way through her chest. She had to do something, but what? There was no telling what Jenny might do if Mindy took the same approach Sam just had.

"Of course you don't need my help," Sam said, taking her hand and hooking it in the crook of his elbow. "I was merely offering to walk you there. Or perhaps we can head out to the lobby and get out of this stuffy ballroom."

Jenny's sights narrowed on Sam. "You're trying to get rid of me."

"Not at all. I only sense that maybe you're not enjoying yourself. We could go get a drink in the bar. You can tell me all about yourself."

Jenny was weaving again. "You're lucky you're so tall. I have a thing for ridiculously tall men."

"See? We make a perfect pair." Sam wasn't taking no for an answer. He began walking Jenny out of the ballroom and she had no choice but to stumble along.

Sophie appeared at Mindy's side. "What is he doing? Where is he taking her?"

"From the looks of it, he's saving your wedding reception."

"Oh, give me a break. Everyone's having a lovely time."

Mindy turned to her sister. "Would you like to bring back Aunt Jenny? Because I can gladly go get her."

Sophie pursed her lips. "No. I don't want that."

"Then I think we both know that Sam has done you a favor."

"That doesn't count for that much, Min. It'll take him a lifetime to make up for everything else he's ever done."

"I'm sure he's keenly aware of that. Now if you'll excuse me, I'd like to at least go offer to be his backup." Mindy didn't wait for another comment from her sister and rushed through the ballroom doors, down the hall and out into the lobby. She spotted Sam and Jenny sitting at a side table with cups of coffee.

Sam subtly waved Mindy off, and so she hung back, watching him do this magic. Whatever he was saying, Jenny was clearly amused. She was warming up to him, smiling. Laughing, even. After a few moments, Sam beckoned one of the bell captains with a curl of his finger, gave him a tip and, before Mindy knew what was happening, Sam was walking Jenny outside. Mindy made her way across the lobby and peeked through the revolving doors just in time to see Sam put Jenny in a town car.

The look of victory on his face when he returned to the lobby was pure magic. It made Mindy's entire body tingle from head to toe. "Feeling pretty good about yourself, eh?" she asked.

"Shouldn't I be? I kept a bundle of dynamite from exploding in your sister's wedding reception. I'm pretty proud of myself, to be honest. I'm not usually that good at calming people down."

Mindy pulled him closer, drawing in his scent. It was even more intoxicating now than it had been out on the dance floor. His effect on her was more potent now, too. There were no prying eyes on them now. She felt free. "It's because you turned on the charm. Most women have no defense for that."

Sam's eyes darkened. "And what about you, Mindy? What are you keeping up your defenses for? We kept Gerald from asking you to dance. Your sister's wedding has gone off with only the most minor of hiccups. Looks to me like you're in the free and clear."

He was exactly right. She didn't need to be there for the cake cutting. She didn't need to worry any more about the bad things that might happen and her role in stopping any of them. She smoothed her hand over Sam's lapel and dared to look him square in the eye. "I think you're right. I think I can do whatever I want right now."

"And what is it that you want, Min?"

She bit down on her lower lip, a million ideas zipping through her head. Could she present Sam with a list of what she wanted? Because she certainly had enough material to make one. "Right now, with nobody watching us, I want to take you upstairs and get you out of this tux."

Five

The elevator door hadn't even closed before Mindy was kissing Sam, and he eagerly returned the favor. Lucky enough to be riding alone with him, Mindy saw no point in waiting, going straight for his tie and undoing the knot. She'd spent a lot of time and effort fighting this moment. It felt so good to simply give in to it. As she started to unbutton his shirt, she banished the little voice in her head that said this was just going to create problems. Problems were for tomorrow. Tonight, now that the weight of Sophie's wedding was gone, all she wanted was to get lost in Sam.

She flattened him against the wall, but he countered with a kiss that nearly blinded her. "I don't care that this is crazy. I want you." Her voice was a gasp, so desperate and breathless that it was as if it no longer belonged to her. She waited for Sam to respond, her chest heaving. She needed to hear him say that he needed her, too.

"Are you sure you want to do this, Min?" He reared back his head, leaving his mouth out of reach. At this point, even in heels, she would need a stepladder to kiss him. It felt mean and cruel, like he was showing off his masterful self-control. Mindy possessed so little of it when it came to him.

The elevator door slid open and she grabbed his hand, stealing down the hall to her room. "Am I sure I want to have sex with you? Yes. I didn't say that to be cute or coy." She waved her key in front of the lock and they were quickly inside. "Why? Are you not sure you want to have sex with me?" It felt like forever ticked by while she waited for his answer. She braced for the possibility that he would reject her. It was a mortifying prospect, but she could imagine him doing it. To get even. To have the upper hand.

Without a word, his hands went to her hips, which gave her a sliver of hope. She knew Sam. He wouldn't touch her if he didn't want her. "I'm sure I do. I just needed to ask."

Mindy was more than a little relieved. "Oh, good. I was worried there for a minute." She sensed that wasn't enough of an answer. She did want him to know that the things he'd done for her over the last forty-eight hours had meant something. "Thank you for being such a sport about the wedding, and having to pretend to be my real date, and dealing with the moms. It really means a lot to me. Honestly, I don't know what I would have done without you." It was the truth. He was so much of the reason she'd found a way to enjoy herself.

"I'm not a bad guy. Maybe you can remember that the next time someone tries to convince you that I am."

Mindy really didn't want to get into this again. Such serious topics would ruin the impetuousness of the moment. She took his hands from her hips and walked backward, leading him farther into the room. "You know, Sam, right now it's just you and me and a beautiful bed. I don't think we should think about other people or let this go to waste." Mindy came to a stop when the backs of her legs hit the mattress.

Sam let go of her hands and rolled his shoulders out of his suit jacket, tossing it aside. He kicked off his shoes and took off his socks, then untucked his shirt, not taking his eyes off her. "The rest of my clothes are up to you."

Now they were getting somewhere. Mindy took her time unbuttoning his shirt, standing close to him and drawing in his warmth and masculine smell. She loved having his eyes on her as she spread her hands across his firm chest, using her fingers to trace the defined contours. She'd really missed seeing him without a shirt. She'd missed having her hands on his bare skin. If she were being honest, she'd simply missed being around him. His presence, when there were no outside forces between them, was comforting—like being wrapped up in a warm blanket. Paradoxically, being with him was also a thrill, causing her pulse to race and her head to swim.

He watched her as she unbuckled his belt, then unbuttoned and unzipped his pants, letting them drop to the floor. The look on his face, full of his unflinching restraint, made her that much more eager for the main event. She not only needed every inch of him, she wanted to put a smile on his face. Make him happy. Remind him that she was worth missing.

She wrapped one arm around his waist and, with her other hand, began to gently touch him through his boxer briefs. Her fingertips rode along his steely length, so tense she could feel how hard he was through the fabric. Sam groaned and closed his eyes, a mix of frustration and satisfaction crossing his face when she made it to the tip and rolled her thumb over the top, back and forth. She had no idea when this would happen again, if ever. There was too much standing between her and Sam. She wanted to enjoy every second of this.

"I have to sit," he mumbled. "You're making me dizzy." Sam slid onto the bed and leaned back on his elbows, his long body splayed out for her.

Mindy followed his cue and slipped his boxers down his hips. He was so magnificent it was hard to know where to look first. So she let her eyes rove over the landscape of his chiseled body, the long and muscled legs, his perfect abs, his sculpted shoulders. She wanted nothing between them and there was still a big something—her dress.

"I need to get out of this thing," she said.

"Yes, you do. I'll watch."

"I can't do the zipper on my own."

"Okay. Come here." He sat up and scooted to the edge of the bed.

She perched next to him and turned to provide access to the zipper. He first undid the clip in her hair and set it on the bedside table. He carefully uncoiled her hair from the twist, letting it fall down around her shoulders.

She felt his presence, and not just his warmth, right behind her. His breaths were heavy, his heavenly smell
swirling around her. He drew down the zipper, then
peeled the dress away from her skin, blazing a trail of
kisses along the channel of her naked back as he went.
He had no idea what that did to her, the way it made the
heat pool between her legs and the need double, then
triple. She pulled the bodice forward and Sam reached
around from behind, cupping her breasts in his hands,
rolling her nipples between his fingers and pressing his
chest against her back. She rolled her head to one side,
relishing the jolts of electricity traveling between her
breasts and her apex. It was as if her entire body had
just come back to life. He kissed her neck with an open
mouth, using his tongue, kneading her breasts and letting her get lost in the heavenly sensations. As amazing as it was, Mindy wanted more of him. She wanted
to be able to see him. Kiss him.

She twisted her torso, then lay back on the bed,
her dress still covering her from the waist down. Sam
rose to his knees, hovering over her, then lowered his
head, drawing her nipple into his mouth, swirling his
tongue perfectly. He switched to her other breast and
it was just as mind-blowing, especially when he would
stop every few seconds and blow cool air against her
overheated skin. He kissed the flat plane between her
breasts, then dragged his mouth along her centerline.
When he reached her waist, she wished her dress could
just disappear.

Sam was on the case, though, standing and pulling the garment down her hips and tossing it away.
He quickly kneeled on the floor in front of the bed

and tugged her panties along the length of her legs, leaving her bare to him. He lifted one leg and placed it on his shoulder, then kissed his way along from the inside of her knee, down her inner thigh. Mindy's head rolled back when his lips found her apex and his tongue flicked at her center, then rolled in firm and steady circles. Sam had an incredibly talented mouth and he knew exactly how to please a woman. She wasn't sure if he was just good at reading her cues or if he just naturally knew what she liked. She only knew that he did.

Her head rocked back and forth over the silky bedding while her fingers massaged his scalp and combed through his thick hair. She was already heading toward her peak when he slipped a finger inside her, curled into her most sensitive spot. He was careful with her, and precise, staying homed in on the place that brought her the most pleasure. Mindy's mind was a blur of colors and blissful thoughts of Sam, and then the tension broke and she felt every muscle in her body go tight and let go, pulsing over and over again. He was unbelievable. And she intended to give him every bit of pleasure he'd just given to her.

Sam stretched out next to Mindy on the bed and kissed her softly. She quickly amped things up, hitching her leg over his hip and taking the kiss deeper, urging his tongue to coil with hers. He didn't need a single word of praise from her. She was telling him everything he wanted to hear with her actions as she rolled him to his back, kneeled between his legs and took his erection into her mouth.

That instant when her velvety tongue hit his skin made him lose all sense of time and place. How could one touch feel so impossibly good? She held him tightly between her lips, riding his length and rolling her tongue over the swollen head when she reached the tip. As good as it felt, he wasn't going to last long if she kept this up. That was a simple fact.

But he didn't even need to express it because Mindy did it first. "I love making you happy, but I really need to have you inside me."

My sentiments, exactly.

"I'm still on the pill, and I hate having to ask this question, but I need to know if you used a condom with any of the women you've dated since me."

"Believe it or not, it was only that one woman, and we didn't have sex."

Mindy sat back on her haunches. "You. Didn't have sex. With a woman."

He shook his head. "I swear."

Mindy cocked her head adorably, like one of those puppies with the big ears. Her gorgeous hair spilled over her shoulder. "I'm amazed."

He wasn't. He'd been there. He could explain the whole thing if needed. "Can we stop talking? I want you."

Mindy smiled and planted her hands on each side of his chest and her knees bracketed his hips. She leaned down into him, kissing him slowly. Softly. Like they were starting all over. It was a deliciously painful exercise in patience as her sumptuous lips glossed over his, and she put none of her body weight on him, hovering above him like a butterfly. From head to toe, he pulsed with need. Having only the softest brushes of her skin against his made it even more intense. Her breasts grazed his chest. Her nose nudged his cheek. Her knees squeezed his hips. His hands caressed the silky skin of her back, his fingers following the channel of her spine. But it wasn't enough. He needed her in a way he couldn't begin to describe.

He pulled her firmly against his chest and rolled her to her back, her red tresses splaying against the white bedding. She responded with a more intense kiss, one born of recklessness. It was the perfect reflection of the idea that they did not fit well into each other's lives, and yet they couldn't stay away from each other, no matter how hard they tried. He positioned himself at Mindy's entrance and drove inside, all while his mind spun out of control. Mindy gasped, then hummed with pleasure, a near mirror for everything going through his head. He hadn't forgotten how incredible she felt, but he had forgotten the magnitude of the moment when everything felt right and he couldn't have asked for another thing in the whole world.

Their bodies tumbled into a steady rhythm that suited them both perfectly. Mindy coiled her legs around his hips, pulling him closer, and he obliged, driving as deep as he could with every pass. She curled her fingernails into his back, the sting keeping him in the moment and heightening every sensation. Every muscle below his waist was contracting and releasing in an unceasing pattern. More intense. Closer to the brink. He listened to Mindy's breaths and moans, waiting for the moment when he got his body weight on just the right spot. Closer. And closer. And then he hit it. She tilted her hips and curled herself into him even more, holding on to him like she would never let go.

"I'm so close," Mindy mumbled into his neck. She kissed him fitfully, her mouth gaping.

Sam was so close it felt as if he was being teased by his own body. His peak was a whisper away but he focused on Mindy, rocking against her center and staying deep inside her. Her body pulled on his tightly and in a sudden rush, Mindy's head knocked back and she called out. Sam clamped his eyes shut and let his body take over, the climax rolling through him like a tsunami coming on shore. Over and over again, surges of warmth pushed him into contentment. A place where nothing else mattered but her.

He collapsed when the final waves washed over him. He rolled onto his back, right next to Mindy. He clasped his fingers around hers and raised her hand to his lips. He wasn't sure that this had been the smartest decision, but right now, he wasn't worried about being wise. He was too exhausted.

"Why does this always end up happening between us?" she asked.

He knew it wasn't a rhetorical question. It was real. And he also didn't know the answer aside from the obvious. "Because you're gorgeous and sexy and we have crazy chemistry?"

Mindy rolled onto her side and swished her hand across his chest. Even that mostly innocent touch threatened to get him going all over again. "You're sweet. I feel the same way about you. You're too enticing. I can't not kiss you. Which is sort of a problem, if you think about it."

Sam gave himself a minute to consider her answer. It didn't have to be a problem at all if she would stop letting her family come between them. There was a nagging sense deep inside him that there could be more between them than just sex. But he wasn't about to bring it up first. It had been hard enough to be rejected by her when she jettisoned him from her life. He was tough, but he wasn't impervious to pain. Plus, her mother had flat out told him exactly what he had suspected all along about Mindy—she needed her free will. The minute she started to feel trapped or obligated, she got panicky.

"Sam. I need to tell you something."

Sam couldn't begin to imagine what was coming next, but he feared she was about to do the thing he most dreaded—tell him to put his clothes on and leave. "Yeah. What?" If that was what she was about to do, it was best to get it over with. Maybe he'd finally learn his lesson this time.

"When I first told Sophie and Emma that I was bringing you to the wedding, they were concerned."

"They didn't understand that we struck a deal and you wanted to buy the Mercer from me?" Sam looked right at her as she pressed her lips together, waiting to answer his question.

"I didn't tell them that part. I worried that Sophie would think it was uncool that I was essentially leveraging my plus-one to her wedding. Plus, I didn't want her to question your motives. I figured it was good enough that they thought I had asked you because I was trying to keep Gerald away."

"Something tells me you would have had no problem dealing with him."

"Maybe. Probably. He was more of an annoyance than anything, but that's not what I'm trying to tell you. I'm trying to tell you that Sophie and Emma were worried that I was going to fall under your spell."

Sam laughed. He couldn't help it. "I have a spell? I had no idea."

"Oh, you do. You definitely do. You make me a little bit crazy, Sam."

He reached out and cupped her bare shoulder, trailing his fingers down her arm. "Mindy, sweetheart, I'm pretty sure you're crazy on your own. It's not my fault if I bring it out in you."

Mindy swatted his chest. "Hey. Let me finish." She then closed her eyes tight and scrunched up her face. "This is so stupid. I'm not even sure I can say it out loud."

"What?"

"My sisters and I made a bet. We made a bet that I won't fall for you again. If I do, if I get involved with you, I have to stay at Eden's for an extra year. Which obviously I don't want to do."

There was a lot about this that Sam needed to unpack. It might take him hours to sort this out in his head. "Again? Does that mean you fell for me before?"

Mindy unleashed a groan. "Well, yeah, but you had to have known that."

Sam shrugged. "How could I have possibly known that?"

"Don't guys always know when a woman is gaga over him?"

"Gaga? No. I knew you liked me enough to sleep with me. That was about it."

"Well, it's not like I even had the slightest idea how you felt about me. Everything always felt so temporary. You were always coming into town, then leaving again. It was hard to watch you go."

If she thought it was hard to watch him go, she needed to know what it felt like to be asked to leave. Sam realized just how little time he and Mindy had spent talking about anything of substance when they'd been together before. They'd given in to the physical side of their attraction, but they hadn't bothered to explore anything deeper. He'd always assumed that was what Mindy wanted. Now he was starting to wonder if he'd been wrong. Under any other circumstances, this revelation could have made this the perfect time to wade into those deeper waters, but the bet with her sisters made everything infinitely more complicated.

"How serious do you think Sophie and Emma are about the bet?"

"Dead serious. They don't want me to get hurt and they don't want me to leave the store."

"So why did you take it in the first place?"

Mindy sat up and pushed away, distancing herself from him and resting her back against the headboard. "It was supposed to be insurance. I was trying to protect myself."

"From me?" He knew he'd done things that had been construed as bad, but he'd never had anything less than Mindy's best interests at heart.

"More like from my weakness for you."

Six

In the breaking light of day, Mindy felt Sam's presence in her hotel room, and with that came the worry. Had she made a mistake? Had last night been a grave error? She didn't want to think so. She and Sam worked well together, at least for short stretches. Last night had been an amazing one and her thirst for him wasn't nearly quenched.

From the other side of the bed, he stirred. He'd be awake soon, which meant he'd be leaving. He never stayed for long. Her sister Sophie was off to the airport for her honeymoon in Bali later that day. Her sister Emma was also about to embark on a romantic getaway—a trip to England to visit Daniel's parents. Mindy, however, would be returning to work. Yes, she loved staying busy and being productive, but where was her fun? Why couldn't she have a love life like her sisters did?

It would be easy to blame her drive and determination. She'd always had a need to succeed, and that had gotten in the way of love many times. Had it gotten in the way with Sam? If so, the bet made things even messier. If she lost the bet, she would be stuck at Eden's for an extra year. Sophie would never let her off the hook, in part because she was so set on having Mindy on board at the store forever.

Sam wrapped his arm around Mindy's waist. He pressed his long body against hers, his heat pouring into her. She loved these moments together, when it was just the two of them, and all in their world was relatively calm. When everyone else wasn't weighing in on her choices. Sam nuzzled the back of her neck with his nose and pressed a soft kiss against her nape. She closed her eyes and inhaled deeply, relishing every second of this moment. It would be gone soon. Quite possibly gone forever. However complicated, Sam was an amazing man. There were only so many times she could shoo him away before some smart woman, somewhere, would keep him around.

But maybe Mindy could have some more of this blissful feeling with Sam, at least for another week, while her sisters and their watchful eyes were away.

Mindy rolled to her other side and faced Sam. "Hey, handsome. You awake?" she whispered.

He nodded, his eyes still closed. "Getting there."

"Can I ask you a question?"

"You just did."

"Okay, fine, funny guy. What do you have going on this week?"

He cleared his throat and their bodies pressed against

each other again. "The usual. There's a bullheaded woman who wants to buy a building from me. I guess I need to follow through on that one, huh?"

Mindy smiled and settled her face in his neck. "I do plan on holding you to that. I wasn't kidding when I said I wanted that building."

"Oh, believe me. I know. Any time I know what you want, I don't let it go. You can be very difficult to figure out."

Mindy didn't see herself that way at all. "I'm so easy to figure out, it's ridiculous."

"Then I must be spectacularly stupid."

"What's that supposed to mean?"

"Any time I ever think I'm doing right by you, I end up falling flat on my face. I ended up kicked out of your life."

"But we're talking about big missteps, Sam. Interfering with Eden's. Leaking information about Emma to the press."

"Both done at times when you were deeply unhappy and I was trying to find a way to turn that around."

Had his actions really been so secretly benevolent? Mindy still had her doubts.

"Sam, what happened with you and Jake?"

He drew a deep breath through his nose. "I'd call it a misunderstanding. He thought we were full partners, but I didn't see us that way. I felt that we were helping each other out. It's just something people do to get by, right? Especially when you're starting out?"

"I don't understand why he would feel so betrayed by that. He's clearly still holding a major grudge."

"I made a lot of money with the deal he thought I'd cut him in on. Money makes grudges stick."

"So why didn't you include him?"

Sam took another breath and rolled to his back, away from her. She missed him the instant he was gone, in part because she sensed his anger bubbling to the surface. "I needed the money. Not for myself, but for someone else. And for a good reason. So I did it. If I had cut Jake into the deal, I wouldn't have made enough money to take care of the problem."

From the tone of Sam's voice, Mindy could only infer that he preferred this to be the end of the subject, but she didn't want it to be. She wanted to know more. If he was ever to be redeemed in the eyes of her family, she had to know the truth. "If you were helping someone, why didn't you just tell him that?"

"Because it's none of his business. This was personal and although we were friends, this wasn't something I wanted to share with anyone." Sam's voice now had an edge of agitation that Mindy had never heard. He threw back the covers and climbed out of bed.

"Where are you going?"

"I'm getting dressed. I'm leaving."

"Wait. Don't. Don't go."

He stood before her, naked, every inch of his stunning body on display. "I don't want to play this game anymore, Mindy. It's not fun and I have the distinct impression that I'm always going to lose. I don't like to lose. Ever."

Mindy sat up and scooted to the edge of the bed, clutching the sheet to her chest. She couldn't sit before him feeling so exposed. "I don't think it's unfair of me to question you on certain things."

"But you do nothing but question me, Mindy. My motives. My tactics. The things I say. It's exhausting. You know, you and I got along perfectly until you started talking to Sophie and Jake. Nothing has been the same since then. I live under a cloud of suspicion and I can't take it."

Mindy couldn't begin to form a response. There were too many thoughts whirring around in her brain. He was right about Sophie and Jake. She hadn't formed her opinion of Sam fully independent of others. And that certainly wasn't fair. She wouldn't like it if someone had done that to her. "You're right. I need to take the things you say for what they are and stop reading into them. If you tell me that you believe you had no choice but to cut Jake out of that deal all those years ago, I believe you."

Sam arched both eyebrows and lowered his chin. Even in the soft early-morning light, she could see exactly how skeptical he was of her. "That doesn't change the fact that you made a bet with your sisters that you wouldn't fall into my clutches. Whatever you may think of me, Mindy, I'm not a spider waiting for its prey to make a fatal error."

Mindy exhaled, a bit exasperated. He was right again. It was only a fear of her own weakness that had made her take the bet in the first place. She couldn't blame Sam for it. "The bet was stupid. I never should have agreed to it." It was especially pointless since the entire aim had been for Mindy to force herself to stay away from Sam. Judging by the state of the bed, she had failed spectacularly. If Sophie knew what happened last night, she would already have Mindy on the hook for another year. Sisterly guilt goes far. "But I'm stuck in it. Sophie will never let me out."

"Well, think of it this way. At least you know she wants you close. That counts for something." He knocked his head to one side and folded his arms across his chest. "From where I sit, it counts for quite a lot."

"I want *you* close." Mindy could hardly believe she'd had the nerve to say it. Even she marveled at the conviction with which she'd uttered the words.

"I love morning sex as much as anyone, but maybe we need to stop doing this. Last night was incredible, but I can't take everything that goes with it."

Mindy carefully peeled back the covers and stood, facing him, taking the zaps of electricity that pinged back and forth between them. "I'm serious, Sam. I do want you close. The last few months have been miserable. And I want a chance to spend time with you again like we did at the beginning, out from under the microscope of my family."

"What are you suggesting?"

"Sophie's out of the country for a week. So is Emma." She took his hands in hers, rubbing her thumbs back and forth across his knuckles. "Let's use this time to be together."

Sam nodded slowly, but she knew he wasn't agreeing to this—he was thinking. By the dark look in his eyes, it was difficult for him to reach a decision. "Then what? After the week?"

That was the question she'd feared most, but she owed him an answer. "If we still like each other after a week, I'll go to my sisters and try to work out a compromise."

He shook his head. "I'm not a compromise. I refuse to be one. Either you tell them we're together because we are, or we aren't."

Mindy was more than a little taken aback. It wasn't like Sam to draw such a hard line in the sand. But she'd backed herself into a corner here and she had to keep her eye on the prize—she wanted to give Sam yet another chance. "Okay. It's a deal."

"And we stay at my apartment. Not yours."

"I wasn't aware you were in a position to make demands."

"Those are my rules. You've never even been to my apartment."

"Did you ever invite me over?"

"I did. Many times."

After their long and meaty conversation, Sam headed back to his apartment to prepare for Mindy's arrival that afternoon. He had never before cohabited with a woman, and although this was only for a week, it did make him unsettled. His place was his retreat. He'd purposely bought in Tribeca and avoided the social posturing of Central Park or the Upper East Side, where Mindy lived. Of course, his neighborhood was the most expensive in the city at the moment and one of the trendiest, but at least he felt as though he was mingling with people who'd made their money and were enjoying it, rather than acting as though they were made of it.

His apartment occupied the top two floors of a renovated warehouse. There were exposed brick walls, tall arched lead-paned windows and beautifully restored hardwood floors. The kitchen was a showpiece, with white marble countertops, an industrial range and espresso-brown custom cabinetry. His favorite part of the apartment was the library, perched on an elevated platform circling his entire living room, with his home office occupying one corner. There were thousands of books, many original editions, and several places to curl up and get lost in a good read. He spent more time in that part of the house than any other, and he used his time before Mindy's arrival to unwind in his favorite chair, a chocolate-brown antiqued leather recliner, with a good mystery.

He was so immersed in the story that he jumped when his cell phone rang. He fished it out of his pocket and consulted the caller ID. He'd thought perhaps it was Mindy, but it was his sister, Isabel. "So you finally call me back," he answered. "I was beginning to worry."

"I know. I know. Work is crazy. What can I say?"

"You can say that you're sorry. You can say that you won't wait more than an entire week to call me back next time. I do worry, you know."

"About me?" Isabel laughed. "I'm the oldest. It's my job to worry about you."

"Somehow I don't think that applies anymore now that we're both in our midthirties."

"Unfortunately, I'm more like late thirties. And you'll always be my little twerp of a brother. I don't care if you are six foot six. It'll always be like that. No matter what you do."

Sam laughed and set his book on the side table next to his chair. He didn't know what he would do without his sister in his life. She was not only a rock, she shared his past. It was so nice to be able to talk to someone without having to skirt topics. It was so much easier to just be completely open about everything. "I guess I should let you know why I called," he said.

"Whatever works. I'm fine with just catching up, too."

"I got a call from the woman who runs the fundraisers for ALS research. You know I make at least one major contribution every year. Anonymously."

"Of course. Mr. Secretive has to keep things under wraps."

"Hey. That's not fair. It's just a lot easier for me from a business perspective if people don't know about my involvement with the charity. I don't need anyone's pity."

"I've heard this story from you before."

Sam grumbled under his breath. "Anyway, they need a new sponsor and host for this year's gala. They found themselves in a precarious situation. The original hosts were Senator Miles and her husband. That's not the best optics right now."

"Ouch. Yeah. A big public sex scandal doesn't really sell charity fundraiser tickets, does it?"

"No. It does not."

"And you're hesitating because you don't want to deal with putting your name on the event."

"I'd also have to make a speech and get people to open up their checkbooks. That means telling a sad story. That means talking about Mom in front of a room of hundreds of people, many of whom I would like to be able to do business with."

Isabel sighed. "That does sound like a lot to deal with."

"They keep calling me about it and I haven't given them an answer. I need to decide soon. I don't want to be the reason they get held up."

"Well, let me say this. First off, nobody in that room is going to be anything less than sympathetic to what happened to Mom. And it might help people see a softer side of you. You do have a bit of a reputation. We've talked about this before."

"Yes. I know." Sam shifted in his seat and crossed his legs, feeling surprisingly uncomfortable in his favorite chair. "And you also know that there are details surrounding Mom's death that don't reflect well on Dad. Or could create a scandal if they ever came out. I don't want to give anyone an excuse to dig."

"That was nearly twenty years ago at this point. And I don't think there's anything that anyone could find out. Dad's accident was found to be exactly that. The insurance company and the police both did a thorough investigation and reached the same conclusion. You took care of the whole thing later. You destroyed the note he left. I mean, you and I will always know what really happened, but nobody else ever will."

Sam drew a deep breath through his nose. "I suppose you're right. It still worries me. I just…" Sam had to choke back a surprising lump of emotion. "I would never want anyone to ever speak ill of him. He did everything for us."

"I know, honey. I know."

Sam closed his eyes and willed his bad memories away. Still it was hard to do—there were so many images permanently emblazoned in his mind. Especially the note. He might have burned it, but it would always live on in his head. He could still see his dad's chicken-scratch handwriting, the way the words became more difficult to read as it went on about the reasons why he'd decided to do the unthinkable. "So you think I should do this? Is that what you're saying?"

"I do think you should do it. I think you will feel good about it when it's done. I think it will ultimately be a good thing when it comes to your business. It might even bring you some new opportunities. And most important, it'll give me an excuse to come to New York and brag about my little twerp of a brother."

Sam couldn't help but be excited by the prospect of seeing Isabel. It didn't happen nearly enough. "That would be amazing. I'd love to have you here. For moral support, if nothing else." He started to realize exactly how much of an undertaking this would be. He would be expected to bring in ticket sales, and, of course, there was the matter of the speech.

"I wouldn't miss it. I promise to be there, looking amazing, and clapping louder than anyone for you."

He breathed a sigh of relief. This would be a lot of work, but at least he'd made a decision. That part didn't need to weigh on him anymore. "You sure you'll be able to get away from work?" Isabel was a high-powered attorney in Washington, DC. She was also a bit of a fixer. If an important person got in trouble and needed a discreet way out, she was there, for a price.

"Yes. I'm sure. Honestly, I need to take a few days

off anyway and I'd love to spend some time in New York. I'm so tired of DC. There are far too many politicians here."

"Aren't they your bread and butter?"

"Annoyingly so. I'd rather just get back to working with regular rich people. They're far more interesting and far less predictable."

"Maybe you should think about moving here. It is your firm, after all."

"Funny that you should mention it. I've been thinking about exactly that for a while now. It would be nice if you and I lived in the same place again. We haven't done that since we were kids."

"It would be amazing."

"Plus, I need to find a man. I think I've already exhausted the dating pool here."

"I'm surprised you have time."

Isabel laughed. "Oh, honey, I make time."

Sam closed his eyes and shook his head. "And I do not need to know anything more than that."

"What about you? Anyone new since the few women you dated after Mindy Eden stomped all over your heart?"

Sam had confided in his sister about Mindy. Not everything. Just basic venting. Isabel was his only personal confidante, unless you counted Mindy, and they had only ever skimmed the surface. He knew he was going to catch some crap for having Mindy back in his life, but he also knew he couldn't hide it. There were likely stories about Sophie's wedding in the tabloids today. At the very least, the rumor mill was always running. "Yeah. About that. I, uh, went to Mindy's sister's wedding yesterday. I went as Mindy's date, actually. Well, it was more of a business arrangement, I guess." With every passing word, Sam realized just how convoluted his situation with Mindy was. There was no putting a label on it. He couldn't even explain it to his own sister.

"Have you seriously let her back into your life? You already know I'm not a fan."

Sam couldn't hide anything from Isabel. "We had a really good time together at the wedding. And, well, we've decided to spend some time together on a trial basis. We'll see how it goes."

Isabel did not respond to that bit of information.

"I can hear you breathing," Sam said.

"I'm thinking. About how badly I want to lecture you. And whether or not it's worth it to get on a plane and read you the riot act in person."

"Save it. I love you, but I can handle this. If nothing else, I feel like Mindy and I have unfinished business. Hopefully this will at least give me a chance to have some closure."

"Closure is a myth. Like unicorns and leprechauns. Closure is just a word for learning to ignore pain."

Was Isabel right? Was Sam putting his heart on the line for all the wrong reasons? His phone beeped with a text and he pulled it away from his ear to see the message.

I'm here.

He couldn't help it—his heart rate picked up at the idea that Mindy had arrived.

"Hey, Is. I have to go."

"Okay. Keep me posted on the Mindy Eden situation. And send me the link to buy tickets for the fundraiser."

"Will do. Love you."

"I love you, too."

Sam hung up and raced down to his door to let Mindy in. Her driver was unloading the back cargo area, setting three…four…five suitcases on the sidewalk. "Wow. You came prepared."

Mindy peered up at him from behind oversize Jackie O sunglasses. She cracked a dazzling smile. "A week for me is like a month for anyone else."

Sam had more than a passing thought that at least with this much stuff, it would be harder for her to run out the door. At the very least, it would slow her down. He took two of the bags, Mindy wheeled one, her driver the rest, and Sam led them to the elevator.

"I can take everything from here," Sam said to her driver.

"You sure, Mr. Blackwell? I'm happy to ride up," Mindy's driver said.

The reality was that Sam was too eager to finally have Mindy all to himself. He didn't want to wait. "I'm sure. I'll take it from here." He held the elevator open by leaning into it and reached into his wallet for a twenty, hoping a tip might encourage him to go.

The driver waved it off. "Oh, no sir. Thank you. I'm just fine."

Mindy turned to him. "Pick me up outside at eight tomorrow morning for work?"

"You got it, Ms. Eden. Have a nice night." With that, the driver departed.

Sam stepped on board, punched in his access code, and they rode to his main floor. He let her go first, then quickly offloaded her bags. Now, finally, he and Mindy were alone in his apartment. And he wasn't quite sure where to start. Their usual routine was to start taking off each other's clothes, and he certainly hoped that would happen at some point. But there was another part of him that was hoping he and Mindy could start breaking a few old habits. Perhaps they could finally get down to a different kind of business...the one where a man and a woman learn how to be friends.

"Your apartment is stunning," Mindy offered, walking through the foyer and into the open living room. Sam rarely had visitors, so it was fun to watch as her eyes were immediately drawn up. "Ooh. What's up there? A library?"

"My favorite part of the house. Can I show you?"

"Yes. I can't wait to see it."

Sam took her hand and led the way past his sectional sofas and fireplace, to the far side of the room, and up the modern wrought-iron staircase to the loft.

When they arrived up there, Mindy ran her hands across the spines of the leather-bound volumes. "I had no idea you were such a reader."

"I can spend hours up here. Days. It's my escape."

She turned to him, her perfume wafting gently to his nose and wrapping around him like an embrace. Having her here made everything different—the air was charged with something warm he couldn't describe. "Do you feel like you need an escape?" she asked.

"I did when I was a kid. I guess I just got in the

habit." Panic overtook him as he realized he'd opened himself up to questions about his childhood. He wanted to open up to Mindy, but not about that. Not yet. "What's your escape, Mindy?"

"Judging by the number of suitcases I brought, it looks like you are."

Seven

It took less than twenty-four hours for Mindy to feel at home with Sam. They'd spent their Sunday afternoon and evening in and out of bed, enjoying each other's company in ways that left Mindy so relaxed, she'd never felt more prepared to tackle her Monday and the rest of the workweek. They'd had dinner in, which Mindy had prepared, while Sam was in charge of pouring wine and distracting her with his hands on her hips and his lips on the crook of her neck. They'd stayed up late, bodies twined under the covers, watching old movies. Mindy learned that Sam not only had a penchant for books, but he knew quite a lot about film, as well. She cherished the chance to learn these new things about him, little details that helped to color in her sense of who he was.

Things were certainly different being at Sam's place

as opposed to her apartment, and Mindy couldn't help but wonder if it was about more than a change of location. They were still keeping things secretive as they'd had to do many times before, but there was a sense of freedom that hadn't been there before. Sophie and Emma were far away. There were no prying eyes watching over her, questioning her time with Sam and making her second-guess herself at every turn.

Now that it was Monday morning, and this would be Mindy's first time running Eden's on her own, it was time to see if this newfound freedom extended to her work life, as well. Mindy's driver, Clay, was waiting for her outside Sam's apartment right on time, and Sam walked her out to the curb to say goodbye. It was another gorgeous fall day. The sun was strong, the sky clear, and the air crackled with autumn crispness. "I guess it's time for me to head in," Mindy said, peering up into Sam's face.

His arms circled her waist, pulling her closer. She loved the way he always sought this physical closeness. It was more than hot—it made her feel wanted. Needed. "Before you go, do you think you can get away for a few hours at lunchtime?"

Mindy smoothed her hand over the lapel of Sam's jacket. "What did you have in mind? Meet back here?" She and Sam had just spent a good half hour in the shower together. The memory of his soapy hands all over her body sent a zip of excitement along her spine. Still, she was amazed that his mind was already back on sex. Apparently he was just as determined as she was for them to squeeze as much into their week together as possible.

"Actually, it's a surprise. I'll pick you up at Eden's? One o'clock?"

This put Mindy in a bit of an awkward situation. If he was at the store, people would see him. But she also knew that the employees were not prone to gossip, and with Sophie and Emma in far-flung corners of the globe, she decided it was a chance she could live with. "Sounds great. I can't wait." She kissed him on the lips and he stole the chance to squeeze her backside with one of his massive hands. She mentally pinched herself, feeling incredibly lucky.

Clay got her to the store much faster than she ever arrived from her place on the Upper East Side—another unexpected bonus of staying with Sam. The morning went smoothly—a meeting with the department heads, a conference call about a new exclusive designer the store was courting and a preliminary chat with Reginald about the store's Christmas displays, especially the world-famous windows. Sophie, the self-appointed duchess of all things Christmas at Eden's, would be brought in later. Reginald merely wanted to run a few ideas by Mindy. She was "far less picky," as he put it.

With about a half hour before Sam was to arrive, Mindy switched to some BMO emails, and that was where her day became decidedly complicated. There had been endless internal strife lately, and it seemed to be getting worse rather than better. There were arguments over creative directions, battles over production schedules and dismal reports from the finance department about supply costs. The company had been firing on all cylinders a year ago and now they were barely keeping their collective head above water.

She shot off an email to acting CEO Matthew, offering suggestions as to how to fix their problems, and asking him to give her an update on everything. She didn't want to micromanage him, but she did want him to take some ownership of the situation and stop letting her employees argue with each other forever. She was tempted to call a staff meeting and give everyone a pep talk about cooperation and teamwork, but she didn't want to undermine Matthew. If this was going to work, he had to appear to be in charge. Still, it made her that much more eager to get out of Eden's and back to running BMO. Fourteen months was all she had left. Of course, there was the bet to worry about, but right now, that was a fleeting thought. It was easy to ignore without Sophie and Emma exerting their sisterly pressure.

Five minutes before Sam was due to arrive, Mindy shut down her laptop, grabbed her Birkin bag and ducked into the ladies' room to freshen up. Her hand trembled a bit as she reapplied her lipstick. She couldn't help but be excited by the notion of Sam surprising her. What did he have up his sleeve? A fancy lunch? Shopping trip? With the city at their feet, the possibilities were endless.

Mindy emerged from the bathroom and Lizzie flagged her down from reception. "Ms. Eden, there's a man on the phone named Benjamin Summers. He asked to speak to either you, Sophie or Emma. He said he's calling about a promissory note. Something about a loan your grandmother took out?"

"I have no idea who that is. Is he from a bank?" Mindy hooked her bag on her arm and walked over to Lizzie's desk.

Lizzie shook her head. "He wouldn't tell me where he was calling from. He only gave his name."

"Sounds like a scam to me." Ever since Gram had passed away, there had been countless people attempting to get their hands on Eden's in any number of ways.

"That's what I was thinking. What would you like me to do?"

"I guess you should take a message, but between you and me, I'm not going to call him back."

Behind Mindy, the elevator dinged. Mindy's heart did a flip in her chest and she whipped around only to see Sam step through the doors. There was something about that moment when he walked into the room—everything around her became fuzzy, and he was the only thing in focus.

"Lizzie, I'm headed out to lunch." Mindy turned for a second, catching that "good for you" look in Lizzie's eye. "I might be gone a few hours."

"No worries, Ms. Eden. We'll hold down the fort."

"Ready?" Sam asked.

"Absolutely."

Mindy's escape was perfect. Everyone else in the executive offices was at lunch and Lizzie would never breathe a word of this to anyone. Mindy was the one who'd gotten her the biggest raise she'd ever received. Not that she didn't deserve it—she absolutely did. She put up with the three sisters and their constant drama, and never let it faze her.

As soon as they were alone in the elevator, Mindy took Sam's hand. "Where are we going?"

"I told you. It's a surprise."

She couldn't have hidden her smile if she'd wanted

to. This made her happy. Normal relationship stuff. Could she and Sam have that? Could she talk Sophie and Emma out of the silly bet? If her week with Sam continued like this, Mindy was going to have to sit her sisters down and explain to them that they were going to have to put her happiness before the things that they wanted.

Mindy and Sam were soon in the back of Sam's black stretch SUV with his driver at the helm. They'd traveled only a few blocks west from Eden's Thirty-Sixth Street entrance before it became apparent where they were headed—the Lincoln Tunnel. "We're going to New Jersey?" she asked.

"I should have blindfolded you," Sam quipped.

Mindy was momentarily distracted by the idea. "Wait. Are we going to see the Mercer?"

Sam reached down for his black leather messenger bag and produced a thick envelope, which he handed to her. "Here you go. The purchase agreement."

"Seriously? You got it done already?" Mindy took the packet from him, hearing the excitement in her own voice. So many of the problems with BMO could be solved with the purchase of this building. Every issue she'd had to grapple with that morning would improve simply by having her entire operation in one place.

"Of course I got it done already. A promise is a promise." He gestured at the envelope with a nod. "Go ahead. Read it."

"Right." She unhooked the metal clasp and pulled out the sheaf of papers. "Of course, I'll have to wait to sign it until I have my lawyer look at it." Everything between Sam and her was going so well, but surely he understood that this was business. "You get it, right? I have to make sure everything is in order."

"Absolutely I understand."

She was glad that it didn't feel as though there was any subtext in his answer, one of her not trusting him. She began to look through the pages, skimming the key points and clauses, until she reached the section with the purchase price. She nearly passed out when she saw the number. "A dollar?" Mindy had no idea her own voice could reach such a ridiculously high pitch. "You're selling me the building for a dollar? Seriously? Is this a joke?"

Sam frowned, which made Mindy feel horrible. "I wanted to do something nice for you. Something sort of romantic." His response was adorably tentative. Sam was always so self-assured, it was humbling to see this hint of vulnerability.

"Flowers are romantic. A building that could save my entire mess of a business? I don't even know what to say, Sam. This is beyond romantic. It's so generous of you. I don't know if I can accept this. It's such a huge gift." She set the papers down on the seat between them and took his hand. "It's seriously the nicest thing I think anyone has ever done for me. Thank you." She leaned over and gave him a soft and sensuous kiss. She wanted him to know that she truly appreciated the sweet gesture.

"You're welcome. I'm just happy that you're happy. Seeing that look on your face is all the reward I need."

"I'm curious why you did this, though. Is there something you want or need?"

"I don't need anything more than you right now, Mindy."

Mindy's heart fluttered so fast it made it feel as though she might float away. She was seriously starting to feel light-headed from Sam's brand of romanticism, but the driver turned into the drive for the Mercer and this was no time for letting her head stay in the clouds. She peered out the window to look at the building she hadn't seen in over a month. An old sugar processing plant, the Mercer had character for days—five floors clad in red brick with sky-high factory windows and a hint of art deco architecture. It was going to be a real showstopper once she turned it into everything they needed it to be. "I can't believe this is going to be mine. Everything under one roof. It's amazing."

Sam's driver parked the car and they climbed out. That was when Sam unveiled his second surprise of the day. His driver had a blanket and picnic basket in the front seat with him. "We shouldn't be much more than an hour," Sam said, taking the items from him and closing the door.

"A picnic? You are full of surprises."

"I want us to enjoy our week, and this is part of that. Plus, a businesswoman's got to eat, right?"

"I am slightly starving. So yes."

He took Mindy's hand and led her around back to the door next to the loading dock bays. He unlocked it and presented the key to her. "You should probably be in charge of this. It's your building."

"I haven't even signed the contract yet. How do you know I'm good for that dollar?"

He bounced his eyebrows up and down and they

stepped inside. "Something tells me I'll get it out of you one way or another."

The main floor was a cavernous, empty space with the building's highest ceilings—twenty-two feet. "This is where all of the shipping and fulfillment will go," Mindy said. In her mind, she could see her employees packing boxes with wedding invitations, birth announcements or Christmas cards. The idea filled her with hope, something she hadn't been feeling about BMO in recent weeks.

"Sounds perfect," Sam said as they walked over to the back stairs. "I guess we'll have to hoof it."

"No electricity, no elevator."

They carefully ascended the five flights, which were dimly lit right now, narrow beams of sunlight filtering through windows that needed a good wash. Still, Mindy was struck with the feeling that things were turning around. She hadn't worried that Sam would go back on his promise to sell her the building, but she'd certainly never expected him to sell it to her for a song. More than anything, she'd never imagined he would take something so important, yet decidedly *not* romantic—an old factory—and turn it into such a sweet and sentimental outing. He knew exactly how much this meant to her and he'd gone the extra mile to make it special.

"I scouted out the perfect location for our picnic. Up here, fifth floor." Sam pulled open the heavy metal door at the top of the final landing, which creaked loudly on its hinges. "Ladies first."

Mindy blinked several times while her eyes adjusted to all of the light. The sun positively poured through the windows lining the straight shot of what would eventually be the executive floor. "It looks like somebody cleaned up here." Mindy turned and took it all in. This was not what it had looked like when she and Matthew had walked the space before making an offer. The windowpanes were crystal clear. The original wide-plank hardwood floors weren't covered in dust and dirt like they had been downstairs.

"I knew we were going to have lunch. I didn't want you to get whatever you were wearing all dirty," Sam said.

"When did you have time to plan all of this? Or even have it done? It must have taken days."

One corner of Sam's mouth turned up and Mindy saw something she'd never seen on his face—a blush in his cheeks. "It took about a week."

She had been staying at Sam's apartment for only a day. It had only been yesterday morning that they'd decided to try at all. "You planned this before the wedding? Back when we were keeping things platonic and focused on being friends?"

"Well, yeah. I like doing nice things for you, but I know I haven't done a great job of it in the past. Plus, I know how much this means to you. I hear it in your voice. I see it in the way your eyes blaze when you talk about it. Not many people have a vision. Not many people are capable of being passionate about what they do. I wanted to reward that. It's not something you see every day."

Mindy gazed up at Sam, overwhelmed with a feeling she never flirted with—love. Did she love him? Was that what this was? She was certain she was at least falling under Sam's spell again, this time harder than all of the others put together. Could she have the happy ending her sisters had managed to get for themselves? Or was she once again allowing herself to be swept away by the handsome man with the inexplicable pull on her?

Sam hoped he hadn't overstepped. The look on Mindy's face was hard to decipher—he'd expected smiles, not sadness, and certainly not a tear rolling down her cheek. Before he could ask if she was okay, she flung her arms around him.

"Thank you so much. I don't even know how to express how much this means to me."

He set the picnic basket down on the ground and took his chance to wrap his arms around her. "Any idiot could figure that out, Min. All I had to do was pay attention."

She eased her head back, arms still circling his waist. Her gaze met his, her eyes bright and crystal clear. "I feel like I spend my entire day trying to justify my dream to my sisters. They don't understand it. But you do."

Sam pulled her a little closer and kissed her on the forehead. His heart was unfortunately heavy, despite her happy reaction. There was information about BMO he had to share with her today. But for right now, he would enjoy every minute of her gratitude. He rarely felt so rewarded for his efforts.

"Of course I understand it. In fact, I probably get it more than the average person. There are plenty of days when you're leading the charge on everything on your own. I'm in that same boat with my company. The rewards are great when it works out, but it's incredibly stressful when it isn't quite what you want it to be."

"Yes. You are so right. Today feels like one of those days when everything is working out exactly like I want it to."

Sam cringed inwardly, knowing what he had to tell her about Matthew and the way the original sale of the Mercer had happened. But he would let himself savor this beautiful moment for a little longer.

"This corner of the building has an incredible view," Sam said, nodding toward the windows. "Is this where you planned to put your office?"

Mindy trailed over to the corner, glancing outside. "You know, it's funny, but I've envisioned everything else about BMO moving into this space. Except for my office. That part hasn't really registered. Maybe because I've been stuck at Eden's this whole time."

"So you're having a hard time remembering what it used to be like to run BMO." Sam took the checkered blanket he brought and spread it out on the hardwood floor. He took a seat and offered his hand to Mindy.

She settled in right next to him, tucking her legs under her skirt. "Sort of. I mean, I still get to deal with the headaches. Some things are not going well."

Sam had worried that might be the case. He opened the basket and handed Mindy a sandwich from the gourmet shop down the street from his office. He got out a bottle of wine, one that came with a screw cap, and poured some for both of them in small plastic cups. "Cheers."

"To the Mercer," Mindy said.

Sam knew that was his opening. "Min, I need to tell

you something about the building. I got the building for a steal. Way under its current value. And I know you said that you were trying to buy it, but I talked to the head of my acquisitions team and he told me that there were no other offers on the property."

Mindy finished chewing a bite of her sandwich, then wiped her mouth with a napkin. "No. That's not right. I signed our offer. I had to as majority owner of the company."

"Do you think it's possible the offer was never actually submitted?"

Mindy reared back her head. "No way. Matthew told me he did it. Why would he lie to me about that? He wanted the building just as badly as I did."

Sam nodded. "I don't know why he would lie, but I'm worried he did."

"What? I can see those gears turning in your head. You're thinking something and I need to know what it is."

"How much do you trust this Matthew guy?"

"He came very highly recommended. Every company he's ever run has been nothing less than supersuccessful. And he's brought a bunch of companies back from the brink of failure."

"That's not what I asked. I asked if you trust him. Do you?"

Mindy sighed and she hunched her shoulders. "Not really."

"I see."

"I figured that was just because it's my company and I'm a control freak and don't really trust anyone when it comes to this."

"Okay, well, here's the other piece of this puzzle that I know about. Our acquisitions team got a tip about the Mercer. We were told to bid quickly and bid low but do an all-cash deal. They checked it out, the building was a great buy and they pulled the trigger. But nobody can tell me exactly where the tip came from."

"None of this makes sense. Why would Matthew want to sabotage the attempt to buy the building? Our only other option was looking at new construction or hoping something better came along. It was a huge setback when we didn't get it."

"Maybe he's trying to sabotage you. Either he's in a competitor's back pocket or, what I think is a more likely scenario, he's seen firsthand that you have a real gem on your hands, but you're in a vulnerable position right now. This is pretty much the time when businesses like yours either fail or flourish. I'm wondering if maybe he's pushing you just close enough to failure to make you want to sell to him."

"People do that?"

"Are you kidding? All the time. Especially guys like Matthew. He runs companies. He doesn't come up with ideas. He has no expertise in building a team. He only knows how to run with existing ones. But you have a pretty amazing setup, you have unlimited growth potential and, most important, he already knows that you're distracted by another big business."

"Eden's."

"Right. You have another year where your attention has to be divided between the two. I'm guessing that he's hoping that you'll give up on one."

"But I would never give up on BMO. It's my baby."

Sam felt a sharp pain in his chest just hearing the distress in Mindy's voice. "I know that. And I'm sure he knows that on some level, too. But he's hoping that at some point, you're going to give your baby up for adoption."

Mindy's jaw was set tight. She seemed confused and stressed out. "Can you help me figure this out? Help me try to decide if this is what's really going on? You're the only one who can do it. If my sisters get involved, he'll know something is up."

"What about me, though? He knows we're exes."

"And maybe that's why he picked you to tip off. He knew it made it a plausible story that you would have swooped in and bought the building."

"We were seen at your sister's wedding together. So it looks like we're back together." Sam didn't say it, but it felt that way, too. It felt like they were a couple, for real. He didn't want to think about what was coming at the end of their week together, when Mindy would once again be under the influence of her family.

Mindy took another bite of her sandwich, and Sam took his chance to eat something, too. Meanwhile, the gears were clearly turning in Mindy's head. He did love seeing her spring to action. "If your hunch is correct, maybe it's a good thing if he thinks we're back together. That should make him plenty nervous, shouldn't it?"

Sam smiled wide. He loved the way she was looking at this. "Yes. And nervous people make mistakes."

"Which means it'll make him even more nervous when he finds out you sold me the building for a dollar." Mindy sipped her wine, then leaned over and kissed him, her sweetness lingering on his lips. "Thank you again, by the way."

"You're so sexy when you're being calculating," he said.

"You're so sexy when you're helping me squash all of my problems. Now we just need to figure out how to squash this one."

Eight

Two days after he sold the Mercer to Mindy, Sam arrived home from work to what was becoming a regular occurrence in his apartment—Mindy, cooking in his kitchen. In heels and a designer dress, no less.

"I see you're at it again," he said, coming up behind her and kissing her neck.

"I had the worst day."

"Most people just have a drink." He reached around to the countertop to a pile of grated parmesan she'd left on the cutting board. "Ooh. Why is cheese so good?"

"I don't know, but I do know that cheese is the best part of anything with cheese in it." She took a wineglass from the cabinet, poured some for him and topped off her own. "Cheers. Here's to letting the day fall away."

"Cheers." To anyone else, this scene might be nothing but mundane, but to Sam, it was extraordinary. So this was what cohabitation was like. So this was what it was like when Mindy and Sam didn't have anyone between them.

Although Mindy had said she'd had a bad day, she seemed to be in a good mood. Much better than he tended to be when things at work became overwhelming. She buzzed around the room, opening the fridge, adjusting burners and cutting vegetables.

"What happened? Something at Eden's?" he asked.

"Actually, stuff at Eden's is pretty much on autopilot at this point. So much of the staff has been there forever. It's BMO stuff again. Stupid stuff. Totally preventable. The art director not talking to the marketing team. The head of production letting us run out of things a printing business should never run out of." She took another sip of her wine, looked up at the ceiling shaking her head, then pointed her sights at him. "Like paper. Actual paper."

"Seriously?"

"Seriously."

Sam sat down on a bar stool next to the kitchen peninsula. "Do you think it's Matthew?"

Mindy shrugged. "I honestly don't know. I had a call with him today. He claims that he's working on it, and everything he tells me seems to check out, but I just don't know. It feels like somebody is setting little fires everywhere, just so I can run and put them out."

Sam felt a bit like he was about to set a big fire square in the middle of Mindy's work life, and he hated it. But he also knew that the truth would ultimately be so much better for her. "I have some info I want to share with you. I did some digging into Matthew. And I discovered some interesting stuff."

"Good interesting or bad interesting?"

"I don't think you'll be happy. But maybe this is for the best." He unzipped his laptop bag and pulled out a file folder. "Here's what we found."

"We?"

"I'm no detective. I mean, I found some of this on my own, but I also have people who work for me who are exceptionally good at digging." Saying it out loud made him feel bad that he'd taken this step without asking her first.

Mindy wiped her hands on a kitchen towel and joined him at the kitchen peninsula, settling in next to him. "Okay, then. Show me what you found."

Sam opened the folder and walked her through the documents—a mix of online articles about businesses Matthew had run, financial reports and timelines, all of which had a recurring second character—a man named Zeke Anderson. There was a very regular pattern of one of them working their way into a high position within a promising start-up, things going from good to great and then suddenly starting to take a downward turn. At which point the other person, either Matthew or Zeke, swept in and offered to buy a majority stake in the company, just to "rescue" a struggling owner. The companies all miraculously recovered and went on to record earnings.

Mindy clasped her hand over her mouth. "Oh, my God, Sam. This is not only exactly what's happening with BMO, but Matthew suggested to me today that I should consider selling the company before we do the move. So I wouldn't have to deal with the hassle and could just cash in."

"Did you tell him that I sold you the Mercer?"

"I did. He didn't seem fazed by it, but he did bring up the idea of selling right after I told him."

Sam worried that Mindy had a real mess on her hands. He hoped he could figure out a way to help her through it. "I wish I had better news to deliver."

"Me, too. I also wish this had never happened. I feel like a complete idiot for putting my company in jeopardy like this. I clearly didn't do a good enough job vetting this guy."

Sam shook his head emphatically, wanting her to understand that the situation she was in was not of her own doing. "You cannot blame yourself for this. It's not you, Min. You're a brilliant businesswoman. Look at the companies these two have gotten involved with. Most are hugely successful. That's how they get the next gig and keep themselves looking like geniuses."

"Meanwhile, they're orchestrating the whole thing."

"That's my gut."

"I don't want to let him get to the point where he gets to be the hero. I want to stop him as soon as we can."

"Well, yeah. Of course. If anyone is going to be the hero in this story, it has to be you. I'm here for whatever you need."

Mindy looked at Sam, her eyes bright and full of life. No one could blame her if she were feeling down or defeated by any of this, but she wasn't. She was leaning into the wind, ready to tackle her problems head-on. "Will you help me figure out how to catch him at his own game? At least enough for me to force him out? He has a pretty ironclad contract with us. Unfortunately, I worried more about him not sticking around than I ever worried about needing to get rid of him."

Sam hadn't sorted out how they would do this, but he was fairly certain he could come up with something. "I'm sure I can think of something. Might involve some cloak-and-dagger work. Corporate espionage is no small matter."

Mindy's eyes glinted with mischief. "Ooh. I feel like I'm fully stepping into your dark and sexy underhanded world, Sam."

Sam laughed quietly. "Trust me, it's not that sexy." He cleared his throat when he saw the way Mindy's mouth went slack. That vision of her mouth made him want to take her, right then and there. "Scratch that. With you in it, it's supersexy. Like unbelievably sexy."

Mindy slid off her bar stool and stood between Sam's legs, wagging her hips back and forth, knocking herself against his knees. "You are amazing. Truly amazing. Thank you for showing me the light of day with Matthew. If it wasn't for you, I would be barking up the wrong tree right now, worried about little stuff while much bigger issues were going on under my nose."

"We make a great team." The words had left his lips before he'd really had a chance to think them out.

She smiled and leaned into him. "We make an amazing team."

Once again, Sam was overcome with relief. He'd made so many mistakes in the past and he wanted to prove to her this week that he wasn't that guy. He *was* capable of making her happy. He felt like he'd done that today.

He lowered his head, she raised her chin, and their lips met. Passionate and eager, this kiss felt far more potent than any other. A kiss on steroids, turned on at full blast. Mindy combed her fingers into his hair at the nape, digging in her nails, driving him wild. Her tongue wound in circles with his, the kiss wet and hot. He inched forward on the bar stool and she pressed right against his crotch with her hips, rocking into him as the blood in his veins went from warm to red hot.

He tugged down the zipper of her dress and didn't wait until the garment was off before he was unhooking her bra. Mindy let go of their kiss and shook the straps from her arms, leaving both items of clothing to fall to the floor. He dropped his feet to the floor and picked her up at the waist, plopping her down on the kitchen counter.

She was as tempting as could be sitting before him in nothing more than heels and a pair of lacy black panties. "Much better," he said, taking her breasts in his hands. Her skin was soft as the finest silk, her nipples hard beneath his touch. He drew one tight bud into his mouth, swirling his tongue, savoring her sweetness. How he loved feeling the reaction of her body against his lips, her skin puckering from his touch.

He reached down and curled his fingers into her perfectly round bottom, urging her closer to the edge of the counter. He put one of her legs on his shoulder, then the other, and using his thumb, pulled aside her panties, leaving her bare to him. Mindy planted her hands back behind her, tilting her pelvis and giving him the perfect angle. He lowered his mouth against her center, and licked, slowly at first, listening to her soft moans—pure music to his ears. Making her happy, bringing her close to the brink of orgasm, left everything in his body impossibly tight. It felt as if the blood had left his head and feet and instead raced to his hips, pulsing hard. Mindy bucked her hips, her breaths becoming short and fast.

"Come for me, darling," he said, slipping two fingers inside her. She was so warm, so wet, and he could hardly wait to be inside her, especially as his erection grew harder and heavier between his legs. Still, he wasn't willing to do anything but focus on her pleasure, so he returned to his charge, swirling his tongue in circles while his fingers glided in and out of her body. She gasped loudly when she came, pressing her calves against his back, nearly squeezing his head between her knees. He gave her center one more kiss, which made her suck in a sharp breath.

She lowered her legs and he stood, kissing her deeply. Mindy wrapped her legs around his waist and pulled him closer. "I need more of you," she said. "All of you."

That was exactly what he wanted to give her, but as tall as he was, the cabinet was still in the way. So were his clothes and shoes and far too many other things. "I don't want to have sex in the kitchen, if that's okay with you." He didn't wait for a response, wrapping one arm around her waist and scooping her legs up in his other arm. Mindy wasn't a damsel in distress. She didn't need to be saved. But he loved having the chance to feel for at least a few moments like he might be her knight in shining armor.

* * *

Mindy curled into Sam as he carried her down the hall to his bedroom, his strides long and confident. She felt so sexy in his arms, especially in that postorgasm glow. The man had the most talented tongue, the sexiest mouth. And he knew exactly how to send her over the cliff. When it came to the physical, he knew exactly how to make her happy.

They arrived in his room and he left the light behind, setting her down on the mattress. She wasn't about to get settled, though. Sam had taken off his shirt, and shoes, but his pants had to go. She scrambled off the bed and shimmied her panties down her legs. Then she went to work, getting rid of his pants and boxer briefs. Sam spent most of his day looking perfectly yummy to Mindy, but tonight he looked even better than usual. Maybe it was because she knew now that he wanted to protect her. No man had ever wanted to do that, let alone try. She was strong and independent, but there was still this part of her inside that was soft and gooey and needed to know that somebody would be there to catch her fall.

She took Sam's erection in her hand, which immediately produced a deep groan from his lips. She stroked firmly, trying to match the tension beneath his skin with pressure of her own. She felt a little bit like she was losing at this idea, but Sam was more than pleased, his lips humming with approval. She kneeled on the bed and took him into her mouth, skimming her wet lips along his steely length, gripping his hips with her hands. She pressed her thumbs into his skin hard, and that made him growl. She'd learned by now that Sam really liked the contrasts—the hard with the soft, the rough with the tender.

She wrapped her hand around the base of his erection and gently pulled him from her mouth. She rubbed her thumb along the tender underside, enjoying the power she wielded in this situation. She knew she could do anything she wanted and he would be happy. But the reality was that she was most interested right now in what would make them both happy—him inside her. So she eased back on the bed and stretched her arms high above her head, clasping her hands. She was his for the taking and he did exactly that. Descending on her, blazing a hot trail of kisses from her stomach up to her breasts, then settling in her neck just as he drove inside.

The pressure was intense from the very beginning. He filled her so perfectly and they once again fell into that rhythm that made them both happy. He used one hand to keep her in place, leaving her deliciously defenseless. Meanwhile he slipped his other hand between their bodies, resting his thumb on her center, backed by his complete body weight. Mindy already felt like she was about to rocket into the upper atmosphere, but she told herself to relax, to savor every deft stroke he took inside her.

He had his head turned to one side, breathing hard, pressing one shoulder against hers while bucking his hips.

"Kiss me, Sam," she said. As close as they were right now, she needed more of him. She was desperate for all of him the way a person wants cool water on a hot day.

He claimed her mouth with his, their tongues tangled, and the pressure in her hips coiled so tight she nearly bit Sam's lips. His thrusts were as deep as she could imagine, and she pressed hard on his backside with her feet, raising her hips to meet his. The pleasure was making her light-headed, like she was fading into dark and coming back to light. As good as she knew the climax would be, there was a part of her that wanted this to go on forever. She never wanted to be anywhere else but right there. With Sam.

His hips moved faster and his breaths followed suit. Mindy was on the edge, but she wanted to wait for him. She wanted to get there at the same time. Still, her body was chipping away at her resolve, going tight. Then tighter. And even tighter again. It felt as though fireworks were going off in her body, a chaotic onslaught of electric pulses. Sam froze for a moment and buried his face in her neck, then he took labored thrusts, pulsing inside her over and over again. Mindy didn't dare let go of her legs around him.

When he tried to roll to her side, she followed.

Sam laughed. "It's okay to let go, you know."

"I don't want to," she said, kissing his chest and drinking in his smell. She'd just had two powerful orgasms and she wanted only more of him.

"Well, I'm going to need at least a half hour to recover from that. Maybe more."

Mindy sighed. "Okay. But I just want to stay in bed for the rest of the night, okay?"

"What about the dinner you made?"

"Oh, yeah. I forgot about that. Okay. I just need to pop in some pasta, then we can eat in bed and watch TV and have sex again."

Sam kissed her on the forehead. "Pasta and sex. You really are a dream woman, aren't you?"

He traipsed off to the bathroom and Mindy grabbed one of Sam's T-shirts, then scurried out to the kitchen, turning on the flame under the pot of water she'd left out earlier. The sauce was already prepared. It wouldn't take much more than ten minutes once the water came to a boil.

Sam appeared moments later in his boxers and poured them each another glass of wine. "I don't think I've ever seen you in just a T-shirt. I'm so used to the designer version of you."

"I can go get my robe if you want. I just grabbed this because it was quicker. I'm highly motivated by the idea of eating in bed."

Sam grinned. "No. I like it. It gives me this idea of what you might have been like when you were younger." He set down his wineglass and formed his fingers into a frame, peering at her through it. "I see seventeen-year-old Mindy Eden, making spaghetti in the kitchen of the family mansion."

"I wouldn't call it a mansion. It was a penthouse." Mindy always got a little defensive when the privilege of her youth was brought up. Yes, she'd had anything material she could have ever wanted, but there hadn't been a lot of love and affection in that household, aside from what was between Sophie and Mindy. It was a big part of the reason they were so close.

"What were you like as a teenager?" he asked.

"Pretty much the way I am now. I've always been focused on accomplishing things. Staying busy. Keeping myself occupied. Otherwise, I get bored."

"So you weren't running around with your friends chasing after guys?"

Mindy gave the pasta sauce a stir. "Oh, no. I did my fair share of that."

"Lots of boyfriends?"

"Lots of dates. Not many who stuck around very long. I had a tendency to pick guys who thought like my dad. Guys who didn't like the fact that I was driven. They wanted a girl who would sit back and let them be at center stage. I'm just not like that. I don't have to be the center of attention, but I'm not going to set aside my dreams for a guy."

"How could your dad not admire that in a daughter?"

"He had a lot of preconceived ideas about what a girl should be like. I also think he wished I'd been a boy. I was the firstborn. I wasn't much of an heir in his mind." Mindy fought back the sad feelings that came along with this topic. She had enough confused thoughts and guilt about her dad to last a lifetime. She'd never felt loved by him. Not once. Still, she wanted to share this part of herself with Sam. Maybe it would help him see that she wasn't as indestructible as he thought.

"I guess you eventually got past the stage of picking guys like your dad?"

"Not really. Honestly, you're the first one who wasn't entirely like him. Of course, it was a little different with you. You pursued me. I'm not sure I would have had the guts to approach you the night we met."

Sam reared back his head. "You don't strike me as a woman who has any problem introducing herself to a man."

She smiled and lifted the top off the pot of water,

dumping in half a box of bucatini pasta. She gave it a healthy dose of salt, a stir, and set the timer for nine minutes. "You're a little too intimidating, Sam."

"Physically, maybe. But I'm not once you get to know me."

She shook her head. "No. You can still be intimidating. You play things very close to the vest. You get closed off sometimes. In that way, you're a lot like my dad."

"I don't mean to be that way. It's just my personality."

He turned away from her, walking across the kitchen, getting a water glass from the cabinet and filling it at the fridge. It was a perfectly innocent act—he was thirsty. But she couldn't help but feel like he was doing the exact thing she'd just brought up. He was closing himself off, when all she wanted was to talk. He'd mentioned in passing at Sophie's wedding that his mom had passed away when he was a teen. She wondered if he'd open up to her about it.

"What about you? What were you like as a teenager?" she asked.

He drew a deep breath through his nose, then downed the rest of his water. "Sullen. Moody."

Mindy didn't want to immediately jump to the conclusion that he was that way because of his mother. Surely there had been some happy times. "What about girls?"

"Not until college."

"Really?"

"Really."

Mindy was getting the distinct impression that he did not want to talk about this. She didn't want to push.

Not when they were having such a perfect night. She wasn't going to ruin it with questions and prying. If Sam wanted to open up to her, he would. She only hoped it would happen eventually. She needed to be close to him. In more ways than one.

Nine

By Sunday night, Mindy was cooking again. She couldn't help it. It was the only way she could cope with her anxiety, and it was much healthier than downing entire bottles of wine. Sam had gone for a run, which left Mindy to do nothing but think about the week ahead. Being pulled in so many directions was making her feel like she was losing her mind. She couldn't handle the constant push and pull—she was stuck between Eden's and BMO, stuck between wanting to believe Matthew and not trusting him at all, and most difficult of all was the spot she was in between her sisters and Sam. Sophie and Emma would both be back at Eden's tomorrow, which meant that a storm was moving in.

She and Sam had given themselves a week. Tomorrow morning was supposed to be the end. Logic said that she should move her things out, that these seven days had been nothing but a fantasy fulfilled. But that thinking was too focused on logic and right now she was feeling more like she wanted to follow her heart. She didn't want to leave. She wanted to stay put. But was that her wanting to hide from her problems? It wasn't like she and Sam were ready to move in together. Not for real. Plus, she knew exactly what Sophie and Emma would say if they knew where she was right now. Forget the bet—even if that had never existed, they would be shaking her out of her dream state, reminding her that she had deluded herself many times when it came to Sam. She and Sam had enjoyed stretches of happiness before and it always went south. Always.

Sam's home phone rang, and Mindy jumped at the sound. Sam always got calls on his cell. She hadn't heard this line ring once while she'd been here. She shuffled to the far side of the kitchen counter and squinted at the caller ID, but it displayed Private Number, so she let it go to voice mail. Back at the stove, tending some sautéed mushrooms, the phone stopped ringing, but only for a few seconds before it started up again. Once more, Private Number. Whoever was calling certainly wanted to get through. Maybe there was some sort of emergency. Maybe it was Sam and his cell was acting up again.

"Hello?" she answered, cradling the receiver between her ear and shoulder while carefully trimming the ends of green beans.

"Uh, hi. I'm looking for Sam. Who's this?"

It was a woman's voice, one Mindy did not recognize. "Who's this?"

"Sam's sister. Isabel."

Sister? Sam had never, ever mentioned that he had a sister. Not even the other night when she'd tried to ask what he was like as a teenager. What the hell was going on?

"I don't want to be a jerk, but again, I'd like to ask who's answering my brother's phone," Isabel said. "And is he there? I need to speak to him."

Mindy stopped working and set the knife on the marble counter. "Sorry. I was in the middle of making dinner and got distracted. This is Mindy. Mindy Eden." For a moment, she considered whether or not she should label herself—girlfriend? Houseguest?

"Oh, my God. You're the one who broke my brother's heart."

"Excuse me?" This was all too much to process at one time. A sister? And Mindy as the heartbreaker? More like the other way around. It was officially time to pour herself a glass of wine. Sam might have kept his sister hidden from her, but he'd apparently had no problem telling his sister about her.

"He told me all about you," Isabel said. "I know every last thing about you and your crazy family."

Mindy didn't even know what to say. Part of her wanted to defend herself, part of her knew that it was the truth—she loved her family, but crazy things did tend to be part and parcel of being an Eden. "Sam's not here right now. He went for a run. Would you like me to tell him that you called?"

Isabel laughed quietly. "You're changing the subject. I'm sorry. I shouldn't have said that. I'm just very protective of Sam. I don't like to see him get hurt."

"Understandable. I'm the same way about my sisters." Mindy turned off the burner on the stove and took a seat at the kitchen peninsula. "I don't know how to say this, but he never told me about you. He never mentioned anyone but his mom. And that was only in passing."

"Interesting."

"What? Tell me why that's interesting." Mindy realized how desperate she was for information. It was like a portal into Sam had opened up before her and she wanted to peer inside before it closed. "Please."

"If he didn't tell you about me, it only means that he doesn't trust you. Not completely, anyway. Sam's secretive, but most of that comes from things that happened when we were kids. He had to grow up very fast. And I couldn't always be there to help."

None of this was answering anything. It was only leaving Mindy with more questions. It was also saddling her with a growing sadness, one so big it was threatening to swallow her whole. Sam didn't trust her. That wasn't a guess. She had hard evidence of it. "Can you tell me more?"

"If you know about the fundraiser he's hosting, that explains a lot of it."

"No. I don't know anything about it." Now her sadness was becoming outright despair. She'd really fooled herself, hadn't she? She'd thought she and Sam were getting closer this week. Now she knew she was wrong.

"Well, you might want to ask him about that. Or not. I don't know the state of your relationship, but considering the fact that you're answering his home phone, I'd guess you two are back together."

"It's complicated." Mindy hardly knew Isabel. She wasn't going to offer more.

"I'm guessing he would say the same thing."

"Probably."

"Well, let him know that I called, please. I tried his cell but I couldn't get through."

"I will." Mindy said goodbye and returned the phone to its cradle, but was left with a more unsettled feeling than she'd had before she answered the call. She'd been looking forward to a nice night with Sam. Clearly there were things that needed to be discussed.

From the other side of the apartment, Mindy heard Sam's front door close. "Hello?" Sam called out, appearing in the kitchen moments later, sweaty from his run and with a wide grin across his face. Mindy simply watched him as he closed in on her, the unease from the phone call abating for the moment, replaced by the thrill of being in the same space with him.

Sam surveyed the landscape of the countertops and island, where Mindy's cooking project was strewn about. "Hi. I'm looking for Mindy Eden. She's tall. Gorgeous. Real ball of fire. The last time I saw her was a little less than two hours ago and she had not yet turned my kitchen into a war zone."

She stepped closer to him, feeling even more conflicted than she had when she'd come home to start dinner. She was over the moon to see him, but there were uncomfortable subjects ahead. Big decisions to be made. "You're funny. So funny." She didn't care that he was sweaty. She just wanted to be close to him. She wrapped her arms around him, pressing herself against the hard plane of his chest. It was hard to escape the feeling that this was where she belonged, but was that just wishful thinking? Was she pinning hope on a situation that wasn't real? That didn't really exist? Isabel's phone call right before Sam walked in the door certainly felt like a sign. It was without question a reminder—Sam had secrets. She knew it.

The kitchen timer buzzed, pulling them out of their quiet moment. "That's the gratin. Time to take it out of the oven." She hustled over to the stove.

"Smells amazing."

Mindy placed the ceramic casserole dish on the stove, wanting to get past the mental block that was stuck in her head. "Before I forget, you got a phone call."

"You answered my phone?"

"Well, yeah. I've never heard it ring before. It startled me. And I guess I thought it might be important. Your cell phone is always acting up."

"Next time, you can feel free to let it go to voice mail."

Now this was officially not sitting well with Mindy. "It was your sister. Isabel? The sister I had no idea you had."

Sam craned his neck, looking up at the ceiling, drawing a breath through his nose. "I really wish you hadn't answered the phone."

"Do you want to tell me about her? Or would you rather keep expressing the idea that I have somehow crossed the line by daring to answer your phone?"

"Well, you did cross the line. I would never do that at your place."

"So you trust me to sleep in your bed or make dinner in your kitchen, but you don't trust me to take a message? You trust me with a key to your apartment, but you don't trust me with this?" Mindy was more than hurt. She'd thought she and Sam had been making progress. Moving forward. Now it all felt like a lie. "I'm sorry, but that's insulting, and I can't help but be hurt. You have a sister and you never told me about her."

"Min, I really don't think you should be lecturing me about trust. It's more than a little hypocritical considering that there have been many times when as soon as something goes wrong, you look to me."

Sam was right. He was absolutely right. "I'm sorry. I don't know what I'm doing anymore. I shouldn't have answered your phone. Especially when we both know that what's between us has been temporary."

"Oh, right. Tomorrow is the day you surrender to your sisters."

"Don't you understand? I'm not giving in to my sisters. I'm not letting them determine my future, just because they think they know what's right for me. I'm not letting them keep me from everything I've worked so hard for, but I need to be able to do it on my own terms. No guilt."

"You realize a future is about more than what you do for work all day."

Mindy just looked at him, his words tumbling around in her head and getting stuck in a perpetual loop. "You live for your work."

"I do, but after this week, I'm starting to see that maybe I want more."

More of what? Her? Was that possible? If so, that meant that he needed to stop hiding things from her.

"If you're suggesting you want more with me, I don't see how we're going to make that work if you're getting upset with me for answering the phone. And especially not when you're keeping family members a secret, especially ones who know about me. Who know about us."

"Oh, no. Did Isabel say something?"

"She referred to me as the woman who broke your heart."

"She doesn't have much of a filter. I'm sorry."

"Is that true, Sam? Did you talk to her about me? Did you say that? And I don't understand why you wouldn't tell me about her. I don't think you realize how much it hurts to have you shut me out like that."

Sam then did the same thing he did the other night—he turned away from her. Except this time, he walked right out of the room, over to the bank of tall windows in the living room. A person could accuse Sam Blackwell of many things, but he did not shy away from confrontation. You could call him out on the most horrible thing in the world and he would own up to it if the deed was his own. This secretiveness was making Mindy sick to her stomach. This was all wrong. "Sam? Are you going to talk to me?"

He shook his head, not looking at her.

"Are you serious?" She stepped closer and attempted to look him in the eye, but he avoided her. And he did not say a thing.

Mindy couldn't stay. She couldn't endure this. Not the quiet. This was the sort of thing her dad always did when he was angry—he'd kill everyone with silence. It was the cruelest form of punishment to have someone refuse to engage. "If you aren't going to talk to me, I can't stay."

Sam didn't move. Not a single twitch of a muscle. He just stood there in the dim light of the living room, staring off through the windows at the city.

"Okay, then," she said, her voice shaking. She turned on her heel and walked out of the room, past the kitchen and away from the meal she'd prepared. It would just have to go cold. Sam would have to clean up the mess himself. She had to get out of this apartment. Sure enough, the end had come for them. She'd thought it would be tomorrow. But what was the difference? In the end, this thing with Sam was made of glimpses of happiness strung between everything else that was wrong.

She stalked into his bedroom, flipped on the light and grabbed one of her garment bags, spreading it out on the bed. She took her clothes from the closet in handfuls, tossing them in haphazardly and not caring that she was going too fast and rumpling everything. If she did this quickly enough, she and Sam wouldn't have to speak another word to each other. That was clearly what he wanted. With her clothes gathered, she went into the bathroom, scooping up makeup and dumping it into her cosmetic bag. She avoided her own reflection in the mirror. It would be hard enough to live in her own brain tonight. She wasn't going to give herself a visual reminder of how much she hated some of the circumstances of being Mindy Eden.

Sam appeared at the bathroom door. "Don't go. Please don't go."

Mindy clamped her eyes shut, wishing she could

ward off the effect of his voice. "I refuse to stay if you won't talk to me. I won't do it."

He stepped closer and she dared to look up into his dark eyes. "Let me tell you about Isabel. Let me tell you about everything."

The absolute last thing Sam ever wanted to be was vulnerable. Life was easier when you played everything close to the vest. He never let anyone see his soft spots. It not only made his weaknesses easier to ignore, it made it that much more difficult for anyone to hurt him. He'd been knocked down plenty in his first eighteen or so years. He wasn't going to intentionally invite it on himself.

But that was before Mindy started packing her things and preparing to walk out of his life.

"I'm serious," he said. "Don't go."

Mindy took the armful of makeup she had and set it all back down on the bathroom countertop. "I can't deal with the silent treatment. My dad used to do that to Sophie and my mom and me and it's the absolute worst."

"I know it's bad."

"I tried to be respectful the other night when you didn't want to talk about what you were like as a teenager, but I can't deal with secrets, either. I'm not expecting you to tell me everything, but I at least expect there to be some attempt at showing me the boundaries. Half of the time I feel like I'm stumbling around in the dark with you."

Funny, but Sam felt the exact same way about Mindy. And not just half of the time. All the time. "What do you want to know?"

"For starters, I want to know about Isabel. I want to know why you didn't tell me about her. I also want to know about this fundraiser you're hosting. You haven't said a peep about that to me."

Wow, Isabel had really gotten her mouth running. "She jumped the gun if she told you about that. I haven't committed to the fundraiser. And it's all intertwined. It's all connected."

"Okay, then. Just tell me. You can trust me, Sam. I promise."

Sam took Mindy's hand. "Am I going to ruin dinner if I tell you about Isabel? And my mom? It's not a short story."

"I couldn't care any less about dinner right now, Sam. If you want to share even the tiniest bit of yourself with me, I'll take it."

Had Sam left Mindy feeling like she was scrounging for crumbs? That had never been his intention. "Okay. Let's sit." He led her over to the bed, where they both settled in on the edge. He wasn't sure where to start—he had never, ever told anyone about his mom, except for the woman at the ALS Foundation, and that was still only the broadest of strokes. He hadn't told her about losing his dad as a direct result of his mother's illness. He hadn't told her how his entire family, the only family he'd ever known, completely fell apart.

"Isabel is three years older than me. We were always close, but we became more so when our mom was diagnosed with ALS."

"Lou Gehrig's disease?"

"Yes. Exactly. I was fourteen. Isabel was just finishing high school. Our mom was young. Only thirty-nine. She'd been losing strength in her hands and had a hard time holding on to even the simplest of things, like the handle on a coffeepot. When her voice started to change, a neighbor suggested she see a doctor." Just getting that much of his story out felt like a huge accomplishment, especially as visions of his past shuttled through his mind—the morning his mom dropped the coffee carafe on the kitchen floor and it shattered. The day their parents gathered his sister and him in the living room to deliver the terrible news, trying to frame it as something they would all get through. And, ultimately, the sacrifice their father decided to make to save his children's future.

"Sam, I am so sorry. You mentioned at the wedding that she passed away when you were still a teenager."

"She lived a little more than three years after that. So I was seventeen. It was halfway through my senior year of high school. It was not easy, especially since I was the only one around to care for her at that point. Isabel was away at college."

"What about your dad? Was he not a part of your life? You don't talk about him, either."

This was the cruel twist of fate in Sam's life story. In a way, his mother's disease claimed his father, too. "He died in a car accident almost a year before our mom passed. Went right into a guardrail on his way to work. But it wasn't an accident. He took his own life. I know this because he left me a note and told me he was doing it for the life insurance money. He did it for Isabel and me." Sam heard his own voice crack, and he wasn't sure which was worse—the actual sound or the way Mindy's expression morphed into profound sadness. "The medical bills had piled up and I'd gotten early acceptance to Stanford. Isabel was already at Columbia and had applied for law school. He told me to take care of my mom, pay off the house and the bills, and to get myself to Stanford. He also told me to burn the note. So that's what I did."

Sam cast his sights up to the ceiling, fighting back the tears that were welling in his eyes. He hadn't truly broken down since the day his mom passed away. He'd told himself that he couldn't afford to show emotion. He'd never felt weaker than on that day, not even on the day when his dad had died. That day had been more about shock than anything.

Mindy scooted closer and pulled him into her arms, cradling the back of his head with her hand and letting him rest his cheek on her shoulder. She held him so tight it felt like she might squeeze the life out of him, and maybe that was for the best—the only times he'd truly felt alive in recent history were when he was with her. And she was going to leave tomorrow and there was nothing to be done about that. She'd never been anything less than crystal clear about her priorities—family first, job and career a close second and Sam a distant third. Not that he could blame her for her choices. Except for selling the Mercer to her for a dollar, he'd done nothing but put his own business front and center. But he had his reasons. Money bought security. It bought permanence in a world where everything is fleeting. He wouldn't apologize for needing that.

"I wish I knew what to say." Mindy sniffled and he

felt the dampness of her tears on his nose when he raised his head and kissed her cheek. "I had no idea. That's the saddest story I think I have ever heard."

"I don't want you to feel sorry for me, Min. I really don't. It was a long time ago and everyone has a sad story, don't they? I'm no different than anyone else."

"But you keep it all bottled up inside. It's not good for you. And the only support system you have is your sister, and you hid her, too."

"Are you trying to make me feel better? Because it isn't working."

Mindy cracked a small smile and laughed quietly. "Sorry. My bedside manner isn't the best." She took one of his hands and pulled it into her lap. With her other hand, she combed her fingers through his hair.

It was such a sweet and tender gesture, it made Sam want to say that he never ever wanted Mindy to leave. But he knew for a fact that if he were going to scare Mindy, that was the way to do it. She didn't want to be tied down. Her own mother had told him as much. "So now you know why I clammed up the other night. As for the fundraiser, they've asked me to host, stepping in for the original sponsor. I've always been a big donor, but I don't want to be the public face of the event. I just don't think I can do that. I told them I'd give them the money, but I'm not sure about the rest of it. I'd have to make a speech and really put myself out there. You know it's more my inclination to hide in the shadows."

"But you've attended the fundraiser before? Listened to other people give those speeches?"

"Yes. And they're gut-wrenching sometimes. So sad."

Mindy nodded patiently and Sam suspected he knew where she was headed with this. "But does it make you feel less alone when you hear other people tell their stories?"

"Well, yeah. I guess."

"So maybe it's your turn, Sam. If you shared your story, it would be another way of giving back. It might help other people deal with their own circumstances or at least come to terms with a loss like the one you experienced."

"That was exactly the pitch the foundation made to me. But I just don't know if I can get up on that stage and talk about all of that."

"If you can tell me, you can tell anybody."

He wanted to tell her that she was the exception in all of this. She was the one he could trust. "That's my point. We know each other and it was still hard. Plus, I'd have to write the speech and it's only a few days away. That's not my area of expertise at all."

"Then let me help you. You can practice on me. I made a great speech at Sophie's wedding. The truth is that you and I make a great team and I think you should let me help you."

Sam wasn't sure what this meant for their relationship, but right now, he wasn't willing to push for anything more than time with her. "What about your sisters? What about the bet? We're going to end up spending time together if we do this."

"As far as I'm concerned, I'm helping a friend. Nothing else."

"So you really think I should do it?"

"I think it could help you heal. And that's important. So yes, I think you should do it."

"Okay, then. I'll call the foundation first thing tomorrow."

Mindy looked at him, scanning his face with her beautiful eyes. "The only other thing we haven't talked about is that bit about me breaking your heart. Does your sister hate me?"

"If she does, at least you know how I feel. Sophie and Emma hate me. I know that."

"I don't know that *hate* is the right word. And maybe the fundraiser will help to change that. I can tell them about it and get them to buy tickets."

Oh, no. It was bad enough to have one member of the Eden family feeling sorry for him. "Don't do that. Please, don't. That'll just make me more nervous anyway."

"Okay. Okay. I won't say a thing." She stared down at her own hands for a moment. "You didn't really feel like I broke your heart, did you? Not really, right?"

Sam had spent more than enough time this evening tearing open his soul and letting Mindy see it all. He didn't think he could take any more. This was a talk for another day. Another time. If she wanted to have the conversation. "*Heartbroken* is such a melodramatic word. *Disappointed* might be more accurate."

Mindy nodded slowly, taking it all in. "Okay. That makes me feel better. I would never want to do that."

Sam would cling to that much from this moment forward. Even if it ended up happening, he would at least know she hadn't wanted to do it. "Are you still going to leave tonight? Or can I at least convince you to stay until morning?"

Mindy pulled her legs up onto the bed and curled into his chest. "For right now, I'm not going anywhere."

Ten

The morning after Sam's big confession, Mindy got up early and reluctantly moved her things out of his apartment. Their week together had not been what she'd expected. She'd thought this might be their last gasp, or at least an escape from her everyday life. To her great surprise, they'd grown closer. She'd seen sides of Sam she'd never known.

But she was hesitant to push for more with Sam. Was one week enough to change everything? She couldn't imagine a scenario in which it would be enough to convince Sophie and Emma to change their minds about him. And if Sam couldn't be folded into her family life, he couldn't be a real part of her love life. No matter the problems with her sisters, they were the two people she could always count on. They stood by her. More than anything, they loved her.

Love was looming large in Mindy's mind. Was that what she was feeling with Sam? She wanted to think so, but was a week enough time to fall in love? There was also the question of how he felt about her. He'd expressed affection in a million unspoken ways, but the words had not passed his lips. There had been no *I love you*, and as brave as Mindy could be, she couldn't be the first to put that out there. Not as the person who'd long questioned whether she was lovable at all.

Standing on the sidewalk outside Sam's apartment, this game of goodbye was a sad one, one in which she was afraid to bring up anything about their relationship. It was easier to talk about the excuses they had to see each other. "You'll call the foundation today? Tell them you'll make a speech at the fundraiser?" she asked.

"As long as you'll be my date. Isabel is going to be there, but I've spent so many years leaning on her. It's difficult for her, too. I need to know that you will be there for me." He had his sunglasses on again, hiding behind them, leaving her with only his words.

"I'll be there. And don't forget your speech," Mindy said, a transparent attempt at stealing a few more precious seconds. "I promised I would help you with that."

"At least let me practice on you. Maybe tomorrow night?"

There was the glimmer she needed—the promise of time with him. Something to look forward to. "Yes. That sounds perfect."

Fighting sadness, Mindy kissed him, but she made it quick. She didn't want a tear to roll down her cheek and cross her lips. She didn't want him to know just how melancholy she was about leaving. With her driver waiting at the curb, this wasn't the time for an extended goodbye anyway. And maybe that was for the best.

Clay rushed Mindy off to Eden's, and she spent the entire car ride fretting over how to handle the Sophie and Emma situation. She was in deeper with Sam. There would be no denying that. Mindy's trust issues with him were fading away. But what would it take for Sophie and Emma to trust that Sam might be good for her? Under the burden of the silly bet, it would be next to impossible. They would use any excuse to keep Mindy at Eden's. Mindy had to convince them to drop the whole thing. Sophie would be the hardest nut to crack.

About an hour after Mindy arrived at the office, Sophie trailed in, so radiant and relaxed it was like she walked on air. "Knock, knock. I'm back." She plopped down on the chair and grinned from ear to ear at Mindy.

"I take it you had a good time?"

"The best. The absolute best. The villa we rented was unbelievable. Right on the water. Private pool. We had the most amazing chef, who cooked for us morning, noon and night. We snorkeled. We spent hours on the beach every morning, then a nap in the afternoon, and that, of course, led to—"

"I don't need to hear every last detail." Mindy not only didn't want to hear about what came after nap time, she couldn't help but be a bit annoyed. She may have had an incredible week with Sam, but it was all in hiding. No matter how good things were, it hadn't been out in the open. They weren't free.

"Are you jealous?" Sophie grimaced. "We were on our honeymoon. I don't know what else you expect me to talk about."

"No. I just don't need to know the blow-by-blow. Literally." Of course, she was at least a little bit envious. She was only human, and she wanted the things that Sophie had in her life—love and commitment.

Emma poked her head into Mindy's office. "Are you guys meeting without me?"

"I just got here." Sophie hopped up out of her seat and Mindy walked out from behind her desk, so the three of them could embrace. "Bali was amazing, but I'm happy to be home. I'm happy we're all back together."

"How was England?" Mindy asked Emma while returning to her place behind her desk.

Emma perched on the empty chair and Sophie sat again. "Well, let's just say I spent a fair amount of time feeling sick." Emma's eyes darted back and forth between Mindy and Sophie.

Oh, my God.

"Wait a second," Sophie blurted. "Are you?"

Emma nodded. "I'm pregnant."

Sophie squealed. Mindy was excited, but that feeling of being left behind also managed to crop up somewhere in the middle of her reaction. Once again, her sisters had their personal lives on track while she was making only small strides in figuring hers out.

"I took a test while we were there," Emma said. "I thought about texting you guys the news, but I didn't want to interrupt the honeymoon, and Mindy's always working, anyway. I thought I would wait until I could tell you both in person."

"When are you due?" Mindy asked.

Emma shook her head. "I don't know, exactly. I just

made a doctor's appointment. This wasn't planned at all, but we did have a condom malfunction and that was all it took, apparently."

"What does Daniel think about all of this?" Sophie asked.

"He's so thrilled. He already bought a stuffed animal for the baby. A little bulldog that looks just like Jolly." Emma's cheeks blushed bright pink. "And his mom is warming to me now. A baby changes everything."

"Such amazing news," Mindy said. She meant it, but damn... It was hard to keep a stiff upper lip right now.

"It really is. Congratulations to you both." Sophie crossed her legs and bobbed her foot up and down. "So get us up to speed, Min. What happened during the week?"

"Everything was smooth sailing. Not a single problem." That was a lie, of course, but Mindy had handled the few problems that had cropped up. The one thing Mindy did not need to do was to convince her sisters of her capabilities. "The store practically runs itself."

Sophie narrowed her eyes. "Are you sure? Absolutely nothing bad happened? How did the big cosmetics sale go? I haven't seen the numbers."

"Sales were up seven percent over last year. So definitely a move in the right direction."

"Well, great. That's good." Sophie shrugged and looked over at Emma. "I guess we just get back to work as usual."

"I want to hear about your week, Mindy," Emma said. "Not everything is about us."

Mindy did appreciate Emma's generosity. Sophie was the one who often put on the blinders. Mindy could have easily launched into a talk about what was going on at BMO, but she didn't want to ignore the one good thing in her life—Sam. It wasn't right that she couldn't talk about it. It wasn't right that she felt like she had to hide.

"I spent the entire week with Sam. I stayed at his apartment, and it was amazing."

"Oh, my God." Sophie sat back in her seat, shaking her head. "So you're giving up? You're ready to lose the bet and have your heart broken? Because you know that's what's going to happen, right? It's always the same thing with him."

Mindy had to stand up for herself. And she had to stand up for the only chance she had right now for personal happiness. "I'm not losing the bet. It's silly, Sophie, and you know it."

"I know nothing of the sort. It's meant to keep you from making a bad choice."

"Sam and I really had an incredible week together. He's not the way you think he is, Soph. I don't care what Jake says."

"It's not just Jake who's coloring my opinion of Sam. It's lots of people. Including you, at times."

"He has made some poor choices," Emma said. "Do you really want to give him another chance? Is he worth it?"

When Emma put it like that, Mindy had to defend him. "He deserves another chance. I believe that. You know, he sold me the Mercer Building for BMO. He sold it to me for a dollar."

"Wait. What? Sam's involved with the deal on the Mercer?"

Mindy had purposely not told Sophie about this before, just so she wouldn't have any reason to question why Sam was her date at the wedding. But now she had no choice but to reveal what was going on behind the scenes. "Yes. It turns out that Sam bought the building before we had a chance to. It was a mix-up on Matthew's part, but it all got worked out. I asked Sam about it and he agreed to sell it to me for BMO."

"Did you know all of this before the wedding? Is that why you brought him? Did you seriously trade him an invitation to my wedding for the right to buy the building?"

"Technically, yes, but he also solved my Gerald problem. And you should be glad he was there anyway. He kept Mom and Emma's mom from killing each other at your reception."

"I don't know that my mom would have actually resorted to that," Emma said. "She's mostly harmless."

"Regardless, Sam does not earn a free pass for calming down a woman at my wedding. And I have to question his motives for selling you the building for a dollar. Who does that?"

"Maybe he's in love with you," Emma said.

"Is he?" Sophie asked. "Did he say that he loves you?"

At first, Mindy experienced a tiny blip of hope. Was giving her the building Sam's way of saying he truly and deeply cared for her? It would be amazing if that were the case, but it felt foolish to hope for such a thing. If Sam wanted to say something, he came out with it. She could only imagine that if he was thinking about something as serious as love, he would have said it. The only secrets he kept were the painful ones.

Love wasn't painful. Or at least it wasn't supposed to be. "No. He didn't."

"So again, I'm left with the question of his motives," Sophie said.

Mindy had a deep need to prove to her sister that Sam really was a good guy. "Look. I'm telling you that he's got a big heart. He's hosting a charity fundraiser for ALS research in a few days. He's one of their biggest donors, but this year, he's going to give a talk about losing his mom to the disease. I'm going with him as moral support."

Sophie looked at Mindy with such pity that Mindy felt sick to her stomach. "So he's going for sympathy now? Is that why he has you wrapped around his finger, again?"

Mindy's queasiness had turned into a feeling of hurtling toward earth headfirst. Everything she said got turned back on her. "Why are you being so mean about this, Soph? Is this about winning the bet?"

"Would I love to declare the bet a done deal? Absolutely. But it's not about winning. I'm tired of not knowing that you're going to stay at Eden's for the long haul. Emma and I want you here by our side. We love you, and frankly, we're worried about what you're doing to yourself."

"We know you feel pulled in several different directions," Emma said "We understand that's hard. But maybe if you made a decision on the business side of your life, the personal part might fall into place. You might meet the perfect guy."

Mindy wasn't foolish enough to tell her sisters that she was starting to feel like she had met the perfect guy.

It was easier to focus on the business part of this discussion. "But it's not a decision, is it? It's not a choice I get to make," Mindy asked, hating the way her voice was starting to crack. "My inheritance is tied to these two years at Eden's. I can't walk away from that."

"Is it just the money?" Sophie asked. "I'd like to think that you want to be here because of us."

Mindy closed her eyes for a moment. Of course it was about more than that, and it was far more complicated. "I do want to be here because of you two. I actually really enjoy my job at the store. I like feeling like I can fix things. I sure as hell can't fix things at BMO right now."

"I thought things were going great," Sophie said.

Mindy shook her head. "They're not. They're falling apart. And the worst of it is that I think the person who might be making it fall apart is Matthew Hawkins, the man I hired to keep the operation afloat. And I think he's doing it on purpose."

"Why do you think that?" Emma asked.

Mindy told her sisters everything—every last embarrassing detail, including the fact that it had been Sam who figured it out. "So I have to figure out if Matthew really is trying to poach my company."

"How will you do that?" Emma got up and pulled three bottles of water from the small fridge in Mindy's office, handing one each to Mindy and Sophie, then taking a drink of her own.

"I don't know, exactly," Mindy answered. "Do you guys have any ideas?"

Sophie twisted her lips into a tight bundle, clearly putting on her thinking cap. "You could offer to sell him the company. See how he responds. That's what he wants, isn't it?"

"That sounds risky," Mindy said. "He'll want it in writing and then I'll be stuck. I'm not giving that guy any leverage over me at all."

"Do you have an employee you trust?" Emma asked. "Someone who's been there from the beginning and knows the ins and outs of the business? Maybe they can shed some light on what's going on. Or help you figure it out."

It was typically Mindy's last resort to trust anyone. It was easier to rely only on herself. But this situation called for extreme measures. "Carla Meadows. She was my third employee. She oversees the production. In fact, she's the person Matthew has blamed a lot of our problems on. He's been dealing with her."

"Talk to her," Sophie said. "And most importantly, tell him that you're talking with her. Make him nervous. That's when people start making mistakes."

"That's exactly what Sam says."

"I don't make a habit of agreeing with Sam, but I might have to on this one." Sophie leaned forward, placing both elbows on her knees. "Frankly, I'm surprised he didn't come up with a plan to help you catch Matthew. That seems like his wheelhouse."

"You know, all of that is way more about Sam knowing how to get what he wants, rather than him being particularly underhanded. I have to admire that in him."

"Yeah, well, Jake doesn't."

All Mindy could think was that this would all be solved if Sophie, Jake and Emma were able to see Sam in a different light. She wanted them to see the Sam that she adored. The man she was falling for, even when that was the scariest thing to admit. "I want you all to come to the fundraiser. I'll buy the tickets."

"Seriously?" Sophie asked, seeming incredulous.

"Yes. It's for an amazing cause and I think it will be good for you to see what he's really like. He's going to give a speech and I think it'll all do us some good." She knew this was a huge gamble. It could very easily backfire.

Lizzie appeared at the door. "I don't want to interrupt, but we just got this letter from a lawyer's office. I had to sign for it. It looks important."

Sophie reached out for the envelope. "I'll take it."

Mindy sat back in her chair, her previous hurt morphing into panic. She was going to have to find a way to break it to Sam that she had not kept the fundraiser a secret. In fact, she'd gone so far as to invite her family to the event. He was going to be horrified. And quite possibly furious.

"Oh, my God," Sophie said, her skin going starkly pale. "A man named Benjamin Summers claims to have a promissory note against Eden's. Not just the building. The land, too. It belonged to his father and it's his now." Sophie stood and placed the letter on Mindy's desk. Emma got up out of her seat and read over Mindy's shoulder.

Unfortunately, one line into the letter Mindy realized she'd made a mistake when she didn't speak to the man who called the day she was going to the Mercer.

"Gram took out a private loan? Why would she do that?" Emma asked.

"I have no idea," Sophie said. "We have to bring in

our lawyers right away to look at this. The tone of the letter is so aggressive. And I need to talk to Lizzie. It says that they tried to reach us by phone but were unable to get through."

Mindy raised her hand. "That was me. My fault. I thought it sounded like a scam, so I told Lizzie to just get the guy off the phone. I had no idea it was real."

Sophie blew out an exasperated breath. "Well, now we've apparently made Benjamin Summers very angry. We're going to have to figure this out. Right away."

Mindy was desperate to redeem herself in the eyes of her sisters, not only because of this gaffe, but because she wanted to find a way forward with Sam. She'd never be able to forge a lasting relationship with him if her sisters weren't on board. "Let me handle it. I need to talk to the legal team about some other things, anyway."

"Are you sure?" Sophie asked. "You're the one who's already stretched way too thin."

Mindy shrugged. "I work best under pressure."

"So you really want us to come to this fundraiser? It's going to take some doing to convince Jake," Sophie said.

"Just tell him that if he comes that night and still hates Sam by the time it's all said and done, then I'll drop the whole thing."

"You mean you'll drop Sam?" Emma asked.

Mindy wasn't willing to go there. Not yet. "I'm not saying that at all. Frankly, I've had enough of wagers and bets."

Eleven

Within twenty-four hours, the situation with Benjamin Summers grew even more complicated and inexplicable. This mysterious man claimed that Gram had an affair with his father, and that he had loaned a great sum of money to her because he was in love with her and she was trying to get out from under Sophie and Mindy's grandfather's gambling debts. It was both hard to believe and nearly impossible to prove. Most of the people involved in the tale Mr. Summers was weaving were dead and gone. Still, none of that mattered for the present day. Mr. Summers was moving forward with a lawsuit. He wanted the store or the money owed, a sum that had yet to be determined—the way the interest was to be calculated was still subject to debate. One guess put it north of several hundred million dollars.

Mindy didn't have that kind of cash lying around. Sophie and Emma didn't, either. There was a big difference between a person's net worth and the size of a check they were able to write. Regardless of what happened, the Eden sisters had a huge legal battle on their hands and if things didn't go their way, a massive financial problem to fix. One that could destroy their grandmother's legacy. In that scenario, Mindy worried most about Sophie. Both her heart and her sense of self were wrapped so tightly around the store, it was impossible to know where one started and the other ended.

For now, Mindy couldn't entertain worries about Eden's. She was on her way to Sam's to help him with his speech for the fundraiser. There was a lot riding on Friday night, especially since Mindy had slipped up and not only told Sophie and Emma about the event, but then dared to tell them to attend it. All sorts of things could go wrong, like Jake and Sam getting into another staring contest, but Mindy had no choice. If the gap between her family and Sam wasn't bridged in some way, it would never, ever work. No, she didn't know if Sam was built for love or marriage, and she had the same reservations about herself, but she couldn't bear to think of the alternative—walking away from him. They'd made so much progress. She had to keep trying.

He buzzed her into the building as soon as she arrived and was waiting, wineglass in hand, when the elevator doors opened into his apartment. "I hope you're ready to work."

Mindy's first thought was that she wanted to get to work on Sam's shirt, but she had to focus. She stepped inside and let him take off her coat. "Of course. That's what I'm here for."

"Good. Because my writing is a disaster."

"I'm sure it's great. I'm sure you're overreacting."

"I'm not. I read it over the phone to Isabel. She told me it stinks."

Mindy placed her hands on both of Sam's biceps, telling herself this was not the time to give them a playful squeeze, however much she wanted to. "It's going to be okay. I'll stay all night if I have to."

He knocked back the last of his wine and grabbed the bottle from the kitchen counter, refilling his glass. "This is not my area of expertise. I'm not good at pulling heartstrings. And that's what this requires. If I'm going to get people to open their checkbooks, I need to leave an entire roomful of people in tears."

"Stop making excuses and show me what we're working with, okay?"

Sam waved Mindy into the living room and they headed up the stairs into the library, where his home office sat at one end of the loft. He pointed to his laptop, which was sitting on the desk. "Go ahead. Take a look. I'll be over here, dying a quiet death."

Mindy laughed quietly. She thought Sophie could be dramatic. Sam was giving her a solid run for her money. She pulled back his black leather desk chair and took a seat in front of his computer. She read carefully, trying to imagine Sam standing onstage behind a podium, looking as handsome as he had the day of Sophie's wedding, delivering these words he'd written. His work was indeed well composed, but this was not the sort of speech that would leave anyone clamoring for a tissue, and most certainly not their wallet. It was too clinical. Too safe. Sam was hiding again, this time behind words.

She turned in the chair when she finished reading. He was a good ten feet away, sipping on wine and pacing back and forth in front of the bookshelves. "I told you. It's terrible. Be honest. Be brutal. I need it."

Mindy had to figure out how to frame this. She didn't want him to be discouraged. It would make it far too easy for him to back out of delivering this speech and she sensed that he needed this, however much he was putting up a fight. If he hadn't wanted to do it, he never would have run it by his sister. He never would have asked for Mindy's input. When Sam was certain, he acted, without hesitation.

"I think you need to tell some stories, Sam. I think you need to tell people how it felt to be in that situation, with your mom sick and your sister away at school, and your dad struggling with it in his own way."

He kneaded at his forehead, the most stressed she'd ever seen him. "I don't know where to start. There are a million stories, and the ones that are the most memorable are also the most painful. I'm not really in the right mental space to sit in front of a computer and just bleed."

Mindy grabbed his laptop and wheeled the desk chair in front of the leather recliner he loved so much. "You sit and I'll ask you questions and when you answer, I'll type out what you say. We can use that as a starting point."

"I don't know, Min. I was sort of hoping we could just have a nice night together. Drink some wine.

Drink some more wine." He bobbed his eyebrows up and down.

She was absolutely on board for that, but they had to stay on track. "There will be plenty of time for that. Let's finish this first. The fundraiser is only two days away and you need to practice before then. If we don't get this done, you won't be able to be as polished as you want to be."

Sam bunched up his lips, scrutinizing her with his dark eyes. She wasn't sure what he was looking for, but she met his gaze with her own, unflinching. She was going to be here for him, but she was also going to drag this out of him if necessary. Even if it took all night. "Okay. Fine. Let's get this done." Sam plopped down in the leather chair and crossed his long legs at the ankle. "What do you want to know?"

Mindy hadn't experienced a lot of personal tragedy, but she did know pain. She did know what it was to be vulnerable and helpless. She'd felt both many times over the years. "Tell me about the first time you cried about your mom's illness. The first time you were pushed to the brink and you felt like you couldn't take it anymore."

"Wow. You do not mess around."

"I know it sounds horrible, but this is the relatable moment. This is where people will hear your words and see some part of themselves."

Sam avoided making eye contact, picking at his pants leg. "It was the day I looked up ALS in the library at school." His voice failed to carry its usual strong timbre, but when he looked up at Mindy, she could see on his face that his heart was doing the heavy lifting here.

"Our parents had told us that our mom would get better, and I wanted to believe that. But I didn't need to read very far before it became obvious that it would take her life."

Mindy typed every word as he said it, not commenting, only letting him run. She was usually very good at soldiering through hard work, but this was a battle. All she wanted to do was cast aside the computer and wrap him up in her arms.

"I remember there was a small group of students at one of the big tables. Four or five kids. Freshmen like me. They were talking. The librarian kept shushing them and they would snicker and laugh, then go back to having their fun. That was the first time it really hit me. They had this life that I'd once thought I had. And for me, it was gone. It was hard to imagine myself ever laughing or goofing around like them because there was this dark cloud moving in overhead. My mom was going to die. That was a fact and there was no getting past it. That seemed like it would never be me again. I guess it was innocence lost. I just grabbed my backpack and hightailed it out of there. I didn't even go back to class. I went straight home so I could spend time with my mom."

Mindy finished typing a few seconds after he stopped talking. It was good to have her hands occupied. She otherwise only wanted to hug Sam and take care of him. Tell him how sorry she was, even when she knew he didn't want her pity. "That must have been such a hard day."

"One of many."

"I've never been to this event, but is that the sort of thing people talk about?"

He cleared his throat. "It is."

"Okay. Then let's keep going."

Mindy pressed on and Sam talked, continuing through several other retellings of the events of his past. She marveled at how far he had come with her in a short amount of time. A few weeks ago, and certainly the first time they'd been together, he never would have done this. Part of her wanted to believe that it was the timing that was off the first time for them. He wasn't ready and she wasn't sure she had been, either. Were things finally coming together for them? Would it all work out? Friday was a big test. Then, like everything else in her life, she'd reevaluate and figure out her next step.

A few hours later, Sam had a working draft of the speech. He read it back to her from his laptop, and she did her best to stay objective and not get swayed by the emotion of the story. Still, it was impossible to not feel the pressure in the center of her chest, right in the vicinity of her heart.

"Practice a few more times and you'll be all set," she said. "You're going to do an incredible job. I know you will." Now that the speech was wrapped up, Mindy wanted to get herself wrapped up in Sam, but there were other things that needed to be addressed. She needed to tell him about her sisters coming to the event, even when she knew that he had trusted her to not say a thing. As to how he would react, she did not know. But she was done with having barriers between them. It all had to go.

* * *

Mindy had succeeded at something no one else had—she'd gotten Sam to shed his hard exterior. Not even Isabel, who was especially good at getting people to do things they did not want to do, had ever been able to convince him that baring his soul was a good idea. He'd always been so convinced that letting down his guard would somehow make his pain worse. It wasn't better now, but it was different. Oddly, he felt more comfortable with it. And that was all because of Mindy.

"I really don't quite know how to thank you for this. I'm starting to feel like you're my therapist."

"Before you get too appreciative, you should know that I had to tell Sophie and Emma about the fundraiser."

Sam's stomach sank. One minute they were on the same wavelength, and the next they were running off the rails. "Why did you do that? I specifically asked you not to."

Mindy wheeled herself closer to his chair and took his hands. "I know. And it was my intention to honor that. But I didn't want to hide the fact that you and I had spent the week together."

"Despite the bet?"

"Yes. Even with the bet. So I spilled that detail and, of course, they protested."

Sam couldn't listen to this. He got up out of his seat and distanced himself from her, but something stopped him when he got only a few feet. "Of course they did. They hate me, Min. I don't see how we're ever supposed to get past that."

Mindy rushed up to him and forced him to look her

in the eye. "They don't hate you. They don't hate the real you because they don't know the real you. That's why I told them."

"I don't need their sympathy. I don't need anyone's."

"I know that. But I need them to see you the way I see you. Or at least some of the way I see you. Which is why I also asked them to come to the event."

Sam could hardly believe what she was saying. "You did what? Is Jake coming?"

Mindy shrugged sheepishly. "I guess? I don't know for sure."

Again, Sam needed his space, and he took it, doubling back to his chair, picking up his laptop and returning it to the desk. "I can't believe this. I shouldn't have agreed to any of this. It was a mistake."

"Sam. Don't shut me out. Listen to me. Please." Mindy didn't let him off the hook, storming up right behind him. She gripped his shoulders and leaned into his back, pulling him against her. "I know this is going to be hard, but I want you to do it for us."

Sam stood frozen, keenly aware of his breaths as they shuddered in and out of his lungs. *Us.* She said *us.* "For us?" He turned and circled his arms around her. "Is that what this is? Because it feels like I'm the one who's going to be on trial with everyone there."

"Hey. I'm on trial here, too. My sisters are convinced I've made a bad choice. And I need to prove them wrong. Because if you're going to be in my life, Sam, I need it to work with my family. There is no compromise that works for me. All or nothing."

Sam wasn't quite sure what emotion he was supposed to be feeling right now. There were bits of hope running around in his head—Mindy had suggested she wanted him in her life. But she'd also suggested it wouldn't work if her family didn't approve. And it was difficult to be content with that. There was part of him that wanted her to risk it all for him, even when he knew that was foolish. It seemed like that was the only way to know it was real. It seemed like the only sure sign of love.

"Do you want to know what happened between Jake and me?" he asked.

Mindy's eyes went wide with surprise. "If you want to tell me, of course I do."

"I did cut him out of the deal. He's not wrong about that. But I did it so I could pay back the insurance company the claim on my father's life insurance. I couldn't live with myself, knowing that I'd received any reward at all for his death. And I couldn't let Isabel live with it, either. My conscience needed a clean slate and I saw an opportunity and I took it. So when I told you that I did it to help someone, I was helping me."

Mindy clasped her hand over her mouth. "Oh, my God, Sam. You did that?"

He nodded, willing the shame to go away. "If I would have known how much trouble it was going to cost down the road, I wouldn't have done it. I guess I figured that Jake would eventually forgive me. But he put up such a wall after that happened, there was no way for me to get back in."

"Jake has his own issues," Mindy said. "He grew up with a horrible home life and his mother abandoned him with his grandmother, who was not a nice woman. I'm sure he simply can't handle betrayal."

Sam clamped his eyes closed, letting his mistakes

tumble around in his head. "I had no idea. He never told me."

"That's the problem here. People don't tell each other stuff. And then it ends up getting one hundred times worse. Do you want me to tell Sophie and ask her to tell Jake?"

Sam shook his head. "No. If they're coming on Friday night, I'll do it myself. It has to be man-to-man. Either he'll forgive me or he won't. I can't focus on what other people think, even if it is your family, Mindy. Even if they might never let me have a moment's peace."

"Okay. Whatever you think is right."

"Just so you know, I'm not the only one who's going to fall under some scrutiny at the fundraiser. Isabel is going to be there and I'm afraid that her opinion of you isn't much better than what your sisters think of me."

Mindy sucked in a deep breath, her shoulders rising up near her ears. "Oh, God. She's going to put me on the spot, isn't she?"

"Probably. That's her personality. I mean, she's mostly harmless, but I'm not saying it won't hurt. It might. She doesn't have a great opinion of the Eden family in general, but most of that falls on you."

Mindy wrapped her arms around her midsection as if she was trying to shore up her defenses. "I'm getting a stomachache just thinking about it. Why did you have to tell me this? I might have been better off if it was a sneak attack."

Sam pulled her into a hug, rocking her back and forth. He didn't want to torment her, but he didn't mind giving her a small taste of what he lived with on an everyday basis. He'd shielded her from Isabel before.

That couldn't happen anymore. Not if they had any shot at all of a future. "If I have to worry for two days about what will happen, then you do, too. Plus, now you know how it feels to go without the unwavering support of family."

"This feels a little bit like payback."

"I'd say it's more like the final test." He reached up and smoothed her hair, committing the feeling of the silky strands beneath his fingers to memory. If things didn't work out between them, he could look back on this moment and try to cling to it.

"Now who's the one with the bad bedside manner? That does not make me feel any better. At all."

He knew it was harsh, but he'd grown accustomed to dealing with some pretty damn unpleasant things lately. Now was no time to quit. "It's our shared reality, Mindy. Either our families decide to get in line on Friday night, or they continue to get in the way. And if that's the case, it'll be time for you and me both to decide if we were just having fun or if we're willing to go to battle with the people we love most." He hated putting that spin on it, but in many ways, he was only filling in the blanks for her. He might be willing to go against Isabel in the end, but he feared Mindy would never shake the iron grip of her family. They were both better off if it was out in the open.

"I know. You're right."

If only she knew he took zero solace in that fact. "Will you stay tonight? I don't want you to go."

"I don't have any clothes with me. No toothbrush."

"No excuses tonight, remember? That's what you told me about the speech." When it came to excuses, he had no more when it came to the real confession he wanted to make—that he loved her. The words were right on his lips, waiting to be uttered. But this wasn't the right time. They still had their hurdles ahead. If he went down in flames on Friday, she would likely side with her family. Which meant that all he could do was cherish tonight with Mindy. It was the only certain thing he had to hold on to.

Twelve

The fundraiser was being held at a midtown art museum. The event space was beautifully appointed—fifty round tables dotted the room, all topped with candles and ruby-red floral centerpieces, just waiting for the hundreds of guests to arrive at any minute. Sam's mood did not reflect the relative calm and elegance of the room he was standing in. In fact, he was already freaking out. He paced back and forth in front of one of the bar stations while a bartender dumped ice into bins and waiters polished glassware.

Ms. Parson, the charity's representative, the woman Sam had given such a hard time when she'd called him at the office, approached. "Are you sure you're okay, Mr. Blackwell?" She peered up at him from behind frameless glasses, seeming nothing short of gravely concerned.

"Yes. Absolutely. Just going over the speech in my head. No problems at all." He had to lie. He'd already put Ms. Parson through the wringer.

"Okay, then. I'm going to go back and check with the caterer on a few things. I believe they have just opened the doors. Guests will be arriving any second now."

Great. That's not helping. "Perfect. Thank you."

Isabel had apparently been one of the first people through the door. She marched up to him in a stylish white gown with silvery beads, her long black hair back in a sleek ponytail. "If it isn't the man of the hour," she said, kissing him on the cheek.

"Do not call me that. That's the exact last thing I want to be."

"All ready to give your speech?"

"As ready as I will ever be. Which isn't saying a lot, but it's better than nothing."

"When do you have to get up and speak?"

"It's the first thing, but they wait about an hour, until everyone has a few cocktails in them. After that, it's dinner and dancing."

"They probably worry people will eat and take off. Gotta put on the thumbscrews as early as possible."

The thought of medieval torture was a nice one right now. He'd much rather have dealt with that than anything else. "I'm glad you could be here. I appreciate you coming." Sam had to decide how to best frame what he had to say to his sister. "Mindy's going to be here tonight and I'd like to introduce you two. I'm hoping you can find it in your heart to be nice."

"This is definitely a thing, isn't it? Not just a fling?

Are you sure you want to go there? What if she spins you out of her life again?"

Sam could handle only so many questions at one time, especially questions for which he had few answers. "Yes, it's a thing. I like her a lot. In fact, I think I love her." Sam choked back the admission. He hadn't said it out loud before that moment.

Isabel grinned and elbowed him in the stomach. "You're such a sap. It's adorable."

"I thought you didn't like Mindy."

"Oh, I don't. I mean, I won't if she does one single thing to hurt you. But if you've fallen in love, of course I support that." She smoothed Sam's lapel and patted him on the shoulder. "Just be careful. These Eden women are not to be trifled with."

Sam knew that very well. And he was not certain about what she would say if he finally just made his admission. Would she think he was softhearted like his sister did? She was not a woman who got wrapped up in typical romantic gestures—she was the sort of woman who swooned when you sold her a building. And as her mother had pointed out, she was also someone who viewed commitment as a trap. Although Sam was buying that line of thinking less and less. He suspected that Mindy's mother didn't know her like he did. The woman who was willing to stay up all night to write a speech, or was willing to push him past his comfort zone, was not a person who shied away from the more complicated things in life. And if anything was complicated, it was love.

"Speak of the devil," Isabel muttered under her

breath. "Your lovely date and her sister are fast approaching. Along with your nemesis, Jake Wheeler."

"He's not my nemesis. He's just stubborn. I don't need everyone in the whole world to be my friend." Except that he did need to patch things up with Jake. He was part and parcel of the Eden clan.

Sam chose to focus on Mindy as she approached, and what a sight she was in a stunning black gown that shimmered in the candlelight. She'd worn her hair up in a twist similar to the one she wore to Sophie's wedding. He only hoped he'd have the chance to later take it out exactly like he had the first time.

Mindy winked at him when she was about ten feet away, then went right in for a kiss. Sam was stuck between getting what he wanted, that close physical contact with Mindy, and the audience who was witnessing it. This was more than just a kiss. She was showing her sister and his that she meant business about him. He had to wonder if she had any idea how comforting that was to him. It was like taking fifty deep breaths.

"Hi," she muttered against his lips. "You look very handsome tonight."

"You look incredible. Absolutely gorgeous. I want you to meet my sister, Isabel."

Isabel did her sisterly duty, but Sam could tell that her smile was an act. Behind it was Isabel the protector, the one who would not let him get hurt. He wanted to tell her to back off, but he knew it was of little use. "It's nice to meet you, Mindy, after talking to you on the phone while you were staying with Sam."

Isabel glanced over at Sophie and Jake and went right

ahead and introduced herself. "Hi, I'm Isabel Black-well. Sam's sister."

"Sophie Eden. This is my husband, Jake Wheeler," Sophie said, seeming confused by everything going on before them. "I'm Mindy's sister."

"Oh, I know," Isabel said.

Sam both hated and loved his sister for pushing the envelope. Isabel knew very well the undercurrents between this group of people. She knew that Sophie's and Jake's opinion of him had caused Mindy to break up with him before. She wasn't testing the boundaries for spite. She was testing them to make sure they didn't break.

Sam wasn't particularly keen on talking to Jake after the run-in the night of the rehearsal dinner, but he also didn't want to let their feud go on any longer. "Jake. Hey. Nice to see you. Thank you for coming tonight."

Jake did offer a handshake with a minimum of hesitation. That was a positive sign. "Sam. I had no idea you were so involved with charity."

Sam nodded. "Well, I am. And I'm making more of a point of putting these things out in the open."

Isabel took Sam's arm and snugged herself close for an instant. "I'd say it's more a matter of him not wanting to brag about himself. He's been doing it for years."

"I wish I'd seen this side of you before," Sophie said, still seeming entirely skeptical.

"All I can tell you, Sophie, is that I will try to do better." He put his arm around Mindy, hoping Sophie would catch the double meaning. He was trying to do better on all fronts. "Speaking of which, Jake, I was hoping that you and I could get together some time soon. Maybe grab a drink. Hash out a few things."

Jake looked to Sophie, almost as if he was seeking her approval. Mindy might have been the oldest of the sisters, but Sophie played the role of matriarch. "That could be good," Sophie said, again sounding uncertain. "As long as it fits in your schedule, of course."

Jake turned back to Sam. "I'll have to take a look at my calendar."

Sam wasn't about to make any more of an overture than that. He'd tried to extend the olive branch. It was up to Jake to take it.

"How soon until you have to make your speech?" Mindy asked.

Sam glanced at his Rolex. "Half hour or so."

"Do you have a minute to talk?" she asked. "Just the two of us?"

Sam couldn't think of anything he wanted more than to be alone with Mindy. "Yes. Of course." He took her hand and led her to the far corner of the room, away from the bustle and noise of the crowd.

"I debated about whether or not I should kiss you in front of my sister and Jake. But you know what? The second I saw you, I knew that it was stupid to not kiss you. I want to kiss you. I should just kiss you, right?"

Sam had to laugh. "Yes. You should kiss me whenever you want. I'm hoping it's often."

She gathered both of his hands in hers and squeezed them tight. "You are going to rock this speech. I know you will. And then we can drink a bunch of wine when you're done and say mean-spirited things about our siblings behind their backs."

He pulled her against him in a snug embrace. "You are so funny." *I love you.* It was right there. Within reach. "I think you did pretty well with Isabel."

"Something tells me she won't be quite so nice if you're not around."

"I will do my best to keep you safe." He muttered the words against her ear, meaning it in a much greater sense than the here and now. He wanted the chance to do it for the long haul.

"I'm glad you made an effort with Jake. I think he'll come around eventually. I really do."

"What about Sophie? Do you think she's given up on the bet? I should hope so."

Mindy shook her head slightly. "Giving up on the bet would mean giving up on me staying at Eden's, and that's the last thing she's going to do. But that's okay. You know, I'm over it. My sister and I will reach an understanding somehow. Some way. We always do. There might be some yelling and hair pulling, but that's nothing new."

"Hmm. Now this hair pulling, is that something I can watch?"

Mindy smacked his arm. "Be serious. You have to put on a straight face in a few minutes."

"Don't remind me."

"Oh, come on. You'll be perfect. I know it." She leaned into him and gave him a big kiss. "Daniel and Emma just got here, so I should go say hi. And we need to find our table. I'll talk to you after you're done?"

"You will be my reward." *In more ways than one.*

Sam watched as Mindy sauntered off. She was a truly remarkable woman. Strong and smart, funny and sexy. He'd be a fool if he didn't put everything on the line for her. The how and when were still up in the air, but he knew it had to be soon. She wouldn't wait on him forever.

Sam crossed over to the other side of the room and checked in with Ms. Parson.

"I'd say it's time for you to go on up and welcome everyone and make our first big pitch of the night for donations."

"Got it. Thank you for the opportunity," he said, shaking her hand.

She knocked her head to one side quizzically. "It's you I should be thanking, Mr. Blackwell."

He shook his head. "No. I'm sure I got it right the first time. And please, call me Sam."

Her face lit up with a ready smile. "Break a leg, Sam."

Sam took the stairs up onto the stage, squinting into the bright lights. He took deep breaths as the music faded, reminding himself that no matter what, he would get through it. He had been through things more difficult. This would be over in a matter of minutes and he would ultimately wonder why he'd ever allowed himself to get so worked up about it. As he looked out into the crowd, full of expectant faces about to hang on his every word, his heart thundered in his chest. He had to orient himself, search for the table where Mindy sat with her family. Two rows back. On the right-hand side of the room. He found it and his sights flew right to her. There she was in that heartbreaking dress, looking more beautiful than ever. How was that possible? For a woman to be more gorgeous now than even a week ago? A minute ago? Was it because he knew what was behind the beautiful shell? Was it because he truly knew now what she was made of?

The answer to those questions was an absolute and resounding "yes." And so he did what he had to do. He adjusted the microphone, took a sip of water and prepared himself to throw away the speech he'd written with Mindy. Tonight he had a different plan.

Mindy shifted in her seat as Sam stood on the stage, the audience eerily quiet. Mindy's pulse pounded, making it hard to hear. She wished she could send Sam a psychic message. *You'll do great. I believe in you.*

It was almost as if he'd heard her thoughts. His gaze connected with hers and he seemed to say something in return. Something along the lines of how they had done this together. How this might be his night, but she'd helped him get here. She couldn't have been more proud.

"Good evening, I'm Sam Blackwell. I'm honored to be here tonight to share the story of my family's struggle with ALS. I'm not the sort of guy who opens up, so I hope you all take notice, especially when I ask you to be as generous as humanly possible this evening. Because I am going to ask that of you. Each and every one of you." Sam methodically pointed to a few people around the room, and everyone started to laugh, lightening the mood. "And with that, I'll get started."

The speech Sam and Mindy had written together rolled smoothly from his mouth. He was as confident as could be, and Mindy could not have been any more proud. He delivered the heartbreaking stories about how he had to watch his mother's decline and the way his father had struggled with watching his wife fade before his very eyes. He spoke of Isabel. He spoke of being on his own. He spoke of love.

"And years later, after having gone through that unbelievable loss, I had to ask myself where the love in my life was. Had it disappeared?"

Mindy sat, transfixed. This was not part of the speech they had written. Sam had gone off script. And she had to wonder where in the world he was going with all of this.

"Yes, I had my sister, but she has her own life. And the love I have inside me is bigger than one person. I no longer had my parents. And although I love them every day from afar, there's still a surplus. There's something in my heart that's about to burst. Every day. I think we all experience that on some level, and it's impossible to measure the emptiness it creates when you have love in your heart and there's nowhere for it to go."

Sam took a sip of his water and let out a breathy laugh. He lowered his mouth to the microphone and said, "I'm sure you're all wondering where I'm going with this."

The crowd laughed in kind, as did Mindy, nervously. Where was he going?

"I've learned a lot about myself while preparing for tonight. I'd once thought of the journey I made with my family as a dead end. But the truth is that experiencing it for a second time while writing this speech, I realized that it was only a single point in my life. That there was more ahead if I just opened my heart to it. I needed a very special woman to show me how to do that, and I couldn't be more thankful to her if I tried. She not only makes me a better person, she makes me the sort of person who gets up in front of a room of strangers and asks them to write a big fat check."

Again, the audience laughed. Meanwhile, Sophie caught Mindy's attention by bugging her eyes. Mindy shrugged. What was she supposed to say? Sam had gone so far out on a limb. In front of her entire family. In front of these people he'd once been afraid to open up to. And he was putting it all on the line in the most public way possible, probably because that was what their relationship had become—too many people weighing in, too many people deciding they had a voice. It was best to put it all out there. For the people who knew them and cared about them, they would know what he was talking about. They knew the context and what this meant.

"So in closing, just remember what brought us all here tonight. It isn't a disease that brought us together. It's not sad stories, and it's not the promise of finding a cure. It's love. Love made us walk through the door tonight and open ourselves up to the possibilities. Take your loved ones and hold them close. Make sure that they know what they mean to you. And let everything in your heart free. Thank you."

Sam had hardly finished uttering that final syllable when the audience rose to their feet en masse and erupted in thunderous applause. Sam looked out over the crowd in Mindy's direction, and their gazes connected. It was a miraculous moment and not just because Mindy could hardly see, the tears absolutely pouring from her eyes. How he managed to smile at her after the speech he'd just delivered, she did not know. But that was Sam—always surprising her with his amazing ways. He walked down off the stage, only to be greeted by a throng of people who had left their tables to shake his hand.

Mindy had to get to him right away. She had to tell him that she loved him. She couldn't let him go another minute wondering if she did.

"Mindy. Wait." Sophie grabbed her arm. "Is he talking about you?"

"If he isn't, I'm about to put my foot in my mouth, big-time."

"You guys are in love? You didn't tell me that the other day when we talked about it."

"I know. I guess I was just too scared to admit it."

"Oh, Mindy. You had to know that I would let you out of the bet if you really wanted that. I'm not going to hold you hostage."

Mindy leaned over and kissed her sister on the cheek. "Thank you. I appreciate that. But that's not what I mean. I was scared to tell you I love him because I couldn't tell you that he would ever say it back. I was a big chicken."

"And now?"

"And now it's time for me to put it all on the line." Mindy wound her way past the tables, dodging waiters and other guests, until she was standing outside a ring of people waiting to talk to Sam.

He saw her and smiled, then reached past several guests for her. She put her hand in his, which left her with a tingle. That zap of electricity. It would never grow old. He pulled her through until she was right by his side. "I'm sorry. I know we need to talk. This will only take a second. I promise."

"It's fine. I'm not going anywhere." She held on to his hand like it was her lifeline, and in many ways it was. No, she hadn't fully talked this through with Sophie, but quite frankly, she didn't plan to. Sam was the right man for her. She knew that with every bone in her body.

As the crowd around Sam dwindled, Mindy spotted her sister and Jake standing on the periphery. She certainly hoped there would be nothing but well-wishes from them. Sam deserved nothing less.

Jake pushed forward and held out his hand to shake Sam's. "Incredible speech. Absolutely amazing."

"Thank you. I appreciate that."

"I, uh… I'm sorry about earlier. I'm sorry about the wedding. I would like to have coffee. I would like to see if we can patch things up."

Sam smiled wide. "Sounds like a plan. I will give you a call in a day or two."

Jake cast his sights at Mindy. "No hurry. I have a feeling you have other things you need to deal with."

Sam squeezed Mindy's hand. "I do. In fact, right now." He leaned down and muttered in her ear, his breath warm against her neck. "We have to go somewhere where we can talk."

"God, yes." Mindy led the charge, towing Sam back to the entrance and right outside into the night air.

"I will have to go back in at some point," he said.

"I love you, Sam." She didn't want to wait any longer. She didn't want any more buildup to the words that should have come out of her mouth before. "I loved you before you made that speech. And I don't know why I was scared to say it other than I feared that you might not return the words and that was going to crush my heart."

"Shh. Shh. It's okay." Sam placed a hand on each side of her head and kissed her on the lips, making Mindy rise up onto her tiptoes just to be closer. "I love you, sweet woman. I love you more than I ever thought possible. And I'm just as guilty of holding back. At first it was your family, then the bet, but in the end, I think it was all that same fear. I worried that I wouldn't be enough. I worried that I wouldn't be right for you."

Mindy smiled so wide her lips hurt, her chest heaving with happiness. "I'm so glad you said all of those things in front of everyone. It was perfect. We had to put everyone on notice, and you did that. Now we let the chips fall where they may. I defy anyone to tell us that we don't deserve to be in love."

Sam arched both eyebrows at her. "I am very happy to hear you say that. I was worried you would get angry with me and say that I put you on the spot with your sisters, but I also figured that there was no way things were going to get any worse, right?"

"Absolutely right."

Sam sighed and wrapped his arms around her. "You know what?"

"What?"

"I'm happy. Actually, completely and totally happy. I can't think of a single thing in the entire world that I would want right now."

"Nothing?" Mindy asked with a pointed stare.

Sam laughed. "Well, yeah, of course. That." He tugged her even closer and kissed her softly. "I always want that from you."

"I suppose we have to go back inside first, though, huh? Say our goodbyes. Let people fawn all over you."

He took her hand, leading her back to the museum steps. "I say one more hour. Then I want you to come home with me, Mindy."

Her heart absolutely swelled, right there in the center of her chest. "I'll come home if you promise me one thing," she said, stopping right in front of the door.

"What's that?"

"That you'll clean out one side of your closet. If I'm coming home with you, I'm staying. For good."

Epilogue

One month after the fundraiser, so much in life had changed. For starters, the renovations on the BMO offices had begun. As had the restructuring of the company, starting with Mindy installing Carla Meadows as the new CEO after Carla cleverly not only got Matthew to admit he was trying to undermine the value of the company, but also ask if he could bribe her to help him. The best part? Carla had been smart enough to record the whole conversation on her phone. Pushing Matthew out of the picture had ultimately proved a very simple thing, just as Sam had suggested.

Sam and Mindy were at the Mercer late Saturday morning to check out the progress. The first floor had been completely cleaned out and had all-new industrial lighting and a fresh coat of paint. Soon enough they would start moving the printers in, as well as the shipping department. The second, third and fourth floors were also well under way with refinished floors and a more open layout after knocking down many walls. But Mindy was most excited to see the top floor. Where her office would be. They reached number five and, although it was still weeks away from being complete, Mindy could see the space taking shape. They'd installed glass walls for her office, right in the sunniest corner. It would be a very cheery place to work.

Sam put his arm around her while they surveyed her little kingdom together. "You must be proud," he said.

"Still a long way to go, but yes. I'm feeling a big sense of accomplishment right now."

To Mindy, this felt like a very full-circle moment. This old building that had once seemed like nothing more than a pawn in a complicated game of business had really brought her and Sam back together again. She might hate Matthew Hawkins for what he tried to do, but she had to appreciate him on some level. If he hadn't tried his underhanded trick, there was no telling if Mindy would have ever been smart enough to try again with Sam. She worried that she wouldn't have dared to cross her sisters. Now she was so glad she had.

"And maybe a little bit of relief?" he asked.

"More like a whole lot. The Matthew thing is resolved. Sophie backed off the bet. Technically, I'm free to do whatever I want in a year."

"But?" he asked. "I'm sensing a *but* at the end of that sentence."

"But I feel guilty. And I feel bad. Will I just be abandoning Sophie and Emma? What about this Benjamin Summers guy and the lawsuit? What if we end up losing the store?" Mindy knew she sounded frantic, but that was the one unsettled area of her life. Yes, it was a big improvement over a month or two ago when her entire existence was in disarray. But still, she didn't like having such a big thread dangling.

"First off, I don't want you to feel guilty. If you make it to the end of the two years, you can still decide to stay at the store. A lot could happen in twelve months. There's no telling where you'll be."

"You're right. Things change. They always do." Mindy gnawed on her fingernail. "I think I'm going to need some lawyer recommendations from you for Eden's. Our in-house legal team plays it totally by the book and I think we're going to need to outmaneuver the issue of this lien against the store."

"So you come to me for the less-by-the-book people?"

"You know what I mean."

He chuckled warmly. God, she loved that sound. Happy Sam Blackwell was the absolute best. "I actually have an idea, but I think it'll be more than a little controversial."

"Oh, good. Just what you and I need. Controversy."

He dropped his arm from her shoulder and stood to face her. "Just promise me you'll hear me out."

"I promise."

"Isabel."

Mindy blinked. "As in your sister?"

"She's an unbelievable lawyer and she's made the decision to move to New York. She could handle this thing no problem. I swear."

Mindy had not been prepared for this idea at all. "I don't know. My family has just gotten used to one Blackwell. I'm not sure the idea of putting the fate of the store in the hands of your sister is going to fly."

Sam shrugged. "Think about it. I know she could do an amazing job."

Mindy would have to ponder that thoroughly, as well as find a way to run it by Sophie and Emma. "Okay. I will."

"Ready to head out?" Sam asked. "I was thinking we should go for a drive. It's such a beautiful day."

With nothing else planned aside from a quiet dinner at home, Mindy was game. "Sure. Sounds fun."

They locked up the building when they got downstairs and walked over to where Sam had parked his Bugatti, near the loading dock. He'd said that he wanted to give his driver the day off, but Mindy also wondered if he'd just used this excursion as an excuse to drive. He loved his car, and living in the city didn't make it a very practical choice.

He drove north and eventually hopped on the Palisades Interstate Parkway, which ran parallel to the Hudson River. She just enjoyed the colorful scenery of a late-autumn day, but after about a half hour, Mindy had to ask, "Where are we going? I can't help but feel like you have a destination in mind."

"I have something I want to show you." He glanced over at her, but his eyes were hidden behind sunglasses, revealing nothing.

"Something like what?"

"It's a surprise. We'll be there in a few minutes, okay? Just relax. I promise you it's a good thing."

Mindy sat back in the seat. She wasn't big on surprises, but she figured that whatever Sam had up his sleeve had to be something she would like. He'd figured her out pretty well by now. After another ten or fifteen minutes, he pulled off the main road and they were soon in a residential area with sprawling lawns and extravagant, elegant homes. He turned on a side street and pulled up in front of a house at the very end of the road. He put the car in Park and killed the engine, then turned to her.

"Well? What do you think?"

Mindy looked out the window. "It's beautiful. And massive. And way outside the city." She turned back to him. "Do you know the person who lives here?"

He shook his head and removed his sunglasses. "No. But I know the person who wants to live here. And I know the person he's hoping will move in with him."

Mindy didn't want to be slow to figure this out, but this wasn't adding up. "What are you saying, Sam?"

"Come on. Let's get out of the car and take a look."

"Okay." Mindy climbed out and joined Sam as they walked up to the gate. The house was still very far away, down at the end of a long cobblestone drive. There was a stone fountain in the center of a large courtyard, manicured landscaping as far as the eye could see. Dozens of windows dotted the front of the home, suggesting that there were an awful lot of rooms.

"I'm sorry. I wish I had the keys so we could look at it," Sam said, gripping the wrought-iron gate. "Although part of me doesn't want to look at it if you aren't into the idea."

"You're saying you want to buy this house?"

"I'm saying that I want to know what's next for us. I guess I'm asking you what's next. I found out the other day that this house was for sale and I looked at it on the website and all I could think is that I loved the idea of getting out of the city, and I loved the idea of doing that with you."

"Oh, my gosh. That's amazing. And also a little surprising. What exactly would we put in a house that big, Sam?"

He shrugged. "I don't know. Kids? A bunch of pets? We could do whatever we want."

Kids. Wow. That was a leap she had not seen coming. Forget work priorities, she would need to rethink everything. Still, she turned to Sam and her heart melted. It was a lovely idea, especially with him. She suspected he was eager to build the family he'd always wanted, so he could remember the one he'd once had.

"You and I have spent so much time worrying about business and family," he said. "Now that we're together, I want to know where you see us going. I cleaned out half of my closet for you, but this would be a lot more than that."

Mindy cast her sights at him again. She would have been surprised, but she knew that they would eventually have the commitment talk. When she asked herself the question—what do you want?—the answer was him. She wanted him by her side every day. She wanted to be able to come home to him at night and wake up next to him the next morning. She wanted weekends and holidays, good times and bad. She wanted everything she could get from Sam. Every last drop. "You sound like you're unsure of what I want."

"It's always easiest if you tell me. I'm a man, Mindy. Not a mind reader."

"You're also a guy who overflows with confidence. You don't always have to follow my lead. Why don't you tell me what you want. You're entitled, you know."

Sam pressed his lips together and looked through the gate again, the breeze blowing his hair back from his face. He was so handsome in profile, his strong nose and jaw. The lips she loved to kiss. He turned back to her and she could see just how much he had dropped his defenses. A single tear rolled down his cheek. "I want the fairy-tale ending, Min. I want us to promise each other that we'll always be there for each other. And I want us to do it in front of everyone we love with rings and champagne and vows. I know you see marriage as a trap, but I promise you that I will never let it be that way for us. I will always be true. I will always be open and honest. I will always make sure you know that you're loved for the incredible woman you are."

Mindy stood perfectly still. This scene between her and Sam was so unimaginable the first time they were together, and the second, and the third… And that was all on her. She'd told herself she wanted him to stick around, but the truth was that it was only at the moments when he said he would that she ended up getting nervous.

But not anymore. That was the old Mindy. She was not letting Sam walk out on an emotional ledge without being there to catch him. "So you want to get married? Buy a big house and start having kids?"

He nodded. "I know it sounds ridiculous coming from me. I know this is probably the last thing you ever expected, but it is what I want. I love you, Mindy. From the moment I met you, there was no one else. We are meant for each other. We fit together perfectly."

Mindy leaned into him and gave him a kiss. "In more ways than one."

"So what do you say? With every other bit of uncertainty ahead, what do you say we place all bets on us?"

Mindy's heart felt as though it was doing cartwheels and backflips, a feeling she'd never expected to feel at the prospect of marriage. But she knew now that it wasn't about the institution or the promise, it was all about the man she loved more than anything. "I'll take that bet, Sam Blackwell. I'll take it every single day."

* * * * *

POWER
PLAY

ANNA DePALO

For my editor, Charles Griemsman.
Your editorial guidance has been invaluable!

One

Sera disliked smooth operators, bad in-laws and unwelcome surprises.

Unfortunately, Jordan was all three, and his sudden appearance in her offices on a sunny spring day in Massachusetts meant she'd better start preparing herself for the unthinkable.

"You!"

The exclamation was out of Sera's mouth before she could stop it. It had been just another day at Astra Therapeutics until Mr. Hotshot-NHL, Underwear-Ad-Hottie Jordan Serenghetti had crashed the party like an errant puck arcing through the air.

Jordan smiled lazily. "Yes, me."

Arms folded, he lounged against the treatment table, as if striking sexy poses was second nature to him—even when propped up by crutches, as he was now. Clad in a casual long-sleeved olive T-shirt and jeans, he emanated charisma. The shirt outlined the hard muscles of his arms, and the jeans hugged lean hips. Not that she was noticing. Not in *that* way.

Sera was wary of men who were too good to be true—as if everything came easy to them. Nowadays, Jordan Serenghetti would be at the top of her list. He was smoother than a skate blade hydroplaning over ice. With dark, ruffled hair clipped short, moss-green eyes, and a sculpted face with a chiseled jaw, he could score anywhere.

Sera had seen him in underwear ads, showing off his package on supersized billboards and fueling thousands of dreams. But she'd learned the hard way to deal in reality, not fantasy.

"What are you doing here?" she blurted, even though she had a sinking feeling she knew. She'd been told her next appointment was waiting for her in room 6, but she'd had no idea it was Jordan.

She'd heard he'd suffered a sports-related injury, but figured he was in good hands with the New England Razors hockey-team staff. She *so* was not going to worry about him, even if her *second-worst mistake* was now related to her by the marriage of her cousin to Jordan's brother. In the annals of her bad history with men, Jordan ranked number two, even if it had become clear to her that he didn't remember their chance encounter in the past.

She eyed his wrapped left knee. She wasn't used to seeing Jordan Serenghetti vulnerable...

"Now, that's a refreshing change from the usual greeting. Too often I get enthusiastic fans yelling my name." He shrugged. "You're an antidote to the monotony, Angel."

Sera sighed. Fans? Women screaming his name was more like it. *Terribly misguided, deluded women.* "Don't call me Angel."

"Hey, I'm not the one who named you for a heavenly being."

She'd never had occasion to rue her name so much. *Se-*

rafina served as a topic of easy cocktail-party conversation, but the nickname Angel irked her, especially when uttered by Jordan. So what if she was named for the seraphim?

"Your type of angel is supposed to be heavenly and fiery," Jordan went on, unperturbed. "Someone had a kismet moment when they named you. Beautiful and hot-tempered."

Serafina rolled her eyes, refusing to be swayed by the way *beautiful* rolled off Jordan's tongue. "Am I supposed to be impressed by your grasp of biblical trivia…or backhanded compliments?" Then she scowled at the thought that her response had just proven his point. She dropped her clipboard on the counter. "So you're here for a physical-therapy session…"

"Yup."

She quelled her irritation. "And I'm supposed to think it's mere chance that you were assigned to me?"

Jordan held up his hands, a smile teasing his lips. "No, I'm not going to lie about that part."

"Oh, good."

"I want the best—"

Sera was sure Jordan was used to the best in women. No doubt eager females were waiting for him when he exited the New England Razors' locker room.

"—and you've already got a great reputation. The clinic manager couldn't stop singing your praises."

With a pro athlete of Jordan's caliber, Sera was sure Bernice had given him his choice of staff. And the clinic's manager probably thought she was doing Sera a favor…

Sera thought back to her conversation earlier in the week with Bernice. *We're trying to land a contract with the New England Razors. Their management is looking to outsource some therapy work and supplement the team's staff. They're auditioning three outfits, including us. If we land this deal, it could open the door to work with other sports teams in the area.*

Ugh. At the time, she'd dismissed her chances of encountering Jordan, even though he played for the Razors. The gods couldn't be so cruel. Apparently, however, gods laughed at angels. Jordan had been sent—or volunteered—to test the quality of the clinic's services. With her. She should have known the minute she stepped into this room, but she'd been in deep denial.

"You asked for me?" Sera said slowly.

Jordan nodded and then cracked a grin. "The fact that, when I booked my appointment for today, your receptionist couldn't stop extolling your cooking skills just sealed the deal for me."

"She mentioned my cooking?"

"And baking," he added. "Apparently, the homemade dishes that you sometimes bring in for the staff earn you brownie points. So you were clearly the right choice."

"Let me remind you of something…we don't like each other."

"Correction," Jordan said, lips quirking. "You don't like me. I have no problem with attractive and passionate women. You, on the other hand, have issues—"

"Right." She narrowed her eyes.

"You should feel safe around me," Jordan said easily. "We're practically related."

Right. Jordan's older brother Cole had recently married Sera's cousin Marisa Danieli. Jordan loved to joke about the couple's long and winding path to the altar. At one point, Marisa's former fiancé had been dating Cole's ex-girlfriend, and Jordan had kidded that his brother and Marisa were engaged by proxy. It did *not*, however, mean that *she* and Jordan were related in any meaningful sense of the word.

Up to now, Sera had done her best to ignore the fact that she and Jordan were technically cousins-in-law. Marisa and Cole had had a surprise wedding, so she'd been spared having to be the maid of honor to Jordan's best man.

"I'll drive you into the ground, Serenghetti," she harrumphed, changing tactics. "You'll sweat like you've never worked before."

It was only a half-idle threat. She expected a lot from her patients. She was good, she was understanding, but she was tough.

Jordan's smile stayed in place. "I wouldn't expect any less."

"Are you always so sunny?" she grumbled. "Do the clouds ever come out in Serenghetti Land?"

He laughed. "I like to rile you, Perini. I may not have clouds, but I can rock your world with thunder and lightning."

There it was again. The sexually tinged double meaning. And then a traitorous voice whispered, *You already have. Once.* The fact that he didn't remember just made it all the more galling. "You don't want to get involved with me." *Again.* "I'm not a woman you can conveniently walk away from." *This time.* "I'm your sister-in-law's cousin."

He arched a brow. "Is that all that's stopping you?"

She threw up her hands—because no way was she going to remind Jordan about the past. *Their past.* And with her bad luck, in the future she and Jordan would be named as godparents to the next Danieli-Serenghetti offspring. As it was, they'd dodged that bullet the first time around since Jordan's brother Rick and his wife Chiara had done the honors. It seemed Cole was going down the line by order of birth in naming godparents from among his siblings.

Jordan shrugged and then glanced around. "At least we'll have the memory of a few good physical-therapy sessions."

"All you'll be remembering fondly is the pain," she practically snarled.

"I'm a good listener if you ever want to…you know, talk instead of spar."

She swept him a suspicious look—unsure if he was joking or not. *Better not to take chances.* "As if I'd open up to a player like you," she scoffed. "Forget it."

"Not even when you're off duty?" he teased. "It could be therapeutic."

"When I need to unwind, I'll book a vacation to the Caribbean."

"Let me know when you're going. I'll reserve a seat."

Argh. "It's a vacation—as in, I don't want to be irritated!"

He quirked an eyebrow. "Irritated isn't your natural state?"

"No!"

"So where do we go from here?" he said. "You're irritated…"

As he said the words, Jordan watched Serafina with bemusement and not a little lust. With blond hair swinging past her shoulders and amber eyes, she was a knockout. He'd been around plenty of beautiful women, but Sera's personality shone like an inner light. Of course, she directed snark at him, but he enjoyed tangling with her.

She was a puzzle he was interested in solving. Because if he'd ever met a woman with a boulder-sized chip on her shoulder, it was Sera Perini.

"Listen, I'll make you a deal," he joked. "I'll try to behave if you stick around and help me out."

"You will behave," she said firmly. "And your coupon is valid for today's session only. After that, the sale is over."

His eyes crinkled. "Hard bargainer."

"You have no idea."

"But I guess I'm going to find out."

"True, but first you need to sit on the treatment table so we can take a look at that knee." She paused. "Let me help you."

"No need."

Even though they were now related by marriage and had

seen each other at the occasional family gathering, they'd never come close to touching. Not a pat, not a brush of the arm, and certainly not a peck on the cheek. *Nada.* It was as if by tacit agreement boundaries had been drawn, because they were more like warring in-laws than the friendly kind. And maybe because they understood that, it was dangerous to cross some unspoken line.

Now, bracing his arms, he hopped up onto the table using his good leg.

"Nice stunt," she commented drily.

He tossed her a jaunty grin. "More where that came from."

With a last warning look, she turned her attention to the paperwork he'd brought with him to the appointment and had dropped on the counter before she'd walked in.

He took the opportunity to study her again. Today, she wore nondescript, body-concealing light blue scrubs. When she'd sometimes waitressed at the Puck & Shoot, the popular local sports bar, she'd usually kept her hair pulled back in a ponytail or with a headband and had had a black apron tied around her waist. But thanks to the fact that they were now related by marriage, he'd seen her in other getups: body-skimming dresses, tight-fitting exercise attire... She had an hourglass figure that was fuller on top, so everything flattered her. More than once he'd caught himself fantasizing about what it would be like to run his hands over her curves and skim his palms over her endless legs.

Yet he didn't know what to make of her. He was attracted as hell, but she was an in-law...and she didn't like him. Still, the urge to tease her was as natural and unavoidable as breathing, and as irresistible as the impulse to win a hockey championship. And on top of it, he needed her physical-therapy skills. Already the companies behind his endorsement deals were getting nervous because he'd been off the ice. For the umpteenth time, he pushed aside the thought that his career could be over. He'd work like hell in therapy to make sure that possibility would never become a reality. Sure he'd made some savvy business investments with his earnings, but his plans depended on continuing to play.

With a grimace, Jordan turned and stretched out his legs in front of him on the treatment table.

Sera looked up, seemingly satisfied with what she'd gleaned from his intake papers. "So how did the ACL tear occur?"

"A game three weeks ago against the New York Islanders. I heard a pop." He shrugged. "I knew what it was. Cole's been through this before."

His older brother had suffered a couple of knee injuries that had ended his professional hockey career. These days, Cole was the head of Serenghetti Construction, having taken over after their father's stroke had forced Serg Serenghetti to adopt a less active lifestyle.

"You're lucky it happened at the end of the hockey season, and the Razors didn't advance in the playoffs this year."

"I've never thought of getting knocked out in the playoffs as a lucky break," he quipped. "Especially when I wasn't there to help."

"It's a tear, not a break," she parried. "So who performed the ACL surgery on your knee?"

"Dr. Nabov at Welsdale Medical Center, and it was last week. In-patient for a day. They insisted I stay overnight. I guess they didn't want to take any chances with my recovery. Hockey fans, you know."

"Mmm-hmm." Sera flipped through his paperwork again. "Did you sign autographs while you were there?"

He cracked a smile and folded his arms over his chest. "A few."

"I assume the nursing staff went wild."

He knew sarcasm when he heard it and couldn't resist teasing back. "Nah, they've seen it all."

"You've been icing the knee?"

"Yeah. The staff at the hospital told me what to do post-surgery."

"Until you could get yourself into more expert hands?"

He flashed a grin. "You. Right."

She might totally be his type if she wasn't so thorny… and since she was related to him by marriage, a casual fling was out of the question. Still, there were layers there, and he enjoyed trying to peel them back.

Sera set aside his paperwork and approached him, her expression all business. "Okay, I'm going to unwrap your knee."

For all her prickliness up to now, her touch was light as she removed his bandages. When the bandage was off, they both studied his knee.

"Good news."

"Great."

"No signs of infection and very little bleeding." She pressed on his knee as he remained in a sitting position on the table but leaned back propped up by his arms.

"Am I hurting you?" she asked, not looking up.

"Nothing I can't handle."

"Manly."

"We hockey players are built tough."

"We'll see." She continued to press and manipulate his knee.

"I'm your first. Otherwise you'd know."

"I've never been curious about how tough hockey players are."

"You're mentally disciplined."

"We physical therapists are built tough."

Jordan smiled. "Built pretty, too."

"Behave."

"Right."

Then she reached over to the counter for an instrument. "I'm going to take some baseline measurements so we know where you are."

"Great." He waited as she straightened his knee a little, measured, and then bent his leg and measured again.

After putting the measuring instrument aside, she said, "Okay, not a bad starting point considering your knee has been wrapped since surgery. Our goal today is to improve your quad function and the mobility of the patella, among other things."

"What's a *patella*?"

She tucked a strand of hair behind her ear. "Your knee-cap."

"Of course."

"Let me know if I'm causing you too much pain."

Her tone was surprisingly solicitous, so he joked, "Isn't that what you promised? Pain?"

"Only the intended and expected variety."

He was a high-level athlete—he was used to pain and then some. "How many ACL tears have you treated?"

"A few. I'll let you know at the end if you were my best patient."

He stifled a laugh because she'd deftly appealed to his competitive instincts. He wondered if she used the same technique to cajole all her patients. Probably some played sports—since a torn ACL wasn't too unusual an athletic injury—even if she'd never treated a professional hockey player like himself before. "Will you dock me points for irreverence?"

"Do you really want to find out?" Methodically, she taped two wires to his thigh. "I'm going to set you up with some muscle stim right now. This will get you started."

In his opinion, they'd gotten started with the electricity when she'd walked in the room. But he sensed that he'd teased her enough, and she wasn't going to take any more nonsense, so he kept mum for the next few minutes and just followed her directions.

After the muscle stim, she taught him how to do patellar glides. He followed her instructions about how to move his knee to gain more flexibility. They followed that up with quad sets and heel slides, which she told him to do at home, too.

Overall, he found none of it too arduous. But at the end of half an hour, she announced that his ability to bend his knee had gone from around ten degrees to eighty.

He grinned. "I'm your best?"

"Don't flatter yourself, Superman. Your knee was wrapped in bandages that interfered with motion until now, so you were bound to make some significant improvement."

"I'll take that as a yes."

"You're impossible."

"No, I'm very possible if you'll consider your options. Now, insufferable, that's another thing…"

Sera seemed to grit her teeth. "You'll need weekly appointments."

"How long will my therapy last?"

"Depends on how it goes." Her expression was challenging—as if she'd been referring to his behavior, good or bad, as well as his recuperation. "Usually three to four months."

"Nothing long-term, then?"

She nodded. "What you're used to."

A fling. The words drifted unspoken between them. She'd met his double entendre and raised him. *Ouch.*

Two

"I can't do it. There's no way I can be Jordan Serenghetti's physical therapist." Sera drew her line in the sand. Or rather, on the hockey ice—or *whatever*.

"You have to," Bernice, the clinic's manager said, her short curly brown hair shining under the overhead fluorescent light.

"He needs a babysitter—" *of the centerfold variety* "—not a trainer. Or a physical therapist."

"We're counting on you to help us land this client."

And Jordan Serenghetti was counting on landing her. His appointment had ended over an hour ago, and still she was suffering the lingering effects. Annoyance. Exasperation. Indignation. She'd spent the time since naming her emotions.

True, Jordan emanated charm from every pore. She wasn't immune. She was still a woman who liked men, and she wasn't dead. And okay, maybe she was the one with long-suppressed needs. But that didn't mean Jordan was getting anywhere with her. *Again.* She still remembered the feel of his lips on her. And he didn't have any recollection—*none whatsoever.* She'd just been another easily forgotten face in a cast of thousands. That much had become clear once she'd reencountered him years later while waitressing at the Puck & Shoot, and there'd been not even a flicker of recognition in his eyes.

She knew the score these days, and this time she was determined that the game would end Sera 1, Playboy 0.

Endure months of close contact with Jordan? It would test her nerves and more. So after her session with him had ended, Sera had sought out Bernice in her office to plead her case. Standing just inside the doorway, she focused on the bobblehead dolls lining her boss's bookshelves. All the major sports were represented there—including hockey. Scanning them, Sera didn't see Jordan. It gave her hope that she had a small chance of convincing Bernice. How big a fan could her boss be?

"How about you reassign me and I bring you another baked lasagna to thank you?" Sera cajoled.

"Ordinarily I'd consider a small bribe," Bernice parried, her desk chair turned toward the office's entrance, "especially if it's one of your homemade dishes. But this time, no. The staff has been enjoying the big pan of baked ziti you brought in for lunch today, though."

Sera lowered her shoulders.

"If we do a good job," Bernice continued, "we should get regular business from the New England Razors. It'll be a huge boost for Astra Therapeutics and for your career."

Sera held back a grimace. As far as her boss was concerned, there'd be no getting out of this gig.

Bernice tilted her head. "You've dealt with difficult clients before. We all have."

Sera opened and closed her mouth. This was different. *But she could hardly explain why.* "Isn't this like nepotism? I get the plum client because he's related to me by marriage?"

Bernice chuckled. "The fact that you're practically family should make this assignment a piece of cake." Her manager looked thoughtful. "Or if he's a bad in-law, well then, we've all had those, too."

Sera pressed her lips together. *Damn it.* She'd worked so hard to get her physical-therapy degree. She'd moonlighted as a waitress and endured three grueling years back at school for a graduate degree. And now Jordan Serenghetti stood in the path of her advancement.

Bernice gave her an inquisitive look. "On the other hand, is your problem that Jordan has too much magnetism? Some people get starstruck by celebrities and have a hard time focusing on the job."

Sera spluttered. "Please. The fake charm is a big turn-off."

Her manager raised her eyebrows.

Sera's face heated, and she quickly added, "I'm not taking it personally. There isn't a woman alive Jordan doesn't try to charm."

"You know, if I were a little younger, and my husband would let me, I'd consider dating Jordan Serenghetti."

"Bernice, please! You've got gold with Keith. Why trade it in for pyrite?" Sera knew her manager had just celebrated her sixtieth birthday and thirtieth wedding anniversary.

"What makes you think Jordan isn't genuine?" Bernice countered.

Sera threw up her hands. She wasn't about to dig into her past with her boss—and explain how she'd honed her instincts about men the hard way. She was wise enough these days not to be taken in by ripped biceps—hadn't she seen them up close an hour ago?—and hard abs. Probably those lips were still magic, too. "The problem is he knows he has the goods."

Bernice laughed. "There's nothing wrong with a man who's confident."

"Try arrogant." Sera knew she had to talk to Marisa. Perhaps her cousin could convince Jordan that this work arrangement wasn't a good idea. If she couldn't get out of this assignment herself, maybe Jordan would back out.

Knowing she wasn't going to get anywhere with Bernice, Sera decided to back off and change the subject. But when her workday ended at four, she made the short drive from Astra Therapeutics' offices outside Springfield to Marisa and Cole's new home in Welsdale.

Sera pulled up to a classic center-hall colonial and thanked her lucky stars for May in western Massachusetts. The breezy, sunny day could almost erase her mood. She had texted Marisa in advance, so when she got out of her beat-up sedan, her cousin was already opening the front door.

Marisa wore a baby sling and raised a finger to her lips but exchanged a quick peck on the cheek with Sera. "Dahlia just fell asleep. I'm going to lay her down in her crib and be right with you."

"You and Cole have gone all Hollywood with the baby naming," Sera remarked wryly, because even months later, the baby's name brought a smile to her lips.

"If Daisy is acceptable, why not Dahlia?" Marisa said over her shoulder as Sera closed the door and followed her into the house.

"And here I thought Rick and Chiara would go all name crazy, but no, nope, they had to settle on something traditional like Vincent." Frankly, it wouldn't have surprised her in the least if the middle Serenghetti brother and his new wife, actress Chiara Feran, who resided in Los Angeles most of the time—home to the weird Hollywood baby-naming craze—had come up with something like Moonlight or Starburst.

Sera bore only a passing resemblance to her cousin. They shared the amber eyes that were a family trait, but she'd grown a shade taller than Marisa by the time she was fourteen—and her dark blond hair set her apart from her cousin, who had long curly brown locks. When Sera had been younger, she and Marisa had been deep in each other's pockets, and sometimes she'd wished the similarities had been strong enough that they could easily pass as sisters.

"I'll be right back," Marisa said as she started up the stairs from the entry hall. "I'll meet you in the kitchen."

As Sera made her way to the back of the house, she noted once again that it bore the stamp of domesticity. The new home was still sparsely furnished, but the signs of baby were all around. She figured that Jordan must break out in hives here.

When her cousin came back downstairs moments later, Sera put down her glass of flavored water and braced her hands on the granite kitchen countertop. She wasted no words. "Marisa, Jordan is about to become a client of mine."

Her cousin's expression remained mild as she turned on a baby monitor. "They're sending him to you to help recover from his torn ACL."

Sera didn't mask her surprise. "You know? And you didn't warn me?"

"I found out just this morning. Cole happened to mention Jordan was heading to Astra Therapeutics. But I wasn't sure he would definitely be assigned to you." Her cousin wrinkled her brow. "Though, come to think of it, he did make an offhand comment to Cole about possibly asking for you…" She shrugged. "We thought he was teasing because, ah, you two have always seemed to rub each other the wrong way at family gatherings."

"Well, it's no joke, but someone has made a mistake." Wanting to spare her cousin any awkwardness with her in-laws, and because, frankly, her first encounter with Jordan had been embarrassing, she'd never mentioned to Marisa that she and Jordan had briefly crossed paths in the past. It was bad enough that others could sense tension between her and the youngest Serenghetti brother.

"If anyone can whip Jordan into shape, it's you," Marisa teased.

Sera scowled as she pushed away from the kitchen counter. "This isn't funny."

"Of course not, but maybe you've met your match."

Sera shuddered. "Don't say it."

The last thing she needed was for anyone to think Jordan was a work challenge that she couldn't conquer. First off, she didn't want to conquer anything—especially him. Second, no way was he her *match* in any other sense of the word—not that Marisa could mean *that*. The fact that Jordan had found her infinitely forgettable at twenty-one was evidence enough that they weren't fated *in any way*.

Her cousin glanced down at some paint chips fanned out on the kitchen counter. "Who knew there were so many shades of beige for a guest bedroom?" she asked absently. "I just want a soothing tone, and Cole is kidding me about using Diaper Brown."

"Is that the name of a paint color?"

Marisa pinked. "Paint colors are a running joke in this house ever since Cole and I redid the kitchen cabinets in my old apartment."

Her cousin and her husband had only months ago moved into the new colonial in Welsdale that Cole had built for their growing family. They'd moved in right before Dahlia was born, and Sera knew that the process of decorating weighed on Marisa, especially as a new mom. "Most of us can use a professional. Get a decorator."

Marisa looked at her thoughtfully. "Isn't that why Jordan is coming to you? Because you're a professional?" She tugged on the hem of her top and rubbed at a stain. "Why are you so reluctant to help him?"

Sera opened her mouth and then clamped it shut. Because…because… No way was she getting into any embarrassing past *incidents*. "He's obnoxious."

"I know you two have a testy relationship, but he'll have to do what you tell him."

"He's a smooth operator." *Happy-go-lucky.* With a bad memory to boot. And he didn't know the meaning of struggle.

Marisa glanced at her keenly. "You're protesting too much."

"Paraphrasing Shakespeare? Spoken like a true English teacher."

"Former English teacher. And I'm on maternity leave from the assistant principal position at the Pershing School." Marisa yawned. "Something to eat?"

"No, thanks. And you're doing great in your leave as a new mom."

Her cousin gave a rueful laugh. "I know, but family history and all. At least Cole is on board."

Sera gave her cousin a reassuring pat. Marisa had been raised by a single mom, Sera's Aunt Donna. Marisa's father had died before she'd been born—having already made clear that a baby didn't factor into his plans for pursuing a minor-league baseball career and maybe getting to the majors.

Men. These days, Sera didn't need more confirmation that they could be fickle and untrustworthy. Her awful experience with Neil had taught her enough. Jordan had just been the start of her bad track record—one she seemed to share with the women in her family. *Must be in the genes.* "You and Cole have to convince Jordan this is a bad idea."

"Sera—"

"Please."

* * *

Jordan shifted in his seat next to his brother and glanced around the crowded bar. Business was humming as usual on a Thursday evening at the Puck & Shoot. None of his teammates from the Razors were around, partly because many had scattered for home or vacation in the postseason.

Sera also no longer moonlighted here as a waitress—and *that* was a good thing, he told himself. He could still recall his reaction when he'd first discovered, shortly before Cole's marriage, that the hot blond waitress at his favorite dive was Marisa's cousin. The fates had a twisted sense of humor.

Still, tonight, even without his teammates and Sera at the Puck & Shoot, it almost felt like old times. He nearly felt like his old self—*normal*. Not injured and off the ice, with brothers who'd suddenly morphed into fathers—though he was happy for them. It felt good not to be holed up at home, which would have just given him more time to mull his uncertain future and push away his regular companion these days—unease.

If he could only take out his frustration and pent-up energy the way he normally did, things would be better. "Man, I miss our evenings at Jimmy's Boxing Gym."

Cole, sitting on the bar stool next to him, smiled. "I've got better things to do with my after-work hours these days."

"Ever since you got hitched, you've become boring, old man," Jordan grumbled good-naturedly. "And fatherhood has just added to your—" he strangled out the word "—domesticity."

"Dahlia is brilliant," Cole countered. "Did I tell you she rolled over the other day?"

"No, but she clearly takes after Marisa. Beauty and brains."

Cole just smiled rather than giving as good as he got—

and that was the problem. Jordan wished for the old days. It was as if his brother didn't even miss hockey. What was the world coming to?

"The only reason I'm here at the Puck & Shoot is because of Marisa," Cole said. "She's the one who encouraged me to come keep your sorry butt company."

"You owe me one. More than one. You might not be wallowing in wedded bliss if it weren't for me."

"Yeah, how can I forget." Cole's voice dripped sarcasm. "Lucky for you, it all ended well. Otherwise, you could have been sporting a broken nose."

Jordan grinned because this was a spark of the old Cole he was used to. "Luck had nothing to do with it. You and Marisa were destined to be together. And for the record, a broken nose would have just added to my sex appeal."

Jordan had seen how unhappy his older brother had been when his reconciliation with Marisa had headed south, so he'd fibbed and told Cole that Marisa was looking for him—sending his unsuspecting brother to her apartment. Jordan had hoped that once the two were alone, they'd have a chance to talk and patch things up. They'd realize they were made for each other. In fact, Cole and Marisa hadn't made up then, but shortly afterward. And in the aftermath, they'd invited everyone to an engagement party that had turned out to be a surprise wedding.

Sera had been at the event, of course, looking sexy and tempting. He'd only discovered at a fund-raiser a short time before that she was Marisa's relative; there he'd recognized the attractive waitress from the Puck & Shoot whom he'd never had a chance to speak with and who always seemed to avoid him. The physical resemblance when she was side by side with her cousin had been unmistakable.

He'd gone slack-jawed, however, at Sera's transformation from waitress to temptress in a blue satin halter-top cocktail dress. Makeup had enhanced her unique and arresting features—full lips, bold eyes and fine cheekbones that any model would have wept for. And the halter top on her dress had emphasized her shoulders and toned arms before skimming down over testosterone-fueling curves to endless legs encased in strappy, high-heeled sandals. Seeing an opportunity to make his move, he'd approached the two women, but Sera had swatted him away like a pesky fly that night…

Cole slapped him on the back. "You look pensive. Buck up. It's not all doom and gloom."

Jordan didn't think his thoughts were showing, but maybe he was wrong. "Since you got married and gave up the mantle to become nauseatingly cheery, someone has to take over the role. And now both you and Rick are fathers."

Cole's face broke into a grin. "Yup."

"Someone has to uphold the family reputation."

"What reputation are you referring to? Being depressed and down?"

"No. Sexy and single." If he wasn't a professional hockey player and all-around chick magnet, who was he? He gave an inward shudder. Best not contemplate the abyss.

"All right, but from the looks of you, I've got to ask. What's throwing shade on sexy and single?"

Jordan waved his beer. "The obvious."

His latest injury had kept him off the ice for the end of the season, and his corporate partners—with contracts for endorsement deals—were starting to get restless. Not to mention his injury didn't put him in a great position to negotiate his next contract with the Razors. Everyone knew that one Serenghetti had already had a career-ending ACL injury.

"I'm proof there is life after the game," Cole said quietly.

"Yeah, I know, but if I can get over this injury, I should have a few more good seasons left." He was on the wrong side of thirty, but he was still at the top of his game. Or rather, he had been. In the last couple of years, he'd shifted position from right wing to center and had had some of his best seasons ever. The one that had recently ended might have been just as good, except it had ended abruptly for him with a knee injury. Still, at thirty-one, he figured he could squeeze out another half decade at the top—if he had better luck than in the past weeks.

"Speaking of injury," Cole said, nodding to the crutches that Jordan had propped against the bar, "what's your game plan for this one?"

Jordan took a swig of his beer. Fortunately, since it was his left knee that had needed surgery, he'd been able to start driving again this week. "I'm doing physical therapy."

Cole took a swallow of his own beer without glancing at him. "Yup, I've heard. Sera. So you weren't joking when you mentioned it might be her you'd see at Astra…"

"News travels fast," Jordan murmured. "I was just in to see her yesterday."

"And I'm supposed to be here to convince you not to see her."

Jordan tossed his brother a quick look. "Wow, so this is what it feels like."

"What?"

"The first time a woman has tried *not* to meet me."

"Sera is special."

"Tell me about it."

"You don't want to tangle with her. She's Marisa's cousin and not someone you can easily walk away from."

"Hey—" Jordan held up his hands "—all I'm asking is that she cure my knee, not date me." So what if Sera had already made a variation of Cole's argument?

His brother's tone was light, but there was also an undercurrent of warning. He wasn't sure whether the note of caution was because Cole was thinking about Jordan's best interests, or because he was naturally protective of his wife's relative. Cole had always been the responsible one, *relatively speaking*, and Jordan had chalked it up to oldest-child syndrome.

"Face it, Jordan. You can't turn off the charm. You love to get a rise out of Sera."

"I thought I was helping her career by asking for her."

"Apparently she doesn't want the boost."

Jordan twisted his lips in wry amusement. If he didn't have a healthy ego, he'd be feeling a twinge of wounded pride right now. "Look, when the Razors' management discovered I'd need physical therapy, they wanted me to try out a new outfit for them. I remembered Sera worked at Astra Therapeutics, so I mentioned the only name I knew when it was time to set up an appointment."

"Except Sera doesn't want to work with you."

Jordan put a hand to his chest. "Be still my heart," he said mockingly. "A woman who doesn't want me."

"You'll get over it. Trust me, you don't want to get involved with Marisa's cousin. I've seen her in the boxing ring. She throws a mean left jab."

"Which one?" Jordan joked. "Marisa or Sera?"

"Sera, but take my word for it, it's in the genes."

"And you know this how?"

Cole gave a long-suffering sigh. "Marisa and I met Sera at her gym once before having lunch nearby. She was finishing up her workout." His brother's lips quirked. "The rest I know because I'm married to one of the parties involved. Marisa is no pushover herself."

So Sera boxed. Like him. Interesting. She liked to take out her frustrations on a punching bag?

Still, Jordan quieted. He hadn't expected Sera to go to the trouble of recruiting Marisa and Cole to make her case. He'd thought he was doing her a good turn by asking for her by name. He was surprised by her level of opposition, and not for the first time he wondered what was behind it.

Maybe he should let her off the hook about this physical-therapy gig if she was that panicked about it. But possibly not before finding out why she was so dead-set against him…

Three

"Guess what?"

Sera regarded her older brother, Dante, with a wary eye. There'd been many *guess what*s in their lives. *Guess what? I brought your hamster in for show-and-tell... Guess what? I'm dating your volleyball teammate... Guess what? You're getting your own car—my old wreck.* She loved her brother, but sometimes it was hard to like him.

This time, they were at Dory's Café in downtown Welsdale, and she had some major armor against an unwelcome surprise. Namely, she was sitting down, already fortified by morning coffee ahead of brunch. And Dante was lucky—there was a table between them, so she couldn't kick him in the shins as she might have done when she was six—not that she was above trying if things got out of hand.

"Okay," she mustered, "I give up. What is it? Winning lottery numbers? One-way ticket to Mars? What?" She stuck out her chin and waited.

"Nothing so dramatic, sport." Dante chuckled. "New job."

Sera breathed a sigh of relief. "Congrats. That makes two of us in less than three years. Mom will be doing the happy dance." Frankly, her mother could use good news. Rosana Perini was still putting the pieces of her life back together—rearranging the puzzle that had broken and scattered when she'd become a young widow. The whole family had needed to regroup when Joseph Perini had died six years ago when Sera was twenty-three. It was one of the things that had made Sera decide to start a new chapter in her life by going back to school for her physical-therapy degree.

"You're looking at the new VP of Marketing for the New England Razors."

Sera's stomach plummeted as she was jerked back to the present. No, no and *no*. Dante's working for the New England Razors meant only one thing: another connection to Jordan Serenghetti. Still, she managed to cough up the critical word. "Congratulations."

"Thanks, Sera. It's my dream job."

Her brother had always been a sports nut. His teenage bedroom had been decorated with soccer, football and hockey memorabilia. No wonder someone had thought he was perfect for the Razors marketing position.

A dream come true for Dante. A nightmare for her. She didn't need her life further entangled with Jordan Serenghetti's. Her brother would be offering up free game tickets and suggesting a family evening out. Or talking nonstop about Jordan Serenghetti's prowess—on and off the ice.

Dante, though, appeared oblivious to her discomfort. "I wonder if Marisa can grease the wheels for me with Jordan Serenghetti. You know, maybe invite us both to a family barbecue at her house again soon." Her brother shrugged.

"Making sure that Jordan and the Razors are happy with each other is part of my new job description."

"She doesn't need to," Sera managed to get out, volunteering the information because Dante would find out eventually anyway. "I'm seeing Jordan myself."

Dante's eyebrows shot up. "Oh, yeah?"

"Jordan is my new client at Astra Therapeutics. The Razors are farming out some of their physical rehab, and Jordan is their guinea pig."

A grin split her brother's face. "You mean your guinea pig."

Sera tossed her hair. "Hey, I'm a professional."

"Then why do you eye him at family gatherings as if he's the first case of the plague in five hundred years?"

"Professional distance."

Dante snorted. "I'll buy that as fast as a counterfeit trading card on an online auction site."

"Whatever. I'm giving him the boot to another therapist in the office."

"Why?"

"You just said it yourself. We don't get along."

"What about family loyalty?"

"To Jordan Serenghetti? He's only a cousin-in-law." As if she could forget.

"Jordan could end up owing you a debt of gratitude for getting him back on his feet."

Just then, the waitress arrived with their food—a lumberjack breakfast of eggs, sausage and toast for Dante, and an egg-white omelet for her. Sera liked to practice what she preached to her clients—healthy eating and clean living. She also made sure to thank the waitress because she knew what it meant to be on your feet for hours.

Her brother took his first bite and then tilted his head and studied her. "You don't like him because women fawn over him."

"I hadn't noticed, and anyway it's none of my business." She gave all her concentration to seasoning her food with the pepper mill.

"You shouldn't let one bad experience with what's-his-name Neil sour you."

True…if she could trust her instincts. But she still wasn't sure her radar was working right. And Dante had no clue that she and Jordan had shared more than casual conversation in the past. Not that she wanted her brother to ever find out. It was bad enough he knew the basics of her drama with Neil.

Dante waved his fork as he swallowed his food. "You should at least tell Jordan that your attitude isn't personal."

"Never…and you're not going to, either." Because it was personal—and wasn't just about her unsavory experience with Neil.

"Okay, play it your way, but I think you're making a mistake."

She shrugged. "Mine to make."

"Ser," Dante said, suddenly looking earnest, "I could use your help."

"Wow, this is a change."

"I'm serious. I need Jordan back on the ice, and the sooner the better. It would make a great start to my new job if I could claim some credit. Or at least if I could say my sister—the physical therapist with the golden touch—helped get him back in shape."

Sera made a face. "Ugh, Dante. That's asking a lot."

Dante cleared his throat. "I got the position with the Razors…but there's already a higher-up who is gunning for me." He shrugged. "We have some bad history together at a prior employer, and I'm sure he'd be happy if I screwed up."

Sera sighed. "What kind of bad history?"

Her brother looked sheepish. "We were in competition

at a sports agency…and there might have been a woman involved, too."

Great. She took a bite of her omelet. She could just imagine her brother involved in a love triangle. *Almost.* She didn't want any more details.

"Fans come to see Jordan in action," Dante cajoled.

"Whatever." From what she could tell, Jordan was still in fantastic shape despite his injury, and she didn't care how much money he had on the table. The guy had major bank already—what was a few million, more or less, to him?

"Sera, I'm asking."

Sera shifted in her seat. Because, for once, the tables were turned. Her brother needed her help—unlike when he'd stepped in to bail her out when they were younger. Sure, he'd been a thorn in her side with his antics—keeping her on edge—but he'd also cast a protective mantle. Unlike her, Dante remembered the child their parents had lost at birth, and it was almost like he'd absorbed their unspoken worries about losing another loved one. So, he'd issued warnings about situations to avoid at school, stood up for her when she'd been picked on as a kid and, yes, kept some of her secrets from their parents.

On the other hand, Jordan threatened the safe and tidy world that she'd worked hard to build for herself. She knew just how potent his kisses could be, and she was nobody's fool. Not anymore. If she stepped up for Dante, she'd be walking a fine line…

Sera folded her arms as she stepped into the examining room. "So you're stuck with me."

Jordan was leaning against the treatment table, crutches propped up next to him. He was billboard-ready good-looking even under the fluorescent lights of the room. She, on the other hand, was in her usual shapeless scrubs. Clearly, if he didn't enjoy toying with her, she'd be beneath his notice—which ran to models, actresses and reality stars these days, if his press was to be believed.

Jordan's expression turned to one of surprise, and then he gave his trademark insouciant grin. "I'm stuck with you? And here I thought the best part of the day was getting to sample your cannoli bruschetta mash-up recipe along with the rest of the staff. It was delicious, by the way."

"Well, you were wrong," she deadpanned. Why did she feel a thrill at his compliment?

"What prompted the change of heart? Don't keep me waiting. This is the most suspense I've had in ages."

"I'm sure it's a rare occurrence for a woman to keep you cooling your heels."

Jordan's smile widened. "What do you think?"

She ignored the question and gritted her teeth instead. *Best to get this over with.* "My brother, Dante, just got a job with the Razors. Marketing VP, to be exact."

Jordan raised his eyebrows and then his lips quirked. "You Perinis can't seem to stay away from professional hockey players."

She gave him a frosty smile. "Let me remind you that I was initially recruited for this job. I didn't volunteer."

"The end result is the same."

"Now I'm helping out Dante by getting you back on your feet."

"Of course."

Well, that was easy.

"Do I get anything in return for helping you out?"

Sera narrowed her eyes. She'd spoken too soon. This was more like the Jordan Serenghetti she expected. "Don't be evil. The chance to spread some beneficence should be good enough for you."

Jordan laughed, looking not the least bit insulted. "Now I understand why you showed up for my appointment today as scheduled—instead of, you know, feigning typhoid or something."

"Count your blessings."

"So you're going to agree to be my physical therapist, and here I was about to let you off the hook."

"You're not going to make this easy for me, are you?"

"Is that a rhetorical question?"

"The silver lining is that I get to make you sweat."

"Some people pay to see that, you know."

Of course she knew Jordan got paid millions for his skills on the ice. Still… "Don't you ever stop?"

"Not when it's this much fun."

"Well then, I guess it's time for me to stop making it so enjoyable for you."

"You know, I really was going to let you off the hook today." Jordan shrugged. "Cole came to see me because you were adamant about not being my therapist. Obviously, you've had a change of heart."

Now she looked like an opportunist. She didn't know that Marisa had followed through and told Cole to have a talk with Jordan. "Why didn't you cancel your appointment? Or ask for someone else before your scheduled time?"

"I didn't want you to look bad at the office. I figured it would be better if the word came from you."

Sera lowered her shoulders. She felt bad—guilty… Damn him. She was only trying to help her brother!

Jordan just stood there, being himself—all sexy. Badass abs and chiseled pecs under a formfitting T-shirt, square jaw, magnetic green eyes and all.

Sera gritted her teeth again. She could do this. She… owed him. "Thanks."

He cupped his hand to his ear. "What was that?"

And just like that, they were back to squabbling. She knew she was rising to the bait, but she couldn't help herself. "Thank you…for giving me the opportunity to see you grunt and sweat."

Jordan laughed but then started leveraging himself onto the treatment table. "Ready when you are."

She moved aside his crutches and then helped him stretch his legs before him. When he was settled, she examined his knee. After a few moments of poking and prodding, she had to admit he was coming along nicely. "The swelling is about as good as we can expect at this stage."

"So I heal well?"

She looked up. "You're a professional athlete at the top of your game. It's not surprising." When he looked pleased, she added, "Today we're going to focus on increasing mobility and improving your quad function even more."

"Sounds…fun," he remarked drily. "You know, it's amazing we didn't know each other in high school. You lost some opportunities to kick my butt."

"*Amazing* isn't the word I'd use." *More like a relief.* Her teenage self could have gotten into big trouble with Jordan. As it was…but she was older and wiser now.

"Marisa mentioned you grew up in East Gannon. Right next door."

"And yet a world away." East Gannon was Welsdale's poor cousin. People had small clapboard homes, not mansions with expensive landscaping.

Jordan looked thoughtful. "Welsdale High played East Gannon plenty of times."

"I didn't pay much attention to hockey in high school. I left that stuff to Dante."

Jordan's expression registered surprise. "And you call yourself a New Englander?"

She stuck out her chin. "I played volleyball."

Jordan's eyes gleamed. "An athlete. I knew there must be something we had in common."

Sera stopped herself from rolling her eyes.

"And you also box to stay in shape, from what I understand," he murmured. "So two things we have in common."

"I doubt there are three," she countered, and he just laughed.

She could get used to the way his eyes crinkled and amusement took over his entire face.

"You went to Welsdale High?" she added quickly. "I figured you'd gone to a fancy place like Pershing School along with Cole."

Cole Serenghetti had been a star hockey player at the Pershing School. It was where he'd met Marisa, who'd attended on scholarship. They'd had a teenage romance until Marisa had played a part in Cole's suspension. Then they'd led separate lives for fifteen years until fate and a Pershing School fund-raiser had brought them together again.

"Serenghetti Construction wasn't doing well during a recession, so I decided to take the financial burden off my parents by switching to Welsdale High for my junior year."

"Oh." She tried to reconcile the information with what she knew of Jordan Serenghetti. *Self-sacrificing* wasn't a word that she'd have associated with him. And she didn't want a reason to like him.

Jordan gave her a cocky grin. "I had an excellent run at Welsdale High School. You missed it all."

"No regrets." Then, giving in to curiosity, she asked, "Do you ever wish you'd gone to Pershing School?"

"Nope. Welsdale High had just as good a hockey team, and we were the champs twice while I was there."

This time, Sera did roll her eyes. "No doubt you think it was due to the fact you were on the team."

Jordan smiled. "Actually, I was a lowly freshman for the first win."

She shrugged. "Maybe you thought Pershing School was second-best to Welsdale. After all, the suspension that Marisa earned Cole meant that Pershing hadn't won a championship in a while."

Jordan held up his hands in mock surrender. "Hey, I don't blame Marisa. She had her arm twisted by the fates." He gave her a cheeky look. "And no, I didn't transfer because I thought Welsdale High had a better hockey team. I figured whichever side I played on would have the superior team."

"So I was right, after all. You claim all the credit."

Jordan relaxed his teasing expression. "As I said, since the two teams were about equal, I decided to do my parents a favor by saving on tuition. But I let them believe that the hockey team was the reason for my switching schools."

Sera got serious, too. "Well, it was a nice thing to do. Apparently, you do have a pleasant side…occasionally."

He angled his head. "Want to help me brush up on my manners?"

"I'm not a teacher, and something tells me you'd be a poor student. But actually, right now I have something to show you."

He perked up.

"Heel slides," she said succinctly, all business. "The first exercise for your knee."

"Oh."

She guided him in a demonstration of sliding the heel of his foot along the treatment table, extending his knee for twenty seconds. After that, as he reclined on the table, he did repetitions by himself while grasping a belt that was anchored with the heel of his foot.

"Great," she said encouragingly. "This should improve your quad function."

He grunted as he continued, until she felt he'd done enough.

She took the belt from him and put it aside on the counter. "Now I'm going to teach you something you can do at home by yourself."

He arched a brow, and she gave him a stern look even as she felt heat rise to her face.

"Great," he managed. "I suppose I should be glad that there are no paparazzi around, angling for a picture of me on crutches."

"Exactly." Putting her index finger at the location of one his incisions, she moved her finger back and forth, her touch smooth but firm. "This scar massage is to reduce inflammation. You should continue to do this daily." She started a circular motion. "You can also vary the direction."

Sera kept her gaze focused on his knee, and Jordan was quiet for a change—watching her.

"So I have a question," he finally said, his tone conversational. "Have any of your clients flirted with you? Before me?"

"We haven't flirted. Well, you have, but it takes two to tango." With an impersonal touch, she placed his hand where hers had been on his knee. "Now you try."

He inclined his head in acknowledgment, imitating her motion. "Okay, what about before me?"

She covered his hand to guide him a bit, ignoring the sudden awareness that came from touching him again. "Some have tried, none have succeeded."

"Wow, a challenge."

"You would see it that way. But nope, a futile endeavor is more like it."

He looked up. "Throwing down the gauntlet."

She met his gaze. "You're too incapacitated to bend low enough to pick it up."

"But not for long," he replied with a wicked glint.

"Now we're going to try the stationary bike," she announced, ignoring him.

Jordan raised his eyebrows. "I'm going to be biking already?"

"Your good leg will be doing all the work." She was relieved they were moving to the wide-open gym. Verbally tangling with Jordan Serenghetti while they were alone was like walking a tightrope—it took all her focus, and she needed a break.

He followed her over to the gym on his crutches, and she helped as he gingerly got on the bike.

Because he exuded so much charisma, Sera could almost forget Jordan was injured. She refocused her attention and instructed him in what to do.

He slowly pedaled backward and forward with his right leg, his left knee bending and straightening in response.

"How's the pain?" she asked.

He bared his teeth. "I've had worse in training sessions with the Razors."

"Good. You want to push but not too hard."

"Right."

She watched him for a few more minutes until she was satisfied with his effort. "Good job."

"Effusive praise from you," he teased.

"We're not done yet," she parried.

After several more minutes, they returned to the treatment room, where she instructed him on how to do straight-leg raises while resting on his back. She followed this up with having him do raises from the hip while he was lying on his side. Then she helped him sit up to do short arc quads, raising his leg from the knee.

As he was finishing up his last exercise, she glanced at the clock and realized with some surprise that their time was up.

She tucked a stray strand of hair behind her ear and exhaled. "Okay, that's it for today."

He raised his brows. "I'm done?"

She nodded. "You're making excellent progress. You've gained some more motion in your knee since the surgery, and that's what we're going to continue to work on."

He smiled. Not mocking, not teasing, just genuine, and Sera blinked.

"Glad things are working out," he said.

That made two of them. For her peace of mind, Jordan couldn't get well fast enough.

Four

"The companies behind the endorsement deals need reassurance. When do you think you'll be playing again?" Marvin Flor's worried voice boomed from Jordan's cell phone.

Jordan shifted on his sofa. Marv had been his agent since his professional hockey career had started nearly ten years ago. He was good, tough and a whiz at promotion. Hence Jordan's promotional contracts for everything from men's underwear to athletic gear and sports drinks. Marv was in his sixties and a dead ringer for actor Javier Bardem—and well into his third decade as a top-notch sports agent.

"Why don't you partner with your sister, Mia, for a line of men's apparel? Isn't she an up-and-coming designer?"

Jordan stifled a laugh, pushing aside the thought that Marv's half-joking suggestion—at least, he thought it was only semiserious—might be a sign of desperation. His house phone rang, and he ignored it. "First off, I don't think Mia's ready to branch into men's sportswear just yet.

And second, we'd throttle each other if we worked together. Sibling rivalry and all that."

Jordan gazed at the lazy, late-afternoon sunlight filtering through the floor-to-ceiling windows of his Welsdale penthouse. Usually in the off-season, he was a whirlwind of energy. Vacationing in Turks and Caicos, making personal appearances…working out to keep fit. Now the weights in his private gym lay unused, and he hadn't met Cole at Jimmy's Boxing Gym in weeks. At least he'd been able to shed his crutches the other day, since he was close to four weeks postsurgery.

Marv sighed. "So, okay, what's the latest on when you'll be back on the ice?"

"Doubtful for the beginning of the season. We're looking at three months of therapy at least." Jordan winced. His endorsement contracts had clauses in them, and if he wasn't on the ice, he'd stand to lose a cool few million. And then there was the upcoming negotiation of his contract to continue to play for the Razors…

"What's the prognosis?"

"There's no reason not to expect full recovery." *At this point.*

Jordan could almost hear Marv's sigh of relief.

"Good. Because everyone is aware of the family history."

Meaning Cole. Meaning ACL tears ran in the family. And had been career-ending for at least one Serenghetti already. Not good. "I'm in great hands, Marv. The best." He couldn't complain about his doctors. His physical therapist, on the other hand…

Sera had surprised him at their last session. He was happy to help smooth Dante's way with the Razors. And Sera was going to be his reluctant physical therapist for the duration…even if she sometimes acted as if she wanted to take a few shots at him in the boxing ring. The thought made Jordan smile. In fact, the biggest problem with his prolonged recovery was that his plan for what to do with the endorsement-deal money might be in jeopardy. He'd had a few restless nights about his career hitting the rocks, but he was a fighter.

"Well, if we can't get you on the ice, we need to keep you in the public eye with a positive spin," Marv continued. "That should help keep the companies that you've partnered with happy."

Jordan heard his landline ring again and told Marv to hold on even as he picked up the receiver with his free hand. After building reception announced that his mother was on her way up, Jordan switched back to his agent. His day was about to get more interesting, and Jordan knew he had to wrap things up with some quick reassurances. "Don't worry, Marv. With this banged-up knee, I'm not likely to be partying hard in Vegas."

"Yeah, yeah. But good press with your name attached to it would be better. It's not enough to stay out of trouble."

Jordan knew Marv would love his plan for what to do with the paychecks from his endorsement deals, but he wanted to keep his idea to himself for the moment. He hadn't mentioned his intentions to anyone, and anyway, good publicity and Marv's worries weren't the reason he wanted to go ahead with his plan. No, his reasons were deeper and personal, which was why he'd kept a lid on his goal till now.

"I suppose a semiserious relationship isn't in the cards."

Jordan coughed. "No."

He intended to enjoy his pinnacle of fame and fortune. He'd spent enough years being the sickly kid who'd been stuck at home—or in the hospital. That was, until he'd grown into a solid teenager who could slap the puck into the goal better than anyone.

On top of that, his current lifestyle wasn't conducive to

home and hearth. He was on the road half the time when he was playing, and the NHL season was long in comparison to other sports. He wasn't ready to settle down. He was still Jordan Serenghetti—NHL hotshot and billboard model— despite his temporary detour. He'd spent years on the ice. He wasn't sure who he was beyond the identity that he'd taken a long time to carve out for himself.

Marv grumbled. "Well, at the moment you are staying in one place for a while. There's hope. A relationship with a hometown sweetheart would give us some positive ink in the press. Work with me here."

The only woman Jordan was seeing lately was Sera... and she was hardly the type who'd be mistaken for his girl-friend, given that her typical expression around him was a scowl. She'd probably slam the door in a paparazzo's face—and then issue a vehement denial and threaten liti-gation about linking her good name to Jordan Serenghetti. The last thought made him smile again.

He figured they could have some fun together—what was the harm in a little flirtation? And he was curious about the basis of Sera's prickliness. At least it should make her happy that he'd been doing the exercises that she'd assigned for him. He was also looking forward to seeing her next week—sparring with her and peeling back some more of the layers that made up the complex and intriguing Sera-fina Perini.

Jordan heard the private elevator that led straight into the penthouse moments before the door opened and his mother appeared, casserole dish in hand.

"Gotta go, Marv," he said before ending the call on his agent's admonition to keep in touch.

Jordan straightened, lowering his bad leg from where it was resting on the sofa's seat cushions. "Mom, this is a surprise."

Everyone but his mother knew better than to show up unexpectedly.

Camilla Serenghetti smiled as she stopped before him. "I brought you something to eat."

Because his mother still bore traces of an Italian accent—as well as having a habit of mixing words from two languages in a single sentence—the *eat* came off sounding as if there was a short *a* vowel at the end of it.

"Mom, it's my knee that needs help, not my stomach." Still, whatever she'd brought smelled delicious.

"You need to keep up your strength." She moved toward the kitchen where a Viking range was visible from the living area. "Lasagna."

"With béchamel sauce?"

"Just like you like it."

"The staff on the show must adore you if you're always sharing special dishes." *Like someone else he knew.* Except his mother had her own local show, *Flavors of Italy with Camilla Serenghetti*—her name had been added to the title in recent years.

His mother turned back from the kitchen and frowned. "It's not because of the staff that I worry. It's the new television station owners. I'm not sure they like my cooking."

"You're kidding."

"There's talk, *chiacchierata*, about big changes. Maybe no cooking shows."

"They're considering canceling you?"

Camilla's hands flew to her cheeks. "*Per piacere*, Jordan. *Please*, watch what you say."

Jordan knew this show was his mother's baby. And his father had made a guest appearance—finally coming out of the funk into which he'd sunk after his stroke.

"Mom, they're not going to cancel you. They'd be crazy to."

"Not even if they want to bring the television station in a new *direzione*?"

"You mean *take* the station in a new direction." He was so used to correcting his mother's English, it was second nature. She'd been doing a mash-up on her adopted language as long as he could remember.

"*Take, bring*, whatever. *Open* the light means *turn on*. You understand me, *sì*?"

Jordan smiled. "More importantly, your viewers understand and love you. You speak the international language of food."

A look of relief passed over his mother's face. "Years of trying recipes on my family paid off. And you ate my *pastina con brodo*. Always. Good kids make great cooking skills."

He loved his mother's pasta in broth. He'd grown up on it. Even today, the aroma of it brought him back to childhood. He'd been served the dish every time he'd been ill or injured—anything from the common cold to the more serious episodes that had landed him in Welsdale Children's Hospital.

He also knew how much the show meant to his mother as far as giving her a late-life second act. Jordan schooled his expression. "How's Dad? Besides drowning in *pastina con brodo*, I mean."

His mother served the same dish to every ill family member. And because his father had never fully recovered from his stroke, his mother could continue with her culinary cure-all indefinitely. In fact, Jordan was surprised she hadn't brought more of her signature dish with her today on her visit to his apartment.

"Giordano, don't be fresh. Your father is okay with his health. The show, not so good."

Jordan relaxed a little at news of his father. Serg Serenghetti's health had been a cause for concern for his family ever since his stroke a few years ago. For his mother's benefit, however, Jordan teased, "Next you'll be telling me that you're vlogging to build up your audience."

"No, *mia assistente* on the show already does it for me."

"And a star is born." He was surprised his mother even knew what vlogging was, but he supposed he shouldn't be astonished that a cooking show would have already been posting videos online.

"Hmm. Tell that to your father."

Jordan crinkled his eyes. "What does that mean? You just said Dad was fine."

"Yes, with his health."

"Wait, don't tell me… He's having a hard time with the fact that you're the breadwinner now?"

"You know we don't need the money."

"So what is it?" Jordan kept the smile on his face.

For once his mother looked hesitant. "I think—"

"Your star is outshining his?"

Camilla nodded. "He suggested a regular segment about wine on my show. Starring him."

Jordan bit back a laugh. "Delusions of grandeur."

"He built Serenghetti Construction," his mother pointed out.

"Right." Frankly, the wine-segment scheme seemed right in line with his father's outsize personality. "Rope him in, Mom, before he can get away and strike a deal with bigger fish. Cole can get you a lawyer. Tie him up with an exclusive arrangement." He was joking—sort of.

Camilla looked heavenward as if asking for divine intervention. "We already have a long deal. We're married."

Jordan shifted on the sofa, masking a grin.

When his mother's gaze came back to him, she swept him with a sudden, appraising look. "You seem better. More robust. Sera is doing therapy for you."

It was a statement, not a question. His mother was more in the know than he'd realized.

"Yes, what a coincidence," he said cautiously as he straightened, slowly and deliberately.

"Such a lovely woman."

Here we go. But he refused to rise to the bait. "Yup, Cole inherited a great set of in-laws."

"She could have provided rehabilitation for your father."

"Too late. Besides, Dad's stroke happened before Marisa reconnected with Cole." Grimacing, he started to rise, and as he expected, his mother transitioned from hovering in front of him to moving forward, filled with concern.

"Careful, don't hurt yourself. You still need to finish healing."

He waited while she placed a helping hand under his elbow before he stood fully. "Thanks, Mom."

Rick might be the Hollywood stuntman and his new sister-in-law Chiara an actress, but it didn't mean he couldn't call upon his own acting powers when necessary—like diverting his mother from a topic full of pitfalls.

Stepping back, his mother said, "Come and eat."

Mission accomplished.

Why was she here tonight? Her days moonlighting at the Puck & Shoot were supposed to have ended long ago when she'd become a physical therapist. But she was still being roped into helping out from time to time when the bar was short-staffed. She just couldn't say no to the extra cash.

Balancing a tray of beers, she kept sight of Jordan out of the corner of her eye.

Angus, the bar's owner, had called in desperation because they were down two waitresses, and it was going to be a busy Saturday night. The Puck & Shoot was the type of place where the saltshaker was either nearly empty or ready to shower your fries in an unexpected deluge. Still, the regulars loved it.

The part-time gig had helped pay for her education, but at some point, the tables had flipped so that the job was what was holding her back from starting her new life—one which she'd thought involved *not* seeing certain regulars. But she felt she owed Angus.

Jordan sat at the bar, as usual, and held court with a couple of Razors teammates who happened to be around even though hockey season had ended. Sera recognized Marc Bellitti and Vince Tedeschi.

Since Jordan had a habit of not taking a table, she'd almost never had to serve him. It had been years since their brief encounter during spring break in college, and when she'd first started working at the Puck & Shoot, it had become clear that Jordan hadn't recognized or remembered her. She'd been angry and annoyed and then somewhat relieved—especially after Neil had confirmed her opinion about certain types of men. They were players who moved from one woman on to the next, juggling them like so many balls in the air.

Now that Jordan knew who she was, though—Marisa's cousin and his new therapist—even the little bit of distance afforded by his customary seat at the bar seemed woefully small. As she served the beers to a table of patrons, she was aware of Jordan filling the room with his presence. He had that high-wattage magnetism that celebrities possessed. With his dark green gaze, square jaw and six-foot-plus muscled frame, he could make a woman feel as if she were the only one in the room. *Damn it.*

And Sera knew she wasn't imagining things. More than once, she caught his gaze following her back and forth across the crowded bar. It made her aware of her snug-fitting T-shirt and short skirt only partially hidden by an apron. Even though she wasn't dressed up or showing much skin, she wasn't in the shapeless light blue scrubs she wore at Astra Therapeutics, either. And her hair caught back in a ponytail for convenience just meant that she couldn't hide her expression from Jordan.

Already she was regretting her decision to stay on as Jordan's therapist—news that she'd broken to Marisa in a brief text. Only sheer strength of nerves had gotten her through a total of four therapy sessions with Jordan so far—and counting. In the past two weeks, he'd shed his crutches—though he still wasn't close to being completely recovered, of course. In therapy, he'd done the exercises that she'd shown him, including doing hamstring stretches, using a stationary bike and walking on a treadmill. They'd worked on gaining balance, extension and strength in his knee—with a minimum of quips thrown in.

She admired his powers of recuperation. She ought to be pleased. And yet…her only defense was that she was in charge during their sessions. He was all taut, lean muscle—in his prime and in great shape.

After making sure that everyone at her table was satisfied with their order, she wound her way back across the bar with her now-empty tray. She again tried to shake off the prickly sensation of being watched in a sensual fashion. Jordan had done it in the past, before he'd known who she was, but now it was more pronounced—blatant, even. It should have been the opposite since they were in-laws. He *knew* she couldn't be just a casual hookup, because they'd see each other again. Didn't the guy ever obey a DANGER sign?

She frowned. She ought to remind him about what had happened during spring break eight years ago. She'd been tempted to on several occasions, but her pride had stopped her. The last thing she wanted to do was tell Jordan that she'd been one in a long line of forgettable women.

From the periphery of her vision, she noticed a young

brunette sidle up to Jordan and strike up a conversation. After a moment, Jordan smiled and slid into flirtatious mode. *Naturally.*

Sera belatedly recognized the other woman as Danica Carr, an occasional patron. Not too long ago, she'd been approached by Danica with questions about getting into a physical-therapy program. Angus had told Danica that Sera had worked her way through school by waitressing.

Sera determinedly ignored Jordan and his new friend and kept busy as the bar got more crowded. The distraction of work was a relief, but almost an hour later, she had the beginnings of a low-grade headache. It was a lot of effort pretending Jordan didn't exist. And he was *still* talking to Danica.

As she paused at the corner of the bar at the end of her shift, Sera felt her temper spike, or at least lick the edges of her conscious. She untied her apron and stuffed it behind the counter. Once upon a time, she'd been Danica. Young, trusting and on the cusp of making a significant career choice.

These days, she didn't even go on dating apps. All that swiping left at the end of a long day was exhausting. If she couldn't trust her instincts about a guy even after months of dating, how could she put her faith in a mere photo on her phone?

Jordan was probably a dating-app star. The thought popped into her head, and she could feel her mouth stretch into a sour line. Whether Danica knew it or not, Jordan was a lion playing with a kitty, and Sera suddenly knew it was up to her to be the lion tamer. She couldn't stand by and do nothing while another naive young woman got taken in by Jordan Serenghetti.

Sera watched as Danica walked away and rejoined her party at their table. Straightening away from the bar, Sera moved toward Jordan, and at the last moment, he turned his head and noticed her—almost as if he'd known all along exactly where she was.

He was dressed in jeans and a crewneck T-shirt that showed off his biceps—how did he manage to be a walking billboard even injured? His gaze flicked over her, quick but boldly assessing, missing nothing from her breasts to her hips. Still, she refused to be unnerved or to succumb, where most mortal women would be tongue-tied and giggly.

When she stopped in front of him, Jordan remained silent, watchful, his expression for once indecipherable. Fortunately, Marc Bellitti and Vince Tedeschi were caught up in their own conversations at the bar and seemed too distracted to notice.

"Danica is a naive kid," she said without preamble. "Move on. She's not in your league."

Jordan smiled. "You know my league?"

Serafina pressed her lips together. Jordan Serenghetti really was beyond redemption—not that she was in the savior business. "I don't do bad boys. My mother taught me right."

Jordan's expression bloomed into a grin that shot straight through her. "Straitlaced. You need to loosen up."

Ha! Easy for him to say. He was the guy who was nothing but loose…and went over like smooth cocoa butter with most women.

Though not with me, she reminded herself. *Not anymore.* "And for the record, you're my patient. It's all business between us."

He glanced around him. "We're in a bar, not at Astra."

"But I'm still working."

He rubbed his chin and then teased, "You're not a woman who's bowled over by my charm?"

"Of course not. Far too levelheaded." *These days.* It was hard to explain how she'd fallen prey to Neil not so long ago, but maybe she'd been overdue for a lightning strike… Then again, the more she thought about it, the more she wondered whether she'd fallen for Neil precisely because he'd been smooth and worldly and sophisticated. Maybe she'd been determined to prove that she could play in the big leagues and wasn't helpless little Sera who needed protecting.

"And yet, I sense fire and passion in you," Jordan murmured.

"That's because I put you in the hot seat, Serenghetti. I see right through your game."

He made a show of glancing around him. "You've stolen the Razors' playbook?"

Sera placed her hands on her hips. It wouldn't be good if Angus noticed her in an argument with a customer—particularly a famous hometown favorite—but fortunately the bar was packed. "You know what I mean. I know your type, and I can read your plays off the ice."

"Jealous of Danica?"

"Please."

He swept her a look that she felt everywhere. "You shouldn't be, you know. At the moment, prickly waitresses seem to be my type." He regarded her thoughtfully. "Particularly those that might have had a prior bad experience."

Sera sucked in a breath and clamped her lips together. He didn't know the half of it. "I'm not naive, if that's what you're suggesting."

"I didn't claim you were. But you are…wary."

Yup. Once bitten, twice shy.

Jordan searched her expression and then relaxed his. "Danica isn't my type, but I make it a policy to be nice to fans."

As if on cue, Danica suddenly reappeared. "Jordan, I'm leaving—" she looked eager as a puppy "—and I was wondering, do you need a lift home?"

Jordan gave a killer smile that made Sera want to reach for a pair of sunglasses. "I'm good."

"Oh." Disappointment was etched on Danica's face. "I thought with you being injured and all…"

"I'm off crutches and can drive." Jordan waved his hand at Sera, and the other woman noticed her for the first time. "It's what Sera and I were discussing."

Sera tossed him a speaking look. *Oh, really?*

Danica pushed her dark straight hair off her shoulder. "Hi, Serafina."

"How are those physical-therapy program applications coming along?" Sera asked, dropping her hands from her hips.

Danica's face fell. "I still need a prerequisite or two. I'm never going to pass Chemistry 102."

"Sure, you will. With lots of studying. Then you can spend your days bending players—" she gestured at Jordan "—into shape."

Jordan looked amused. "I need to be straightened out apparently."

"More like set straight," Sera muttered, her gaze clashing with his.

"Oh." Danica looked between them. "Sorry, I didn't know."

Sera blinked. "Know what?"

A small frown appeared on the other woman's brow. "Um…"

Jordan got off the stool, and in the next moment, Sera felt his arm slide around her shoulders.

Danica took a step back and then another. "Well, I think I'll be going." Turning back in the direction where her friends were still waiting, she added quickly, "Nice talking to you."

Sera twisted toward Jordan. *What had just happened?* "You let her think—"

"Yeah, but you gave me the opening."

Sera pressed her lips together.

"Thanks for allowing me to let her down easy."

"I didn't—"

Jordan slanted his head. "You warned her off me. Goal accomplished."

"Not like that!" She didn't want Danica to think that she and Jordan were… *Oh, no…no, no, no. Never. No.*

Jordan leaned in, his face all innocent. "Like what?"

She spluttered. "You know what."

He lowered his gaze to her mouth. "It's what you said."

She bit back a gasp. "You're blaming me?"

He gave a slow, sexy grin. "Thanking you. Let me know when you're ready to…explore what's between us."

Sera had never been in a more frustrating conversation in her life. "Nothing more ego-stroking than the idea of two women competing for your attention, huh?"

"If you say so."

Suddenly, she'd had enough. Enough of a guy who could juggle women with dexterity—even injured.

"You don't remember," she snapped.

"Remember what?"

"Spring break in Florida eight years ago."

Jordan's lips curved. "Am I supposed to?"

"It depends," Sera said sarcastically. "Do you keep a running tally of the women you dally with, or do they just run together in one seamless and nameless highlight video in your mind?"

Jordan tilted his head, looking more intent. *"Dally with?"*

She gestured with her hands. "Flirt with. Come on to… Kiss."

"I'm supposed to remember every woman I ever flirted with?"

"Granted, it must be a long list. How about kissed?"

"Including the fans who've thrown their arms around me?"

She drew her brows together. "Including the ones you've

chatted up on spring break and engaged in some lip-to-lip action with after a couple of beers."

Jordan regarded her thoughtfully. "Are you saying we've kissed…and I don't remember it?"

Sera smacked her forehead. "Give the man a prize for a light-bulb moment."

Jordan grinned. "It must have been some kiss."

"You don't remember it!"

"But you do."

Sera felt herself heat. "Only because you've become famous."

He frowned. "I would have remembered an unusual name like yours."

"I didn't give you my name, and anyway, you probably would have thought I meant *S-A-R-A-H*." It was a common mistake that she was used to.

"So you like to operate anonymously?" he said, enjoying himself.

"I'd just turned twenty-one." *I was young and stupid.*

Jordan rubbed his chin. "Let's see, eight years ago… college break. Destin, Florida?"

"Right," she responded tightly. "Hundreds of students clogging the beach. Beer flowing. Dancing. You angled in…"

They'd locked gazes while she'd danced, and the sexual attraction had sizzled. In swim trunks and with all his smooth, tanned muscles, he'd been an Adonis. And she'd never felt sexier than when he'd looked her over in her aqua bikini, appreciation stamped on his face, and had started dancing with her.

She'd known he wanted to kiss her and had met him halfway when he'd bent, searching her eyes, waiting for her cue. Once Jordan had started kissing her, however, they'd been egged on by the crowd. In minutes, they'd been plastered together, arms around each other, making out to an audience.

"Why didn't you say anything when we met again at Marisa's fund-raiser a couple of years ago?"

"Please, I know your type."

"Of course."

She tossed her head, ponytail swinging. "It wasn't important, except for the fact that spring break experience backed up my impression of your reputation since then."

"Naturally."

Her brows drew together again. "Are you humoring me?"

"I'm still processing your bombshell. Our lips have touched."

"Another reason I didn't mention it. We're in-laws. It would make things awkward."

"Or interesting. I've thought that family gatherings could use some spicing up." His lips quirked. "So I knew you in your wilder, younger days, Perini?"

Her naive days—when she was like Danica.

"What went wrong?"

She folded her arms.

"So let me get this straight. Your grudge against me is that I don't remember kissing you?"

"When it was over, you turned away and laughed for the benefit of your friends." As if nothing had happened. As if she didn't matter. Her heart had plummeted. She'd crashed to earth—sort of embarrassed and humiliated. "And then you merged into the crowd."

Her ego had taken a hit back then—only to be run over by Neil a few years later. She had to face it—she sucked at dealing with men.

"Hey—"

"My job here is done," she said, cutting him off and checking her watch.

This time, she was the one to walk away—fading quickly into the crowd. But all the while, she was aware of Jordan's gaze on her back…

Five

Sera gritted her teeth as she made her way to her car in the dark parking lot. It was an older-model domestic sedan that she'd bought used after dealing with a slippery salesman. Slick men—the world was full of them!

She should never have done Angus a favor by coming in to waitress. Her blood still thrummed through her veins from clashing with Jordan Serenghetti. Or rather, she'd clashed while he'd looked underwhelmed—blowing her off as if he were amused by the whole scenario. Typical.

She fumed. She had a bad experience that she'd been nursing as a secret for *years*. And when her big moment had finally arrived and she'd let loose, Jordan's response had been mild. *What was the big deal?*

It all reminded her of…oh, yeah, her confrontation with Neil about his cheating. Or rather his using her, unwittingly, as the other woman in an affair. Even confronted with the incontrovertible truth, he'd been full of justifications and excuses. *You're special. I meant to tell you.* And her favorite: *It's not what you think.*

Serafina still burned every time she remembered how she'd been taken in by Neil's lies. She'd told Marisa and Dante the cursory details. In fact, she probably shouldn't have divulged anything at all and simply said the relationship had ended. In the aftermath of that debacle, she hadn't wanted anyone to think she still needed protecting and couldn't be trusted to exercise good judgment.

She'd told herself that any woman could have been duped by Neil. He oozed charisma and charm. Just like Jordan Serenghetti.

Oh, Neil had lacked fame, but notoriety would have interfered with his twisted schemes anyway. The press would have made it much harder for him to hide the fact that he had a wife and kid tucked away in Boston. *The rat.*

Do you really know a person if you see only one side of him? Sera had had plenty of time to contemplate that question since breaking up with Neil.

She got behind the wheel and pulled out of the lot for the drive home. She lived in a two-bedroom condo on the opposite side of town that she'd inherited from Marisa. When her cousin had gotten married and moved out, Sera had jumped at the chance to buy the apartment for a very reasonable price. Fortunately, because traffic was light and she knew the route well, she could drive practically on autopilot.

As she started on the main road, Sera replayed the evening. The only reason she'd agreed to help Angus was that she had a whole four consecutive days off from her physical-therapy position. What was one Saturday night helping out a friend and former boss? Plus, she was paying off student loans, so she could use the extra wages and tips from a night moonlighting as a waitress, an aproned superhero saving innocent young women who were easy prey for—

Sera snorted. She should have known it wouldn't be a simple favor. *Of course Jordan would be there.* Saying things she hadn't expected him to say. Looking almost… normal…relatable. She couldn't afford mixed feelings where he was concerned. *Danica isn't my type.* It made her wonder who was—and that was the problem.

Sera flexed her fingers on the steering wheel. The last thing she needed was to be mooning over Jordan Serenghetti. She didn't need to be wondering—mulling—what was on his mind.

Suddenly, she spotted a flurry of movement from the corner of her eye. In an instant, a bear appeared directly in front of her car. Sera sucked in a breath and then jerked hard on the steering wheel to avoid hitting it.

Then everything happened in a blur. Sera bounced around in her seat as the car went off the road in the darkness. She heard and felt tree branches hit the windshield and the car doors. Fear took over, and she hit the brakes hard.

An eternity later—or maybe it was just a couple of seconds—the car jerked to a stop, and the engine cut out.

Sera sat frozen with shock. *What…?* It had all happened *so fast…*

She threw the emergency break and then blinked at the debris marring her front window. Taking a shaky breath, she leaned her head against the steering wheel. Tremors coursed up her arms from her grip on the wheel.

Great, just great.

At least she hadn't hit the bear.

Could this night get any worse? She wanted to cry but instead gave herself a scolding. After several moments, still shaken, she raised her head and stared into the darkness. It wasn't safe to be a lone woman stranded by the side of the road at night. On top of it, she didn't know where that bear was, but with any luck, she'd managed to frighten him off with their near miss.

Of course, she could use her cell phone to call for help. Dante or another relative would come if she called. Still, she hated being poor, helpless Sera again in the eyes of her family—which was how they would see it.

Suddenly, headlights appeared in her rearview mirror. Sera shook off the touch of fear. It was just someone driving by. Someone who would most likely simply keep on going—because she didn't even have her hazard lights on. Statistically speaking, it was unlikely to be an ax murderer.

But the car slowed down as it passed. Then, a few yards down the road, the driver pulled over.

When the person behind the wheel got out, she immediately recognized Jordan Serenghetti even with only the dim illumination of his flashlight.

Sera suppressed a groan. Not an ax murderer, but someone even more improbable. Jordan. Though she supposed she shouldn't be surprised, since he'd been at the Puck & Shoot, too, and the bar was minutes away.

Unsteadily, she got out of the car, determined to put on a brave front. His appearance just added to her turbulent emotions.

Jordan's face was pulled into an uncharacteristic frown as he approached, looking from her to her car and back again. *He even looked attractive with a scowl.*

"Are you all right?" he asked, for once not displaying his trademark devil-may-care expression.

"Isn't that my line?" How many times had she asked him the same thing during a physical-therapy session? She raised her chin, but with horror, she realized there had been a slight tremor in her voice. *Not all right. Damn it.* She cleared her throat.

He came close, and she'd never seen him appear more serious.

"What are you doing?"

"Checking you for obvious signs of injury. Relax. I'll

take it as a good sign that you were able to get out of the car under your own power."

His gaze searched hers in the dim light. "Despite what you think of me, I like to give a hand when I see someone in trouble."

She blinked. "Oh."

"Anything hurt?"

"No." And then she blurted, "What are you doing here?"

Jordan managed to look aggrieved—another new expression for him. "I decided to leave right after you did."

"The fun was gone?" Impossibly, she was challenging him, even though she'd just been in an accident—maybe *because* she'd just been in an accident. She didn't like feeling vulnerable.

"You could say that, but I guess it was good timing—" he gave her a significant look "—because I happened by right after your accident."

"I would have been perfectly fine without your help." No way was Jordan Serenghetti her knight in shining armor.

"Well, judging by your mouth, you're not hurt. And I figure you're going to deny being shaken up. So what happened?"

It irked that he could tell she was rattled. "I swerved to avoid a bear in the road." She grimaced and scanned the woods around them. "In fact, I hope it's not hanging around."

"It's unlikely to view you as a threat." His lips quirked. "I, on the other hand..."

She flushed. Considering she'd just tried to stage a takedown of his womanizing ways back at the bar, she could hardly argue. Next, she expected a critique of her driving skills, but surprisingly it didn't come.

Instead, Jordan examined her car, training his flashlight on the front.

She bit back a gasp as the badly dented front fender was

illuminated. And the headlight had been taken out. Her car was a piece of junk, but now she'd have to add automotive repair costs to her budget.

Jordan tucked the flashlight under his arm and pulled out his cell phone.

"What do you think you're doing?"

"Being practical," he responded mildly, walking a few steps away. "I'm getting highway patrol out here."

"You're calling the police?" she said.

His gaze met hers. "So you don't have to. Your insurance may require a police report."

Sera wrapped her arms around herself. The night was warm, but she suddenly felt chilled. She could fume at his take-charge attitude—or grudgingly accept his help, despite what had just happened between them at the Puck & Shoot.

Within minutes, as Jordan continued his inspection of her car, the police showed up. Sera could only conclude there must have been a highway-patrol car in the vicinity.

When the patrolman got out of his car and approached, he paused a moment, and then obviously recognizing Jordan, his expression relaxed. "Hey, you're Jordan Serenghetti."

"Yup."

"Got into a little fender bender tonight?"

"Not me, her."

Sera watched as the police officer's gaze came to rest on her. She gave a jaunty little wave that belied her emotions. So this was what it felt like to play second fiddle to Jordan's star power.

"What happened?" the officer asked, his gaze now on her.

"I swerved to avoid a bear that appeared on the road." She gestured at her car. "And, well, you can figure out the rest."

The officer rubbed the back of his neck. "Uh-huh."

"She may need paperwork for insurance purposes," Jordan put in.

"Right."

The police officer put up flares while Jordan summoned a tow truck.

When the officer got back to her, she had her driver's license and insurance information ready as another patrol car pulled up.

Again the officer—another middle-aged blond guy— did a double take when he saw Jordan.

The first officer patted his colleague on the shoulder as he went by to his car to fill out the necessary paperwork, and Jordan chatted casually with the new arrival, who obviously couldn't believe his luck at running into a sports celebrity during his shift.

Sera was miserable. The night had gone from bad to worse. She should be slipping between bedcovers right now in soft, worn pajamas. Instead, she was in the middle of a Jordan Serenghetti fan moment.

When the tow truck arrived, the driver slowed his steps as he approached Jordan, and Sera resisted the urge to roll her eyes.

"You're—"

"Jordan Serenghetti," Sera supplied. "Yes, we know."

Jordan's lips twitched. "Don't mind her, she's testy." He shrugged. "You know, accident and all."

The tow truck driver's gaze skimmed over both of them. "Well, at least no one was hurt."

Yet. Yes, she was irritable. Sera waved her hand at Jordan. "He is."

The driver and the police officer still standing nearby both raised their brows.

"Knee surgery," Sera supplied laconically. "I'm sure you two gentlemen have heard about it in the sports news."

Before either man could say anything, Jordan added, "Yeah, and my physical therapist is a badass. I go to bed aching."

The men chuckled, and Sera narrowed her eyes. What had she been thinking about no one being hurt *yet*?

Unfortunately for her, it took another half hour for her car to be towed and the police to be done.

As both officers headed to their cars after the tow truck departed, Jordan turned to her. "I'll drive you."

"Please. The last thing the two of us need is to be in the same moving vehicle together." The police had clearly thought she had a ride with Jordan, though—one they no doubt would have loved to take themselves as his fans. Sera gritted her teeth. "I can use the ride-hailing app on my phone to get a car to pick me up. My apartment is on the other side of town."

"Yeah, you moved into Marisa's old place," Jordan said, ignoring the first part of her reply.

"So you know just how far it is." Sera supposed she shouldn't be surprised that he knew where she lived.

He tossed her a sidelong look. "Great, my place is closer. Let's go."

Wait—what? Had he not heard what she'd said? She was not going to Jordan's place.

As if reading her thoughts, he added, "You're shaken up, and I'm not leaving you alone to be picked up in the dark by a driver you don't even know."

"As opposed to you? Because you're the safer bet? And anyway, chivalry is dead."

"So angelic and yet so cynical," Jordan murmured.

"With good reason!"

"I'll get you a car from my place once I'm convinced you're all right."

It was hard to be mad at someone when you owed them a favor.

And the last person she wanted to be indebted to for help was Jordan Serenghetti.

Somehow, she was going to live down tonight's debacle. Somehow, she was going to get through weeks of physical therapy with Jordan. Her mind ping-ponged, hit by a gamut of emotions as she stepped into Jordan's apartment.

His place had the ambience of an athlete...a jock...a celebrity...a sports star living there. But shockingly, Sera couldn't sniff *playboy* in the air as she paused next to the elevator that had just deposited them in his penthouse. Everything was modern, pristine and orderly. White walls, chocolate upholstery and stainless-steel appliances. It was far from the messy fraternity house existence that she'd been expecting.

And then, because Jordan was watching her as they stood just inside his apartment, she said, "So this is how the other half lives."

"It's not that fancy."

Her gaze drifted toward the back of his apartment. "Your Viking range alone must have cost thousands of dollars. And I'm guessing you don't even really cook."

"No, but my mother does. So she has expectations."

The apartment was dim and quiet...and Jordan was standing too close. So much so that she picked up on the scent that she had started to identify as uniquely his.

As a result of their physical-therapy sessions, she was well-acquainted with the reasons why *some* women found him attractive. He was all toned and sculpted muscle—with a lean, hard jaw and wicked glint in his green eyes. Even injured, he exuded a powerful magnetism. This close, she had to lift her head to make eye contact, making her even more aware of just how *male* he was. Now that he was out of his milieu—a sports bar—she could momentarily forget why she didn't like him. *Almost.*

They stared at each other in the dim light.

The corner of his mouth lifted. "Lost for words?"

"I've spent them all."

"Yeah, I know."

All that remained unsaid hung between them.

"Come on in," he said.

"I thought I was getting a car."

"In a sec." He regarded her thoughtfully. "But first you look like you could use a shoulder to lean on."

"Not yours." To her horror, however, her voice wasn't as strong and steady as she would have liked. The hour was late, she was tired and she'd had one roller coaster of a day. Suddenly, it was all catching up to her and was just too much. Right now, she wanted to be in fluffy socks and battered sweats and holding a cup of herbal tea. Not dealing with the complexities of her relationship with Jordan. No, wait—they didn't have a *relationship*.

Jordan searched her face with an annoyingly penetrating gaze. "Are you okay?"

"Fine." Could that high-pitched voice possibly be hers? But fortunately, he hadn't brought up their conversation at the Puck & Shoot.

"Sera."

She felt as if she were drowning.

"Aw, hell," Jordan said.

In the next instant, he'd folded her into his arms, smoothing his hands down her back as he tucked her head under his chin.

She stiffened. "You're the last person—"

"I know."

"I don't even like you. You are irritating and rude and—"

"—ridiculous?"

"This is a delayed reaction," she sniffed, relaxing into his embrace.

"Understandable."

"If you breathe a word about this to anyone, Serenghetti…"

"Not likely. Your reputation is safe with me."

"Great."

She was more shaken up by her accident than she'd thought. More shaken up by *everything*.

He stroked his hand up and down her back, lulling her. She leaned into him. They stayed that way as time ticked by for she couldn't say how long.

It was quiet, and the lights of Welsdale twinkled outside.

Slowly, though, as she regained steadiness, comfort gave way to something else. She became aware of subtle changes. Jordan's breathing deepened, and hers grew shallower and more rapid.

He shifted, dipping his head, and his lips grazed her temple.

She lifted her head and met his gaze. "So these are the famous Jordan Serenghetti moves these days? A hug?"

Their faces were inches apart, and she remained pressed against him—his long, lean form imprinting her, making her *feel*.

"How am I doing?"

She lifted her shoulders. "Do you usually look for a rating?"

"You still have a smart mouth, Perini," he muttered.

"Weaponized? And you're going to disarm me, I bet," she replied tartly.

He bent toward her and muttered, "Worth risking serious injury for."

"I dare you." She tossed out the words carelessly, but she was all taut awareness because she'd never seen Jordan this focused and intent.

"You know that kiss…"

Her brows drew together. "What about it?"

"Since I don't remember it, I'm curious."

She sucked in a breath and then warned, "Since there's no audience to cheer you on this time, why bother?"

He pressed the pad of his thumb against her bottom lip. "Such a loaded question. Let's find out."

And just like that, he kissed her.

She tried for nonchalance. Still, his mouth was lazy and sensual, coaxing hers into a slow dance.

Eventually, the kiss took on a life of its own. In fact, Sera wasn't sure what possessed her. The need to tangle with a player again—and this time be the one who came out ahead? Perhaps a desire to prove that she was older and wiser and not so green—and therefore wouldn't be hurt? She couldn't say—and maybe didn't want to examine the issue too closely.

Jordan cupped the sides of her face, his fingers tunneling into her hair, and held her steady. His mouth was warm, searching...confident.

He swept his tongue around hers, and she met him, every part of her responding. She gripped his shirt, pulling him in, and he made a low sound in his throat.

She'd wondered over the years whether her memory of their kiss had been dulled by time. Had it really been that good? Not that she'd been looking for a repeat lately, she told herself. It had just been idle curiosity sparked by seeing Jordan again. And since he'd been so annoying and able to bring out her snarky best, she'd assumed her recollection was off.

Wrong, so wrong.

Every part of her came to life, sensitized to his touch, his scent, his taste. And there was no lazy humor to Jordan now. Instead, everything about him said he wanted to strip off her waitress clothes so they could both find bliss...

When the kiss broke off, he trailed his lips across her jaw, and she tilted her head so that he could continue the path down the side of her neck. His hand came up to cup her breast, and she strained against him, wanting more, a sound of pleasure escaping her lips.

He brought his mouth to hers again, and his leg wedged between her thighs. She skimmed her hands along his back, feeling the ripped muscles move under her caress.

Jordan's scent enveloped her—the one she'd started to know so well and had fought against. But his casual devil-may-care persona was stripped away, and all he seemed to care about was getting closer to her, exploring the attraction that she'd often dismissed as just smooth moves on his part.

He tugged her T-shirt from the waistband of her skirt as their kiss took on a new urgency. Pushing aside her bra, he found her breast with his hand and palmed it tenderly.

She moved against him, feeling the friction of his jeans straining to hold back his arousal, and he broke off the kiss on a curse.

Lifting her shirt, he looked down as he stroked her breast, his chest rising and falling with awareness.

She glanced down, too, and watched him caress her, her excitement growing.

"So beautiful," he muttered. "Perfect."

He rested his forehead against hers—and their breath mingled, short and deep and fast. "Let me touch you."

Her brain foggy with desire, she didn't understand for a moment, until she felt his hand slide under her skirt. Pushing aside her panties, he began gently exploring her.

Sera's head fell back, her eyes closing.

"So good," Jordan murmured in a voice she didn't recognize. "Ah, Angel, let me in."

She let him stroke her, building the heat inside her. She shifted to give him better access, and he built a rhythm that she enjoyed…until he pressed his thumb against her and she splintered, her world fracturing, filling with their labored breaths and the scent of Jordan all around her.

They stood that way for moments, and Sera slowly came down to earth, her breath slowing.

What was she doing?

With a remaining bit of sanity, she pulled back, and he loosened his hold. Then she laid her hand on his chest as if to underscore the distance she needed. She felt the strong, steady beat of his heart, reminding her of the sexual thrum between them.

He didn't move. His jaw firm, he seemed carved out of stone, his face stamped with unfulfilled sexual desire in the dim illumination.

She felt like a heel—an uncomfortable and new feeling where Jordan was considered. Still, they couldn't, they shouldn't. "This is so wrong. We—"

"Angel—"

"We shouldn't have done that."

And then she ran. Grabbing the purse that she'd come in with, she turned and stabbed the button for the elevator.

"Sera—"

She nearly gasped with relief when the door slid right open and Jordan made no move to stop her.

As the elevator door closed, she called hurriedly over her shoulder, "I'll summon a cab downstairs with my phone."

Six

Jordan came awake. The bedsheets were a tangled mess around him because he'd had a restless night.

Sera. The one-word answer for why he'd been edgy.

He'd dreamed about her after she'd left in a hurry. At least in sleep, he'd gotten a chance to indulge many of his fantasies from the past couple months. He'd guided her and learned her pleasure points with his hands and mouth. He'd whispered all the indecent things he wanted to do with her, and she hadn't blinked. But unfortunately, none of it had been real. In real life, Sera had hurried out of his apartment.

He was still wrapping his mind around all the revelations from last night. Their kiss had been fantastic enough to fuel fantasies all night long. He'd had a hunch they'd be combustible together, and he'd been proven right. More than right. Things had escalated, and if Sera hadn't broken things off, he had his doubts they would have bothered making it from the entry to his bed. She'd been soft and curvy and responsive, just like he'd imagined. *Better than he'd imagined.* She had the softest skin he'd ever caressed.

Sera was soft despite her seemingly hard shell. Who knew?

And how the hell could he have forgotten someone as hot and memorable as Serafina Perini? He racked his brain for memories from eight years ago. Could he really have been as much of a jerk as she'd made him out to be?

Sera had been pissed off at being so easily consigned to oblivion. No question about it.

The only answer was that he'd been young and stupid and immature. Flush with the first victories of a burgeoning hockey career that had put his sickly childhood behind him, and intent on enjoying his new status and image as a chick magnet and sports stud.

Yup. That explanation would go over well with Sera.

She'd have to deal with him, though, at their next therapy session—and to make matters more complicated, she was now driving his car. After Sera had departed in a rush last night, he'd called downstairs and told Donnie at the security desk to offer her the second set of keys to his sedan. She'd need a car until her beaten-up wreck got fixed, and Jordan would be fine driving his pickup in the meantime. Fortunately, Donnie had later reported that Sera had reluctantly taken up the offer.

Jordan smiled over the irony as he stared at the ceiling. His car had been the fastest and easiest way for her to escape from him.

After a moment, he tossed the covers off and headed to the shower. He needed to clear his head and brainstorm a way out of this bind. *What the hell was he supposed to say to her at their next physical therapy session?*

And then there was the other problem he'd been meaning to get to ever since his last conversation with his mother. He bit back a grimace and figured he was overdue for trying to sort out a different Serenghetti family tangle. Plus, it would take his mind off Sera.

An hour later, after downing a quick breakfast, he headed to his parents' house on the outskirts of Welsdale.

He found his father in an armchair, remote in hand, in the large living room that ran most of the width of the back of the house.

"Hi, Dad. Where's Mom?"

Serg Serenghetti looked up grumpily. "At work. The cleaning service just left."

"Yeah, I know. Conveniently, they let me in as they headed out." Jordan smiled gamely. "So it's just us guys, then."

His father glanced at him from under bushy brows. Then he clicked the remote to change the channel from golf to a commercial.

"What are you going to watch?"

"One of those home-improvement shows your generation loves." He guffawed. "As if any of these TV performers really knows the biz."

"Right." Jordan settled onto the sofa next to his father's armchair.

Serg waved the remote. "If any of my children was interested, you'd be helping Serenghetti Construction with a television show."

"Try Rick. He's got the Hollywood ties these days." Jordan looked around. "Quiet here."

"If your mother was home, she'd just be fussing." Serg turned off the TV. "Now it's quiet."

Jordan shook his head bemusedly. His parents' marriage had lasted decades, producing four kids and now grandkids, while riding the ups and downs of Serenghetti Construction. His parents had met when his mother had been a front-desk clerk at a hotel in Tuscany, and Serg had been on his way to visit extended family north of Venice. So the whole feed-and-shelter hospitality biz was in his mother's blood, and the latest incarnation of that was her cooking show. Until recently, his father had handled the sheltering part with his construction business, while his mother was all about sustenance.

Except that had all gotten upended lately. "So what's got you down?"

"If you spent your days out of a job, sitting here watching TV, you'd be surly, too."

"Right."

Serg lowered his brows. "Come to think of it, that's not too far off from where you are."

Jordan shifted in his seat, because it hadn't occurred to him before now that he and his father might have something more in common these days than sharing a passing family resemblance. An extended convalescence had prevented them both from returning to their old lives. In his father's case, permanently. And in his... Chills ran up Jordan's arms.

He'd thought that his days being sick and bedridden were well past him. But being sidelined with his injury brought back the old feelings of helplessness.

His father was nearing seventy. Not young, but not really old, either. Jordan wondered where he'd be at that age. Certainly not playing hockey, but what would his second act be? At least, he had some plans for what to do with his earnings as long as his injury didn't get in the way.

"You need a second act," he said into the void.

Serg grumbled and shifted. "Your mother doesn't like to share the limelight."

Jordan smiled slightly. "Yeah, I heard. You'd like a segment on Mom's show."

"The audience loved me when I did a special guest spot suggesting wine pairings."

"You should revel in Mom's success," Jordan went on.

"But I get it. She's at the top of her game, and you're at a crossroads."

"Since when are you the family psychologist?"

Jordan chuckled. "Yeah, I know. It's a dirty job, but someone in this family has to do it, and I did well running interference for Cole and Marisa."

Serg lowered his chin and peered over at him. "Jordan, your sport is hockey, not football."

"Okay, fair enough. So…back to you and Mom."

"We're out of your league. Don't try to run interference."

"Right." The message was clear, but he had one of his own. "But maybe instead of wanting a piece of Mom's success, you should develop your own game."

Every once in a while, Sera thought it was a good idea to have Sunday dinner at her mother's house. Today was not one of those days.

The simple three-bedroom shingle house with a post-age-stamp lawn stood on a tidy side street in East Gannon. Its no-frills white appliances were a world away from the high-end stainless steel in Jordan's sleek, modern penthouse. Here, it was all open bookshelves displaying books, mementos and family photos—not unobtrusive panels concealing high-end electronics, as well as its owner's secrets.

And the contrasts didn't end there. Jordan's place was forward-looking, with very little evidence of the past, as far as she could tell. Her mother's place held a hint of nostalgia—now that the kids had grown and flown the coop—and sadness since Sera's father's death from a heart attack a few years ago. His passing had been the wake-up call that Sera had needed to get on with her life and go back to school for a physical-therapy degree.

At the dinner table, Sera twirled some spaghetti onto her fork. Her mother was an excellent cook, and tonight's chicken parmigiana and spaghetti with tomato sauce was no exception. Ever since her mother had been widowed, Sera and Dante had made it a point to visit regularly. They knew their mother appreciated the companionship.

"I heard you had a car accident." Her mother's brow was furrowed with worry.

Sera cleared her fork and started twirling it again because she'd accidentally put on too much spaghetti. Good thing she hadn't had a mouthful already. On the other hand, maybe she should have welcomed an excuse not to talk... "How did you find out?"

"Dante's friend Jeff happened to be at the auto shop earlier today. He overheard the employee there on the phone with you, taking down your personal information to fix your car." Her mother tossed her an arch look across the dining-room table. "There aren't many women running around with the name Serafina Perini."

For the umpteenth time, Sera rued having a unique name. And she sometimes forgot what a small town Welsdale could be. Still, she was lucky that the most popular local auto body shop had Sunday hours because she'd been able to call and get a status report about when she might get her car back. Unfortunately, the news hadn't been encouraging, and it looked like she was stuck driving Jordan's wheels for a while. Too bad every time she climbed into the car, she was unable to shake his scent.

She'd been surprised when the guy at the security desk in Jordan's building had offered her car keys on Jordan's instructions, but after hesitating a moment, she'd chosen the path of least resistance—one that would solve her immediate problems, whatever the longer-term consequences. She now owed Jordan a favor when she should have been mad at him—and then there was the little complication about what else had happened that evening at his place...

"I assume you got a rental car until yours is fixed," her mother observed, "and that's how you got here today."

"Yes, I have temporary wheels." Jordan Serenghetti's.

"Are you okay?" her mother asked.

She schooled her expression with the help of her reflection in the china closet's glass door. "Fine, Mom."

"Why didn't you tell me about your accident?"

"I just did." Her mother would be even more shocked if she knew how Sera had wound up in Jordan Serenghetti's arms in the aftermath of her fender bender.

"You know what I mean. The mothers are always the last to know." Rosana sighed. "I bet your cousin Marisa would have told your aunt right away."

Her mother knew how to play the guilt card... And if there was one thing that Sera had grown up hearing about ad nauseam, it was the close relationship that Aunt Donna had with her cousin Marisa. Never mind that Aunt Donna had raised her only child as a single mother, making her and Marisa a family of two, relying on each other. Rosana Perini looked up to her older sister, even as she took her sibling's life as a cautionary tale. Ever since Donna had been left pregnant and alone by a professional minor-league baseball player who'd died unexpectedly soon after, Rosana had worried about her. But she'd been thrilled when her older sister had finally found love again with Ted Casale.

"Do you want me to ask Dante to go down to the auto body shop?"

"No. I'm capable of handling my own car repairs."

"Do you need some money?"

Sera deployed a tight smile. "No, I can handle it, Mom."

The last thing Sera wanted was for her family to think they needed to come to her aid. She'd spent most of her twentysomething years trying to shed the image of poor Sera who needed rescuing and protecting.

"Thank goodness you got home okay." Her mother frowned again. "You should have called me."

If only her mother knew that she hadn't gone directly home but had been sidetracked at Jordan's place. A detour that had risked turning into an all-night change of direction, if she hadn't put the brakes on their intimate encounter. Then, to cover her bases, she volunteered, "I was lucky that Jordan Serenghetti happened to be driving by. I got a lift."

Not straight home. But her mother didn't need to know that. Sera had been offering up information on a strictly as-necessary basis to her family for years. But it wouldn't do if word somehow got back to her mother that Jordan had been at the scene of the accident and Sera hadn't mentioned it. Dodging suspicion—that was what she'd been doing ever since she'd been a rebellious teenager cutting the occasional high-school class to hang out with friends.

Rosana Perini shot her a disapproving look. "Another reason I worry about you living alone. Who'd know for hours if you didn't make it home?"

Exactly. Who'd know she'd almost spent last night at Jordan's place? She couldn't believe how quickly things had gotten hot and heavy. She'd been thinking all day about it, in fact. *Reliving the highlights.* He'd brought her to satisfaction right there in his foyer. Sera felt her face flame and hoped her mother didn't notice.

Jordan's power to charm and seduce was beyond her understanding. The realization had unnerved her and sent her hightailing it out of his apartment.

She'd already resolved to treat last night as an aberration never to be repeated. She'd had her guard down and had been running on emotion from an evening capped off by having her car banged up. *Yup, that was her story, and she was sticking to it.* She just needed to convince Jordan to treat last night as if it had never happened and swear him to silence about the whole comforting-embrace-leading-to-fringe-benefits thing.

"It was another story when you and Marisa were room-mates," Rosana Perini continued, jerking Sera back to the present, "but now you've got no one nearby."

Except for Jordan. Sera kept her tone light. "I bought Marisa's condo when she got married. I've still got the pro-tective family aura that she left behind."

Her mother heaved a sigh. "You were always sassy, un-like your brother."

"I know. Dante is an angel. I guess you just got the names wrong, Mom."

"Speaking of Dante, he has a new job."

"Yes, I know, he told me." How could she forget? Her brother's new employment was what had gotten her into her current fix. Her gig as Jordan's physical therapist meant she'd have to spend time again and again with the in-law she'd been intimate with.

The doorbell sounded, and her mother got up. "I won-der who that is."

Moments later, Sera heard voices, and then her brother followed her mother into the room.

"Dante, this is a wonderful surprise," her mother said. "We were just talking about you."

Dante filched a piece of bread from the table and bit into it.

Rosana's face was wreathed in smiles as she headed for the kitchen. "I'll set another plate and heat up some more food. I always make extra."

Dante winked at Sera and swallowed. "And today, your just-in-case habit paid off. Thanks, Mom."

As their mother disappeared, Sera regarded her brother. "You made her happy."

"Anything for Mom." Dante took a seat opposite her,

polishing off the last of his bread in the process. "I didn't know you were here. Your car wasn't out front."

"It's there," Sera mumbled. "I parked around the corner."

Dante snagged a piece of cheese from an appetizer plate. "Why would you do that?"

Sera sighed. This was why she was careful around her family. It was always lots of questions—with a subtext of questioning her judgment. And then, because she figured Dante would find out anyway, Sera said, "I got into a little fender bender last night, so I'm driving Jordan Serenghetti's car."

Dante stopped and swallowed. "Whoa, hold up. I'm still processing the cause and effect. How do you go from a little fender bender to driving the Razors' top gun's fancy wheels?" Her brother grinned. "That's some fast work, sis. I'm employed by the Razors organization, and I haven't even had a chance to grab a beer with Jordan yet."

"Hilarious, Dante." She cast a quick look at the kitchen to make sure their mother wasn't coming back. "Jordan drove by right after the accident."

"Just happened to drive by, huh?"

"Yes," she said, holding her brother's gaze but nevertheless lowering her voice. If she couldn't convince Dante there wasn't the scent of a juicy story here, she was doomed with everyone else. "After my car was towed, Jordan lent me his. It was generous of him."

Dante nodded. "Generous."

Sera tilted her head. "What's the matter with you? Have you turned into a parrot?"

Her brother coughed. "Just trying to understand the facts."

Sera smiled brightly. "Well, there you have it. End of story."

"I thought the goal here was to get Jordan Serenghetti

feeling indebted to the Perinis, not the other way around," her brother teased.

Tell me about it.

"By the way, how's it going with my favorite hockey player?"

"Who?" she joked.

Dante bit off a laugh. "Jordan Serenghetti, of course."

Sera debated how to answer. Obviously, *I nearly slept with him* was not the right choice. "He's visiting the clinic weekly and...coming along nicely."

"And you're still his physical therapist?" her brother asked gingerly.

Therapist, in-law, hookup—did the label really matter? "Yup."

Dante relaxed and sat back in his chair. "I knew I could count on you, Sera."

"I didn't say he'd be able to start the season. We're still weeks away from any medical clearance." She took a bite of her chicken parmigiana.

Dante nodded. "But you're helping me get off on the right foot at the office. I've dropped the information into key conversations that my sister is Jordan Serenghetti's physical therapist."

"Yup, you owe me one." Wouldn't Rosana Perini be surprised to know that Sera was helping Dante instead of the other way around? "Don't worry, I'll keep your dirty little secret from Mom. The halo will stay intact."

"You're priceless, sis."

"It's a big favor." Probably the biggest that Dante had ever asked of her, come to think of it. All her instincts had told her to dump Jordan as a client as soon as possible— he was too much for her to handle on every level, and she'd been miserable at keeping it professional—but she was sticking it out for her brother's sake.

"Oh, come on, Jordan Serenghetti isn't that bad. I'll bet

there are plenty of hockey fans in the ranks of physical therapists who'd love to have him as a client."

"I'm not one of them." She just planned to survive the coming couple of months or so at her job—somehow—and be done. Before anyone discovered *her* dirty little secret— which she'd make Jordan swear to take to the grave.

Seven

She could do this. Sera sucked in a breath as she prepared to face Jordan Serenghetti again for the first time since *that night*. It was already Wednesday afternoon and time for their next therapy session. Somehow, she had to do an impossible balancing act between remaining professional and having a frank conversation that addressed moving forward from Saturday's events.

If their families caught even a whiff of this… *situation*, that there was more to it than Jordan just lending her his car, it would be like a powder keg exploding. She'd never hear the end of it, never live it down. Everyone would look at her and Jordan and *know*.

She had to make the potential repercussions clear to Jordan—if he didn't understand them already. *And* she also had to put the genie back in the bottle regarding what happened eight years ago—all in the hour or so they had for their therapy session.

She rolled her eyes. *She could do this.* How hard could

it be? She was dealing with a love 'em and leave 'em type who tossed baggage overboard and bailed... He should have no trouble agreeing to keep things under wraps, right?

But yesterday's delivery from the florist, arranged by Jordan, had made her think she had her work cut out for her.

And unfortunately, she was still driving his car—inhaling his scent and touching his belongings. She told herself that was the reason she couldn't get him out of her mind. And she had to concede it had been a nice thing to do to lend her his ride—a *very expensive* luxury sedan tricked out with leather upholstery and all the latest gadgets that made her beat-up secondhand car look like a horse and buggy. Her own vehicle continued to be in the shop for repairs, and she'd had to make time-consuming calls to her insurance company.

As she stepped into the exam room at Astra Therapeutics, her gaze came to rest on Jordan leaning against the treatment table. Having no need for crutches anymore, he looked even more formidable.

He was dressed in a T-shirt and jeans. Really, what the man could do to a pair of jeans—let alone underwear—was sinful. And he was looking at her as if she were a pint of his favorite ice cream and he was a spoon.

Being this close to him for the first time after Saturday night caused memories to flood back. Her pulse picked up, and she fought the sudden visceral urge to fit back into his arms and pick up where they'd left off. *Have mercy.* This was going to be even harder than she'd thought.

"Hello, sunshine."

"We're here for your rehab." She set down her clipboard. Staying businesslike helped her not lose her mind. She planned to address their never-to-be-repeated Saturday night. *Just not quite yet.* She needed to work up to it and then make it short and sweet.

He looked deep into her eyes. "I missed you after you left."

So much for steering him in a different direction. "Well, I'm here now."

"How's my car working out for you?"

"Fine." And that was the problem. She'd felt enveloped by him for the past four days.

He took her hand, surprising her, and ran his thumb over the back of her palm.

She swallowed. "What happens in the penthouse stays in the penthouse."

He stopped and gazed at her.

She could see herself daydreaming about his changeable green eyes. The whimsical thought passed through her head before she opened her mouth and got back to her script. "You and I are taking what happened on Saturday night to our graves."

Jordan's lips twitched. "The car accident?"

"You know what I mean." She extracted her hand from his because unnecessary touching was a no-no. "The ban includes flowers like those that arrived yesterday." The bouquet had been delivered after she'd gotten home. A lovely bouquet of lilies and… "Achillea Angel's Breath."

Jordan smiled. "I asked the florist for a flower with *angel* in the name."

"Of course."

"You mean a long line of boyfriends has been sending them to you?"

"No, you're the first." *Rats.* Most guys went for the familiar and easy—roses, carnations. She didn't want to give him bonus points for being imaginative. "The flowers were…lovely, but I'm glad you didn't send them to me at work."

Jordan winked. "I'm not going to blow your cover."

"Right." And getting back to the point: "Just erase Saturday night from your mind. Treat it as if it never happened."

Jordan looked amused. "You're asking to rewind the clock. I don't think I can un-remember how soft your skin is, the way you feel in my arms, how you respond to my touch."

She ignored the flutter of awareness at his words. "Really? You can forget eight years ago, but you can't delete last Saturday?"

"Ouch."

She folded her arms. "Save it for when you're doing leg presses."

Jordan sobered. "I'm sorry I came off as a jerk when we first met years ago."

Sera blinked because an apology wasn't what she was expecting. Still, she couldn't let him think it mattered all that much to her, so she waved a hand dismissively. "Please. The only reason I brought it up was because I was annoyed by your smooth-player ways."

Jordan twisted his lips wryly. "The truth is that I've gotten used to laughing off fans' attention or giving them a brief brush with fame and then moving on."

"And those were the moves you were showing Danica at the Puck & Shoot?"

He tilted his head. "As I said, it's easy to fall back on some safe maneuvers."

"So eight years ago, I might have been just another fan coming on to you?" she persisted.

Jordan looked pained. "Okay, that may have been my ego talking."

She dropped her hands. "Exactly."

Jordan held up his hands. "Hey, I'm trying for some honesty here, even if I can't make amends."

Sera lowered her shoulders and sighed. Because, yeah, she'd thought of him as a jerk, but he'd made her look at things from a different perspective. And really, wasn't it best that she accept his explanation and they drop the whole subject—so they could move on as she wanted to?

"So where do we go from here?" Jordan asked, seemingly reading her thoughts.

She pasted a bright smile on her face. "We get started on your physical therapy for the day."

He regarded her thoughtfully for a moment, and Sera held her ground.

"If that's the way you want to play it," he said finally.

"Play is not what I had in mind." Then, seeking a distraction, she concentrated on her clipboard, focusing on her notes and flipping through his paperwork. As if she needed reminding about his file and all the details weren't carved in her memory. Just like Saturday night…

On the fifth page, though, something that she'd initially skimmed over caught her attention. For the question on prior hospitalizations, Jordan had marked *yes* and jokingly written *Too many to mention.*

Hmm. Sera looked over at him. "This was not the first time you've had surgery."

"I'm a professional athlete. What do you think?"

"I think you're familiar with doctors, even if I'm your first physical therapist."

He flashed a brief smile. "I've been giving my mother trouble from day one. Literally. I had a collapsed lung as a newborn. I had some respiratory issues because I inhaled meconium."

She blinked in surprise because this information didn't fit the image she had of Jordan Serenghetti. Cool…invincible.

"And to top it off—" he started counting on his fingers "—a broken arm at age eight, pneumonia at age ten—or wait, was that eleven? And a ruptured appendix at fourteen. I was also in and out of the ER for more minor stuff like an ear infection and a sprained wrist."

"Wonderful."

"Memorable. Just ask the staff at Children's Hospital."

"I'm sure it was for them and you."

He grinned.

Sera felt herself softening and cleared her throat. "Let's get to work."

Jordan followed her from the treatment room to the gym, where they worked on normalizing his gait and improving strength with step exercises and leg presses, among other repetitions. More than a month past surgery, he was regaining mobility.

"So how am I doing?" he asked as they were wrapping up. "Think I'll be able to rejoin the team in the fall?"

Sera tilted her head and paused because, despite his casual tone, she knew the answer mattered to him—a lot. "Mmm, that's a question for your doctor. You're recovering nicely, but there's always some unpredictability post-op. And you're expecting your knee to perform at a high level in professional hockey."

Jordan shrugged. "The PRP therapy that my doctor is doing is helping, too."

"Good. Injections can help speed up recovery." She regarded him, and then offered, "You'll get there eventually. Does it matter when? The last thing you want to do is exacerbate an injury or sustain another tear by getting back on the ice too soon."

"I have some endorsement deals up for negotiation, and my contract with the Razors is coming up for renewal in the next few months. There's a lot on the table."

Oh. Now he told her. Talk about pressure. Not only did Dante need Jordan on the ice—he was a big draw for the fans, obviously—but now there were other deadlines. For a big star like Jordan, his contract and endorsements would be everything.

She'd heard stories about his lucrative investments in business ventures, but still, she was sure that continuing to play hockey was integral to his plans. She knew about other sports celebrities who had gone on to invest in everything from franchises to restaurants to car dealerships, after playing as long as possible.

"Thanks for sharing," she quipped.

Within the four walls of Astra Therapeutics, she'd almost forgotten what a different life he led from the one she did. It was about big money and celebrity and high stakes. Jordan's physical prowess and athleticism had landed him at the pinnacle of professional sports.

"Have dinner with me," he offered, "and I'll tell you all about it. There's a new place in town I've been meaning to try." He shrugged. "But, you know, the knee injury put me off my game."

"Another hockey pub? Angus will be jealous," she parried before getting serious, because she needed to drive this point home. "And we're not dating—remember? Saturday night was a never-to-be-repeated blip on the radar."

"It's not a date. It's friends having dinner. And no, I have someplace a little more sophisticated in mind."

Sera fought the little prick of awareness at his words. He was a master of the segue. "That was smoothly done."

Just like the other night. She'd been replaying the feel of his hands moving over her…again and again. *No…just no.* She wouldn't let herself go there. She was putting Saturday night into a tidy little box and sealing it tight. She took a deep breath. "We're not even friends." *Are we?*

"Okay, in-laws dining out," he responded, but the gleam in his eyes said he recognized she hadn't said no yet.

"We've got nothing to talk about."

"Sure we do." He consulted his watch. "We've talked our way through this therapy appointment. Time flies."

She looked heavenward. Were all the Serenghettis this stubborn?

"There's plenty to discuss. The latest news from our joint family for one," he said, counting on the fingers of his hand again. "And your aversion to hockey and wariness around men."

Around him. "I have nothing against hockey."

"What about men?"

She sighed. "I'm not allergic to men. Saturday night should have put that notion to rest."

He lifted the corner of his mouth. "Yeah."

She took another deep breath. "Obviously, physical therapy isn't the only type you need. We need to add mindfulness because you have to learn to live in the present and stop cycling back to the past."

"I am living in the moment. And aren't you the one caught in a loop about being burned in the past?"

Back to that, were they? Still, she knew Jordan was only guessing if he was referring to anything beyond their kiss on a beach. There was no way he could know about Neil.

"I want to prove you wrong about me."

She was suspicious, cautious...curious. "Why?"

Jordan gave a small smile. "You're funny and smart. You're a hard worker who went back to school to earn her degree while putting up with smart alecks like me at the Puck & Shoot. You're caring. You trained for a profession that makes a difference in people's lives."

She started to melt and then straightened her spine. Still, she couldn't help asking, "Smart alecks? How about glib lotharios?"

He leaned forward, his look intensifying. "I know I have a reputation, but the other night between us was special. I've never felt a connection that fast with a woman before."

"Because I'm good with a comeback?"

"Angel with a smart mouth, yeah. You're one of a kind."

How many times had she wanted to be special and valued for herself? And she especially didn't want to be known as Sera who needed to be protected—as her family saw her. Still, she had to keep these sessions focused on business—she had her work reputation to think about, even if Bernice was the kind of boss to appreciate a good-looking guy. "I'm a therapist, and you're my client. We have to keep this professional."

"We are. I've been doing the homework that you've assigned."

Sera nearly threw up her hands. He was persistent and had a counterargument for everything.

"I hear that you box," Jordan teased. "I'd ask you to meet me for a date at Jimmy's Boxing Gym so we can hit the punching bags together. It's one of my regular haunts but—" he nodded at his knee with an apologetic expression "—I doubt I'm up to that kind of exercise yet."

"Let's take a rain check, then," she said, dodging the invitation before glancing at the clock on the wall. "I'm about to be late for my next appointment."

Jordan looked at her as if he saw right through her.

She wished she could take that rain check for their therapy sessions. Because if Jordan kept on with the charm offensive, it was going to be hard to keep up her walls against him…

By the next week's session on Wednesday afternoon, as he waited for Sera's arrival, Jordan had realized he needed a plan B. The problem was he'd so rarely had to resort to a backup strategy where women were concerned, he wasn't even sure what plan B was. Except that he needed one.

Ever since their fateful Saturday night encounter, he couldn't get Sera out of his mind. Her scent lingered, her touch tantalized, her taste made him yearn for more. Sometimes a great memory was a curse. He must have been an ignoramus eight years ago.

The direct approach—an invitation to dinner—hadn't worked with Sera. She wasn't biting, so he needed to sweeten the offer for her. How? Couldn't Cole and Marisa invite some family over for the baby's sleeping-through-the-night celebration or something? He'd debated his options, had searched his brain during interminable repetitions of his physical-therapy routine at home—when all he could think about was her—and had finally come up with a scenario that involved recruiting his mother.

Needing help from his mother to score a date was as low as he'd ever gone. Frankly, it was embarrassing and humbling…and all part of the new territory he was in with Sera.

When Sera entered the treatment room, her expression was all business. Still, she looked fresh and perky and delicious. He now knew she responded to him as no other woman ever had. She was attuned to him on a level he'd never experienced before. So it made it impossible to even pay lip service to her ridiculous plan to forget that Saturday night ever happened.

"Nice move leaving my car keys with the security desk in my building," he observed.

She swept her hair off her shoulder. "Thank you again for the loan of a set of wheels. My car is out of the shop."

"Congratulations. But I thought I'd at least find some memento of your stay." He shrugged. "You know, a forgotten lip balm or a pair of sunglasses. Or at least your lingering scent on the upholstery."

"I wasn't able to do a complete makeover in a few days," she deadpanned right back. "Your imprint was hard to eradicate."

He loved her sass. "But you tried?"

"I'm sure you'd like to be considered unforgettable."

"I'll settle for immortality," he teased.

She scrolled on the tablet she'd brought to their session this time instead of a clipboard with paperwork.

He eyed her. "I've got a request."

She looked up. "I give you points for being direct."

Jordan laughed as he leaned against the treatment table. If Sera wanted to pretend their close encounter hadn't happened or was an anomaly, then he was willing to play any of the limited cards he had left. "I'd like you to appear on my mother's cooking show."

Sera's eyes widened. "What? You can't be serious."

He shrugged. "Consider it a thank-you for the use of my car."

"Sneaky." She took a deep breath. "Anyway, Marisa may have appeared on the program once, but it's not for me. I've caught your mother's show a few times on television, and I consider it a spectator sport."

"My mother's station is under new management. Mom is worried about being canceled and wants to make a good impression. And I'm trying to help her out by coming up with some ideas."

"Why doesn't she just switch to online? She can go viral." Nevertheless Sera contemplated him thoughtfully. "Still, it's nice of you to try to help her."

"I was an Eagle Scout. Good deeds are my forte."

"Are you sure you want to involve your mother? Who knows what I might tell her?"

He smiled lazily. "That's the point. You'll be on the show, so I'll be on my best behavior…because you'll be doing me a kindness."

"You've thought of everything," she remarked drily.

"And it'll be a good show," he pressed. "Just what my mother needs right now."

"How do you know I'd be appropriate? I might burn the calzones."

"C'mon, you bring homemade dishes to the office, and your coworkers praise your cooking." He'd found a bargaining chip in her baked ziti.

"Remind me to tell them not to be so loose-lipped," Sera grumbled, nevertheless looking flattered. "No good deed goes unpunished."

Jordan snapped his fingers as an idea hit. "You might teach me how to cook. There's no format yet, but the audience would eat up a show about a pro hockey player bumbling his way through the kitchen."

"Well, somehow I doubt any acting would be involved on your part. But anyway, your mother can teach you how to cook on the show." Sera frowned. "In fact, why hasn't she?"

"When the equivalent of Julia Child is at home, why would she let anyone else mess around in the kitchen?" He shrugged. "Besides, I was always at hockey practice. I only made my own breakfast when I slept in. Everyone was doing what they did best. Mom in the kitchen, me on ice."

She smiled too sweetly. "You remember that scene in one of the *Star Wars* movies where Han Solo undergoes carbon-freezing...?"

"I know you'd love to put me on ice—" his expression turned seductive "—but you've heated me up instead."

"Jordan—"

"I like my name on your lips almost as much as your hair down." Instead of her usual ponytail, her hair was swinging loose for a change. Somehow, even with the scrubs she was wearing, the style made her look seductive. He fought the urge to touch her.

As if on cue, she held up a staying hand, and he schooled his expression.

"Right. Behave."

"As if you can."

"I'm trying. And your appearance on my mother's cooking show would help hold me to the bargain."

She sighed in exasperation. "Let's get started on your exercises for today."

He flashed a grin. "So that's a yes? You'll do it?"

"It depends."

"On what?"

"Your behavior. Fortunately, we're already in phase two of your rehabilitation."

"Great, so you're rehabilitating my knee and my playboy ways at the same time. Impressive."

She arched her brows. "I didn't say yes, but just call me a multitasker anyway. Today we'll be focusing on improving your strength base and balance."

As it turned out, the exercises she introduced him to in the gym were some he was familiar with from his pre-injury workouts. He had no trouble with leg squats and glut extensions, and then the various resistance exercises that she threw at him. All the while, Sera evaluated and corrected his body alignment and positioning.

Jordan concentrated on keeping his mind on the exercises. Focus was something that he normally excelled at, but with Sera nearby, he found that his concentration was shot. Instead, his mind wandered to the fullness of her lips, the softness of her skin and the pleasure of her occasional touch.

"We're looking for symmetry of right and left in your gait," she told him.

And he was looking for a *yes* to his proposition, so he aimed to please. At the end of their session, he couldn't resist asking, "So how did I do?"

"Great."

He winked. "And my reward is…?"

"I'll speak to the agent who handles my public appearances and get back to you."

He just laughed—because he was willing to chalk up anything other than an outright *no* as a win.

Eight

Sometimes it was good to catch up with teammates. Marc Bellitti and Vince Tedeschi lived just outside Springfield, where the Razors were based, so even in the off-season, they were good for an occasional beer at the Puck & Shoot, or for lunch like they were having today at another of their customary haunts, MacDougal's Steakhouse.

Except today, Jordan had a motive for asking them to meet up. "I need your help."

With a cooking show. He'd debated how to float the idea of making an appearance on her program to his mother. He knew she'd be delighted to have one of her children back on the air. And Jordan's star power in particular couldn't hurt—just as when his new sister-in-law, Chiara Feran, the Hollywood actress, had gone on the show. Debating what tactic he'd take since talking to Sera and finally getting a tentative commitment, he'd hit upon the idea of a cooking competition—among hometown-team hockey players. Sort of like *Iron Chef* with an ice-puck spin, and Sera as the judge. *Brilliant.* His mother had loved it.

All he needed was to recruit a couple of his teammates—and c'mon, they had to have time to burn in the off-season, and a little positive publicity couldn't hurt.

"When don't you need our help?" Marc joked, snagging a remaining fry from their burger lunch. "Need advice on how to talk to women? I'm your man."

If there was anyone who could best him in the smart-aleck department, it was Marc. But Jordan held his fire, because—as much as this pained him—he needed Marc to play along here. And not in the way his teammate probably imagined. Aloud, he said, "It involves Vince, too."

From across the table, the Razors' goalie held up his hands. "I'm good. Whatever scheme you two are coming up with, count me out."

"Vince, if it's about women, believe me, you could use all the help you can get," Marc shot back.

On that score, Jordan had to agree. Vince Tedeschi was a big, hulking, taciturn guy. He was the team's rock, but he let others do the razzle-dazzle.

"It's 'cause you're such a straight arrow that you're perfect for this gig, Vince," Jordan said.

"Which is?" the goalie asked warily.

"I need you and Marc to cook." Jordan paused. "On air. On my mother's show."

Vince groaned.

"Hey, you're used to being on television."

"But not cooking, man."

"It'll impress the ladies. They'll be calling and writing in."

Vince knitted his brow. "What's the demographic of *Flavors of Italy with Camilla Serenghetti*? My grandmother watches."

Next to Vince, Marc swallowed a snort. "And there's your answer right there."

"You won't be the only ones on it."

Now Marc looked intrigued.

"My physical therapist will be judging our cook-off."

Now Marc burst out laughing. "Great, I'll have a chance to kick your butt on air."

"Yeah, think of it as a golden opportunity," Jordan said drily.

Marc liked to indulge in the occasional prank, and Jordan had had his butt slapped by a hockey stick on more than one occasion.

"You've recruited your physical therapist, too?" Vince seemed perplexed.

"Serafina Perini," Jordan said. "She's an in-law."

Marc's brows shot up. "Do tell."

Jordan shrugged. "She's Cole's wife's cousin."

Vince grumbled. "Jeez."

Marc raised his hand. "Hold up, Tedeschi. Is this Serafina under eighty?"

"Yup." Jordan was tight-lipped.

"Single."

"Yeah." Jordan didn't like the direction this conversation was heading.

"Attractive?"

Jordan narrowed his eyes.

Marc rubbed his chin again. "Sounds like a woman to get to know."

And Jordan was feeling the urge to rearrange Marc's pretty face. He hadn't been able to get Sera out of his mind ever since their night together. Being around her was like a euphoric high that he'd only experienced one other place— on the ice. He was restless to see her, touch her, spar with her again.

"Wait, wait." Marc rubbed his chin. "Serafina Perini is

ringing a bell… Was she the gorgeous ash-blonde poured into a satin dress at Cole and Marisa's surprise wedding?"

The way Jordan saw it, Marc's great memory could be a pain in the ass sometimes. He made a mental note not to invite the Razors' defenseman to any other weddings—not that he was planning to host one himself. "Her hair is a honey blond."

"You noticed." Marc flashed a knowing and triumphant grin.

"Just setting the record straight."

"Hey, is this the same Serafina who recently waitressed at the Puck & Shoot?" Vince suddenly piped up. "That woman you were chatting up during our last time there addressed the waitress as Serafina, and that's kind of an unusual name."

Jordan bit back a grimace—now Vince had to get all verbose on him? "I was not chatting up Danica. She walked over to me, and I was being polite."

"*Polite* is not the adjective that comes to mind, Serenghetti," Marc joked.

Jordan sat back and draped his arm along the top of their booth. "Hilarious."

"Serafina didn't seem particularly friendly toward you at the Puck & Shoot," Vince observed.

Jordan regarded both his teammates. Since when had the Razors' goalie become an astute observer of human interactions? "So are you guys going to do the show?"

Marc looked like he was enjoying himself and not ready to give up the fun. "So this Serafina is an in-law, your physical therapist, a waitress at the Puck & Shoot who, come to think of it, I should have recognized from your brother's wedding even if she was dressed up…and the special guest on your mother's show?" he drawled, rubbing his chin. "Seems as entangled as you've ever been with a woman, Serenghetti."

Jordan shrugged and adopted a bored tone. "Sera cooks, and Mom's liked her since her cousin married Cole."

Marc looked at Vince like he wanted to crack up. "Well, if your mother likes her, I guess that seals the deal."

"Not quite," Jordan replied drily. "I've got to get you two jokers to add some suspense to the whole episode."

"Not romance?" The defenseman adopted an exaggerated expression of shock.

"It's a cooking competition, Bellitti."

"And has this honey-blond physical therapist ever wanted to be on air?" Marc joked.

"No. And she's not into hockey guys." It couldn't hurt to drive the point home.

Marc's eyes crinkled. "Meaning you've failed with her? The legendary Jordan Serenghetti charm hasn't worked."

"I haven't tried." He hadn't tried to get to bed with her. Not really. Not yet...

"This I might have to see," Marc said, warming to the subject.

"If you go on the show, I'll prove that I can make Sera melt." A little extra motivation would be good for Marc.

The defenseman laughed again.

"Guys..." Vince said warningly.

"You're on, Serenghetti," Marc said, his eyes gleaming. "I'll let my agent know. Because I think you're not going to win."

"Don't be too sure."

"And when you do lose," Marc persisted, "what do I get?"

"The satisfaction of knowing I failed."

The Razors' defenseman laughed again. "I'm magnanimous. I'll hold to my side of the bargain, even if you haven't accomplished yours by the time the show tapes."

"Merciful is your middle name, Bellitti," Jordan remarked drily.

Vince shifted in his seat and muttered, "I've got a bad gut about this..."

"We know, Vince. You're out of this bet," Jordan said resignedly. "As far as you're concerned, you've seen no evil, heard no evil. Just do me a favor? Show up and do the program. And if you can outcook Bellitti, it'll be a bonus."

Sera couldn't believe she'd agreed to this. But here she was, in Camilla's office, eyeing Jordan and waiting to tape a cooking show. They'd already gone through the necessary paperwork with producers, and they'd met with Jordan's mother. Camilla Serenghetti was her usual bundle of energy.

Tipped off by Jordan, Sera had dressed in what she considered appropriate: a solid blue sweater and slacks—soon to be covered by an apron, anyway. Jordan had mentioned, and she'd known herself, that busy patterns didn't work on camera. She'd donned some delicate jewelry and had done her own hair and makeup—though she figured the show's staff would do some touch-up before she went on air.

They were in a lull while Camilla spoke with her producers on set and they waited for other guests and the audience to arrive and taping to begin. After she'd reluctantly committed to doing the show—thinking of Dante, Camilla and the favor she owed Jordan after her car accident—Jordan had informed her that the taping would be a cooking competition with him and a couple of Razors teammates as contestants *and her as the judge.* It had been too late to back out, but she couldn't help feeling a little bit like the star of *The Bachelorette*, being asked to choose among several single men.

Still, she felt poised, professional...and sexy under Jordan's regard. She had to put that night behind her—even though every time she was near him now, she had to fight the urge to touch him, slip back into his arms, and... *No, no, no.* Still, his magnetism was so strong, she could feel the pull as if it were a tangible force.

Ignoring the frisson of awareness that coursed through her at the thought, she focused on a framed photo of Jordan and his brothers when they were younger that rested on a nearby windowsill. Picking it up, she asked, "Is this you around age ten?"

Jordan tossed her a surprisingly sheepish smile. "No, that was me at twelve. I've hidden that photo every time I've been to Mom's office, but she keeps setting it back out." After a pause, he added, "I was a late bloomer."

Sensing a chance to rib him, Sera felt her lips twitch in a smile. "In other words, for the longest time, you were an underdeveloped, small and scrawny kid?"

"Going for the jugular with three adjectives, Perini? How about we leave it at *small*?"

"Wow, so you came late to your lady-killer ways…"

He bared his teeth. "How are they working?"

She resisted reminding him that he'd agreed to be on his best behavior today—her sanity depended on it. And she was still processing this new bit of information about Jordan. She'd assumed…well, she didn't know what she'd thought, but she'd always figured he'd sprung from the womb as a natural-born charmer. Apparently, she'd been— and, wow, it hurt to admit this—*wrong*.

"Braces on your teeth?" she asked, setting the photo back down.

"Check."

"Glasses?"

"Sometimes, until laser-vision surgery."

"Acne?"

He nodded. "I'll cop to the occasional teenage blemish."

"Nose job?"

"Now we're going too far."

She smirked. Rumor was, back in the day, all the Welsdale girls got boob jobs and cars for their birthdays—because they could.

"I leave the cosmetic surgery to the models and Hollywood starlets," he added, as if reading her mind.

At the reminder of the types of women he'd dated, she folded her arms. Because now they were back on comfortable ground. He'd started late, but he'd made up ground in the playboy arena with a vengeance. "Making up for lost time these days?"

"Let's not get all pop psychology on me."

No way was she backing off. She was enjoying this. Nodding at the picture, she asked, "How many of your dates have seen this?"

"None, fortunately. Not one has been in Mom's office. But *WE* Magazine ran a Before They Were Famous feature not long ago, and they dug up an old Welsdale newspaper article of me posing with my team in a youth-league photo."

"Horrors," she teased.

Jordan shrugged easily. "I got over it. Not even a nick in the public image."

"The carefully constructed persona stayed in place?"

"Fortunately for my sponsorship deals. Image is everything."

Sera widened her eyes. "Wow, so I just put it all together…"

"What?"

"Doctors, nurses, therapists. They're all uppermost in your subconscious."

"Hold on, Dr. Freud."

"You have a fixation with those in the health-care field because of your own sickly childhood."

Jordan arched a brow. "So you're saying that the reason I'm attracted to you is because you're a physical therapist?"

"Bingo," she concluded triumphantly, feeling a tingle of awareness at his admission that he wanted *her*.

"How much psychology have you studied?"

"I took a few courses on the way to my PT degree, but that's irrelevant."

"Right," he responded drily. "Here's another theory for you. I like blondes. See? My theory even has the beauty of simplicity."

Sera dropped her arms. "You're not taking me seriously."

Jordan tilted his head. "Don't you want to argue that my attraction to blondes stems from the newborn period? You know, when I might have been placed next to babies with wisps of light hair in the hospital?"

Sera resisted rolling her eyes.

"Hey, you started this. Anyway, does it matter? You're here, about to go on television—"

"Don't remind me."

"—and whether I like your physical-therapist scrubs or just women with cute blond ponytails is beside the point."

Sera reluctantly admitted he had a point. Still, if she could pigeonhole and rationalize their—uh, *his*—attraction, it would be easier to manage. Aloud, she said, "Why do you like me? You shouldn't, you know. We're bad for each other. I come with strings attached as an in-law, and that's contrary to your MO. And you're the type of on-and-off the field player that I think should come with a warning label."

"Maybe it's the forbidden aspect that drives the attraction."

"Maybe for you." *Damn it, he was right.*

"Okay, for me," he readily agreed and then checked his watch. "Ah, I've got to warn you before you go on—"

"What?" Sera's sublimated nervousness kicked up a notch.

"My father will be in the audience, and he has delusions of getting on television."

"He doesn't know your mother's show may get canceled?"

Jordan shook his head. "After his one guest appearance, he thinks he can make it better by becoming a staple on the program."

"And why not?" Sera asked. "He's about the only Serenghetti who hasn't been on television regularly."

Cole and Jordan had both been on televised NHL games, not to mention postgame interviews. Their brother, Rick, was a stuntman with movie credits who was married to a famous actress. Jordan's younger sister had done fashion shows that had been broadcast. And Camilla had her own television program, of course. Sera could understand why Serg felt left out of the limelight. He wasn't only dealing with his poststroke infirmities but also with not appearing on the marquee alongside the rest of his family. As a physical therapist, she'd seen his frustration in plenty of patients and could sympathize.

"If he wants to be on television, he should consider commercials for a construction industry supplier instead," Jordan muttered.

"Then why hasn't he?"

"Because he fancies himself a sommelier these days."

Sera felt a tinkling laugh bubble up. "A wine expert?"

"Bingo. And guess whose show he thinks would be perfect for a regular guest segment."

"Oh."

"Right."

"Your father just wants to be understood."

Jordan snorted. "He's tough as nails and ornery."

Sera tilted her head. "So you're telling me this because he might spring up from his seat in the audience and shout something?"

"He can't spring up from anywhere these days," Jordan muttered. "And believe me, the only reason he'd shout a comment is to tell me I'm doing something wrong."

"Does he do that at your hockey games, too?" Sera asked, amused.

"If he does, he's too tucked away in the stands for people to really notice. Anyway, my point is he may try to insert himself into the show somehow, and I don't want you to be surprised by anything…unexpected."

"How does your mother feel about this turn of events?"

"Like the breadwinner who has a temperamental kid on her hands."

Sera laughed.

"Suddenly she's the star, and he's cast in her shadow. Though, I don't think he'd even admit to himself that's what he's feeling."

Sera tapped a finger against her lips. "There's got to be a solution to this."

Jordan shrugged. "If there is one, I haven't thought of it."

Just then, one of Camilla's producers stepped into the room to call them on set.

"Ready?" Jordan asked, searching her gaze.

Sera shrugged. "As ready as I'll ever be."

Showtime. In more ways than one…

Nine

She was supposed to have had one rule: never get involved with a player.

Except Jordan actually seemed kind of cute and endearing at the moment wearing an apron, but still looking masculine. He was prepared to make a fool of himself under the bright television-studio lights. All for the sake of his mother. *Aww.*

Sera straightened her spine against the traitorous thought. She needed to get him in top shape and marketable for Dante and his team—and his sponsors. *Nothing more.*

"Hi, Sera!" Marisa waved as she stepped into the studio with her husband and scanned for an empty seat.

Sera's eyes widened. "What are you doing here?"

"Returning the favor," Cole replied, shooting a look at Jordan.

"What favor?" Sera knew she sounded like a parrot, but she couldn't help herself.

She'd avoided mentioning her appearance on the show

today to Marisa, which meant… She focused her gaze on Jordan, who wore a bland mask.

Cole cast his brother a sardonic look. "Jordan came as comic relief when Marisa and I were guests on Mom's cooking show before we were married."

"Oh." Sera remembered teasing her cousin about the significance of that appearance for her relationship with Cole—which was why she hadn't wanted to mention her own cameo today in return to Marisa, who might get the wrong idea.

"We thought about bringing Dahlia," her cousin went on, oblivious to Sera's distress, "but we figured she was too young to—"

"—watch her uncle Jordan get outmaneuvered." Cole chuckled.

"Thanks for the vote of confidence," Jordan replied.

Cole flashed a smile. "Payback, little brother."

"And thanks to the fact that Mom still has a show, you have the chance," Jordan grumbled.

Just then, Serg Serenghetti walked into the studio, all the while chatting with a producer.

"Excuse me," Cole said. "I'm going to help Dad find a seat."

Jordan watched his brother walk away and shrugged. "The Serenghettis have arrived in force."

Sera bit back a groan. *Great.*

As if on cue, more Serenghetti family members entered the studio. Rick and Chiara Serenghetti were followed by Jordan's sister, Mia. Even though Chiara wore glasses and a baseball cap, so as not to be identified as a well-known actress, Sera recognized her immediately.

Sera swung back to Jordan and asked accusingly, "What is this? A Serenghetti family reunion?"

Jordan shrugged. "News to me, too." Then he stepped

forward and addressed his middle brother. "What are you doing here?"

"We're here for moral support," Rick replied sardonically.

"For whom?" Jordan replied.

Sera was wondering the same thing. In this wilder-than-dreams scenario, it was hard to tell who needed help more: her, Jordan or Camilla, whose show might be in the crosshairs of new management.

Mia Serenghetti walked up, holding a cup of coffee and looking on trend in the way only a budding fashion designer could. She caught Sera's gaze. "Nice job bringing my youngest brother to heel."

Sera blew a breath. Despite her best intentions, it was as if she and Jordan wore bright neon signs: *Get These Two Together.* Still, as everyone laughed, Sera pasted a smile on her face. "Thanks, Mia, but I'm not in the market for—"

"—reforming bad boys," Jordan finished for her wryly. "Yes, we know."

Mia's gaze swung from Sera to her youngest brother and back. "Finishing each other's sentences. Interesting."

That comment earned a laugh from Rick and Chiara.

Sera held up her hands. "No, we're not. We're boring. Very, very boring."

"Better hope that's not true for the sake of Mom's show!" Mia replied, taking a sip of her coffee.

Fortunately, Sera was saved from the need for further comment because the studio staff—including the middle-aged producer who'd summoned her from Camilla's office earlier—started hustling everyone into position.

Minutes later, Sera pasted a smile on her face for the cameras and went with the agreed-upon script. "Gentlemen, start your kitchen appliances."

The audience chuckled.

Okay, so she was here as an *alleged* cooking expert to

judge Jordan's kitchen skills against those of two Razors teammates he'd cajoled, charmed or blackmailed into appearing as contestants today.

Jordan was so in trouble. And frankly, so was she. When she'd agreed to this, she'd thought she was volunteering for some sedate affair. She should have known better with the Serenghettis.

"Jordan, let's start with you," Camilla said in a drill-sergeant tone as she stopped at his counter station.

"Playing favorites, Mom?" Jordan asked, and then winked at the camera. "I always knew I was first."

Camilla ignored him. "What will you be making?"

"*Pasta alla chitarra* with fresh mackerel ragù, capers, tomatoes and Taggiasca olives."

Sera couldn't help a look of surprise. She was shocked Jordan even knew what a Taggiasca olive was.

Jordan winked at the audience. "You can call this dish The Jordan Serenghetti Pasta Special."

Sera raised an eyebrow because Jordan seemed not the least bit nervous about his ambitious recipe. *Fine, let him try.* Shouldn't she have known by now that he was always up for a challenge?

Marc Bellitti volunteered that he'd be making a ravioli dish with a secret family recipe for vodka sauce. And Vince Tedeschi said he'd prepare *pollo alla cacciatore* with mussels.

"Thank you, Vinny." Sera tossed the Razors' goalie an encouraging smile because he seemed the most nervous of the contestants.

Jordan's brows drew into a straight line. "That's Vince."

"She can call me whatever she wants," Jordan's teammate responded with an easy grin.

Sera tossed him a beatific smile. "I'm a fan of turf and surf."

"It's *surf and turf*, not *turf and surf*," Jordan said.

Sera ignored him. "Apparently, the only one who is allowed to make up names is Jordan himself."

"Oh, yeah?" Marc asked interestedly. "What does he call you?"

Sera and Jordan stared at each other for a moment, their gazes clashing.

The entire studio audience—including, heaven help her, Marisa, Cole *and* Camilla Serenghetti—seemed to lean in for the answer.

"Angel," she and Jordan said in unison to much laughter.

"Hey, I think this contest is rigged," Vince protested.

"Yes, but not in the way you think," Sera cooed. "I don't like the name."

"Great, we've neutralized the famous Serenghetti charm," Marc put in.

"We'll see," Jordan remarked drily.

Camilla Serenghetti hurried forward. "Let's get down to cooking."

"Before this show degenerates into slapstick comedy," Sera added.

When Vince groaned, Jordan arched a brow. "Don't you mean *hockey stick*?"

"There's no puck," Sera replied crisply.

"We're slapping the joke into the goal for the winning shot."

"Hmm. The only thing you should be slapping is the fish for the entrée you're making."

The show proceeded smoothly after that. And Sera had to give Jordan points for trying. But at the end, after sampling all three dishes, she had to go with Vince's *pollo alla cacciatore* because it was simply superb. For the audience's benefit, she explained, "While I chose Vince's recipe, Marc Bellitti also gets points for a professional-quality family sauce. And Jordan's dish is original. They were all close..."

"I've always said Marc has the secret sauce," Vince joked. "On and off the ice."

"Hey, I thought that was me," Jordan chimed in.

Camilla clapped her hands. "Well, we have a winner—" she fixed her gaze on her son "—and a loser."

"So Jordan is hopeless?" Vince asked jokingly.

Camilla clasped her hands together. "Perhaps Sera would like to give my son a cooking lesson?"

Sera's eyes widened. No way was she signing up for more. "Signora Serenghetti, I—"

Camilla's request was a tall order. And she'd already told Jordan she wasn't into reforming bad boys. But they were on TV with a live audience—and Jordan was contemplating her expectantly. Looking around for a lifeline, her gaze came to rest on Serg Serenghetti in the audience, and an idea struck. "Serg, would you like to come up here and suggest a wine that I could pair with Vince's winning dish?"

She tossed a significant glance at Jordan and Camilla. "After all, if the loser might get a cooking lesson, the winner should receive some recognition, too."

Serg's face brightened.

"Well, *pollo alla cacciatore* is an interesting dish," Serg said, though he was already slowly standing. "It's got many blended flavors that you don't want to overwhelm. You still want to taste the tomatoes and mushrooms."

Cole got up to help him, but the older man batted away his hand.

"Oh, come on, Signor Serenghetti, I'm sure you can suggest something," Sera prompted.

Serg chuckled. "Well, sure, if you insist."

"Oh, I do." Sera was enjoying herself. Beside her, Camilla and Jordan had gone still. *Priceless.* She bit back a laugh as Serg stole everyone's thunder. Jordan was probably wondering whether she'd gone nuts and why she was disregarding his warning from earlier. But she had a plan.

Serg accepted help from a producer who gave him a hand getting on stage and led him to where Sera was standing. "Now, traditional chicken *cacciatore* is made with red wine—"

Sera furrowed her brow at the camera for effect.

"—but Vince went with white instead."

Sera widened her eyes to underscore the point.

"Obviously, he would not have won if the dish wasn't creative and delicious," Serg added.

"Of course."

"Now a Chianti classico is a good red wine to pair with traditional *pollo alla cacciatore.*" Serg paused. "But even a white zinfandel would be good paired with Vince's version."

"A Serenghetti who knows his wine," Sera offered approvingly.

"My son—" Serg jerked his thumb at Jordan "—never offered you a glass of wine?"

Sera heated, and Jordan cleared his throat.

"Well, uh—"

"As a matter of fact—"

The older Serenghetti cut them both off. "A travesty."

"We've had catering at family events. I've never had to bartend," Jordan offered by way of explanation to the audience.

"And I like to pour my own wine," Serafina added quickly, trying to cut off the line of conversation, which could end up...who knew where.

Serg just shook his head in disappointment.

Steering the conversation to safer ground, Sera said, "You're a natural at this."

Serg beamed, while Jordan tossed her a questioning look that said *You're creating a monster.*

Ignoring Jordan's expression, Sera went on. "You should have your own gig, Mr. Serenghetti, not minutes snatched from another show. You could tape commercial-length wine segments." She smiled brightly. "I've even got a name. *Wine Breaks with Serg!*"

The audience clapped in approval.

Before Serg could respond, a producer signaled Camilla, who stepped forward.

"Alla prossima volta," Camilla said, giving her signature closing line. "Till next time, *buon appetito.*"

Seconds later, the cameras switched off, and Sera's gaze tangled with Jordan's.

He gave a relieved and appreciative grin. "Nice moves. Thanks for giving Dad his cameo and for suggesting something else for him to do. I wouldn't be surprised if he went straight home to build his business plan."

"No trouble," Sera mumbled before looking away in confusion. She had the warm fuzzies from his compliment, and she so didn't want that feeling where Jordan was concerned. Even mindless sexual attraction to a marquee brand, a celebrity face and a bad-boy body was preferable. Because emotion meant wading into dangerous, deeper waters.

"If Dad has his own project, it'll take the heat off Mom." Jordan shrugged. "And who knows? In the future, she might feel comfortable enough to partner with him on air, once he's got his own audience. Good going."

Sera blew some wisps of hair away from her face. Why hadn't she noticed how hot it was under the studio lights when they'd been taping? "I like my entertainment with unexpected plot twists."

Jordan laughed. "What a coincidence. So do I."

His siblings came up on stage then, and Jordan turned away to deal with his family.

Sera found herself at momentary loose ends, until her cousin Marisa stepped close, a teasing expression on her face. "You know you're in trouble, right?"

"I was hoping the trouble was over."

Her cousin shook her head. "Nope. Every woman who has been on this show to cook alongside a Serenghetti has wound up married to him."

Sera felt her stomach somersault, but she strove not to show emotion. "Don't worry. There's no chance of that in this case."

She'd sworn Jordan to secrecy, and in any case, their one recent encounter was eons away from a march down the aisle. Marisa angled her head, scanning her expression. "Are you sure there's nothing more between you and Jordan?"

Sera scoffed. "Of course. Positive."

"Well, I'll just repeat what you said to me," Marisa said, and she mimicked Sera's voice. "'He wants you to appear on his mother's cooking show? That's serious.'"

"That's some memory you have," Sera grumbled.

Her cousin just smiled.

Sera bit back a groan. *Out of the frying pan and into the fire.*

Sera hurried out the front doors of St. Vincent's Hospital to greet the sunny afternoon outside. She'd just visited one of her patients who'd had to have additional surgery.

She was back to business as usual—or so she told herself—after taping Camilla's show two days ago. She hadn't heard from Jordan but she was scheduled to see him again soon for their weekly therapy session. Anticipation shivered over her skin.

She'd known her family would eventually see or hear about her appearance on Camilla's show, so she'd played it off as doing a favor for Jordan and the rest of the Serenghettis. Dante had been thrilled.

Head bowed, she dropped her cell phone into her handbag as she blinked against the bright sunshine, and then collided with a rock-solid chest. "Oomph!"

Strong hands grasped her arms and steadied her. "Easy."

She looked up and locked gazes with the last person she expected to see right now. *Jordan.*

"I didn't think I'd run into you here," he said, dropping his arms and stepping aside.

She followed suit so she wasn't standing in the way of pedestrian traffic. "I just finished visiting an elderly patient of mine who needed surgery." Sera searched her brain for pleasantries even as she drank him in—he looked sinfully good. "What are you doing here?"

"I work with the Once upon a Dream Foundation. I'm visiting the pediatric floor."

She couldn't keep the surprised look from her face.

"Want to join me?" Jordan asked.

Sera looked around and noticed he was alone.

Jordan's eyes crinkled. "I don't normally bring a camera crew with me on these visits." He shrugged. "I prefer not to make it a media event. Sometimes the kids like it when they're on the news, but other times it freaks them out."

"I'd think a kid would freak out just because Jordan Serenghetti showed up in his hospital room."

Jordan grinned and nodded toward the entrance. "Then, come inside with me and calm things down. You're good at puncturing my ego."

Sera flushed. "Yup, you're right."

He was easy on the eyes and, now that she didn't have quite as many of her negative conceptions of him, *dangerous.* Today was another blow to her armor—he did charity work with sick kids?

"So what do you say, Angel? Ready to head back in?"

She couldn't even get annoyed about his use of the pet name at the moment. She was a sucker for people in need—and those who helped them. It was why she'd become a physical therapist. "Another appearance with you in front of a live audience? How could I refuse?"

Jordan gave her a lopsided grin. "Before long, you'll be a pro."

That was what she was afraid of. Nevertheless, she turned to follow him into the main hospital building. He placed a guiding hand at the small of her back, and she felt his touch radiate out from her center, heating her.

Upstairs, the nurses broke into smiles when Jordan appeared. As brief greetings were exchanged, Sera wondered how many other sick kids Jordan had visited in the past.

A portly middle-aged woman in scrubs pulled a hockey stick out of a closet next to the nurse's station.

"Thanks, Elsie," Jordan said, flashing a killer smile as he took the equipment from her.

"Anything for you, honey," Elsie teased. "My husband knows I'm a fan."

Catching Sera's expression, Jordan looked sheepish. "I came by yesterday, but it was the wrong moment for a visit. Elsie was kind enough to hold on to the hockey stick until I came back."

Moments later, another nurse directed them down the hall. When they stopped at an open patient-room door, Sera waited for Jordan to enter first.

He rapped on the door and then stepped inside. Immediately, there was whooping and hollering from a handful of adults in addition to a boy who was sitting up in his hospital bed.

Sera paused on the threshold. Of course she knew Jordan had a fan base, but seeing his effect on people in person was another thing. At the Puck & Shoot, he was surrounded by regulars who weren't surprised when he showed up. And Sera had always dismissed a lot of the rest as just the adulation of adoring, unthinking women. But now, when she saw the frail and bald boy sitting up in his bed—he couldn't be more than ten or twelve—and how his eyes lit up at the sight of Jordan, emotion welled up inside her.

Stepping over the threshold, Sera scanned the crowd. An assortment of adults continued to laugh and smile.

"Hey, Brian. What's going on?" Jordan said casually.

Brian broke into a grin. "Number Twenty-six. I can't believe you're here."

Sera recognized the number as the one that Jordan wore. The local shops in Welsdale sold that jersey more than any other.

"Hey, you invited me," Jordan joked. "Of course I'd show up."

"Yeah, but you're busy."

"Not too busy to visit one of my best fans."

Brian looked uncertain. "I am?"

"You used your wish on me."

A grin appeared again. "Yeah, I did. I just can't believe it worked."

Brian's assorted visitors laughed—including two who, from the resemblance, could be Brian's parents.

Sera felt her smile become tremulous. Damn Jordan Serenghetti. He made her mad, sad and bad by turns— she was always riding a roller coaster in his company.

As the adults talked, Sera learned that Brian's prognosis was good. His leukemia was responding to treatment.

"I brought you something," Jordan said to Brian.

"The hockey stick is for me?"

"Of course. What would a visit be without memorabilia? And I'm going to sign it, too." Jordan fished a marker out of his pocket and placed his signature on the widest part. Then he handed the stick to Brian.

"Wow! Thanks."

"I hope you enjoy it."

Brian looked up from his gift. "Do you think you'll be playing again soon?"

"I hope so." Then Jordan turned to nod in the direction

of the doorway. "Sera's the one who's making sure I'll be back on the ice."

"She's your doctor?"

Sera flushed. Such an innocent question, and such a complicated answer. *Hired professional, in-law and...*

Jordan chuckled. "She's medical. Definitely one of the scrubs."

She cleared her throat as everyone's gaze swung to her. "I'm his physical therapist. We, um, crossed paths downstairs after I saw another patient, and Jordan was kind enough to invite me along on this visit. I hope you don't mind."

Her voice trailed off as she finished her lame and rambling explanation. *Not a girlfriend, not a girlfriend, not a girlfriend.* Thank goodness there were no television cameras in the room.

"Hey, Brian, let's get some pictures of you with Jordan," someone piped up after a moment.

Sera was glad for the change of topic.

Obligingly, Jordan stepped forward and leaned in so that someone could snap a photo. Afterward, Jordan lingered for another quarter of an hour, talking with Brian and the others.

Sera chatted with a woman who introduced herself as Brian's mother and also with a nurse who stopped in. A half hour later, as Brian yawned a couple of times, Jordan took his cue, and Sera followed his lead in saying goodbye.

As she and Jordan made their way toward the elevator bank, she remarked, "You were the highlight of his day."

Jordan sighed, suddenly serious. "It's tough sometimes. Not all of the kids get better, but their courage is inspiring."

"You lift their spirits."

His lips quirked. "It's the least I can do if I'm not going to heal their bodies with physical therapy."

Sera flushed as she stepped into an empty elevator, and he followed. "Do you volunteer here because you were a sick kid yourself?"

"Going all pop psychology on me again, Angel?"

"Just an observation based on the evidence," she remarked as the doors closed.

"Okay, yeah."

"So I was wrong," she joked. "You don't have a fetish for Florence Nightingale types."

Jordan quirked an eyebrow. "I don't? What a relief."

Sera shook her head as the elevator opened again on the ground-floor lobby. "No, my new theory is that you want to be Florence."

Jordan stifled a laugh as they crossed the lobby to the exit. "Great. I guess I have my costume for next Halloween."

When they emerged from the building, she turned to face him. "Would you be serious?"

"Would you?"

"Your visit today was a nice thing to do."

He flashed a boyish grin. "See, I'm not all bad."

"No, no, you're not."

"So I'm making progress?"

"Of sorts."

"Good enough."

"I can't fault a guy who visits sick kids." She cleared her throat. "I had an older sister who died as a baby."

Jordan sobered.

She adjusted her handbag. "She died from a congenital defect." She wasn't sure why she was volunteering the information. "Your family may have hovered because you were always sick. Mine did, too, but for different reasons."

"They were protective because they knew what it meant to lose a child," he guessed.

"Exactly, though it was hard for me to appreciate at the time." She didn't want to understand Jordan Serenghetti, but she did—more and more. It was much easier to label him as just another player.

"My sister Mia could tell you all about overprotective parents." Jordan gave Sera a half smile.

She thought back to her brief conversation with Jordan's sister on set the other day, then sighed as she remembered something else from the taping. "I hope your mother isn't still expecting me to teach you how to cook."

Jordan flashed her a teasing look. "Don't worry—"

"Phew! What a relief." So why did she feel disappointed suddenly?

"I've gotten you off the hook by telling her that I'd ask you to attend a wedding with me."

Sera's mind went blank. "Wait—what?"

"A wedding. I avoid them like the plague—"

"Of course you do."

"—but this one I have to attend. It's a cousin, and Mom is all about family."

Well, that might explain why all the Serenghettis were in town—Mia from New York, where she was based, and Rick and Chiara from Los Angeles. They were here for a wedding—as well as to throw moral support behind Camilla *and* bear witness to Sera's on-screen chemistry with the family's baddest bad boy.

"That is some stealthy maneuvering, Serenghetti," Sera said in her sternest voice.

"It was Mom's idea."

"What!"

"She suggested I bring you to the wedding instead." Jordan shrugged too casually. "Because I was planning to fly solo."

"She makes a good accomplice," Sera muttered.

Jordan gave a short laugh. "She's desperate."

"For ratings, or to get you paired up with a woman who likes to use her brain?"

"Maybe both." Jordan schooled his expression. "You have to come with me to the wedding. I'm too injured to find a date."

"Please. You'd be able to find a date even from a hospital bed."

"You're giving me too much credit."

"Modesty. What a refreshing change for you," she teased. "So I'm a last resort?"

He looked like a kid caught with his hand in the cookie jar. "And a first."

She searched his expression, saw only earnestness and then felt warmth suffuse her.

She didn't want to be number one in Jordan's book—did she?

Ten

The last place Sera wanted to be was at an event with more Serenghettis—and yet here she was.

She'd been to enough get-togethers at Marisa and Cole's house or Serg and Camilla's to know the Serenghettis welcomed everyone and anyone. But once a social event ventured into cousin or—heaven help her—even second-cousin territory, like today's wedding, she knew she was in deep. In fact, she'd just met another of Jordan's second cousins, Gia Serenghetti, so now she knew the family's inside joke about the rhyming Mia and Gia "twins."

Still, Sera had to admit the colonial mansion outside Springfield, Massachusetts, was a picture-perfect setting for a June wedding. She'd decided to wear a sleeveless shimmering emerald sheath dress for the evening affair, and she'd caught back her hair in a jeweled clip for a low ponytail.

Jordan's gaze lit as it settled on her again from across the lawn, where he stood chatting with some fellow guests during the postceremony cocktail reception, while the bride and groom, Constance Marche and Oliver Serenghetti, posed for picturesque photos on the lawn. His perusal was a slow burn, full of promises and possibilities as it skimmed her curves.

As she took a sip of champagne, Sera could almost read the thoughts chasing through his mind. She was a flame dancing in the warm breeze of his appreciation. *Wow.*

Still, she felt like a phony. An impostor. She wasn't really Jordan's girlfriend or even his date. She was here as a fill-in, to avoid a cooking lesson that had been asked for on air. And to help Dante. And...*nothing more.*

She was so far from getting married herself, she might as well have been in a different galaxy. Neil had seen to that. And it wasn't as if she and Jordan would ever walk down the aisle. Her heart squeezed, nevertheless. She'd gotten misty-eyed at the exchange of vows earlier. It had been so beautiful, so perfect. The couple caught in the beams of the evening sun behind them and outlined by a trellis with climbing flowers. She couldn't think of a better arrangement if she'd been planning her own ceremony—not that it was in the cards.

On top of it, Marisa kept shooting her quizzical looks—as if her cousin, too, was puzzled about what to make of today and Sera's agreement to appear on Jordan's arm, especially since Sera had sworn that there was nothing romantic between her and Jordan. An appearance on Jordan's mother's show was one thing; a family wedding was another. *That's serious.* Her cousin's words echoed in her head.

Jordan approached, and Sera noticed again how he filled out his dark tailored suit. Only her well-trained eye could detect any lingering unevenness in his gait, since they were now more than two months postsurgery. In the past couple of weeks, since the cooking show, he'd grown stronger and more able with each physical-therapy session. Even she had been impressed at his progress. She knew from experience that there could be many unexpected stumbling blocks to recovery.

"I should never have agreed to this," Sera murmured as Jordan stopped by her side.

He took a sip from his champagne. "Relax. It's not as if we were caught having sex in the closet under the hall stairs."

"There's a closet under the stairs?" she squeaked. Why was she turned on? She wanted to fan herself and instead took another fortifying sip from her glass.

Jordan gave a strangled laugh. "Every old mansion has one."

"There's already open speculation in your family about what the status is between the two of us. I can read the looks on their faces, and they don't even know—"

"—we got it going already?"

Sera nodded, her face warming. "This is getting complicated."

"No, it's simple. You don't like me, and I've got a hard case of lust for you."

"I've been rethinking that part," she muttered.

"What?"

She cast him a sidelong look. "The part about how I don't…don't like you."

Jordan fiddled with the knot of his tie. "Now you tell me?" he joked. "We're at a wedding surrounded by a couple of hundred people. Some of them even related to me."

"And whose fault is that?" she replied. "Isn't there a closet under the stairs where we can hide?"

Jordan gave her a look of such longing and heat that Sera felt as if her clothes evaporated right off her.

He leaned close and whispered in her ear. "Hiding isn't exactly what I had in mind."

"Oh?" she asked breathlessly.

"What's under that dress?"

"It's got a built-in bra," she answered hesitantly.

"Even better. One zipper? I want to know how easy it is to peel you out of it."

"It's on the back. But don't you want to explore and find the exits on your own?"

Jordan took a deep swallow of his drink. "We could do this."

This was so crazy. They were actually contemplating if they could duck inside the mansion for a quickie.

"Dinner will start soon," she tried.

"We won't be missed."

"Is that why you waited till now? Because disappearing from the ceremony would have been too noticeable?" She really needed a fan.

One side of his mouth rose in a slight smile. "You think you were saved by the wedding bell?"

"Maybe you've been." Jordan was a no-strings kind of guy—it would be lethal if he was caught getting it on with her, of all people, and here, of all places.

"Angel, it's not salvation...yet. It's purgatory right now."

Sera forced a laugh. "Hey, you invited me to this event. I'm sure all your relatives aside from your mother are surprised you're here with a date." *Me*.

"Let them wonder all they want. It's been way too long."

"Since you've been at a wedding?"

"Since the two of us have been all over each other with lust," he responded bluntly.

Sera sucked in a breath.

"Don't tell me you haven't been wondering, too," Jordan continued in a low, deep voice. "Fantasizing about whether the chemistry that night in my apartment was a fluke or we're really that good together."

In fact, she had. She'd been working hard to keep up

her defenses, but it hadn't worked. She was having trouble remembering why she shouldn't like him. "Okay, I have. But it's unprofessional of me—"

Jordan gave a dismissive laugh.

"—and wrong." Dangerous, even. To her peace of mind.

He took the champagne flute from her hand and set it down on a nearby table along with his own glass. Then taking her hand, he said, "Come on."

She looked startled. "What? Where? Why?"

"You forgot *when* and *how*." He tossed her a wicked glance as they headed toward the back of the mansion. "*When* is now, and the answer to *how* is that there's a cloakroom off the main hall on the ground floor that isn't being used because it's summer and no one brought a coat. It's also bigger than the closet under the stairs."

Sera's quick indrawn breath was audible. Still, excitement bubbled up within her. They were playing with fire, but she felt alive, all her senses awakened.

They slipped inside the house without drawing attention, and in line with Jordan's expectations, the short hallway to the cloakroom was deserted. He opened the half door and then led her toward the shadowed recesses.

The minute they reached the back wall, his mouth was on hers.

Finally. She exulted in being in his arms again. She'd fought the good fight against his charm, but everything except this moment receded into the background.

Their mixed sighs filled the empty room as the kiss deepened. She tunneled her fingers into his hair, and he pulled her closer. All her soft curves pressed into his hard, lean physique, molding to him.

His scent was so good, his taste even better. And her senses stirred with his kiss, which was hot, warm and enticing.

When the kiss finally broke off, Jordan skimmed his

mouth across her cheek and nuzzled her temple before his breath settled around the delicate shell of her ear, giving her goosebumps and making her weak with awareness.

"Your dress has been driving me crazy all evening," he muttered.

"It's not meant to make men wild with lust."

He gave a strangled laugh. "That keyhole cutout that shows your cleavage. All I wanted to do was this—" he reached to her nape, and her zipper rasped downward "—and bare your gorgeous breasts."

She leaned against the wall, her breath hissing out of her as the top of her gown sagged. She wanted—

In the next moment, Jordan unerringly gave her what she was seeking—cupping her exposed breast and running his thumb over the pebbled peak.

"You're so responsive, Sera," he whispered, his voice reverent.

She shifted, brushing against his erection, and they both sighed.

Jordan bent and covered her breast with his mouth, and her hands tunneled through his hair as she gave herself up to waves of sensation that carried her closer to a shore of paradise...

Suddenly, there was the sound of a door opening, and Sera froze, yanked from a wonderful reverie.

Jordan straightened, and they hastily moved apart.

Sera's gaze met Jordan's in the shadows, and he pulled her closer, yanking the top of her dress back into place as he did so.

"Shh," he whispered into her ear.

Obediently, she stood still, hoping not to be noticed.

"I'll be back in New York on Monday," a woman's voice said. "We can discuss it then."

Jordan relaxed, his hold on her easing.

Sera thought it sounded like—

"Thanks, Sonia." There was a rustle, as if someone was fiddling with her purse.

In the next moment, the cloakroom was flooded with light as someone flipped a switch.

"Jordan."

Sera suppressed a groan. It was definitely Jordan's sister.

"Mia."

While Jordan stayed pressed against her for obvious reasons, Sera looked sideways over her shoulder at his sister, who wore an amused expression.

"I was just helping Sera with her dress." Jordan shrugged. "Stuck zipper."

"Of course," Mia played along. "You don't need to tell me. As a fashion designer, I've seen dozens. Hundreds, even. Those darn zippers. The pesky things give the worst trouble at the most inconvenient moments."

"Right," Jordan agreed.

"Sometimes a zipper will open easily but get stuck closing, or the reverse. Was the zipper going up or down?"

"For God's sake, Mia."

Sera's face flamed. Could things get more mortifying? And of course, it had to be one of Jordan's siblings who walked in on them.

"What are you doing here, Mia?" Jordan asked, going on the offensive.

"I could ask the same thing of you, big brother. But for the record, I was looking for a quiet place to take a call and just wandered in this direction right when the call was ending." Mia arched a brow. "And I'm going to assume you two came this way looking for a sewing kit…to fix Sera's dress."

Sera's hands flew to her cheeks.

Mia laughed. "Don't worry, your secret is safe with me." She gestured near her mouth as if turning a key in her lips and throwing it away.

"Thanks, sis."

Mia winked at them and then flipped the light switch and threw them into darkness again.

A moment later, Sera heard footsteps receding down the hall. She collapsed against Jordan with a small sound of relief, even though she wasn't sure how much longer she could stand their sexual frustration.

As Jordan drove her home after the wedding, Sera was a bundle of tingling awareness. They'd managed to keep their hands off each other and the PDAs to a minimum through the wedding dinner and dancing and socializing, but the tension had built…and built.

Yes, she'd been embarrassed about being caught in a clinch by Mia. And she hoped that Jordan's sister could keep a secret. But she and Jordan were playing with fire, and it just fueled their sizzling attraction.

They got out of his car and made their way to her building, enjoying the fresh air on this warm and balmy night. There was no question she was inviting him upstairs and inside. In the hall outside her front door, she handed him her keys, and the gesture—a mere brush of the fingers—was electric.

When Jordan pushed open the door, Sera entered the silent apartment and turned on a dim lamp. She hadn't changed much of Marisa's decor for the two-bedroom apartment, which had a retro vibe—right down to the Unblemished Yellow wall paint that her cousin had used to give a face-lift to the old kitchen cabinets. She was home, and yet her place had never felt less relaxed. Instead, the air was charged with sexual tension.

She heard every rustle as she set down her evening bag on a console table and Jordan followed her. With a remote, she switched on some flameless candles that sat on a chest in her living room and then turned and nearly collided with Jordan's chest.

He ducked his head and kissed her—all sexy and lingering.

Sera leaned into the kiss. She wanted to taste him, lick him, be enveloped by him.

When they broke apart, he gazed into her eyes. "I want you, Sera. I can't stop thinking about you."

And just like that, the shackles broke, and Sera was in his arms, kissing him back and pressing closer, desperate to pick up where they had left off earlier in the evening.

"Jordan," she breathed.

He smoothed his hands along her curves and skimmed kisses from her mouth to the side of her neck.

She'd resisted him for weeks but had nevertheless felt herself sliding into an attraction that she could not deny. He'd been hard to ignore—at physical therapy, on his mother's cooking show, in the hospital, and now at a wedding—and impossible to resist. He'd seduced her in the process, teasing her out of her shell.

He tugged on the zipper at the back of her dress and it rasped downward, her breasts spilling against him out of the built-in bra.

Bracing his good knee on a nearby ottoman, he bent and drew her closer. Running his hand up her calf in a light caress, he pulled one breast into his mouth.

She held his head close, her eyes falling shut. *Bliss.* The sensations were so acute, so exquisite, and she knew it all had to do with him and their burning, simmering desire for each other.

Jordan transferred his attention to her other breast, and Sera moaned.

He slid his hands up her legs, pushing up the hem of her dress, and then hooked his hands inside the band of her panties and pulled them down.

Sera braced her hands on his shoulders.

He murmured sweet encouragement and words of appreciation. "I've wanted you so long. Waited for you."

Me, too.

It was her last thought before he tugged her down to the ottoman, where she lay back, bracing herself on her elbows as he bent in front of her.

He ran his hands up and down her thighs in a delicious caress. Eventually, he found her with his mouth, and a strangled cry was torn from her lips. She lost all sense of time, just letting herself feel all the wicked things that he was doing to her. And then suddenly, her climax was upon her in a bright burst of energy.

She spasmed, riding an intense crest of pleasure that went on and on until she floated down and went limp against him.

Somehow, after that, they found their way to the bedroom, where they both stripped off the rest of their clothes.

She loved him with her mouth and hands until she could sense Jordan was on the brink of losing control.

"Ah, Sera," he groaned.

"Too much?" she teased as she settled back on her bed.

"Just right." He sheathed himself in protection and braced himself over her.

She quirked a brow at him. "Came prepared, did you?"

He flashed a quick grin. "Wishful thinking, but thank you. It's because of your therapy that we're even able to use this sexual position."

"Sure, blame me," she teased again.

He gave a strangled laugh. "No, I'm going to love you until we're both mindless."

In the next instant, he stroked inside her, and they both sighed.

She took up the tempo that he set. Sera had never felt so close to anyone before.

She'd rationalized away their first encounter on the night of the car accident as the product of adrenaline, annoyance and more.

But this time, there was no denying the truth. She came again, clinging to him as he sent her soaring on a wave of pleasure right before he found his own release.

In the aftermath, she lay in Jordan's arms, content as she'd ever been, until sleep claimed them.

When she came awake, she was surprised to see sunlight streaming through her bedroom windows, but the bed beside her was empty.

Frowning, she looked around the room, but then heard sounds from the kitchen. She cleaned up in the bathroom, donned some sweats and pulled her hair into a messy ponytail before padding out to find Jordan.

He was in the kitchen—at the stove, no less. She let a mix of emotions pass over her—pleasure and, yes, worry. Had she never fully shucked her fears about being disappointed by a man after Neil?

"Hey, sexy." Jordan held a spatula in his hand, and mouthwatering aromas filled the kitchen.

"Back at you."

Sera eyed him; he was tousled and edible-looking. He'd donned last night's suit pants but otherwise he was barechested—all rippling, lean muscle. Sera drank in the view of what was covered up during therapy.

Jordan smiled at her. "Hungry?"

How could he be so cheery so soon after sunrise? Okay, the sex had been spectacular. She felt like a well-sated cat. But still, mornings were mornings. She yawned and moved toward a cabinet to pull down a coffee mug.

"You know, I once asked if the clouds ever come out in Serenghetti Land," she muttered. "I guess the answer is no."

Jordan laughed. "Angel, I'm guessing I'll always need to be the one in charge of breakfast for us."

Retrieving her mug, she answered, "You got that right."

And then she realized...*always?* She hadn't blinked at his allusion to a next time—more than one, in fact—for them. She tested the idea and registered that it made her... happy. Butterflies-in-the-stomach happy, actually. Last night, her relationship with Jordan had taken a big step toward *complicated*, but right now, she wanted to shut out the world for a little bit longer and just experience the moment.

"Grumpy in the morning?"

"Yes." *Well, until seconds ago, anyway.* She poured herself a cup of dark brew that he'd had ready for her.

"I'll file that information away for future reference."

"I bet you've always dated the kind of woman who sleeps in her makeup so she can wake up camera-ready," she grumbled before savoring her first sip of coffee.

Jordan just smiled again. "Don't worry. You're cute in the morning—"

"Only in the morning?"

"—in a tussled-in-the-sheets kind of way."

"Hmm." *Thanks to him.* She looked at the stove. "What are you making?"

"The Serenghetti Brothers Frittata."

"So you do cook."

"Breakfast, sometimes. I think I mentioned it before. Since I often slept in, it was the one meal where Mom wasn't ruling the kitchen."

"Late-night carousing, I bet. I'm guessing you were having a lot of breakfasts later than everyone else. Closer to noon, maybe?"

He tossed her a meaningful look. "I'm not going to incriminate myself."

"Of course."

"When I started living on my own, making breakfast became a survival skill."

"Along with getting the right meal partner?"

"Jealous?"

"Please."

He looked boyishly charmed by her denial. "Something tells me you're going to be my best...meal partner ever."

"Oh?" She kept her tone casual. "Well, you're about to find out."

In fact, his frittata was delicious. And afterward, not least because it was her kitchen, she took charge of cleanup, while he headed to the shower. Wiping down the kitchen counter minutes later, she heard the water running and gave in to the urge she'd been resisting since she woke up.

She stripped off her clothes and headed in the direction of the running water.

Opening the bathroom door, she could see him in the shower stall. He held a disposable razor in one hand and one of her cosmetic mirrors with the other. As he shaved, she slipped up behind him and rested her hands on his hips and her cheek on his back.

When he reached for the shampoo, she stopped him and instead poured a dollop into the palm of her hand and went to work massaging his hair.

He tilted his head back in order to help her reach. And after several moments, he said, "Ah, Sera. Are we going for round two here?"

"Feels good?" she murmured.

"Feels great."

"Mmm." She could feel her body humming and vibrating to life.

"How about you go to work on the ache that's flared up?"

Her brow puckered. "Your knee is bothering you?"

"Right now, I could use your hands on me, Angel."

Concerned, she rinsed the suds from his hair and then bent down to place her hands on his knee.

Laughing, Jordan grasped her arm and pulled her up and around to face him.

Immediately, she realized he was aroused. "I thought you said your knee injury was bothering you."

He gave her a quick peck on the lips. "I didn't mention my knee, but I'm aching in other ways."

She realized she felt the same.

When had she started agreeing with him?

Eleven

Jordan couldn't stop thinking about her. He'd always stuck to casual relationships. What was the saying about best-laid plans?

The sex…it had been fantastic. Mind-blowing, even though that sounded trite. She'd been so responsive, and he'd been able to relieve a sexual frustration that had gone on forever—building up to the breaking point at his cousin's wedding, of all places. Not that he felt relief—now he itched to spend every moment with her.

He'd fantasized about her last night, reliving their evening together, except he'd woken aroused…and to an empty bed. Still, the memories had been vivid. The way she'd looked at the moment of her release—her back arched, her breath coming audibly between parted lips, her eyes half-closed.

Jordan almost groaned aloud, shifted on the bar stool and tightened his grip on his beer. He took a deep breath. If he wasn't careful, he'd embarrass himself or race to find Sera.

Usually weddings like the one the other day were a reminder that he wasn't looking to make a serious commitment himself. He liked his life just fine. At his cousin's
ceremony, though, every thought had fallen by the wayside
except getting closer to the woman he'd wanted to seduce.

He was pensive this evening even though he'd come to
the Puck & Shoot to relax. He couldn't even manage more
than distracted conversation with Vince, who occupied
the next stool.

On days like today, he had to wonder whether the whole
sports celebrity gig was worth it. Because, on top of it,
while he'd gotten a reprieve from the press during the off-
season and because he was out of commission with a bad
knee, lately they'd acted up again.

"Serenghetti." Marc Bellitti slapped him on the back
as he walked up. "It's good to see you nearly looking like
your old self."

"Yup." Jordan took a swig of his beer.

"Sera must be miracle worker." Marc flashed a grin.
"She almost makes me want to have a bum knee."

Jordan's hand tightened on his drink again—because he
had a sudden inexplicable urge to get in Marc's face. Once,
not so long ago, he'd been like his teammate—unable to remember names, but always able to recall a pretty face and
a body to match. But things had changed. *He'd* changed.
Maybe it was the injury, maybe it was Sera, maybe it was
the two together. After all, he had her to thank for his
amazing recovery.

Marc propped his forearm against the bar. "You haven't
even glanced at the blonde at table six throwing hot-and-
heavy looks your way. So I have to say you're only *nearly*
back to normal."

Jordan glanced over his shoulder. "She's not my type."

"Serenghetti, they're all your type. What's wrong with
her?"

"Too young."

Marc gave a mock gasp and clutched his chest. "Be still my heart. You cruised past thirty, and suddenly twenty-five is too young?"

"How do you know how old she is?"

Marc gave a sly smile. "On my way over here to keep company with your sorry cooking-competition-losing self, I happened to find out she's already got her degree and is going for another in marine biology."

"As I said, not my type."

"Well, well," Marc drawled, "look which kitty cat has changed his stripes."

Vince laughed.

"Maybe you're still thinking about that physical therapist," Marc commented.

"Appearances can be deceiving," Jordan responded, refusing to be drawn in.

He'd rather eat a hockey puck or two than admit to... *feelings*. He'd never hear the end of it from his teammates.

"Meaning?" Marc prompted.

Jordan raised his eyebrows but made sure to keep his tone nonchalant. "Maybe Sera's just my biggest challenge yet."

Or he was hers. Damn. He and Sera had never discussed the future, and he'd been content to live in the moment. *And what moments they'd been...* Still, the last thing he needed was for his teammates to latch onto the idea that his relationship with Sera was anything more than casual. Although, how he and Sera were going to continue to keep things on the down low after shattering the final barrier in their relationship on the night of his cousin's wedding, he had no idea. Sera hadn't said anything, but they were already skating on thin ice with Mia in the know.

"What about our bet that you could make her melt?" Marc asked. "Are you conceding defeat?" His teammate tut-tutted. "You're on a losing streak, Serenghetti. First, the cooking show, now—"

"I'm not conceding anything." Jordan made a motion indicating he was zipping his lips and throwing away the key. Let Marc speculate all he wanted. He wasn't going to admit anything—or divulge intimate details.

When Marc just laughed, Jordan glanced over his shoulder and then sobered. "Hi, Dante."

He wondered how long Sera's brother had been standing there and what he'd heard and then shrugged off the thought. His words could be read in many ways.

She'd never felt this way about a guy. There, she'd admitted it. He'd been a laundry list of her *never*s, but Jordan had somehow become her *must-have*. She couldn't wait to see him again, jump his bones and float in a happy bubble of coupledom.

Her former self would have found it all ridiculously saccharine instead of cause for a goofy smile. Few would be able to tolerate her right now—even her own past selves.

Take Marisa, for example.

She'd just run into her cousin in the produce aisle of the local supermarket, Bellerose. Pushing her cart and daydreaming, she'd almost jumped when Marisa had called out her name.

Her cousin knit her brow. "Are you okay?"

"Just peachy," Sera managed, even though all she wanted to do was throw her arms wide and twirl. In the middle of the produce aisle. "It's been ages since I've run into you here."

"That's because I'm normally trapped in the baby aisle comparing package labels and feeling guilty about not pureeing everything myself," Marisa quipped and then tucked a stray strand behind her ear. "These days, if I manage to get out of the house without spit-up on my shirt, I'm good."

Sera smiled. "And where is the marvelous Dahlia?"

"At home with Daddy and, with any luck, napping. Cole had the day off."

As they continued to chat, lingering in the aisle, Sera shifted from one foot to another.

She knew her cousin had to be full of speculation about her appearance on Jordan's arm at the wedding. Plus, this was no longer simply one amorous encounter with Jordan that she'd told him to swear to take to the grave. Any last shred of professional distance was gone. She and Jordan had done the deed, and short of amnesia, she was never likely to forget that night—in all its pyrotechnic glory.

As if on cue, Marisa said, "So how is Jordan these days?"

Sera made herself shrug nonchalantly. "He's been recovering nicely."

"Mmm-hmm." Her cousin looked amused. "He seems to be in great shape. Enough to attend a wedding."

With you as his date. The unspoken words hung in the air.

"I went with him because it got me out of giving Jordan the cooking lesson that his mom suggested," Sera blurted and then could have bitten off her tongue. There was no need to clarify why she'd been with Jordan, and being defensive definitely made it seem like a date. Her face heated.

"Mmm-hmm."

"Will you stop saying that?"

Marisa smiled. "Please. The guy's been tracking you with his eyes."

Sera felt a hot wave of embarrassment. "I didn't even want to be his physical therapist. I tried to get myself out of it."

"Yeah, but the attraction was so strong, maybe you were just afraid to go there."

Sera bit her lip. *Afraid.* She hadn't given more than a passing thought to Neil in…it was probably a new record.

Instead, her mind—and heart—had been consumed by Jordan. She supposed it was all a sign of how far she'd come since her bad breakup. Sure, she'd had boyfriends before, but nothing serious until Neil—or so she'd thought. But her relationship with Neil had been skating on the surface in comparison to the depths she'd plunged into with Jordan.

Jordan had wrung every emotion out of her—annoyance, exasperation, nervousness, need, hunger, joy, pleasure. It was like living life in an explosion of color, especially in bed.

Just then, another shopper came by, and Sera and Marisa separated in order to let the older woman through with her cart. Sera took the opportunity to glance at her watch to try to extricate herself from this tricky conversation. If she lingered, she expected more gentle probing and teasing.

But her cousin just winked at her. "Keep me posted."

Sera rolled her eyes. "Right."

Saying goodbye to Marisa with a promise to catch up another time, she headed to the checkout line.

Minutes later, after she'd loaded the groceries into her car and had gotten behind the wheel, her cell phone rang. Noticing it was from Dante, she turned off the ignition and took the call.

After a brief exchange, during which Sera wondered why Dante was calling, her brother asked, "How are things going with you and Jordan?"

"Great." The trending topic of the day: #JordanandSera.

Dante cleared his throat. "Just be careful."

"Don't worry," she replied, hoping to keep this conversation light, "I promise not to let him break a bone on all that physical-therapy equipment." She hadn't confided in her brother about her true relationship status with Jordan these days, so she wondered what her brother was getting at. Unless Mia had been loose-lipped, despite her promise to button it? Sera tightened her hold on her cell. "Is there anything you're not telling me?"

"No. Yes. I heard you went as his date to a family wedding."

"I did. He needed one. He's injured…and not getting around much." It wasn't a total lie, but she added quickly, "I didn't mention it to you or Mom because it was casual." *And I didn't want you to make too much of it.*

There was a pause. "I know I'm going to regret this, but my loyalty to my little sister is bigger—"

"Than what?"

"I ran into Jordan at the Puck & Shoot."

Sera forced nonchalance. "And so? He was flirting with Angus?"

"You know Angus has been married fifty years."

"Thirty-five."

"Who's counting?"

"He is. When he skipped over his wedding anniversary two years ago, his wife never let him forget it."

"No, Angus is out of the picture. But listen, I overheard Jordan joking with some Razors about you being his biggest challenge yet."

Well, she was. Or did Jordan mean she was just another conquest? It was an ambiguous statement, but the fact that he'd been joking with his teammates when he'd said it wasn't a good sign.

"Right before that, I heard Jordan tell Marc Bellitti that appearances can be deceiving."

Hadn't she thought the same thing about Jordan recently? She'd discovered he volunteered with a children's charity. And she'd been basking in the realization that he wasn't quite the player she'd thought he was. "In what context did he say this?"

"To be honest, Marc was ragging Jordan about being hung up on you."

Even Jordan's teammates were onto them? She strove to keep her voice neutral—bored even. "I've been a waitress at the Puck & Shoot. I've heard it all. They were probably just shooting the breeze."

"Jordan and Matt had a bet—"

"Players often do."

"—that he couldn't seduce you. Or, uh, to be more precise, make you 'melt.'"

She froze. It was like Shakespeare's *The Taming of the Shrew*, and she knew what her role was. Her lips tightened. Yes, she was pissed off. But she was going to hold her fire and question Jordan at the appropriate time. Have him explain himself. *If he could.*

She sighed, conceding her brother's good intentions in telling her all this. "Thanks, Dante." She watched a cloud pass in front of the sun, darkening the inside of her car. "I owe you." *Poor Sera, saved by her family again.*

Surprisingly, though, she didn't get an immediate wisecrack from Dante. Instead, her brother matched her tone of resignation. "What are siblings for? Anyway, these days, you've been coming to my aid just as much. More, actually."

Dante's words were almost enough to bring a smile to her face. Because he was right—and there was the small silver lining to her current predicament.

She was a mature and intelligent woman. Or so Sera kept reminding herself.

In the days since speaking with her brother, she'd come up with a plan—once she was done being miffed. She was willing to give Jordan the benefit of the doubt. After all, she'd witnessed plenty of ribbing banter while waitressing at the Puck & Shoot, just as she'd told Dante. The best strategy might be to beat Jordan and his buddies at their own game.

Could it have been only a week since Constance and

Oliver's wedding? So much had happened, including the buildup of sexual frustration. Work and other commitments had kept her and Jordan apart except for physical therapy, and then Dante's news had led her to bide her time until tonight, when Jordan had suggested dinner out at Altavista.

She and Jordan had been served wine but had yet to order their meal. *Time to have a little fun.*

She leaned close, drawing Jordan's attention, so she could keep her voice low. "I've been thinking all week about Saturday night."

Jordan's eyes kindled. "What a coincidence. So have I."

"Hmm." *And not just so he could claim to have won a stupid bet?*

"I don't want to rush you, but, yeah—" the corner of his mouth turned up "—I've wanted a repeat."

She dipped the top of her finger into the top of her wineglass and then, without breaking eye contact, brought that finger to her lips.

Jordan swallowed, his throat working.

She knew him well enough now to recognize the flare of arousal. They occupied a cozy corner table for two, where they could engage in semipublic flirtation without attracting too much attention. She wanted to have some fun while she made him eat his words.

Deliberately, she let her leg brush against his. Her wrap dress clung to her breasts, and she leaned forward, knowing her cleavage would be on full display. "I want to make you melt."

"Sera," he said in a low voice, his gaze kindling, "the appetizer hasn't even arrived, and you're—"

"Ready for dessert?" She trailed the wine-stained finger from her collarbone to the swell of her breasts.

Jordan cleared his throat and lowered his eyes to follow the motion of her finger.

"I came straight from work. I'm a little…breathless."

He lifted his gaze then and fixed it on her. "You're wearing clingy dresses in your therapy sessions these days? For which client?"

She gave a throaty laugh. "Don't be silly. I changed into my thong and dress in the bathroom before I drove over here."

Jordan sucked in a breath. "You're playing with me, aren't you?"

Yes, she was enjoying turning the tables.

"I don't know what's put you in this mood—"

"Well, it's been a while since we've had sex. Now that I've had a taste, I want more."

He groaned, and she gave him a naughty smile.

Jordan thrust his crumpled napkin onto the table. "That's it. Let's go. I'll leave a big tip for the wine we ordered and for the meal we didn't."

"But we haven't had dinner."

His gaze was hot on her face. "We'll order in. After."

"Jordan," she murmured, "you look a little flushed. Are you hot?"

"Yeah, for you," he growled back, waving away an approaching waiter. "Great invitation, by the way. I accept."

She curved her lips and then shifted in her seat. She took a large swallow from her water glass to steady herself and then regarded him over the rim.

"Sera." There was an edge to his voice. "We need to leave now. Otherwise I won't be able to without—"

"Mmm. Wouldn't want your teammates to see that, would we?"

"Exactly."

"After all, you're the one who's supposed to make me melt."

Jordan stilled and then groaned again. Except this time, the sound was self-deprecating.

Sera tilted her head and regarded him.

"I can explain."

"I'm sure. I can't wait to hear it."

"Who told you? Dante?" he said on an exhale. "Sera, it was a ridiculous bet—"

"At my expense."

"And a flippant remark—"

"To uphold the great and mighty Jordan Serenghetti reputation?"

"Damn it."

"Amen."

"Are you going to make me grovel?"

"Or at least work for it," she replied teasingly. "Let me help you out here. 'I was just being one of the guys.'"

"Check."

"'We don't wear emotion well.'"

"Check."

"'It was false male bravado. Psych 101.'"

"Check again." He took her hand. "I'll take it from here. I'm frustrated about not being on the ice. Getting grief about you from my teammates was heaping—"

"Insult onto injury?" she asked drolly.

He looked sheepish. "Yeah. I didn't want to go there with them…about you. Because it was you, and you're special."

"I'm going to have to get tough with the Razors crew."

Jordan smiled. "They already know you can kick ass on TV."

"Mmm-hmm."

He lifted her hand and kissed her knuckles. "Forgiven?"

"I ought to make you take cooking lessons live for a season."

Jordan shuddered. "Please. The last episode nearly did me in." Then he sobered. "Anyway, this isn't about some asinine bet or tit for tat. The truth is I've lost track of which one of us owes a favor to the other. Because somewhere along the way, I stopped caring. Except about being with you."

Wow. She wanted to believe those words. His bet had cast doubt on what she'd thought was something genuine and true and beautiful. She still had faith in him, but it had been nicked. But then, she hadn't expected him to crack open with emotional honesty tonight.

"I had this germ of a plan to make a major donation to Welsdale Children's Hospital," Jordan went on after a pause. "Thanks to you, I might still have a career that'll make that possible."

She blinked.

"It'll be a hospital addition for rehabilitation facilities. Because I understand how important physical therapy is."

Sera parted her lips on an indrawn breath. She'd started out annoyed and ready to teach him a lesson, but somehow they'd ended up in a place where he held her heart.

Jordan caressed the back of her hand with his thumb. "I have a meeting with hospital management in the next few weeks. I'd like you to be there."

She blinked again. It wasn't a marriage proposal, but this was heady stuff. He was asking her to weigh in on a major life decision—one that would involve millions of dollars. "Why?"

"You'll have a perspective on things that I won't. I value your opinion." He gave a lopsided smile. "You're important to me."

His words were sexier than any underwear billboard. On impulse, she cupped his face and kissed him, heedless of the other diners scattered through the dim restaurant.

When she sat back, Jordan laughed.

"Hey," he said, "I wasn't joking earlier when I said we needed to get out of here fast. Any more PDAs and—"

"—we'll be putting on an R-rated performance?"

"Anyone ever tell you that you have a knack for finishing my sentences?"

"We're on the same wavelength."

"That's not all I'd like to be," Jordan growled.

"Get the check, Serenghetti."

Twelve

By the time he and Sera arrived back at his place, it was all Jordan could do to hold himself in check until they stepped off the elevator inside his apartment.

"This place is different than I remember," she remarked. "But then, I was a little shaken up after the accident and maybe not picking up the same details."

He was shaken up *now*. He kissed the back of her neck and let his hands roam up her body.

He wanted to make love to her again. It was a need he hadn't experienced this sharply...ever.

She'd surprised him with her reaction to the ridiculous challenge he'd taken up with Marc. Another woman might have given him the silent treatment and left him to guess why.

But Sera had...attitude. She drove him crazy and made him ache with need.

Even in his sleep, he could taste her and inhale her scent. And ever since their encounter after the wedding, he's been itching to get her alone. He'd meant it when he said all he could think about these days was being with her.

When they got to his bedroom, he turned her around to face him and kissed her. She met him with a longing of her own, her mouth tangling with his.

He pulled at the tie at her waist and her dress fell open. He drank her in with his eyes. "You're a fantasy come true, Sera."

They kissed again, and he inched her in the direction of his bed. Within a few steps, her dress fell to the floor, followed by his shirt.

He cupped her breasts, feeling their luxurious weight and letting his thumbs move over the twin peaks covered by the thin fabric of her bra.

"Do you like my hands on you?" he murmured.

"Yesss." Her breath was shallow and rapid, her pupils dilated.

He wanted her to feel the depth of his need and reciprocate it. He wanted to bring her pleasure.

Sliding his hands under her arms, he unhooked her bra at the back and watched those glorious breasts spill against him.

Then holding her gaze, he bent and gave attention to each breast with his mouth.

She moaned, and her fingers tangled in his hair. "Jordan…"

He closed his eyes, focusing on drawing one peak into his mouth and then the other.

Sera's knees bent, and she leaned in to him.

Yes. He told her all the things he wanted to do with her, until her breath came in rapid rasps. Her skin tasted flowery, making him want her all the more.

When he straightened, his hand went to the juncture of her thighs. "You are so ready for me, Angel."

She had a half-lidded look, her color heightened, her lips red.

"It's going to be so good. I've been waiting for days for a repeat."

She wet her lips and then stroked her hand up and down his erection. "Please."

He breathed deep. "What do you want?"

In response, she surprised him by undoing his belt and stripping him out of his pants. She pressed kisses to his bare chest, making him groan. And then she stroked him with a sure hand, bringing him ever closer to the brink.

"Ah, Sera."

She bent before him and took him in her mouth, loving him.

Jordan's eyes closed on a wave of pleasure. When he couldn't take anymore—knowing he was unbearably close—he tugged her up and stripped her underwear from her.

She lay back on the beige comforter covering his bed, her hair splayed around her.

Jordan fumbled with some protection from a nearby dresser drawer and then braced himself over her.

Holding her gaze as her legs came around him, he sheathed himself inside her, and they both sighed.

Jordan gritted his teeth. "You're so damn hot and tight. So good."

He began to move, and she met him stroke for stroke. Jordan closed his eyes, intent on drawing out the interlude. Within minutes, however, it was too much for both of them.

Sera lifted her hips and arched her back with her climax, and watching her glorious reaction, Jordan came apart himself, his hoarse groan a testament to reaching a new peak.

Afterward, he slumped against her and gathered her to him, and they were both content to let sleep claim them.

* * *

Sera reflected that the only word that could sum up the past week or so was *idyllic*. She and Jordan had snuck away to spend a weekend at a cozy bungalow he had on Cape Cod, taking a balloon ride over the wooded fields and overall enjoying living in their own new and kaleidoscopic little world.

Now as she and Jordan arrived hand in hand at a local movie theater near Welsdale, Sera found herself both content to enjoy the evening and bursting with plans for their burgeoning relationship. Jordan's recovery was going so well, soon they'd be able to head to the boxing gym together. And in future outings to Cape Cod, they could water-ski, take a boat out on the water and even go parasailing. Jordan had dared her to try the last.

"Jordan, Jordan!"

The paparazzo came out of nowhere, camera flashing like a firearm. Sera bent her head down as she and Jordan headed toward the doors of the theater. So far, they'd been able to duck photographers despite his celebrity. Probably the fact that it was the off-season and he'd been convalescing helped.

Sera didn't delude herself, however, that their honeymoon would last forever. Jordan was too well-known. And while they'd been able to keep their relationship under wraps until recently even from their families, this photographer meant she'd have to figure out fast how to deal with being outed. The fact that she and Jordan were holding hands was a giveaway that they were more than casual acquaintances.

As the photographer snapped away, he also jogged to catch up to them. "Any comment on the news report?"

"Whatever it is, the answer is no," Jordan tossed back.

"Are you denying that you're the father of Lauren Zummen's child?"

Sera stiffened and swung her gaze to Jordan, whose expression had turned grim.

"Anything you want to say?"

"Again, no."

In the next moment, Jordan changed course and was hustling her back to his car—obviously trying to shake the paparazzo.

"No denial?" the photographer called out after them.

"How did you know where we were?" Jordan asked, not looking behind him.

"I have my sources." The paparazzo sounded cheery.

Stunned, Sera silently followed Jordan. Suddenly, what their families might think of their relationship was the least of her problems. And her concern about the stupid bet he'd made with his teammates seemed laughable in comparison.

They both said nothing as they got into the car and Jordan pulled away from the curb, leaving their pursuer far behind them. Obviously, a night out couldn't happen now. They'd be sitting ducks for more unwanted attention.

Sera felt a roaring in her ears. Finally, she forced herself to say, "Do you know what he was talking about?"

She could tell from Jordan's face that he had some inkling at least—and he'd chosen to say nothing to her about it.

"There are rumors…"

She gripped her handbag, pressing her knuckles into the folds. She could've heard those rumors at any time and would have been unprepared to deal with them. She was unprepared to deal with them *now*. "Where are we going?"

"Back to your place because it's closer, so we can talk. Privately."

She took his words as confirmation of her worst suspicions and briefly closed her eyes. "So there's a baby?"

Jordan nodded, not taking his eyes off the road.

"Did you know the mother?" She felt as if she was chewing sawdust as she said it.

"The first time I heard her last name attached to the rumors is when the photographer just said it. Yes, I knew her. But once and for a short time."

"Once is all it takes, isn't it?" she retorted.

This time, he did glance at her. "There's no proof that I'm the father."

"And there's nothing to say you're not."

Jordan hit his palm against the steering wheel. "You're asking me to prove a negative when I haven't even taken a paternity test."

How could this be happening to her again? Was she a marked woman? She'd now dated *two* men who'd had families—children—she hadn't known about. For the second time, she'd experienced the most brutal deception.

"Sera, those kinds of accusations are not that uncommon for professional athletes."

She knew what he was saying. Sports stars were targets for fortune hunters. Her own cousin Marisa was the product of a pro athlete's short-term liaison, though Aunt Donna hadn't asked for or received a penny from Marisa's father, whose minor-league baseball dreams had died along with him in a freak accident.

"The story is that the girl is two and a half," Jordan said quietly.

"When are you going to take a paternity test?"

He didn't take his eyes off the road—didn't glance at her. "This allegation has come out of the blue. I need to have Marv, my agent, arrange to investigate it."

"Why didn't you tell me?"

"I figured it was baseless gossip until now. I want to have the facts first."

Right. Time to figure out how to spin this story for her,

perhaps? There was always a reason—an explanation. Neil had had one, too.

When they arrived at her apartment, she popped out of the car and shot for the door. She heard his car door slam and then Jordan rushing to catch up to her.

"Sera!"

She didn't want to talk about this right now. How could she be so stupid? *Again.*

She must be giving some kind of signal to men: *this one is easy to dupe.*

Jordan touched her arm, and she spun toward him. "Leave me alone."

"We need to talk. Listen—"

"No, you listen." She stabbed a finger in the direction of his chest. "I don't like being had."

He had the indecency to appear surprised. "Neither do I."

"There's a lot about you I apparently didn't know."

"Let's talk somewhere more private."

"I don't think so." No way was she continuing this…*discussion.* Especially inside her apartment. So he could work his *charm* on her and *gaslight* her. There'd be nowhere to run if she was completely broken.

Neil had played with her mind, too. And her feelings—and her heart. *You've got it all wrong, Sera… My marriage isn't real… I adore you.* Afterward, she'd discovered at the bar where she'd first met him that he'd been a longtime customer, and she hadn't been the first woman he'd dallied with. And there'd been a baby, all right—or at least a toddler. A two-year-old who'd lived with his wife in Boston.

Jordan remained silent but sighed and shoved his hands in his pockets.

"What? Nothing to say? This news didn't come as a complete surprise to you."

"I told you what I know. It was sudden, and I just learned the mother's last name. I'm still processing it."

"How stupid do you think I am? These types of scandals are usually percolating for a while before they grab a lot of headlines. And you—" she sucked in a deep breath "—didn't tell me."

"I didn't think you'd be this upset that I'd waited."

"What?" She stared at him. "I wouldn't be upset that you're a father, and I didn't know it?"

"Alleged father. And I recently found out myself."

"But you knew before tonight." She made a strangled sound and then muttered, "I should have learned my lesson with Neil."

"Who's Neil?"

"The guy I had the misfortune to date after he walked into my bar." She paused. "Until I discovered he was married and had a wife and toddler daughter squirreled away in Boston." Her voice dripped sarcasm. "Conveniently far but not too far away from Welsdale, where he traveled frequently on business."

Jordan swore.

Sera gave a humorless laugh. "To think that I thought my biggest problem with you was some ridiculous bet that you'd made with Marc Bellitti about—" she waved her hand "—making me melt. I guess we all know who the fool is, don't we?"

Jordan looked solemn. "Sera... I'm sorry."

"Yes, I guess there's nothing else to say, is there?" she replied flippantly, feeling traitorous tears welling. "Except sometimes *I'm sorry* isn't enough. Goodbye, Jordan."

Jordan stared broodingly at his apartment wall from his spot on the sofa.

When he'd reluctantly driven off earlier without settling things with Sera, he realized that he needed the truth first before he could convince her. Had he really fathered a child he hadn't known about? He'd always been careful. In this case, more than three years ago, he'd been intimate with Lauren once, and he'd used protection. Sure, such measures weren't foolproof, but it gave him reason to question the veracity of the claims here.

He'd met Lauren at a party, and she'd come on strong. She'd had a summer-vacation share on Cape Cod with a bunch of twentysomethings—and his house had been nearby. He'd quickly realized they didn't have much in common, so he'd let her down easy and had never seen or heard from her again. Until now.

Sure, those minimal facts would be small consolation to Sera. But he also wasn't the same person he'd been three years ago. These days, an aspiring groupie held little appeal for him.

He knew what he had to do. If he was already being stalked by paparazzi, the story was spreading quickly. He couldn't afford to wait, even if his agent had flagged the story for him just yesterday—as he often did when his name popped up online, associated with good or negative articles. He'd have to tell his family before they read about it. *Before they had a reaction of shock and disappoint akin to Sera's.*

He winced inwardly. First, though, he had to marshal his resources.

Picking up the phone, he called Marv.

His agent answered on the third ring, sounding sleepy.

"Early bedtime these days, Marv?" Jordan couldn't resist teasing.

"What's up?" Marvin replied in a gravelly voice.

Jordan sobered. "I need you to follow up on the recent gossip story about the baby I allegedly fathered. I can't afford to wait, and we need to move up the timeline about how we react."

"What happened?"

"A paparazzo caught up with me tonight, and the story is gaining traction." He paused, tightening his jaw. "He blurted the woman's last name, and I just discovered that this Lauren is someone I may have known."

He didn't need to spell things out for Marv. Lauren was a common enough name that it had been easy for both him and his agent to initially dismiss this story. But now he was admitting to Marv that this was a woman from his past. And Jordan knew he had to face the consequences, one way or another. "I'm willing to take a paternity test if necessary."

What if he was the father? He weighed the idea. Sure, he figured he'd have kids someday. He liked kids. He loved being the newly minted uncle to his brothers' babies. He cared enough to fund-raise with Once upon a Dream and want to sponsor new facilities at Children's Hospital. But having children of his own wasn't something he'd seriously contemplated up to now given his lifestyle; he was at the peak of his career. Plus, if he was honest, he'd say he'd never met a woman he wanted to have kids with.

An image of Sera flashed through his mind, and he started to smile. His baby and Sera's would be a firecracker, no question.

Marv sighed. "You know, a scandal on top of everything else won't be good for the revenue stream or your contract-negotiating position. I gotta put that out there."

"We're living in the era of reality-TV stars. Don't be too sure," Jordan responded drily. "Anyway, I want the truth—whatever it is."

"Of course."

"I want you to hire a private investigator and find out all you can. I need as much background as possible fast."

He trusted Marv and considered him more than an agent because of their long-standing working relationship. That was why he was asking him to be the point person and hire whomever and do whatever it took.

"You got it," his agent said. "And Jordan?"

"Yeah?"

"No matter what the truth is, you can handle it."

"Thanks for the vote of confidence, Marv."

His life had been turned upside down, but he'd been in worse situations before.

Thirteen

"Bernice, I need to be reassigned."

Sera stood in the doorway of her manager's office, not looking at Bernice but focused on the bobblehead dolls on the shelves. Frankly, she felt a bit like a bobblehead herself lately.

It wasn't every day that a woman had to deal with being outed as a couple in the press and a private breakup *at the same time*. From some angles, it would seem that she and Jordan had the shortest relationship on record. They were the local version of a Las Vegas wedding *and* divorce.

Plus, the juiciness of Jordan being outed as a baby daddy while dating another woman at the same time was making the press slaver.

The twin headlines ran through her head: "Jordan Serenghetti's Secret Love Child." "Jordan Serenghetti's New Mystery Woman."

Bernice swiveled her chair so that she faced Sera more

fully. "You want to be reassigned? Because Jordan may have fathered a child?"

"You know already?"

"Honey, everyone knows. It's Jordan Serenghetti. The news is hard to avoid, especially around here, and I'm not a good gossip-dodger."

Sera wasn't ashamed to admit she'd cried last night. The pain had been a dull throb in the region of her heart. If it had been sharp and awful but over and done within minutes, she might have been thankful. Instead, she had this agonizing aftermath.

It wasn't as if she'd be able to avoid Jordan for the rest of her life. Not unless she declined Marisa and Cole's future invites. And maybe not entirely even then. Welsdale wasn't that big a town, and she was bound to run into Jordan eventually, even if she ducked every event that Marisa and Cole planned for Dahlia or any other child they might have.

Which brought Sera back to the children she and Jordan would never have. Because he may have already plunged into parenthood with another woman, and had hidden it from her—just like Neil had.

Why hadn't she learned? Her inner voice wailed and raged, refusing to be silenced.

Bernice looked at her sympathetically.

"I know you said we need this contract with the Razors…" Sera trailed off and bit her trembling lip. Damn it. *She would not cry.* She'd thought she'd used up all her tears last night.

"Things got a little too cozy with Jordan?"

Sera nodded, still avoiding her manager's gaze. She'd behaved unprofessionally—she inwardly rolled her eyes—and with Jordan Serenghetti, of all people. He was an in-law and a sports celebrity.

"Feelings?"

"Yeah," she responded thickly.

She blamed Jordan—and herself. How had she fallen prey to his charm? She should have known better. She did know better. And even if she had to keep banging her head against a wall, she *would* do better next time.

Bernice sighed. "The smooth-as-honey jocks are always the ones that are hardest to resist."

"You know?" Sera raised her eyebrows. Bernice seemed to be speaking from experience.

"Remind me to tell you about Miguel another time."

Sera's eyes widened because her manager had been married for years. Had Bernice had an affair?

"He was pre-Keith," her manager added. "I learned my lesson."

Sera wished she had, too.

"Okay," Bernice said briskly. "When's your next appointment with the Razors' resident bad boy?"

"Wednesday at two."

"Let me look at my schedule and see who else on staff is available."

Sera relaxed her shoulders. "Thanks, Bernice."

"We can tell him you're unavailable this week and work from there, until this situation gets resolved."

As far as Sera was concerned, this situation was already resolved. She and Jordan were over and done. She shook her head. "This isn't a temporary squabble. There's no hope—"

Bernice waved her hand. "We'll see."

Sera sighed. At least she had a temporary reprieve. "Thanks, Bernice."

Sera did her best to focus on work for the rest of the day. On the way home, she stopped at Bellerose in order to pick up some groceries. She was either going to cook and bake her troubles away or indulge in some premade comfort food—maybe both.

On the way to the ice-cream section, she stopped

abruptly as she caught sight of her cousin Marisa—or rather, her cousin spotted her. She bit back a groan.

"We have to stop meeting this way," Marisa joked, maneuvering her cart out of the way.

Tell me about it. The last thing she needed right now was to run into her cousin. She wasn't sure she had time to put on her *brave face.* "Let me guess. With Dahlia around now, you mostly get to do the supermarket run only in the evenings when Cole gets home."

Her cousin smiled. "Bingo."

Unfortunately, Sera thought, it was also the time when she'd be getting out of work and maybe stopping for milk on the way home. Karma was against her these days in a major way.

Marisa searched her cousin's face and then glanced around them as if to be sure they had some privacy for the moment. "How are you doing?"

"As well as can be expected today," Sera responded noncommittally.

"I was going to call you later on, after I knew you'd be home from work. If you need someone to lend an ear or a shoulder…"

Sera blinked. "To cry on?" She shrugged. "Sorry, all my tears have been washed away."

Marisa sighed.

"How are the Serenghettis handling the news?" Sera damned herself for asking.

After she and Jordan had been ambushed by the photographer, she'd figured it was just a matter of time until the news became really public—though she hadn't expected it to find its way to Bernice so quickly. Perhaps Jordan had called to forewarn his family…a courtesy he hadn't extended to her. Maybe he'd learned something from her reaction to being caught by surprise and decided telling others himself was the better course.

"Jordan has told all of us that he doesn't know what's true yet."

Sera shrugged again. "Well, best of luck to him."

Marisa looked worried. "Oh, Sera, I know you care."

"Do you?"

"I thought, especially at the wedding, that there was a special spark between you and Jordan." Marisa searched her expression again. "Was I wrong?"

"Does it matter now? The only thing that does is that I was a fool. Again."

"Because Jordan may have a child?"

"Because he didn't tell me!" Sera waved a hand. "Like a certain lying ex-boyfriend. I seem to have a special gift for ferreting out impostors."

"Oh, I don't know, the feelings between you seemed very real to me."

As another customer turned into their aisle, they moved apart.

"I need to go," Sera said quickly. "Before someone recognizes me from the news."

"I'm here if you need me."

Sera just nodded as she moved down the aisle, but she mulled over Marisa's words.

Feelings. The magic word. First Bernice, now her cousin. She was hoping these *feelings* would go away soon. Far, far away.

Fool. Sera had called herself the dirty word more times than she could count in the past few days. What kind of pushover got taken for a ride twice by men singing the same tune? Would she ever learn?

She'd taken to the gym with a vengeance. Pilates, yoga, kickboxing, two-mile runs. There was no hurdle that she wouldn't surmount. But she couldn't overcome her fury. Okay, her pain.

Damn it.

And now she was facing Sunday dinner with her family at her mother's house. Not showing up wasn't an option. Her family would just take her absence as confirmation that something was amiss—and perhaps wonder and worry more than they already were. She had to face reality, and the sooner the better.

After serving the spaghetti and meatballs, her mother eyed her speculatively. "I heard the most outrageous story this week. I knew it couldn't possibly be true."

"Hmm." Sera didn't look up from her plate.

"Something about you and Jordan Serenghetti being an item," her mother went on. "I told my hairdresser that the press must have snapped you together because of some invite from your cousin Marisa. You're related by marriage these days, after all."

Yup, and bound to stay that way. It was a gloomy prospect. She was destined to see Jordan again and again. Some traitorous part of her longed to see him again—still—but at the same time, she knew it would be unbearable to maintain a brave front.

"So am I right?" her mother asked brightly, glancing from her to a studiously silent Dante, who'd arrived for the family meal only minutes before.

"It wasn't an event that Marisa was hosting," Sera mumbled.

"And then Natalie—that's my hairdresser—also said she'd heard that Jordan had fathered a child with some woman recently." Rosana Perini heaved a sigh. "Honestly, Natalie hears the worst gossip."

Sera's face grew hot. "Yes, I heard the same story."

Her mother paused and blinked. "You did?"

Sera played with her food. "The photographer who trailed me and Jordan to the movie theater mentioned it."

"Where the Serenghettis were having an outing and invited you. How nice."

Sera held her mother's gaze. "Where Jordan and I were going, just the two of us." *After spectacular sex.*

Dante coughed.

Rosana tilted her head, puzzlement drawing her brows together. "So the story is true? You and Jordan have been dating?"

"Yes."

"And now it turns out he's fathered a child with another woman?"

Sera felt her face heat again. Put that way, it sounded like just another scrape that, in her family's eyes, *poor Sera* would get herself into. "That's what the press is saying."

Her mother seemed to be floundering, unsure of how to process what she was hearing. "You didn't tell me that you and Jordan...were seeing each other."

Right. Precisely to avoid situations like this.

"But he's been injured..." Her mother's voice trailed off, as if shock had left her at a loss for words.

"I've been giving him physical therapy." *And more.*

An uncomfortable silence hung in the air so that every tinkle of a fork sounded loud and clear.

Dante cleared his throat. "Sera got mixed up with Jordan because she was helping me out."

Rosana's bewildered expression swung to her son.

"I asked Sera to take on Jordan as a client so I could look better at work." Dante shrugged. "You know, new job and all."

Sera threw her brother a grateful look. For a long time, she'd been out to stake her independence and competence, and these days her family—or at least one of them—seemed ready to acknowledge her help.

"I don't know what to say," her mother said after a pause.

"Don't worry, Mom," Sera said quickly, because old

habits died hard and she still felt the need to reassure her mother. "Jordan and I are no longer seeing each other."

"Because of the story that's circulating?" Rosana asked.

"That was part of it. More because it took me by surprise. *He didn't feel the need to tell me.*"

Her mother sighed.

Dante helped himself to some more meatballs from the serving bowl. "Well, the world has tilted on its axis," he joked. "Sera is bailing me out these days, and Mom has a beau."

"What?" It was Sera's turn to look surprised.

Her mother suddenly looked flustered.

Dante cracked a smile. "Mom's not the only one who has her sources among the town gossips. The gentleman caller is alleged to be a mild-mannered accountant by day, and one mean parlor cardplayer by night."

Sera tilted her head. "Let me guess. You ran into one of Mom's friends from her monthly card-playing posse?"

"Yeah," Dante said slyly. "One of them let it slip. In her defense—" her brother paused to throw their mother a significant look "—Mom's friend thought I already knew."

"Wow," Sera said slowly, her gaze roaming from her brother to her mother and back. "Anyone else have any secrets to share?"

Dante swallowed his food. "Not me. I play it straight."

Sera resisted rolling her eyes. And then, because her mother continued to look embarrassed, she added, "I'm happy for you, Mom. Really happy. It's about time."

"Thank you, Sera," her mother said composedly before raising her eyebrows at Dante. "We're taking things slowly, despite any rumors your brother may be spreading."

Dante just grinned cheekily.

Her mother then focused on Sera again, fixing her with a concerned look. "Are you okay? This must be a lot to deal with."

"I'm a grown-up, Mom. I can manage."

Rosana Perini suddenly smiled. "I know you are, but if you want to talk, I'm here." She waved a hand. "I realize Marisa has been your confidante, but ever since your father died, I think I know something about being the walking wounded."

Sera tried a smile, but to her surprise it wobbled a little. She couldn't help being touched. First Dante, now her mother. It seemed her family was finally able to give her space as an adult—as well as owning up to their own weaknesses. Her mother showed signs of moving on from her fears after the death of a child and, more recently, of a husband. "Thanks, Mom."

Her mother reached across to give her hand a reassuring squeeze and then stood to take some empty plates to the kitchen.

When their mother had departed, Dante threw Sera a curious look from across the table. "So, you and Jordan…"

"Yes?"

Dante leaned forward, keeping his voice low. "Let me know if I need to challenge Serenghetti to a duel. Job or no job, family comes first."

"Thanks, but I've got this."

"I thought…the bet."

"I know. We patched things up. He seemed to have real feelings for me." *Feelings* again. She was starting to sound like Bernice and Marisa.

"So things were getting real between you and Jordan, and then this happened." Dante cursed.

She leaned forward, too. "He said he doesn't know if he's the father."

Her brother sighed. "For what it's worth, celebrity sports stars are targets for gold diggers and fame seekers all the time. Don't believe everything you read. It might not be true."

Jordan had said as much—or tried to—but at the time, his argument had paled in significance to the parallels to Neil. Except the similarity to Neil wasn't exactly right. Because...because—

"So Jordan has feelings for you. How do you feel about him?"

I love him.

Sera's heart thudded in her chest. She finally admitted to herself what had lingered on the edges of her consciousness despite her pain. Jordan made her sad, mad and bad but vibrantly alive. Sexual tension had given way under her feet like thin ice once she'd gotten to know him.

Yes, she'd been hurt and angry about hearing the bombshell news from a stranger instead of Jordan himself. But unlike her former boyfriend, Jordan hadn't tried to cover up the fact of a secret family for months. And didn't she want to be part of his life, child or no child?

Seeming to read the emotions flitting across her face, Dante continued, "Ser, if you do care about him, you have to figure out what to do."

Sera stared at her brother, and then as their mother reentered the dining room, both she and Dante sat back.

She loved Jordan. The question was: What was she going to do about it?

Fourteen

"I've got news," Marv announced.

"No news is good news," Jordan joked, holding the phone to his ear, "but I'm prepared for anything you have to say. So what did you find, Marv?"

Despite his easygoing tone, Jordan tensed. He'd taken a break from his physical-therapy exercises in his home gym as soon as he'd noticed who was calling. Now the stillness in his apartment on this weekday morning enveloped him. His heart pounded hard against the walls of his chest. Marv's answer had the potential to change his life. If he were already a father, any future—with or without Sera—would be more complicated and a big departure from his life up to now.

He'd agreed to take a paternity test but had told Marv to hire a private investigator and get back to him once they had a fuller story. He could tell a moment of reckoning was upon him.

"I can say with certainty you're not the father. It's not

just the paternity test, but other information that's come to light."

Jordan took a deep breath and lowered his shoulders, the tension whooshing out of him like air from a punctured balloon. Then he silently cursed.

His life had been a roller coaster recently. On top of everything else, Lauren Zummen had given a salacious interview to *Gossipmonger* about their meeting and her subsequent pregnancy.

Jordan winced just thinking about Sera reading that piece. Not that he'd seen her. Bernice had reassigned him to another physical therapist, and he didn't have to ask why.

"Jordan?"

"Yeah, I'm here."

"Lauren wasn't pregnant."

Jordan paced around the gym, wandering aimlessly. "What? How can that be?"

"Her identical twin is the mother of the baby. It took some digging, but the private investigator checked records and talked to people in the small town near Albany that Lauren grew up in."

"What?" He was outraged. "How did they think they were going to get away with this?"

"They weren't. But maybe they'd get a lucrative payment or two from the gossip press for their story and some fame."

"I'm surprised they didn't go for the old-fashioned black-mail route," Jordan remarked drily, curbing another surge of anger. "You know, make me pay hush money."

"Too risky. They're smart enough to know you could have called their bluff and gotten law enforcement involved. The end result would have been a jail sentence."

Jordan tightened his hold on the receiver. "We've got to get the facts out there. At least the fact that I'm not the father."

"I know, I know."

"Wait until *Gossipmonger* finds out they may have paid for a false story."

"The women are identical twins. They can easily come up with some explanation for why they told the story that they did. Given the timing, you couldn't be ruled out as the father. And the women could claim that they swapped identities three years ago for some reason. That the one you met called herself Lauren but was actually her identical twin, and you didn't know it. The possibilities are endless." His agent paused. "Anything to keep the payments they might have received."

"You've got some insight into the criminal mind," Jordan joked.

"Well, I've been talking to the private investigator, and I've been in the business of representing famous people for a long time."

Jordan took a moment to compose himself. "Thanks, Marv. For everything."

The older man gave a dry chuckle. "It's what I do. A sports agent's work is never done. But for the record, you've been a lot easier to work with than some of my other clients. No secret plastic surgery, no sex tape, no drugs."

"Great for the endorsement deals and the contract that are coming up for negotiation."

"Yup."

"I'm a veritable angel."

Marv chuckled. "Go enjoy the rest of your life, Jordan. If your physical therapist keeps working wonders, we'll be in a good bargaining position."

After he hung up with his agent, Jordan reflected on Marv's last words.

Go enjoy the rest of your life. Marv's news today should have lifted the heavy cloud he'd been under, but somehow he still felt dejected and incomplete.

Jordan raked his hand through his hair and cast a glance

around the room. He hadn't bothered mentioning to Marv that Sera was no longer his physical therapist.

She'd worked wonders on him all right, though, and not just with his knee.

He was changed. *She'd* changed him.

Because he loved her.

With a cooler head, and without the issue of possible paternity clouding his judgment, he acknowledged that, given her past experience with men, Sera might easily have felt betrayed by his not initially sharing certain allegations with her. Instead, she'd found out the story from a paparazzo.

He was not that much better than Neil, whoever he was. And wherever the other guy was, Jordan wanted to plant his fist in his face.

Jordan figured his own playboy past hadn't helped him in gaining Sera's trust. He hadn't even remembered their spring-break encounter at the beach, though she definitely had. But he wasn't the same guy he'd been in his twenties or at the beginning of his relationship with Sera—or even a few weeks ago when he'd been brushing off Marc Bellitti's teasing at the Puck & Shoot.

He'd closed himself off from deep involvement—wanting to have fun at the height of his fame and fortune. But Sera was different. She'd challenged him and made him think about the man he was behind the facade of the well-known professional athlete—until his only choice had been to kiss her and fall all the way in love with her.

Crap. His long-standing rule of keeping to casual relationships hadn't protected him—from a gold digger, a paternity claim or anything else. And now, with Sera, he hadn't just *broken* his rule, he'd exploded it with dynamite. By falling in love with a woman who currently wanted nothing to do with him.

He had to do something about that.

* * *

The Puck & Shoot was familiar territory, so it was ridiculous to be tense. She knew that booth two had a rip in its seat cushion and that table four had a chip on its corner. She'd been here a million times.

Except she'd agreed to help out Angus again—and Jordan Serenghetti had just parked himself at table four. Alone.

He looked healthier and stronger than ever. Firm jaw, perfect profile, dark hair that she'd run her fingers through while moaning with desire...

Damn it.

She'd underestimated the power of his appeal. The time that they'd spent apart had either dulled her memory or whetted her appetite.

Still, she tried to draw strength from the crowded environment. At least they weren't completely by themselves.

Sure, she'd been doing some thinking since that night at the movie theater, but seeing him here now was sudden and she wasn't prepared. She expected him to be keeping a low profile with the gossip in the press, and Angus had assured her that he hadn't seen Jordan in a while.

Jordan turned, and his gaze locked with hers.

Steeling herself, notepad at the ready, she approached. "Are you ready to order?"

Her voice sounded rusty to her own ears. This was beyond awkward. Only the fact that she had a job to do kept her moving forward. When they'd parted, accusations had flown and feelings had been hurt. She'd nursed a bruised heart.

"Sera."

Not Angel. Why was he sitting alone when a few of his teammates were at the bar? "What do you want?"

The words fell between them, full of meaning. Then recovering, she nodded at the menu.

"I want to explain."

Flustered, she looked around them. "This isn't the time or place."

"It's beyond time, and it's the perfect place." One side of his mouth lifted in a smile. "And unless you conk me on the head with a menu, I'm in great shape."

She perused him. Unfortunately for her, he was as attractive as ever. Square jaw, laughing eyes, hot body. And Bernice had mentioned that he was continuing to recover well—though Sera had made a point of not asking.

"Fortunately for you," she sniffed, "I'd hate for my hard work in whipping you into shape to be undone."

Jordan laughed, and Sera crossed her arms.

"You have made me better," he said softly. "In more ways than one."

Sera swallowed and dropped her arms. *Ugh.* He could make her mad one minute and want to cry the next.

She glanced around, making sure they weren't drawing attention. "I wish you the best of luck sorting things out with…" She didn't know what to say. *Your baby mama? Ex-lover? Former one-night stand?*

Her heart squeezed, and she felt short of air. All she could manage were shallow breaths.

"I have."

She blinked. "What?"

He looked at her steadily. "I have sorted things out."

"Oh?"

He nodded. "I should have told you right away about the rumors." He paused. "I'm sorry."

She waved an arm dismissively, suddenly emotional and looking anywhere but at him. "Oh…"

He reached into the pocket of his jeans. "The results of the paternity test came back."

She looked down at the papers in his hand uncomprehendingly, her brain frozen.

"The child isn't mine."

Her gaze flew up to his.

"Lauren isn't even the mother."

Beyond the roaring in her ears, she barely made out Jordan's explanation.

"Thanks to Marv, the press should be posting corrected news stories as we speak." He smiled ruefully. "The gossip sites love a story with unexpected twists and turns."

"How can Lauren not even be the mother?" she asked, dumbfounded.

"Her twin sister is."

"How did they think they'd get away with this?"

Jordan's expression darkened. "That was my question. They had to know they'd eventually be found out, but maybe not before they received a fat payment or two to print a juicy story."

Feeling a tremor, she dropped her notepad on the table. "For the record, it doesn't matter. I already made up my mind that whether you were a father already or not was beside the point."

"Sera, I love you."

What? She'd pitched a revelation at him, and he'd hit it right back. And then, because it was all too much and she couldn't think of what else to say, she blurted, "Why should I believe you?"

Jordan stood up and moved closer. "Because you love me, too."

He said it so casually, she almost didn't process the words.

She blinked against a well of emotion and lifted her chin. "Does it matter? You're still…who you are, and I'm who I am."

"And who am I?" he queried, his voice low. "I'm a changed man—"

She opened her mouth.

"—especially since my casual remarks here to Marc Bellitti." He looked contrite.

They both knew which remarks he was referring to.

"At the time, it still seemed safer to play the game, or try to, rather than acknowledge the truth."

"Which is?"

"I love you." He glanced around them and then signaled the bartender.

Sera's eyes grew round. Now they were really creating a scene. "What are you doing? I have to take the order at my next table."

A slight smile curved Jordan's lips. "Already taken care of." He signaled again to someone across the room. "Angus has you covered with another waiter."

"He's short-staffed!"

"Not anymore he isn't. Another employee just stepped out of the back room."

Sera snapped her mouth shut. "You planned—"

"Let's just say Angus is a romantic at heart who's happy to lend a helping hand."

"He called me in when he didn't need me."

"I need you," Jordan said, looking into her eyes. "I've had a chance to sort out my priorities lately. And I've figured out what's important to me besides the career and whether I recover from my injury."

After he gave a sign to the bartender, the music was turned off, and everyone stopped talking. In the sudden stillness, Jordan raised his voice. "I'd like everyone's attention."

Bewildered and worried for him—was it fever? A momentary bout of insanity?—Sera leaned close and whispered, "What are you doing?"

He gave his trademark devilish smile. "In lieu of a jumbotron or big screen…"

OMG.

"I'm making a public declaration—"

Some people hooted.

"—that I think my teammates never thought they'd hear from me."

There was scattered laughter.

"This should be good," someone called out.

"I'm declaring my undying love for—"

Jordan took her hand and kissed it.

"The Puck & Shoot?" someone else wisecracked.

"Hey, maybe it's Angus or his beer." One patron elbowed another.

"Nah, Angus has been married for ages," Vince Tedeschi put in.

"—Serafina Perini," Jordan finished.

"Aww."

"Makes my heart flutter." Marc Bellitti clutched his chest dramatically.

Several women gave audible sighs.

Jordan turned to the peanut gallery lining the far side of the bar, including Vince and Marc. "Hey, guys, knock it off. This is difficult enough. Wearing my heart on my sleeve with no clue about my chances…"

Sera swallowed hard because she'd been getting choked up. Jordan was putting it all on the line for her—in public. She could spurn him, make him pay…or confess that she loved him, too.

Jordan opened his mouth to say more, and Sera impulsively leaned forward and shushed him with a kiss. She could feel his surprise, and then he relaxed, his lips going pliant beneath hers as he let her kiss him.

"Aw."

There were a few laughs, and some women gave audible sighs again.

When she broke the kiss, her gaze connected with Jordan's.

"Is that a yes?" he asked.

She nodded and then slid her arms around his neck. "Yes, yes…yes to everything. I'm all in with you." She looked into his eyes. "I love you, Jordan."

"I think I have a new lease on life in professional hockey thanks to you, and with your help, there are going to be new facilities at the hospital, too."

Sera felt her eyes glisten, so to make up for it, she teased, "They're going to name it the Serenghetti Pavilion?"

"Let's talk. Maybe we should name it after our first-born."

"You've got big plans, Serenghetti."

"Yup."

"Our families will go nuts over the news. And our kids would be double cousins with Dahlia."

He pulled her in for another kiss.

There was a smattering of applause around them.

"I love a happy ending," a woman in the crowd commented.

"Hey, who's going to be the most eligible New England Razor now that Serenghetti has retired?"

"Angus is going to start changing the TV channels from hockey to the feel-good drama of the week," a guy at the bar grumbled.

"What's wrong with that?" a woman beside him demanded.

As they ended their kiss, Sera laughed against Jordan's mouth. *Nothing, nothing at all.*

Epilogue

If someone had told her a year ago that she'd be planning her wedding to Jordan Serenghetti, Sera would never have believed them. Life was good in unexpected ways…

As she stood next to Jordan, Sera surveyed the assorted Serenghettis mingling in Serg and Camilla's Mediterranean-style mansion before the engagement party began. Soon, she'd be one of them. Serafina Perini Serenghetti, or SPS for short. She'd tried out the name numerous times already in her mind, and it always made her heart thrill. It felt right…like she was exactly where she should be.

Of course, the Serenghettis already treated her as one of them. She was Marisa's cousin, but they'd also embraced her as Jordan's fiancée. In fact, they'd been thrilled with news of the engagement months after she and Jordan had reconciled at the Puck & Shoot.

Camilla had exclaimed that she'd known all along that Sera would be a perfect match for her youngest son. Serg had congratulated Jordan on making a wise decision. Cole and Rick had called their brother a lucky man and joked that he'd soon be joining them in the ranks of fatherhood— making Sera flush. And Marisa had been thrilled that she and Sera would be sisters-in-law as well as cousins.

Mia Serenghetti came up and gave Sera's arm a quick squeeze. "Congratulations. I just wanted to say that again before your family and the other guests get here."

"Thanks, Mia."

Glancing at Jordan, Mia added, "You've made my brother very happy…and he'd better behave himself."

"Now that I'm engaged, you're next," Jordan teased.

His sister feigned offense. "How can you say that, after I kept your and Sera's secret at Constance and Oliver's wedding?"

"Simple. Mom. She's ready for her next starring role. Mother of the bride."

Mia rolled her eyes. "Don't jinx me. I'm married to my fledgling design business."

Sera nudged Jordan. "Good luck, Mia. I'll prolong Jordan's wedding planning as long as I can."

Mia threw her a grateful look. "Thanks. I'm glad I'm gaining an additional ally in this family." She gave her brother a baleful look. "It's been rough going."

As Camilla called Mia over with a question, Jordan glanced at his watch. "Your family should be here soon."

Sera squeezed her hands together. Not out of nervousness but excitement. "Yup. And Mom is bringing a date."

Her mother's *male friend*, as Rosana Perini referred to him, had turned out to be a mild-mannered, middle-aged guy with glasses and a quiet sense of humor. Sera had liked him instantly and was glad her mother was taking the next step by inviting him to be her date today.

Dante, of course, wouldn't miss today, either. Once he and their mother had understood that Sera and Jordan had worked out things between them, and how in love they were, they'd been just as excited as the Serenghettis about the relationship. And Dante naturally had been thrilled about becoming the brother-in-law of the Razors' star player.

Sera hooked her arm through Jordan's and beamed at him.

He was having his best season yet with the Razors. And as a result, Marv had had a great negotiating position. In fact, Jordan's new contract with the Razors had exceeded expectations, and his endorsement deals had so far been renewed for impressive sums. The result was that Jordan's plans to fund the rehabilitation facility at Welsdale Children's Hospital were right on track. Even Bernice was happy with all the new sports-team business that Astra Therapeutics was getting after their success with Jordan.

He leaned down to whisper in her ear. "Have I told you recently that I love you?"

"Not in a few hours."

"Maybe it's time to find another cloakroom."

Sera half laughed, half gasped. "We're at our own engagement party."

Jordan straightened and his eyes gleamed. "It wouldn't surprise anyone. And Mia might even be expecting it."

"Something tells me we'll be searching for a cloakroom for the rest of our lives."

Jordan leaned in for a kiss. "I'm counting on it."

* * * * *

COMING SOON!

We really hope you enjoyed reading this book. If you're looking for more romance, be sure to head to the shops when new books are available on

Thursday 5th September

To see which titles are coming soon, please visit
millsandboon.co.uk/nextmonth

MILLS & BOON

MODERN

Power and Passion

Prepare to be swept off your feet by sophisticated, sexy and seductive heroes, in some of the world's most glamourous and romantic locations, where power and passion collide.

Eight Modern stories published every month, find them all at

millsandboon.co.uk/Modern

MILLS & BOON
True Love

Romance from the Heart

Celebrate true love with tender stories of
heartfelt romance, from the rush of falling
in love to the joy a new baby can bring,
and a focus on the emotional
heart of a relationship.

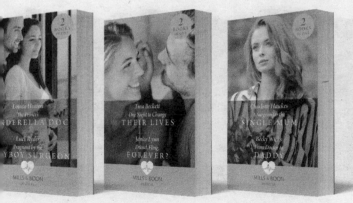

JOIN US ON SOCIAL MEDIA!

Stay up to date with our latest releases, author news and gossip, special offers and discounts, and all the behind-the-scenes action from Mills & Boon...

 millsandboon

 millsandboonuk

millsandboon

might just be true love...